学术顾问

（以姓氏笔画为序）

王　宏　冯智文　李正栓　李丽生　原一川

Academic Advisors

Wang Hong　Feng Zhiwen　Li Zhengshuan

Li Lisheng　Yuan Yichuan

主　编

李昌银

副主编

黄　瑛　彭庆华

General Editor

Li Changyin

Professor of English Yunnan Normal University

Associate General Editors

Huang Ying

Professor of English Yunnan Normal University

Peng Qinghua

Professor of English Yunnan Normal University

云南少数民族经典作品英译文库
Classics of Yunnan Ethnic Groups in English Translation

主编　李昌银　General Editor　Li Changyin
副主编　黄瑛　彭庆华　Associate General Editors　Huang Ying & Peng Qinghua

Manau Jaiwa

目瑙斋瓦

搜集整理◎李向前
英译◎杨慧芳　陈萍　陶玥
译校◎[美]包琼

Collected & Edited by Li Xiangqian
Translated by Yang Huifang, Chen Ping & Tao Yue
Revised by Joan Cecile Boulerice

云南出版集团
云南人民出版社

图书在版编目（CIP）数据

目瑙斋瓦：汉、英 / 李向前搜集整理；杨慧芳，陈萍，陶玥英译. -- 昆明：云南人民出版社，2018.12

（云南少数民族经典作品英译文库 / 李昌银主编）

ISBN 978-7-222-17502-0

Ⅰ. ①目… Ⅱ. ①李… ②杨… ③陈… ④陶… Ⅲ. ①景颇族—叙事诗—中国—汉、英 Ⅳ. ①I222.7

中国版本图书馆CIP数据核字(2018)第277431号

出 品 人　李　维　赵石定
项目统筹　周　祥　殷筱钊
项目组稿　郭木玉
责任编辑　郭木玉　任建红　李东华
装帧设计　马　滨　三人禾
责任校对　王琳淇　崔苡菡　付芳侠　周桉吉
责任印制　陆卫华　代隆参

云南少数民族经典作品英译文库
Classics of Yunnan Ethnic Groups in English Translation

目瑙斋瓦
Manau Jaiwa

搜集整理◎李向前
英译◎杨慧芳　陈萍　陶玥
译校◎［美］包琼

Collected & Edited by Li Xiangqian
Translated by Yang Huifang, Chen Ping & Tao Yue
Revised by Joan Cecile Boulerice

出　版　云南出版集团　云南人民出版社
发　行　云南人民出版社
社　址　昆明市环城西路609号
邮　编　650034
网　址　www.ynpph.com.cn
E-mail　ynrms@sina.com
开　本　787mm×1092mm　1/16
印　张　29
字　数　480千
版　次　2018年12月第1版第1次印刷
印　刷　云南出版印刷（集团）有限责任公司　云南新华印刷一厂
书　号　ISBN 978-7-222-17502-0
定　价　165.00元

云南人民出版社
公众微信号

序　一

◎李正栓

民族典籍英译是传播中国文化、文学和文明的重要途径，是中华文化走出去的重要组成部分。文化与文学的传播，是一个国家提高文化软实力的重要方式，在文化交流和文明建设中起着不可或缺的作用，对提高国家对外话语权、构建国家对外话语体系以及对建设世界文学都有积极意义。

中国各少数民族拥有许多优秀的典籍，具有很高的文物价值、文学价值和文化价值。各民族的先人们通过口头流传或用文字记述了他们各具特色的文化。各少数民族几乎都有自己民族的创世史、史诗和神话传说。

中国民族典籍独具特色，不可替代。重视民族典籍的翻译和研究工作，对于挖掘各民族优秀文化，保护各民族文明，增强各民族之间的沟通和了解，进一步向世界其他地区传播各少数民族优秀文化，乃至提高我国文化软实力都有着重要意义。不少少数民族聚居地处于祖国边疆，有的处在“一带一路”建设关键部位，有的处在与周边国家进行各种交流的重要位置。

中国民族典籍是世界多元文化的有机组成部分，与其他文化共同造就了世界文化的绚丽多姿。世界正因为其文化多样性才变得缤纷多彩。我国各民族典籍中包含的文化多样性极大地丰富了世界多元、特色鲜明的文化。人们对多样性形成全新的认识角度和思维方式。多样性开阔了人们的视野，丰富了人们思考问题的角度。挖掘这些典籍中所蕴含的教育价值和文化价值，对世界其他民族都有指导和借鉴意义，并且有助于建设我国的文化自信。

民族典籍本身蕴含的特殊价值对加强民族文化了解、促进中外文化交流具有重大意义。民族典籍英译具有文学翻译和文化传递之功能，有对外宣传作用，还是一种文学外交。因此，民族典籍翻译和研究对于维护祖国统一、促进民族团结、稳定边疆以及增强国内各民族和中外文化之间的交流都起着极为重要的作用。

中华人民共和国成立以后，中央政府一直十分重视民族典籍翻译和研究工作，提供了强有力的政策支持，并采取了一系列有效措施，加快了各少数民族典籍的抢救、整理、翻译和研究的进程。中央政府多次召开西藏工作会议和新疆工作会议。近年来，国际和国内对于多元文化高度关注，少数民族文学典籍的翻译已然成为业内研究的热点。

近年来，民族典籍翻译和研究迅猛发展，势头良好。国家大力支持，发放国家社科基金课题，教育部和国家民委也发放课题，扶持了一大批研究者。很多民族典籍翻译课题得以立项并顺利开展；为数不少的民族典籍被翻译成汉语、英语和其他语言并出版发行；越来越多的业界人士致力于这个满富生机的学术领域。

在中国文化走出去的国家战略下，全国少数民族典籍英译学术研讨会陆续召开，已经召开三次。

云南是中国民族最多的省份。人口在5000人以上的少数民族有25个，其中有15个民族为云南所特有，分别是：白族、哈尼族、傣族、傈僳族、佤族、拉祜族、纳西族、景颇族、布朗族、普米族、阿昌族、基诺族、怒族、德昂族、独龙族。其中除白族人口占全国白族人口总数的84%以上外，其他14个民族95%居住在云南。

云南还是我国跨境民族最多的省份。在云南的25个少数民族中，有16个民族跨境而居，分别是：傣族、壮族、苗族、景颇族、瑶族、哈尼族、德昂族、佤族、拉祜族、彝族、阿昌族、傈僳族、布依族、怒族、布朗族、独龙族。

云南少数民族创造了辉煌的文化。据不完全统计，云南少数民族文字文献古籍蕴藏量达10万余册（卷），口传古籍4万余种。云南省民委少数民族古籍整理出版规划办公室为了挽救和保护这些古籍，计划在5年内编纂出版100卷《云南少数民族古籍珍本集成》。这是一个令人瞩目的庞大计划。将这些古籍中的珍品翻译介绍给世界，不仅能够弘扬云南省丰富多彩的民族文化，而且有助于增进与南亚东南亚国家的理解与交流，为“一带一路”倡议的实施做出贡献。

云南师范大学外国语学院很重视这一领域的工作。在外国语学院领导支持下，李昌银教授带领一个由教授和中青年学者组成的团队对精选出来的17部云南少数民族经典作品进行英译，计划在5年内（“十三五”期间）翻译出版。这是一项十分有意义的宏大工程。

这17部民族典籍，内容全部为各民族的英雄史诗或神话传说，具有很高的历史意义和文学价值。这些作品涉及阿昌族、白族、傣族、德昂族、哈尼族、景颇族、拉祜族、苗族、纳西族、普米族、彝族等11个少数民族。

云南师范大学这支翻译队伍实力强大，主要由一些多年从事翻译教学、研究和实践的教授和副教授组成，他们是李昌银、黄瑛、彭庆华、孙兴文、吴相如、刘德周、杨慧芳、郜菊、陈萍、包琼（Joan Boulerice）等国内外专家学者。他们在云南翻译界都是风云人物。

在民族典籍英译中，这支队伍异军突起，为我国民族典籍英译壮大了声势，必将为中国民族典籍走向世界而成为世界文学的一部分做出新贡献。

民族典籍翻译与研究事业关乎国家的稳定统一，关乎民族关系的和谐发展，关乎世界多元文化的实现。在中国，民族典籍资源极为丰富，有待进一步挖掘、翻译。因此，民族典籍英译前景光明。同时，我们也应意识到，仍有许多濒临消失的少数民族典籍亟待拯救，民族典籍翻译与研究工作任重而道远。

（李正栓，中国英汉语比较研究会典籍英译专业委员会常务副会长兼秘书长）

Foreword by Li Zhengshuan

The translation of Chinese ethnic classics is an important approach in spreading Chinese culture, literature and civilization. It is a crucial component of Chinese culture going global. The spreading of Chinese culture and literature is a national policy and an important way to improve the cultural soft power of China. It plays an indispensable role in the cultural exchange between China and other countries and the development of world literature.

The ethnic groups in China have countless excellent classics with high anthropological, literary and cultural value. The ancestors of each ethnic group have passed down their distinctive culture orally or in writing. Almost all the ethnic groups have their own story of creation, epics, myths and legends.

Chinese ethnic classics are unique and irreplaceable. It is imperative to attach importance to the translation and research of ethnic classics; to explore the excellent ethnic cultures; to protect the civilization of ethnic groups; to enhance the communication and understanding among ethnic groups; to further spread the outstanding culture of ethnic groups to other parts of the world; and to build the cultural strength of China. Many ethnic groups live in the border areas and thus play an important role in the cultural and economic cooperation between China and its neighbors in the context of the Belt and Road Initiative.

Chinese ethnic classics are an important component of the magnificence and diversity of world culture. It is diversity that makes the world so colorful. The cultural diversity of Chinese ethnic classics has greatly enriched the world's pluralism and its distinctive features. People around the world have formed a new understanding of diversity. This diversity has expanded people's horizon and enriched their way of thinking. Digging out the educational and cultural value in these classics can contribute to the construction of China's self-confidence in culture.

The special value of the ethnic classics itself is of great significance to the strengthening of national culture and intercultural communication between China and foreign countries. The translation of ethnic classics is not just a literary exchange, but also a form of cultural communication. It is diplomacy through literature in that it consolidates the cultural ties between China and other countries.

After the founding of the People's Republic of China, the central government attached great importance to the translation and research of ethnic classics, provided a great deal of policy support, and adopted a series of effective measures to speed up the process of rescuing, collating, translating and studying ethnic classics. The central government has convened several working conferences on Tibet and Xinjiang. In recent years, both China and other countries have paid close attention to multiculture. The translation of ethnic classics has become a hot topic.

In recent years, the translation and research of ethnic classics have progressed rapidly and have shown good prospects. The government strongly supports and grants the research projects of the national social science fund. The Ministry of Education and the State Ethnic Affairs Commission are also issuing research projects and giving funding to a large number of researchers. Many research projects on ethnic classics have been approved and carried out. Many ethnic classics have been translated into Chinese, English and other languages and published. More and more professionals have dedicated themselves to this new sphere of learning.

In this context, the academic conferences on translation of ethnic classics are held one after another all around the country. And up to now three have been held.

Yunnan is the province which has the most ethnic groups in China. Besides the Han people, there are 25 ethnic groups, each with a population of more than 5,000. Among them, 15 ethnic groups are unique to Yunnan, which are the Bai, the Hani, the Dai, the Lisu, the Wa, the Lahu, the Naxi, the Jingpo, the Bulang, the Pumi, the Achang, the Jinuo, the Nu, the De'ang and the Dulong. Among these, 84% of the total number of the Bai people in China and 95% of the other 14 ethnic groups are living in Yunnan.

Yunnan is also the province which has the most cross-border ethnic groups. Of the 25 ethnic groups, 16 live across the border, namely: the Dai, the Zhuang, the Miao, the Jingpo, the Yao, the Hani, the De'ang, the Wa, the Lahu, the Yi, the Achang, the Lisu, the Buyi, the Nu, the Bulang and the Dulong.

The ethnic groups in Yunnan have created splendid cultures. According to statistics, the number of classics of Yunnan ethnic groups is more than 100 thousand volumes and classics in oral tradition are more than 40 thousand. In order to save and protect these ancient books, the Office of Classics Collation and Publishing of Yunnan Ethnic Groups Affairs Commission planned to compile and publish 100 volumes of *A Collection of Yunnan Ethnic Group Rare Books* in five years, which is an ambitious plan. The introduction of the ancient classics via translation can not only promote and develop the colorful ethnic cultures of Yunnan, but also contribute to the understanding and exchange between China and countries in South Asia and Southeast Asia and to the implementation of the Belt and Road Initiative as well.

The School of Foreign Languages and Literature of Yunnan Normal University is paying close attention to this field. With the support of the School and the University, Professor Li Changyin is leading a group of professors and young scholars to do the project of "*Classics of Yunnan Ethnic Groups in English Translation*", which includes 17 ethnic classics selected carefully from Yunnan's bountiful ethnic classics. These books are the heroic epics or myths and legends of each ethnic groups with great historical significance and literary value. They will finish the translation in five years (during "the thirteenth five-year plan"). After that, all the works will be published by Yunnan People's Publishing House.

The 17 works cover 11 ethnic groups: the Achang, the Bai, the Dai, the De'ang, the Hani, the Jingpo, the Lahu, the Miao, the Naxi, the Pumi and the Yi. All of these groups except the Miao and the Yi are unique to Yunnan.

The translation team of Yunnan Normal University is full of strength and vitality, composed of professors and associate professors who have been occupied in translation teaching, research, and practice for a long time. They are Li Changyin, Huang Ying, Peng Qinghua, Sun Xingwen, Wu Xiangru, Liu Dezhou, Yang Huifang, Gao Ju, Chen Ping, Joan Boulerice and other experts and scholars who are representative figures in the translation field in Yunnan province.

This team is a new force that has suddenly arisen in terms of translating ethnic classics. It is expanding the momentum of ethnic classics translation in China and has made a new contribution for China's ethnic classics to go global and become a part of world literature.

The translation and research of ethnic classics are related

to the development of Chinese culture and the realization of multiculturalism in the world. In China, ethnic classics are extremely rich in resources, which require us to make further exploration and research and translate them into other languages. Therefore, the future of translating ethnic classics is bright. At the same time, we should also realize that there are still many ethnic works which are close to extinction and urgently need to be rescued. We still have a long way to go in the fields of translation and research in ethnic classics.

(Li Zhengshuan, Standing Vice Chairman and Secretary General, Classics Translation Committee of CACSEC)

序　二

◎王　宏

好友云南师范大学外国语学院李昌银教授来电嘱托我为“云南少数民族经典作品英译文库”的出版写一序言，并随即发来该文库的背景资料，让我“不着急，慢慢写”。我本人从事中国典籍英译及研究，深知少数民族典籍对外传译的重要性，但又是少数民族典籍翻译的门外汉。因此，我是怀着虚心学习的态度来写此序言的。近年来，在中国文化“走出去”战略工程大背景下，在中央和地方各级政府的大力支持下，我国少数民族典籍的对外传译及研究工作顺利开展，取得了很大的进步。请看以下数据：

2008 年，广西百色学院韩家权教授获批国家社科基金项目《布洛陀史诗》（壮汉英对照）。该项目已顺利结项，并于 2013 年 12 月获得中国民间文艺最高奖“山花奖”。

2012 年，广西百色学院外语系翻译团队翻译的国家级非物质文化遗产《壮族嘹歌》（英文版）由广西师范大学出版社正式出版。

2012 年，东北大学秦皇岛分校吴松林教授主编的《蒙古族系列：江格尔（汉英对照）》（上下册）由吉林大学出版社出版。

2013 年，河北师范大学李正栓教授英译《藏族格言诗》

由长春出版社出版发行。

2013 年，云南财经大学崔晓霞教授撰写的《〈阿诗玛〉英译研究》收入由王宏印教授主编、民族出版社出版的“民族典籍翻译研究丛书”。

2014 年，东北大学秦皇岛分校吴松林教授撰写的《满族档案文献研究》申请到国家社科后期资助，他英译的《英雄格斯尔可汗》由吉林大学出版社出版。

2014 年，中南民族大学张立玉教授主持的“土家族主要典籍英译及研究”获批国家社科基金项目。

2015 年，西安外国语大学梁真惠副教授撰写的《〈玛纳斯〉翻译传播研究》收入由王宏印教授主编、民族出版社出版的“民族典籍翻译研究丛书”。

与此同时，第一届和第二届全国少数民族典籍英译学术研讨会分别于 2012 年和 2014 年在广西民族大学和大连民族学院举行，参加会议的院校分布之广、与会代表数量之众、提交论文数量之多和涉及研究话题之细，十分可喜。2016 年还将在中南民族大学举行第三届全国少数民族典籍英译学术研讨会。

为什么少数民族典籍的对外传译及研究工作在短短几年就受到译界的青睐，取得众多成果？我认为，这在很大程度上归于典籍翻译界乃至翻译界同仁对“中国典籍”的重新思考和认识。中国典籍浩如烟海，卷帙浩繁，举世瞩目，是全人类共同的精神财富。但对于中国典籍的理解，我们以前较多限于汉民族的重要文献和书籍，而对少数民族多有忽略。在讨论中国典籍时，也较多关注古代文学作品。其实，中国典籍指“中国清代末年1911年以前的重要文献和书籍”，这就要求我们从事典籍翻译时，不但要翻译古代文学典籍作品，还要翻译古代哲学、科技、法律、医学、经济、军事、天文、地理等诸多方面的典籍作品，不但要翻译汉民族的典籍作品，也要翻译各少数民族的典籍作品。

民族典籍具有该民族的原型符号的特质，蕴藏着能够“遗传”并不断“再生”的文化基因。民族典籍是中华传统文化的内核，同时还是中华传统文化的符号构成规则。中国是具有56个民族的多民族国家，少数民族典籍是我国少数民族勤劳与智慧的结晶，是中华文明、也是世界文明不可或缺的一部分。少数民族典籍对外传译具有跨文化交流的作用，它不但有助于更多的人了解少数民族的独特文化，而且还有助于保护少数民族文化的独特性、维持少数民族文化多样性、促进各民族团结、提升中华文化软实力等。

中国少数民族典籍涉及宗教、文学、历史、语言、医学、天文历算等领域，内容丰富，版本多样，载体特殊，传承奇特。仅以《中国少数民族古籍总目提要》为例，该书于1997年正式立项，全书总体设计约60卷、110册，目前已出版23个民族卷共20册：纳西族卷、白族卷、东乡族卷·裕固族卷·保安族卷、土族卷·撒拉族卷、锡伯族卷、哈尼族卷、回族卷·铭刻、柯尔克孜族卷、羌族卷、毛南族卷·京族卷、仫佬族卷、达斡尔族卷、土家族卷、鄂温克族卷、鄂伦春族卷、赫哲族卷、苗族卷、侗族卷、黎族卷、朝鲜族卷。该书真实地反映了我国各少数民族古籍赋存的全面情况，充实了中国的历史和文化内容，为后人探索各种文化形式的源流、揭示中国社会文化发展的轨迹提供了极为珍贵的资料，为我国乃至世界各国人文科学研究提供了一套新颖而全面的资料，对于弘扬中华民族传统文化具有深远的历史意义和现实意义。

少数民族典籍的对外传译是一项艰巨的工作，涉及将少数民族语言译成汉语、少数民族语言之间的互译和少数民族语言译成外语（主要是英语）。前两类翻译历史源远流长，最早可追溯到春秋战国时代《越人歌》的翻译，即汉、壮语之间的翻译。少数民族典籍译成外语的时间则要晚一些。据考证，维吾尔族古典长诗《福乐智慧》成书于 1069 年或 1070 年，目前尚未发现完整的原稿，只存留下来三个抄本，分别为赫拉特抄本、费尔干纳抄本与埃及抄本，其中费尔干纳抄本于 12~13 世纪用阿拉伯文纳斯赫体抄写，1914 年发现于今中亚乌孜别克斯坦纳曼干城，现存于该共和国科学院东方研究所。这是少数民族典籍译介到国外的最早纪录。少数民族典籍外译在现代有了较快发展。一些少数民族典籍，如藏族的《格萨尔王传》、蒙古族的《江格尔》和柯尔克孜族的《玛纳斯》等英雄史诗，云南彝族的《阿诗玛》、维吾尔族的《艾里甫和赛乃姆》等民间叙事长诗已先后被翻译成英语及其他外国文字，为世人所知。这对传承少数民族经典，推动中外文化交流起到了不可替代的作用。然而，还有大量的中国少数民族典籍等待我们去翻译和研究。

云南省少数民族典籍资源十分丰富。据不完全统计，云南少数民族文字文献古籍蕴藏量达 10 万余册（卷），口传古籍 4 万余种。“云南少数民族经典作品英译文库”正是依托云南省丰富的少数民族典籍资源，借助云南师范大学外国语学院强大的翻译师资队伍，在云南人民出版社的有力支持下，首次将云南少数民族经典作品成系列对外译介的大力举措。云南师范大学外国语学院对“云南少数民族经典作品英译文库”十分重视，他们首先邀请省内外少数民族语言文化研究专家对云南民族典籍和民族文化经典作品进行筛选，做到“好中选好，优中选优”，同时调配最强的翻译力量承担文库的翻译任务。我粗略看了该文库的选题，发现选题面广，覆盖范围宽，收入了云南省阿昌族、白族、傣族、纳西族、德昂族、哈尼族、景颇族、拉祜族、苗族、普米族和彝族等民族的典籍作品。云南共有25个少数民族，其中11个少数民族的典籍作品都覆盖到了，不少作品还是首次译成英文。这将彻底改变云南少数民族典籍由于对外译介数量较少，不为世界了解的尴尬局面。

对于云南师范大学外国语学院而言，把少数民族典籍英译作为翻译专业的优势特色进行建设，这将对该院的学科建设起到助推作用。“云南少数民族经典作品英译文库”所产生的翻译成果和研究成果将培养出一批优秀的典籍翻译和研究团队，凸显该院在全国的学术特色和学术影响，同时还能将翻译能力和研究能力转化为教学能力，提高云南师范大学外国语学院翻译专业研究生的培养质量，为社会输送高水平的翻译人才，有力地支撑学院翻译专业学科的建设和发展。我对云南师范大学外国语学院的翻译师资队伍较为熟悉。作为云南省唯一获得省级高校优势特色学科建设项目的外国语学院，该院具有雄厚的翻译师资力量，在云南省各高校中当属第一。多年来，该院翻译与跨文化研究团队一直承担着对外交流与合作的各种口笔译项目及任务。由外国语学院精心挑选和确定的“云南少数民族经典作品英译文库”翻译人员绝大多数都是云南省翻译领域里的知名教授或专家，有国外留学经历，且具有扎实的英汉双语语言功底，曾翻译出版多部译著和翻译作品，并且主持和参与过多项翻译项目的研究。我阅读李昌银教授发来的文库翻译人员名单，发现多名我所熟悉的知名教授、博士也在其中，感到格外放心。

“云南少数民族经典作品英译文库”的出版发行是云南省翻译界的一件大事，也是我国少数民族典籍翻译传来的又一佳音。想当年，我和《大中华文库》总协调人李林老师曾在参加全国典籍英译学术研讨会之余一起找到李昌银教授，敦促李教授向学校和同事呼吁，少数民族典籍翻译及研究是富矿，值得快挖、深挖，能早出成果，出大成果。今天，我们当年的心愿变成了美好的现实，心里感到特别高兴。再次热烈祝贺“云南少数民族经典作品英译文库”的顺利出版！

（王宏，中国典籍翻译研究会副会长、苏州大学博士生导师）

Foreword by Wang Hong

My friend Professor Li Changyin of Yunnan Normal University asked me to write a few words for the publication of *Classics of Yunnan Ethnic Groups in English Translation*. I am more than delighted to do it. As I have been doing research in the English translation of Chinese classics, I know how important his work is. In recent years, substantial progress has been made in translating Chinese ethnic classics into English and other foreign languages. Books published in this respect include *The Liao Songs of the Zhuang Nationality* (Nanning: Guangxi Normal University Press, 2008, English Edition), *Mongolian Series: Jianggeer* (Changchun: Jilin University Press, 2012, Bilingual Edition), *Tibetan Gnomic Verses Translated into English* (Changchun: Changchun Press, 2013), and *Geser Khan: a Hero* (Changchun: Jilin University Press, 2014). Several projects in the English translation of ethnic classics have received funding from the National Planning Office of Philosophy and Social Science and, as a result, a number of monographs and PhD dissertations have been published.

Meanwhile, it is encouraging to see that the first conferences on English translation of ethnic classics in China have been held in Guangxi Nationalities University and

Dalian Nationalities Institute respectively. Participants were both many and enthusiastic. Many papers were presented and a lot of topics discussed. The third conference will be hosted by South Central Nationalities University in 2016.

Why, then, has this field attracted so much attention from translators and scholars alike and accomplished so much in just a few years? The answer, I believe, lies in a rethinking of what constitutes Chinese classics as an indispensable part of human heritage. We used to see Chinese classics as more or less equal to the classics of the Han people, excluding works by other ethnic groups. Moreover, when we talk about Chinese classics, we focus too much on the literary works of ancient times. Yet Chinese classics actually refer to "important works and books before 1911, the year when the Qing dynasty fell, bringing an end to imperial rule." This definition requires us to pay attention not just to literary works, but also writings in other subjects, such as philosophy, science, law, medicine, economics, military affairs, astronomy, and geography, not only Han works, but writings by other ethnic groups as well.

The classical works of a nation are its archetypal symbols, the major carriers of its cultural genes. Chinese classics make up the core of Chinese tradition. The Chinese nation consists of 56 ethnic groups. Ethnic classics are an important part of not only Chinese traditional culture, but also of world civilization. The translation of these works into other languages is important in that it helps to promote cross-cultural communications between China and other countries and to protect and preserve the uniqueness and diversity of ethnic cultures by making them accessible to foreign readers.

Chinese ethnic classics cover a variety of areas, such as religion, literature, history, language, medicine, astrology, and calendar, with numerous editions, special media and unique ways of transmission from generation to generation. Take, for example, *An Anthology of Chinese Ethnic Classics*, a colossal project that includes 110 volumes, 20 of which, from 23 ethnic groups, have been published. The anthology reflects the variety and quantity of China's ethnic classics and provides valuable material and resources for studying, understanding and developing Chinese culture and history in a more comprehensive and sustainable way.

The translation of Chinese ethnic classics into foreign languages is a very demanding job, involving rendering from ethnic languages to Chinese, between ethnic languages, and from ethnic languages (often via Chinese) to foreign languages. The first two types of translation can be traced back to the Spring and Autumn Period, when *The Song of the Yue People* was translated from their mother tongue into Chinese. The earliest translation of ethnic classics into a foreign language is *Wisdom of Royal Glory*, a long poem of the Uygurs, which was rendered from the source language into Arabic and is now in the Oriental Institute of Uzbekistan at Namangan. But it was not until modern times that the translation of ethnic classics into foreign languages accelerated. Noticeably, ethnic epics, such as *The Story of Prince Geser* of the Tibetans, *The Story of Jianggeer* of the Mongolians, *Manas* of the Kyrgyz, and narrative poems such as *Ashima* of the Yi people, *Alip and Salam* of the Uygurs, etc., have been published. These translations have contributed to acquainting the world with Chinese ethnic classics, but many remain to be translated.

Yunnan is rich in ethnic classics, boasting more than 100 thousand volumes of written classics and over 40 thousand pieces of oral literature. Relying on such bountiful resources, as a collective endeavor of the translation team of the School of Foreign Languages and Literature, Yunnan Normal University and with the help of Yunnan People's Publishing House, *Classics of Yunnan Ethnic Groups in English Translation* is the first project to translate Yunnan ethnic classics into English on a large scale. The School adheres to a professional spirit and academic standard in carrying out the project by selecting the most authoritative texts in the source language (Chinese) and recruiting the best translators from its huge faculty. The selection of the works, covering eleven of the twenty-five ethnic groups of the province, indicates expertise and insight. The implementation of the project will change the embarrassing obscurity of Yunnan ethnic classics by making them known to the world, many of them for the first time.

In light of disciplinary development, the project is of

great importance, too. Participating in the translation will strengthen the academic foundation of the teachers, enrich their experience and enhance their translation skills and research ability. This in turn will help them become better teachers and thus able to educate students with higher quality. The publication of the books will add greatly to the faculty accomplishments of the School and raise the academic standing of Yunnan Normal University by taking the first step in this direction among the universities of Yunnan province.

This publication project is a great event not only for Yunnan itself, but also for China. Looking back, I remember that Professor Li Changyin, our friend Li Lin, editor of the *Library of Chinese Classics*, and I talked enthusiastically about initiating something like this in Yunnan when we attended a conference on the translation of ethnic classics in Soochow. Lin and I strongly suggested that Professor Li do it as soon as possible. Now I am very pleased to see our talk becoming reality. Again, my congratulations on the publication of *Classics of Yunnan Ethnic Groups in English Translation*!

(Wang Hong, PhD supervisor at Soochow University, Vice Chairman of Classics Translation Committee of CACSEC)

General Introduction

This publication project, *Classics of Yunnan Ethnic Groups in English Translation*, aims at introducing Yunnan ethnic classical works to the world by making them available to native speakers of English who might be interested in them. With the publication of the *Library of Chinese Classics*, which consists only of books written by Han authors in classical Chinese, attention now is being turned to the English translation and publication of ethnic classics, books produced by ethnic writers about their history and culture. Universities in provinces such as Guangxi, Guizhou, Liaoning, Xinjiang, and Xizang, have taken the initiative. We in Yunnan must do something, because Yunnan has the largest number of ethnic groups in China. 15 of the 25 ethnic groups in the province, the Bai, the Dai, the Hani, the Lisu, the Wa, the Lahu, the Naxi, the Jingpo, the Bulang, the Pumi, the Achang, the Jinuo, the Nu, the De'ang, and the Dulong, live in no other place but Yunnan. The classics of these people, either in their own languages or in Chinese translations, are a great treasure house, which should be accessible to English readers and scholars. But what works should be translated first?

All the 25 ethnic groups in Yunnan have their classics, epics, mythology, creation stories, folksongs, folk drama, mountain songs, and funeral lament lyrics, most of which exist in different versions in different places. According to one estimation, there are more than 100 thousand volumes of them, excluding those in oral form. After a thorough survey and extensive consultations with experts of ethnic studies, we concluded that priority must be given to epics and mythologies, as they reflect an ethnic people's philosophy, history and culture more than anything else by narrating the stories of where and how they think they came from. From many epics and mythologies, we selected 17 of the most authoritative and popular classics representing 11 Yunnan ethnic groups, the Yi, the Bai, the Miao, the Hani, the Lahu, the Naxi, the Jingpo, the Pumi, the Achang, the Dai, and the De'ang. These works are all in Chinese, translated from the original by bilingual scholars whose mother tongue is their own ethnic language and who are fluent and proficient in Chinese. Some were recorded from their oral form at rituals and performances. We did not choose texts written in the ethnic language, not least because it is very hard to find a translator who is skilled in both the ethnic language and English. Moreover, some of the classics in the ethnic language were circulated in various oral forms and fragments. The published Chinese versions have been carefully edited and translated, hence they are more reliable. The next question is: how to translate them?

It happens that all of the 17 works except one are in

verse form, with lines more or less the same length and loose rhymes, but no regular meter. A poem must be rendered into a poem; anything less is unacceptable. So here are the general rules we follow when doing the translation.

One. If the original is verse, the translated text must be verse, too.

Two. Reproduce the ideas and the images of the original as completely as possible.

Three. Reproduce the figures of speech of the original as much as possible.

Four. Do not change the number of lines in a stanza unless absolutely necessary.

Five. Do not use standard meters in English, because the Chinese original does not follow any regular meter. Use the natural rhythm of English instead, but most of the lines should look more or less the same length.

Six. Do not use rhyme unless it comes naturally and is faithful to the content of the original.

What we try to do is, to use Susan Bassnett's words, "transplant the seed", not the tree itself. As for the various aspects of form, particularly meter and end rhyme, we reproduce them when it is possible and abandon them when it is necessary.

Who will do the translations? As this is a collective project of the School of Foreign Languages and Literature of Yunnan Normal University, our team consists of a dozen faculty members and two students from our MA translation program who are already teachers in other universities. All the translators have been teaching translation and doing translation research for a long time. They have published not just academic articles on translation, but also translated books from English to Chinese or vice versa.

Traditionally, people translate into their mother tongue, not into a foreign language. But the situation is changing. Many translators today are translating from their mother tongue into a foreign language. The quality can be good, as Nike K. Pokorn and Stuart Campbell prove in *Challenging the Traditional Axioms: Translation into a non–mother tongue* (Amsterdam: John Benjamins Publishing Company, 2005) and *Translation into the Second Language* (New York: Routledge, 2013) respectively. The case of China provides further evidence for their argument. The translation of Chinese classics into English was initiated by James Legge and Herbert Allen Giles in the 19th century and carried on in the 20th century by Arthur Waley, David Hawkes, Burton Watson, John Minford, Stephen Owen and others. It is noticeable that these English and American sinologists were soon joined by Chinese scholars residing in the West, such as Hongming (Tomson) Gu and Lin Yutang, among others. They took up the job because they thought it was their obligation to give English readers more faithful translations than Western sinologists could, who, as their target language is their mother tongue, often misinterpret the original text and misrepresent Chinese culture. Since the 1950s, there has been an increasingly powerful trend for Mainland Chinese translators to render or re-render Chinese classics into foreign languages, English in particular. In our time, this work is gathering momentum, enthusiastically advocated and actively practiced by such well-known translation experts as Yang Xianyi of Beijing Foreign Language Press, Xu Yuanchong of Beijing University, Wang Rongpei of Dalian Foreign Language Institute, Wang Hongyin of Nankai University, Wang Hong of Soochow University, Li Zhengshuan of Hebei Normal University, and many more. These professors are not just translators, but also scholars in translation studies. More importantly, some of them, Xu Yuanchong, Wang Hong and Li Zhengshuan, for example, have had their translations published by Western publishers, which suggests that their English meets the international standard.

In the case of our project, we request that the translators do their best to produce good translations. When they submit them to us, they should represent the highest level that they can attain. Then the general editors appointed by the School read the translated texts and remove inaccurate renderings and grammar mistakes if there are any. On top of that, we've taken an indispensable measure to ensure that our English is readable. We asked Ms. Joan Cecile Boulerice, an American teacher who has been teaching English in our school since

2009, to read every text that we've translated and improve the English by making it more natural and idiomatic. This is the best we can do. Of course any problems that still remain in the translations are ours. They have nothing to do with our American teacher.

As the project is well under way, we would like to thank all those who have helped to make it possible. Ms Guo Muyu, director of the South and Southeast Asia Editorial Department, Yunnan People's Publishing House, has been most helpful in our cooperation. In addition, she has added importance to the project by turning it into a national publication project. Yunnan Normal University has supported us by paying the publication fees so that the translators won't have to be burdened with the financial responsibilities for this project. Professor Li Zhengshuan and Professor Wang Hong not only have always encouraged us to go on but have also written the forewords for the project, putting it in a global perspective. Ms Joan Boulerice's revision has ensured the fluency of the translated texts. Finally, special thanks must be given to Professor Wang Hong, again, and Mr Li Lin of Hunan People's Press for their suggestion that has helped us conceive the project from the very beginning.

(The General Editors, School of Foreign Languages & Literature, Yunnan Normal University, Kunming)

A Brief Introduction to *Manau Jaiwa*

Before the end of the nineteenth century, the history of the Jingpo people's survival and development was mainly handed down by oral chanting and reciting. The epic *Manau Jaiwa*, which was recorded based on what was chanted by a famous Jaiwa, is in a rhythmic and graceful language. It is a precious historical material preserved by the successive Jaiwa chanters generation after generation, offering clues of the ancient history of the Jingpo people. The chanted stories, like beautiful fairy tales, start from the beginning of the world and continue to record the development and evolution of the Jingpo people from ancient times to modern times.

In 1975, Mr. Li Xiangqian, a Jingpo cultural scholar, interviewed the famous Jingpo folk chanter Jaiwa ("Jaiwa" in the Jingpo language means wizard or guru) and compiled the chanted lines into a book in the Jingpo language, which was published in 1982 by Dehong Nationality Publishing House. In 1987, Li Xiangqian, together with Jingpo Professor Shi Rui and Jingpo poet Chen Hong from Yunnan Minzu University, translated it into Chinese, and then the Chinese edition was published in 1991 by Dehong Nationality Publishing House.

The whole book of *Manau Jaiwa* is composed of tens of thousands of lines about the deities creating living things, N-gon Du creating the Sky and the Earth, the flood era, N-gon Du marrying the dragon daughter, the division of the family clans and branches as well as the vivid description of human production and life. It is divided into seven parts: Prologue;

Formation of the Sky and the Earth; Leveling the Sky and the Earth; The Flood; N-gon Du Getting Married; The Origin of the Manau Festival; Life on the Earth.

The epic *Manau Jaiwa* is a masterpiece of Jingpo ethnic literature, which combines mythology, legend and poetry very well. It is not only a living monumental history of the Jingpo people but also a great literary masterpiece of folk literature that has been recited and passed on from generation to generation.

In May 2011, *Manau Jaiwa* was included in the list of the third collection of The National List of Intangible Cultural Heritage of China.

The Translators

目瑙斋瓦

目录

目瑙斋瓦

目录

目瑙斋瓦

目录

Contents

Manau Jaiwa / **Contents**

Manau Jaiwa

Contents

序歌

Prologue

远古，	In remote antiquity,
天还没有形成，	The Sky did not come into being,
地还没有产生。	And the Earth did not take shape.
在朦胧和混沌里，	In haziness and chaos,
有个皮能帕拉①，	While there was Hpri Ninghpa La①,
有个迷能玛木占②；	There was Mi Ningma Majan②;
有个木托拉，	While there was Mahto La,
有个顶山木占；	There was Dingshan Majan;
有个木章拉，	While there was Machyang La,
有个普兰木占；	There was Hpunlap Majan;
有个乌诗拉，	While there was Wushi La,
有个乌卡木占；	There was Wuhku Majan;
有个涛智拉，	While there was Htauji La,
有个涛浪木占。	There was Htaulang Majan.
在朦胧和混沌里，	In haziness and chaos,
上有能万拉，	In the upper world, there was Nengwam La,
下有能斑木占。	In the lower world, there was Ningpan Majan,
能万拉向下漂移，	Nengwam La drifted downwards
落到能斑木占的身上，	On Ningpan Majan.
能万拉在摇摆，	Nengwam La moved on the top,

① "拉"指男性。
② "木占"指女性。

① "La" refers to males.
② "Majan" refers to females.

能斑木占在地下抖动，
创造天地的神已有了。
男神有了，
女神有了，
就要造天了，
就要打地了；
万事该出现了，
万物该产生了。

Ningpan Majan shook at the bottom.
Here were the Gods to create the Sky and the Earth.
Now that the male deity was created
And the female deity was also produced,
It was time to create the Sky;
It was the chance to make the Earth.
All things were supposed to appear;
All things were supposed to emerge.

附记：

目瑙是舞蹈之意；斋瓦是以歌的形式来吟唱历史。目瑙斋瓦即“吟唱史诗的歌”。这种歌一般在举行大型目瑙舞的祭祀活动上由专职的斋瓦吟唱。

“斋瓦”也指能够以歌的形式吟诵历史的祭司，还指以歌的形式吟唱历史的歌手。

序歌中的诸神，均为天地形成之前的阴阳神。由于他们的结合和作用，天地形成了，万物产生了。

Excursus:

Manau Jaiwa: “Manau” means dance, and “Jaiwa” means chanting the history by means of singing or the person who chants the legendary history. When Manau and Jaiwa are combined, it is interpreted as a song of history. Such a song is chanted on the occasion of important ritual activities called the Manau Dance Festival, and it is chanted by the great Jaiwa.

The deities appearing in the Prologue are male and female deities before the Sky and the Earth were created. After the male deity and the female deity interlocked with each other, the Sky and the Earth were created and all things in the world were produced.

第一章 天地的形成

Canto 1 Formation of the Sky and the Earth

一、能万拉和能斑木占的创造繁衍

Ⅰ. Creation and Multiplication by Nengwam La and Ningpan Majan

远古，
能万拉[①]的创造，
能斑木占[②]的繁衍，
生下了像东荣[③]一样的东西，
有了空荡荡的一片。
这是什么呀？
父亲能万拉，
母亲能斑木占说：
“这是将来的全知全能，
潘瓦能桑遮瓦能章[④]

In remote antiquity,
The creation by Nengwam La[①]
And the multiplication by Ningpan Majan[②]
Gave birth to a thing like Dongrong[③].
There was an empty ground.
What was it?
Father Nengwan La
And Mother Ningpan Majan said:
“This is the place named Malan Ting-rong
Where the Know-All saint

① 能万拉：传说中创造万物的男神。
② 能斑木占：传说中与能万拉共同创造万物的女神。
③ 东荣：一种竹编器具。口大底小，呈圆锥体，形容群山环绕的盆地。
④ 潘瓦能桑遮瓦能章：名字，意为全知全能，能创造和解决一切的智慧之神。

① Nengwam La: the male deity who created the world.
② Ningpan Majan: the female deity who helped the male deity Nengwam La create the world.
③ Dongrong: a kind of bamboo utensil which has a large opening and a small bottom. It is a metaphor for an area of flat land surrounded by mountains.

居住的木兰顶荣地方。”

Hpan Wa Ningsang Chye Wa Ningchyang[1] will live."

远古，
能万拉的创造，
能斑木占的繁衍，
生下了十拿长的绳，
有了二十拿长的索[1]，
生下绳做什么，
有了索作何用?
父亲能万拉，
母亲能斑木占说:
“十拿长的绳，
用来拴住木兰顶荣地方，
二十拿长的索，
用来稳固木兰顶荣地方。
生下了十拿长的绳，
有了二十拿长的索，
木兰顶荣地方拴住了，
木兰顶荣地方稳固了。

In remote antiquity,
The creation by Nengwam La
And the multiplication by Ningpan Majan
Made a ten-arm-span[2]-long rope,
And a twenty-arm-span-long cable.
What was the rope for?
What could the rope do?
Father Nengwam La
And Mother Ningpan Majan replied:
A ten-arm-span-long rope
Can tightly tie the place Malan Tingrong,
A twenty-span-long rope
Can make the place Malan Ting-rong stable.
Since the ten-span-long rope
And the twenty-span-long cable were made,
The place Malan Tingrong
Will be more fastened and stable.

① 拿：古时民间衡量长度的方法，一拿约5市尺。这里的十拿二十拿不是实际长度，意为很长。

① Hpan Wa Ningsang Chye Wa Ningchyang: a name meaning "know-all saint, who is regarded to be omniscient and omnipotent".

② Arm span is a unit of measure as long as 1.67 metres. Ten arm spans and twenty arm spans are not real length here. They only suggest that the ropes are very long.

远古，	In remote antiquity,
能万拉的创造，	The creation by Nengwam La
能斑木占的繁衍，	And the multiplication by Ningpan Majan
生下了成卷的东西，	Produced volumes of things
有了成捆的物件。	And bundles of articles.
这是什么呀？	What were these things for?
父亲能万拉，	Father Nengwam La
母亲能斑木占说：	And Mother Ningpan Majan replied:
“成卷的是十卷圣书，	“They are ten volumes of holy books
成捆的是二十捆圣典①。	And twenty bundles of canons.①
谁来看圣书，	Who will read holy books?
谁来用圣典，	Who will use the canons?
看圣书的就要诞生，	The one who reads holy books will be born,
用圣典的就要降临。”	The one who uses canons will be born.”

远古，	In remote antiquity,
能万拉的创造，	The creation by Nengwam La
能斑木占的繁衍，	And the multiplication by Ningpan Majan
生下了一个	Give birth to a creature
还在娘胎里，	Who, when in his mother’s womb,

① 十卷圣书、二十捆圣典：这里不是指实际数字，而是指很多书籍的意思。传说景颇族原来有文字，后来失传。

① Ten volumes of holy books, twenty bundles of canons: Here they don’t mean the exact numbers, but refer to a lot of books. It was said that Jingpo ancestors had their own written languages, but unfortunately they were lost later.

就长出牙齿会说话；	Had teeth and could speak.
还没有出生	Before his birth,
就已经懂事会呼喊。	He was already aware and could shout.
他一出生，	The moment he was born,
就现出一副威严的面孔，	He showed a dignified face,
翘着脚，	Feet stretching
晃着腿，	And legs dangling.
他是谁呀？	Who was he?
他的名字是自己取的：	He named himself:
“我就是看十卷圣书，	“I am Hpan Wa Ningsang Chye Wa Ningchyang,
用二十捆圣典的，	Who can read volumes of holy books
潘瓦能桑遮瓦能章。”	And use bundles of canons.”
潘瓦能桑遮瓦能章，	Hpan Wa Ningsang Chye Wa Ningchyang,
他出生的时候，	As soon as he was born,
他看的圣书有了，	There were holy books for him to read,
他用的圣典有了。	And canons for him to use.
他翻开圣书，	He opened holy books
他打开圣典，	And canons,
来到木兰顶荣地方，	Came to Malan Ting-rong
对父亲和母亲说：	And said to his father and mother:
“父亲能万拉呀，	“Father Nengwam La
母亲能斑木占，	And Mother Ningpan Majan,
你们快创造呀，	Please be quick in your creation

你们快繁衍吧，
你们创造的万事，
我会按着圣书，
指明它们的用处；
你们繁衍的万物，
我会照着圣典，
给它们取下名字。”

远古，
能万拉的创造，
能斑木占的繁衍，
生出了脚蹬的竹桩[①]，
有了手拉的背带。
它们是做什么的呀，
潘瓦能桑遮瓦能章：
这是生育时，
脚蹬的竹桩；
这是分娩时，
手拉的背带[②]。

And your multiplication.
For the things you created,
I will specify their uses
Based on holy books.
For all you multiplied,
I will give them names
Based on canons.”

In remote antiquity,
The creation by Nengwam La
And the multiplication by Ningpan Majan
Produced the bamboo stake[①] for foot stamping,
And the brace for hand grasping.
What could they do?
Hpan Wa Ningsang Chye Wa Ningchyang answered:
“This is the bamboo stake
For women in labor to stamp their feet;
That is the brace
For women in labor to grasp.

① 竹桩：这里指产妇生育时帮助其用力生产的竹桩，立在产床头。
② 背带：这里指生育时，为了帮助生产，两端拴在高处，让产妇拉的带子。

① Bamboo stake: Here it refers to the stake which helps women put their feet on, when they exert themselves in delivery. It is usually set up at bedside.

远古，
能万拉的创造，
能斑木占的繁衍，
生下了一个热水槽，
有了一个冷水槽。
这是做什么的呀？
潘瓦能桑遮瓦能章，
说出它们的用处：
等将来有了太阳，
等将来有了月亮，
太阳不够热，
月亮不够明，
把太阳往热水槽里一淬，
把月亮往冷水槽里一浸，
太阳就够热了，
月亮就够明了。

In remote antiquity,
The creation by Nengwam La
And the multiplication by Ningpan Majan
Made a hot water tank,
And a cold water tank.
What were they for?
Hpan Wa Ningsang Chye Wa Ningchyang
Explained their uses:
In the future, there will be a Sun,
And there will be a Moon.
When the Sun is not hot enough
And when the Moon is not bright enough,
People will soak the Sun in the hot water tank for a while
And immerse the Moon in the cold water tank for a while,
The Sun will be hot
And the Moon will be bright.

远古，
能万拉的创造，
能斑木占的繁衍，
有了最初的太阳，
有了最初的月亮，
最初的太阳不够热，

In remote antiquity,
The creation by Nengwam La
And the multiplication by Ningpan Majan
Produced the first Sun,
And the first Moon.
The first Sun was not hot enough,

最初的月亮不够明。	And the first Moon was not bright enough.
照潘瓦能桑遮瓦能章说的话，	As Hpan Wa Ningsang Chye Wa Ningchyang said,
把太阳往热水槽里一淬，	People soaked the Sun in the hot water tank
把月亮往冷水槽里一浸，	And immersed the Moon in the cold water tank.
太阳够热了，	Then the Sun was hot
月亮够明了。	And the Moon was bright.

远古，	In remote antiquity,
能万拉的创造，	The creation by Nengwam La
能斑木占的繁衍，	And the multiplication by Ningpan Majan
有了热辣辣的太阳，	Produced the hottest Sun
有了明晃晃的月亮，	And the brightest Moon.
但不知太阳做什么，	But what was the Sun for?
也不知月亮有何用。	And what could the Moon do?
潘瓦能桑遮瓦能章	Hpan Wa Ningsang Chye Wa Ningchyang
说出了它们的用处，	Specified their uses,
等将来有了天，	In the future, there would be the Sky,
等将来有了地，	And there would be the Earth.
天不够稳定，	When the Sky was not so stable
地不够坚实，	And when the Earth was not so solid,
用太阳稳定天，	The Sun could stabilize the Sky
用月亮坚固地。	And the Moon could solidify the Earth.

远古，	In remote antiquity,

能万拉的创造，	The creation by Nengwam La
能斑木占的繁衍，	And the multiplication by Ningpan Majan
有了朦胧的一片，	Produced a hazy patch
有了圆圆的一团。	And a round mass.
这是什么呀？	What were these?
潘瓦能桑遮瓦能章	Hpan Wa Ningsang Chye Wa Ningchyang
给它们取了名字，	Gave them names.
朦胧的是天空，	The hazy patch was the Sky,
圆圆的是大地。	And the round mass was the Earth.
天不够稳定，	The Sky was not stable enough
地不够坚实，	And the Earth was not solid enough.
天不停地摇摆，	The Sky kept swaying
地不停地晃动。	And the Earth kept shaking.
按潘瓦能桑遮瓦能章说的话，	As Hpan Wa Ningsang Chye Wa Ningchyang said,
让太阳稳定了天，	The Sun was made to stabilize the Sky,
让月亮坚固了地。	While the Moon was made to solidify the Earth.
天稳定了，	Then the Sky was stable,
地坚固了。	The Earth was solid.

远古，	In remote antiquity,
能万拉的创造，	The creation by Nengwam La
能斑木占的繁衍，	And the multiplication by Ningpan Majan
天空出现了，	Made the Sky appear
大地形成了，	And made the Earth come into being.

天上没有飞的，	But there were no creatures flying in the Sky
地上没有走的，	And there were no creatures walking on the Earth.
天空感到冷清，	The Sky felt deserted
大地觉得寂寞。	And the Earth felt lonely.
潘瓦能桑遮瓦能章	Hpan Wa Ningsang Chye Wa Ningchyang
便对父母说：	Said to his parents:
“父亲能万拉呀，	“Father Nengwam La,
母亲能斑木占，	Mother Ningpan Majan,
创造天上飞的吧，	Please create the creatures flying in the Sky
生下地上走的吧。”	And bear the creatures walking on the Earth.”

远古，	In remote antiquity,
能万拉的创造，	The creation by Nengwam La
能斑木占的繁衍，	And the multiplication by Ningpan Majan
生下了最初的老鹰，	Bore the first eagle
有了最初的乌鸦；	And the first crow;
生下了最初的蛇，	Bore the first snake
有了最初的蟒；	And the first python;
生下了最初的虎，	Bore the first tiger
有了最初的豹；	And the first leopard;
生下了最初的象，	Bore the first elephant
有了最初的象群。	And the first family of elephants.
天上有了飞的，	There were the flying creatures in the Sky
地上有了走的，	And the walking creatures on the Earth.

天空不再感到冷清，	The Sky no longer felt deserted
大地不再觉得寂寞。	And the Earth no longer felt lonely.
天更宽了，	The Sky extended itself wider,
地更广了；	The Earth became broader;
天还在加宽，	The Sky was still widening,
地还在扩展；	The Earth was broadening;
天望不到边了，	The Sky was endless,
地走不到沿了。	The Earth was borderless.

远古，	In remote antiquity,
能万拉的创造，	Due to the creation by Nengwam La
能斑木占的繁衍，	And the multiplication by Ningpan Majan,
宽广的大地，	On the broad Earth,
有的地方凸起来了，	Some places were convex;
有的地方凹下去了。	Some places were concave.
这是什么呀？	What were they?
潘瓦能桑遮瓦能章说：	Hpan Wa Ningsang Chye Wa Ningchyang answered:
“凸起来的是高山，	“The convex places are mountains
凹下去的是峡谷。”	And the concave places are valleys.”
有了高山，	Since there were mountains
有了峡谷，	And there were valleys,
千座山望不到边了，	Thousands of mountains seemed endless
万个坝走不到头了。	And thousands of flatlands had no border.

远古，	In remote antiquity,
能万拉的创造，	The creation by Nengwam La
能斑木占的繁衍，	And the multiplication by Ningpan Majan
有了亮光光的一片，	Brought a bright patch
有了黑漆漆的一团。	And a pitch-dark mass.
这是什么呀？	What were they?
潘瓦能桑遮瓦能章说：	Hpan Wa Ningsang Chye Wa Ningchyang said:
“亮光光的是白天，	“The bright patch is the day,
他的名字叫瓦囊能退拉①，	With the name of Wa-nang Ninghtoi La①.
黑漆漆的是黑夜，	The pitch-dark mass is the night,
她的名字叫能星能锐木占②。	With the name of Ningsin Numroi Majan②.
他们将永远相随，	They will go hand in hand
他们将永远相伴。”	And accompany each other all the time.”

远古，	In remote antiquity,
瓦囊能退拉说	Wa-nang Ninghtoi La said
他要一直亮到底；	He would be bright to the end.
能星能锐木占说	Ningsin Numroi Majan said
她要一直黑到头。	She would be dark to the end.

① 瓦囊能退拉：能退，亮光之意；拉，男性，也即阳性，二者合起来为光明神之意。

② 能星能锐木占：能星，为黑暗之意；木占，指女性，也即阴性，二者合起来为黑暗神之意。

① Wa-nang Ninghtoi La：God of Light.

② Ningsin Numroi Majan：Goddess of Darkness.

他们争来抢去，	They fought against each other.
谁也不相忍让。	Neither could tolerate the other.
潘瓦能桑遮瓦能章	Hpan Wa Ningsang Chye Wa Ningchyang
对他们说：	Said to them:
“瓦囊能退拉呀，	“Wa-nang Ninghtoi La,
能星能锐木占，	Ningsin Numroi Majan,
你们不要再争，	You should not argue with each other,
你们不要再抢，	Or fight against each other.
你们就亮一半，	You two will share
黑一半吧！”	Both light and darkness.”
潘瓦能桑遮瓦能章，	Hpan Wa Ningsang Chye Wa Ningchyang
规定了白天和黑夜，	Specified the time of day and night.
瓦囊能退拉亮一半，	Wa-nang Ninghtoi La was bright half of the time,
能星能锐木占黑一半。	Ningsin Numroi Majan was dark half of the time.
从此，世界上	Since then, in the world
有了白天和黑夜。	Day and night came into being.

远古，	In remote antiquity,
瓦囊能退拉觉得冷清，	Wa-nang Ninghtoi La felt deserted
想要白天的伙伴；	And wanted a companion in the day;
能星能锐木占感到寂寞，	Ningsin Numroi Majan felt lonely,
想要黑夜的朋友。	And wanted a friend at night.
潘瓦能桑遮瓦能章	Hpan Wa Ningsang Chye Wa Ningchyang
便对父母说：	Said to his parents:

“父亲能万拉呀，
母亲能斑木占，
创造白天的伙伴吧，
生下黑夜的朋友吧！”

“Father Nengwam La,
Mother Ningpan Majan,
Please create companions for the day,
And bear friends for the night.”

远古，
能万拉的创造，
能斑木占的繁衍，
生下了黑蚂蚁，
有了黄蚂蚁；
生下了大蚂蚁，
有了细蚂蚁；
生下了小蛐蛐，
有了竹蝗；
生下了灰蚂蚱，
有了绿蚂蚱；
生下了四脚蛇，
有了脆骨蛇；
生下了小青蛙，
有了大癞蛤蟆；
生下了金线蛙，
有了大牛蛙；
生下了夜鸟，
有了蝙蝠；

In remote antiquity,
The creation by Nengwam La
And the multiplication by Ningpan Majan
Brought black ants
And yellow ants,
Big ants
And small ants,
Small crickets
And bamboo locusts,
Gray grasshoppers
And green grasshoppers,
Lizards
And cartilage snakes,
Small frogs
And big toads,
Green pond-frogs
And big bullfrogs,
Night birds
And bats,

生下了长尾鸟，	Reedlings
有了猫头鹰；	And owls,
生下了貂鼠，	Martens
有了穿山甲。	And pangolins.
白天走的归白天，	Those living in the light belonged to the day;
黑夜行的归黑夜。	Those living in the dark belonged to the night.
从此，白天有了伙伴，	Since then, The day got its companions,
黑夜有了朋友。	And the night got its friends.
远古，	In remote antiquity,
潘瓦能桑遮瓦能章	Hpan Wa Ningsang Chye Wa Ningchyang
对父母说：	Said to his parents:
“父亲能万拉呀，	“Father Nengwam La,
母亲能斑木占，	Mother Ningpan Majan,
停止创造吧，	Please stop your creation
停止繁衍吧！	And your multiplication.
让你们的后代	Make your descendants,
瓦囊能退拉，	Wa-nang Ninghtoi La,
能星能锐木占接着创造吧，	Ningsin Numroi Majan continue your creation
继续繁衍吧！”	And your multiplication.”
听了儿子的话，	Hearing their son’s words,
能万拉安息在东方	Father Nengwam La rested in the East.
他在东方发出灵光，	He gave off miraculous brightness in the East,
所以干天从东方开始；	So the dry days began from the East;

能斑木占安息在西方，	Mother Ningpan Majan rested in the West.
她在西方发出灵光，	She gave off miraculous brightness in the West,
所以雨天从西方来。	So the wet days began from the West.

二、瓦囊能退拉和能星能锐木占的创造繁衍
Ⅱ. Creation and Multiplication by Wa-nang Ninghtoi La and Ningsin Numroi Majan

远古，	In remote antiquity,
瓦囊能退拉	Wa-nang Ninghtoi La
接着能万拉创造；	Continued the creation by Nengwam La;
能星能锐木占	Ningsin Numroi Majan
跟着能斑木占繁衍。	Went on with the multiplication by Ningpan Majan.

远古，	In remote antiquity,
瓦囊能退拉的创造，	The creation by Wa-nang Ninghtoi La
能星能锐木占的繁衍，	And the multiplication by Ningsin Numroi Majan
生下了一层层硬壳，	Made layers of shells
有了一团团硬块。	And piles of lumps.
这是什么呀？	What were they?
潘瓦能桑遮瓦能章	Hpan Wa Ningsang Chye Wa Ningchyang
给它们取了名字，	Gave them names.
一层层的是石片，	The layers were scabblings;

一团团的是石块，	The piles were rocks.
把一层层石片放到大地上，	Let's put layers of scabblings on the Earth
大地更宽了；	And the Earth became wider;
把一块块的石块放到大地上，	Put piles of rocks on the Earth
大地更广了。	And the Earth became broader.
远古，	In remote antiquity,
石岩感到太冷清，	The rock felt so deserted
想要伙伴，	That he wanted some companions.
大地觉得太寂寞，	The Earth felt so lonely
想要朋友。	That he wanted some friends.
潘瓦能桑遮瓦能章	Hpan Wa Ningsang Chye Wa Ningchyang
便对白天和黑夜说：	Said to the day and the night:
“瓦囊能退拉，	"Wa-nang Ninghtoi La,
能星能锐木占呀，	Ningsin Numroi Majan,
给石岩生下伙伴，	Please bear some companions for the rock
给大地生下朋友吧！”	And some friends for the Earth."
远古，	In remote antiquity,
瓦囊能退拉的创造，	The creation by Wa-nang Ninghtoi La
能星能锐木占的繁衍，	And the multiplication by Ningsin Numroi Majan
生下了一个凹眼睛、	Bore a creature with sunken eyes
窄脸膛的。	And a narrow face.
它是什么呀？	What was it?

潘瓦能桑遮瓦能章
给它取了名字，
它就是石岩的伙伴，
大地的朋友，
会叫会跳的黄猴。

Hpan Wa Ningsang Chye Wa Ningchyang
Gave it a name:
The Yellow Monkey, who could bark and jump,
A companion of the rock
And a friend of the Earth.

远古，
瓦囊能退拉的创造，
能星能锐木占的繁衍，
生下了一个高眉骨、
短脸膛的东西，
它是什么呀？
潘瓦能桑遮瓦能章说：
“它就是石岩的伙伴，
大地的朋友，
整天蹲在石头上的灰猴。
等将来有了森林，
等将来有了草坪，
它将在森林里玩耍，
它将在草坪上奔跑。”

In remote antiquity,
The creation by Wa-nang Ninghtoi La
And the multiplication by Ningsin Numroi Majan
Gave birth to a creature
With a prominent brow ridge and a short face.
What was it?
Hpan Wa Ningsang Chye Wa Ningchyang answered:
“It is the Gray Monkey squatting on the rock all day,
A companion of the rock
And a friend of the Earth.
In the future, when there are forests
And there is grassland,
It will play in the forests,
It will run on the grassland.”

远古，
瓦囊能退拉的创造，
能星能锐木占的繁衍，

In remote antiquity,
The creation by Wa-nang Ninghtoi La
And the multiplication by Ningsin Numroi Majan

生下了一个圆眼	Gave birth to a creature with round eyes
短脸膛的东西，	And a short face,
它一半像猴，	Half monkey,
一半像人。	Half man.
它是什么呀？	What was it?
潘瓦能桑遮瓦能章说：	Hpan Wa Ningsang Chye Wa Ningchyang replied:
“它就是石岩的伙伴，	“It is the Black Monkey living on the rock,
大地的朋友，	A companion of the rock
居住在石岩上的黑猴。”	And a friend of the Earth.”
从此，居住在石岩上的有了，	Since then, there were creatures living on the rock;
生活在大地上的也有了，	There were creatures living on the Earth.
石岩不再感到冷清，	The rock no longer felt deserted,
大地不再觉得寂寞。	And the Earth no longer felt lonely.
远古，	In remote antiquity,
瓦囊能退拉的创造，	The creation by Wa-nang Ninghtoi La
能星能锐木占的繁衍，	And the multiplication by Ningsin Numroi Majan
生下了平坦的一片，	Made a flat patch
有了椭圆形的一块。	And an oval piece.
它们是什么呀？	What were they?
潘瓦能桑遮瓦能章	Hpan Wa Ningsang Chye Wa Ningchyang
给它们取了名字，	Gave them names.

平坦的是繁衍生命的竹笆①。	The flat was the bamboo fence① for multiplication;
椭圆形的是创造万物的石块②。	The oval was the rock of creation②.
将来的生命，	The life in the future
会在竹笆上繁衍；	Would multiply on the bamboo fence;
将来的万物，	All the living things
会在石块上创造。	Would be created on the rock.
有了竹笆和石块，	With the bamboo fence and the rock,
潘瓦能桑遮瓦能章	Hpan Wa Ningsang Chye Wa Ningchyang
对白天和黑夜说：	Said to the day and the night:
“瓦囊能退拉呀，	“Wa-nang Ninghtoi La,
能星能锐木占，	Ningsin Numroi Majan,
繁衍生命的竹笆有了，	Since there are the bamboo fence for multiplication
创造万物的石块也有了，	And the rock for creation,
你们快繁衍吧，	Please be quick in your multiplication
你们快创造吧，	And your creation.
让生命布满竹笆，	Please make the bamboo fence full of life
让万物遍布石块。”	And the rock covered with living things.”

远古，	In remote antiquity,
瓦囊能退拉的创造，	The creation by Wa-nang Ninghtoi La

① 竹笆：指繁衍生命时用的竹笆，这里泛指宇宙空间。

② 创造万物的石块：形容生产生命的坚硬辽阔的大地。

① Bamboo fence: It refers to the fence which is used when a life is born. Here it means the universe.

② Rock of creation: It symbolizes the vast and hard Earth on which living things grow up.

能星能锐木占的繁衍，
生下了高低不平的一片，
上面长满了绿茵茵的东西，
这是什么地方呀？
潘瓦能桑遮瓦能章说：
“这是长满花草的农斋①地方，
将来的蜂类，
将生活在这里。”

And the multiplication by Ningsin Numroi Majan
Produced an uneven patch.
On it grew the green things,
What was this place?
Hpan Wa Ningsang Chye Wa Ningchyang answered:
“This is the wild①, the field overgrown by flowers and grass.
In the future, the bee species
Will live here.”

远古，
瓦囊能退拉的创造，
能星能锐木占的繁衍，
生下了光出现的方向，
有了光消失的方向。
这是什么地方呀？
潘瓦能桑遮瓦能章说：
“光出现的方向是东方，
那里住着东方木若神②；
光消失的方向是西方，
那里住着西方木若神。

In remote antiquity,
The creation by Wa-nang Ninghtoi La
And the multiplication by Ningsin Numroi Majan
Made the direction where the light appeared
And the direction where the light disappeared.
What were they?
Hpan Wa Ningsang Chye Wa Ningchyang said:
“The direction where the light appears is the East.
There lives the Eastern God Maro②.
The direction where light disappears is the West.
There lives the Western Goddess Maro.

---

① 农斋：泛指野外，蜂类生活的地方。
② 木若神：神的一类，传说多居住在野外。

① The wild: It refers to the field where bee species usually live.
② God Maro: a kind of god, who is often said to live in the fields.

东方木若神是男的，
西方木若神是女的。”

The Eastern God Maro is male.
The Western Goddess Maro is female.”

远古，
瓦囊能退拉的创造，
能星能锐木占的繁衍，
生下了木江阿苦的地方。
生下这个地方做什么呀？
潘瓦能桑遮瓦能章说：
“将来的迷退[1]，
将从这里降生，
将到这里归终。

In remote antiquity,
The creation by Wa-nang Ninghtoi La
And the multiplication by Ningsin Numroi Majan
Made a place called Machyang A Hku.
What was the place used for?
Hpan Wa Ningsang Chye Wa Ningchyang replied:
In the future, the wizard Myihtoi[1]
Will be born here
And will die here.

远古，
瓦囊能退拉的创造，
能星能锐木占的繁衍，
有了宽广的高原，
有了高耸的山峰，
这是什么地方呀？
潘瓦能桑遮瓦能章说：
“这是勒木卢酸能藏贡端[2]

In remote antiquity,
The creation by Wa-nang Ninghtoi La
And the multiplication by Ningsin Numroi Majan
Produced vast grasslands
And towering peaks.
What were these places?
Hpan Wa Ningsang Chye Wa Ningchyang said:
“The resting place of Lamu Lupson Ningtsang

---

① 迷退：神职人员中地位较高的，类巫师或预言家。
② 勒木卢酸能藏贡端：传说巫师去世后其灵魂的安息地。

① Myihtoi: a clergyman with a high position who is also called a wizard or prophet.

地方，	Kungdon①, the Wizard.
等将来生下德如贡散木干贡潘①时，	When Daru Gumsan Magam Gumhpan②, the first King, is born,
他隐藏在这个地方。	This will be the place where he hides himself."
远古，	In remote antiquity,
瓦囊能退拉的创造，	The creation by Wa-nang Ninghtoi La
能星能锐木占的繁衍，	And the multiplication by Ningsin Numroi Majan
生下了长着翅膀，	Gave birth to a creature with a pair of wings
有着白肚子的东西。	And a white belly.
这是什么呀？	What was it?
潘瓦能桑遮瓦能章	Hpan Wa Ningsang Chye Wa Ningchyang
给它取了名字，	Gave it a name.
它就是飞得很快的燕子，	It was a swallow that could fly fast.
等将来有了新的天，	When there was a new Sky
等将来有了新的地，	And a new Earth in the future,
就让它巡视新的天，	It would be made to tour the new Sky
就让它巡视新的地。	And inspect the new Earth.
远古，	In remote antiquity,
瓦囊能退拉的创造，	The creation by Wa-nang Ninghtoi La

① 德如贡散木干贡潘：传说中景颇族的第一个王。

① Lamu Lupson Ningtsang Kungdon: a place where the soul of a wizard rests after his death.

② Daru Gumsan Magam Gumhpan: the first king of the Jingpo people in legend.

能星能锐木占的繁衍，	And the multiplication by Ningsin Numroi Majan
生下了一对伙伴，	Bore a pair of companions
有了一对朋友。	And a couple of friends.
他们是谁呀？	Who were they?
潘瓦能桑遮瓦能章	Hpan Wa Ningsang Chye Wa Ningchyang
给他们取了名，	Gave them names.
雄的叫勒农拉，	The male was named Lanung La.
他是百鸟的父神；	He was the Father God of Birds;
雌的叫勒农木占，	The female was named Lanung Majan.
她是百鸟的母神。	She was the Mother God of Birds.

三、勒农拉和勒农木占的创造繁衍

Ⅲ. Creation and Multiplication by Lanung La and Lanung Majan

远古，	In remote antiquity,
勒农拉的创造，	The creation by Lanung La
勒农木占的繁衍，	And the multiplication by Lanung Majan
生下了勒农省瓦鸟①，	Bore the Lanung Sinwa bird①

① 勒农省瓦鸟：生活在亚热带森林的一种鸟，黑羽毛，长尾巴，景颇族将之视为吉祥之鸟。

① The Lanung Sinwa bird: It has a long tail and black feather, and lives in the subtropical zone. The Jingpo people regard it as the bird of auspice.

有了农鸠郭腊鸟①；	And the Ningkyu Gola bird①,
生下了犀鸟，	The hornbill
有了白凡鸡；	And the Riro bird,
生下了孔雀，	The peacock
有了乌歌鸟②；	And the Ukro bird②,
生下了乌卓鸟③，	The Uchyo bird③
有了阶坎鸟④；	And the Kaihkam bird④,
生下了乌干鸟⑤，	The Ugam⑤ bird
有了斑鸠；	And the turtledove,
生下了登戛日奔鸡⑥，	The Dingga Ribun⑥ pheasant
有了竹鸡。	And the bamboo partridge.
各种鸟生下了，	Then, there were all kinds of birds
各类鸟都有了。	And varieties of fowls.
生下它们做什么呀？	What were they born for?
潘瓦能桑遮瓦能章说：	Hpan Wa Ningsang Chye Wa Ningchyang said:
“等将来有了新的天，	“When in the future there is a new Sky

① 农鸠郭腊鸟：生活在亚热带森林里的一种鸟，头大身小，全身呈灰黑色。
② 乌歌鸟：生活在亚热带森林里的一种鸟，呈暗红色，脖颈上有花纹。
③ 乌卓鸟：生活在山区的一种善于鸣叫的鸟。
④ 阶坎鸟：群居在森林里的一种善飞的鸟，呈灰色。
⑤ 乌干鸟：森林中一种小鸟。
⑥ 登戛日奔鸡：属锦鸡一类。

① The Ningkyu Gola bird: It has a big head and small body and gray and black feather, living in the subtropical zone.
② The Ukro bird: It has maroon all over the body with decorative patterns on the neck. It lives in the subtropical zone.
③ The Uchyo bird: They live in the mountain areas and like tweeting.
④ The kaihkam bird: It is a gray bird living in flocks in forests.
⑤ The Ugam bird: a small bird in the forest.
⑥ The Dingga Ribun: It is a type of golden pheasant.

等将来有了新的地，	And a new Earth,
就让它们飞向天空，	Let's make them fly in the Sky
就让它们扒平大地。”	And level the Earth."
远古，	In remote antiquity,
瓦囊能退拉的创造，	The creation by Wa-nang Ninghtoi La
能星能锐木占的繁衍，	And the multiplication by Ningsin Numroi Majan
生下了直套文仁地方①。	Made the place Jahtau Wunrim.①
这个地方是做什么的呀？	What was the place used for?
潘瓦能桑遮瓦能章说：	Hpan Wa Ningsang Chye Wa Ningchyang said:
“这是将来的凶狠天神	"Here is the place
木夺神浪直卡能旁，	Where Mado Shinlan Jahka Ninghprang,
生活居住的地方。	The God of War, will live in the future."
远古，	In remote antiquity,
瓦囊能退拉的创造，	The creation by Wa-nang Ninghtoi La
能星能锐木占的繁衍，	And the multiplication by Ningsin Numroi Majan
生下了孺木荣皮松统地方②。	Made Ru Marong Hpri Sumhtong.②
这个地方是做什么的呀？	What was the place used for?
潘瓦能桑遮瓦能章说：	Hpan Wa Ningsang Chye Wa Ningchyang answered:
“这是将来的凶狠天神	"Here is the place

① 直套文仁地方：传说中这个地方是个大峡谷。
② 孺木荣皮松统地方：传说中凶残鬼居住的地方。

① Jahtau Wunrim: a grand canyon.
② Ru Marong Hpri Sumhtong: the place where the fierce ghost lives.

<table>
<tr><td>能通诗热能日木接，
生活居住的地方。</td><td>Where Ninghtum Share Ning-ri Matse,
A fierce ghost, will live in the future.”</td></tr>
<tr><td>远古，
瓦囊能退拉的创造，
能星能锐木占的繁衍；
生下了盆南朵丽烈勒旺狄区权地方[①]。
这个地方是做什么的呀？
潘瓦能桑遮瓦能章说：
“这是将来的风神
崩梯格努崩台杜，
生活居住的地方。”</td><td>In remote antiquity,
The creation by Wa-nang Ninghtoi La
And the multiplication by Ningsin Numroi Majan
Made Hpungnam Toli Lawang Dihkyi Hkyet[①].
What was the place used for?
Hpan Wa Ningsang Chye Wa Ningchyang replied:
“Here is the place
Where Bunghti Ganu Bunghtai Du,
The God of Wind, will live in the future.”</td></tr>
<tr><td>远古，
瓦囊能退拉的创造，
能星能锐木占的繁衍，
生下了锋利的圣錾[②]，
有了尖利的钻子，
这是做什么的呀？
潘瓦能桑遮瓦能章说：</td><td>In remote antiquity,
The creation by Wa-nang Ninghtoi La
And the multiplication by Ningsin Numroi Majan
Produced the sharp iron tool
And the sharp drill.
What were they used for?
Hpan Wa Ningsang Chye Wa Ningchyang answered:</td></tr>
</table>

① 盆南朵丽烈勒旺狄区权地方：一个大垭口。
② 圣錾：传说中的一种工具。

① Hpungnam Toli Lawang Dihkyi Hkyet: a great mountain pass.

“用圣錾做项链，	“The iron tool is used to make a necklace
用钻子穿项链。”	And the drill is used to string it together.”
谁来用圣錾？	Who would use this iron tool?
谁来用钻子？	Who would use the drill?
瓦囊能退拉的创造，	The creation by Wa-nang Ninghtoi La
能星能锐木占的繁衍，	And the multiplication by Ningsin Numroi Majan
生下了拉瓦木独，	Bore Laira Madu
有了嫩占木东。	And Ningjan Mutong.
生下他们做什么呀？	What were they born for?
潘瓦能桑遮瓦能章说：	Hpan Wa Ningsang Chye Wa Ningchyang said:
“他们就是用圣錾的，	“They are born to use the iron tool;
他们就是用钻子的。”	They are born to use the drill.”

远古，	In remote antiquity,
瓦囊能退拉的创造，	The creation by Wa-nang Ninghtoi La
能星能锐木占的繁衍，	And the multiplication by Ningsin Numroi Majan
生下了能穿山、	Bore a creature who could go through the mountains
还能入水的。	And jump into the water.
这是什么呀？	What was it?
潘瓦能桑遮瓦能章	Hpan Wa Ningsang Chye Wa Ningchyang
给它取了名字，	Gave it a name.
它就是勒竹格努勒旺阶东杜[①]。	It was Laju Ganu Lawang Gaitong Du[①].

① 勒竹格努勒旺阶东杜：传说中的一种神龙。

① Laju Ganu Lawang Gaitong Du: a powerful dragon in legendary stories.

远古，
瓦囊能退拉的创造，
能星能锐木占的繁衍，
生下了长着尾巴，
浑身有花纹的。
这是什么呀？
潘瓦能桑遮瓦能章
给它取了名字，
它就是生活在树林里，
居住在大树上的树豹。

In remote antiquity,
The creation by Wa-nang Ninghtoi La
And the multiplication by Ningsin Numroi Majan
Bore a creature with a long tail
And covered with decorative patterns.
What was it?
Hpan Wa Ningsang Chye Wa Ningchyang
Gave it a name.
It was the tree leopard
Living in the forests.

远古，
瓦囊能退拉的创造，
能星能锐木占的繁衍，
生下了硬弩，
有了利箭。
谁来使硬弩？
谁来使利箭？
潘瓦能桑遮瓦能章说：
“使硬弩的就会出生，
射利剑的就会降临。”

In remote antiquity,
The creation by Wa-nang Ninghtoi La
And the multiplication by Ningsin Numroi Majan
Bore the hard crossbow
And the sharp arrow.
Who would use the hard crossbow
And who would shoot the sharp arrow?
Hpan Wa Ningsang Chye Wa Ningchyang said:
“The one who uses the hard crossbow will be born.
The one who shoots the sharp arrow will come to the Earth.”

远古，	In remote antiquity,
瓦囊能退拉的创造，	The creation by Wa-nang Ninghtoi La
能星能锐木占的繁衍，	And the multiplication by Ningsin Numroi Majan
生下了身躯高大，	Bore a creature who was tall
长着獠牙的。	And with long teeth.
他是谁呀？	Who was he?
潘瓦能桑遮瓦能章说：	Hpan Wa Ningsang Chye Wa Ningchyang answered:
“他就是使硬弩的力士，	“He is the strong man who will use the hard crossbow.
他就是射利箭的射手，	He was the archer who will shoot the sharp arrow.
他将抬着硬弩，	He will hold the hard crossbow
拿着利箭，	And grasp the sharp arrow,
站在高山上，	Standing on the high mountain
守在峡谷间。”	And guarding in the gorge.”

远古，	In remote antiquity,
瓦囊能退拉的创造，	The creation by Wa-nang Ninghtoi La
能星能锐木占的繁衍，	And the multiplication by Ningsin Numroi Majan
有了巨大的石块，	Produced a gigantic rock
有了沉重的石丸。	And a heavy stone ball.
用它们做什么呀？	What could they be used for?
潘瓦能桑遮瓦能章说：	Hpan Wa Ningsang Chye Wa Ningchyang said:
“等到了将来，	“In the future, the rock can be used to block the gorge
用石块堵住峡谷，	And the stone ball can be used
用石丸塞住石缝。”	To fill in the stone crack.”

远古，	In remote antiquity,
瓦囊能退拉的创造，	The creation by Wa-nang Ninghtoi La
能星能锐木占的繁衍，	And the multiplication by Ningsin Numroi Majan
生下了巨虾。	Bore the jumbo shrimp.
生下巨虾做什么呀？	What was the jumbo shrimp born for?
潘瓦能桑遮瓦能章说：	Hpan Wa Ningsang Chye Wa Ningchyang replied:
“将来水面不干净，	“When in the future,
就让巨虾	The water is dirty,
去清理水面。”	The jumbo shrimp can clean it.”
远古，	In remote antiquity,
瓦囊能退拉的创造，	The creation by Wa-nang Ninghtoi La
能星能锐木占的繁衍，	And the multiplication by Ningsin Numroi Majan
生下了身躯巨大、	Bore a creature who was tall,
脸像簸箕的。	With a dustpan-like face.
他是谁呀？	Who was he?
潘瓦能桑遮瓦能章说：	Hpan Wa Ningsang Chye Wa Ningchyang said:
“他就是山石神，	“He is the God of Rock.
他居住在扎刚崩入拴格登荣石扁地方[①]，	He lives in the Jagrang Bung-ru[①] Valley,
	Where there grow Jagrang Bung-ru vines[②]

① 扎刚崩入拴格登荣石扁地方：传说中林木茂盛的山箐。

① Jagrang Bung-ru: a legendary valley with lush trees.
② Jagrang Bung-ru vines: a kind of vine in legendary stories.

那里生长着扎刚崩入藤①，
那里生长着格登荣石树②。”

And the vine fruit trees called Gading Rumshi①.”

远古，
瓦囊能退拉的创造，
能星能锐木占的繁衍，
生下了面带笑容、
头发伸长的。
他是谁呀？
潘瓦能桑遮瓦能章说：
“他就是德如瓦能用木干兰
　能双，
他居住在江河汇合的地方，
那里生长着能顶能若树。”

In remote antiquity,
The creation by Wa-nang Ninghtoi La
And the multiplication by Ningsin Numroi Majan
Bore a creature with a smiling face
And long hair.
Who was he?
Hpan Wa Ningsang Chye Wa Ningchyang answered:
“He is Deru Wa Ning-yong Magam Lat Ningshong.
He lives in the place where rivers meet.
There grow the trees of Numtin Numro.”

远古，
瓦囊能退拉的创造，
能星能锐木占的繁衍，
生下了一个
拿着金梭板，
带着银梭板的。

In remote antiquity,
The creation by Wa-nang Ninghtoi La
And the multiplication by Ningsin Numroi Majan
Bore a creature
With a golden shuttle board
And a silver shuttle board in his hands.

---

① 扎刚崩入藤：传说中的一种藤子。
② 格登荣石树：传说中的一种树。

① Gading Rumshi: a kind of tree in legendary stories.

他是谁呀？	Who was he?
潘瓦能桑遮瓦能章说：	Hpan Wa Ningsang Chye Wa Ningchyang answered:
“他就是山洼神	“He is Ntam Son Mani Naitam Son Maji,
恩胆算木里乃胆算木直，	The God of Valley.
他居住在昔闵阿苦地方，	He lives in the Samyin Hku Valley.
那里生长着木卡树。”	There grow the tree of Mahka.”
远古，	In remote antiquity,
瓦囊能退拉的创造，	The creation by Wa-nang Ninghtoi La
能星能锐木占的繁衍，	And the multiplication by Ningsin Numroi Majan
生下了头戴犀鸟头的。	Bore a creature with the head of the hornbill on his head.
他是谁呀？	Who was he?
潘瓦能桑遮瓦能章说：	Hpan Wa Ningsang Chye Wa Ningchyang answered:
“他就是德如瓦直来莲木干文布伸，	“He is Deru Wa Jalai Len Magam Wunbu Shen.
他居住在顶木萨浪格那地方，	He lives in the place Ding Masa Lang Gana.
那里生长着萨阴大青树。”	There grow the big green tree of Sa-sing.
远古，	In remote antiquity,
瓦囊能退拉的创造，	The creation by Wa-nang Ninghtoi La
能星能锐木占的繁衍，	And the multiplication by Ningsin Numroi Majan
生下了一个	Bore a creature
穿着金衣，	In golden clothes,
戴着银饰的。	Wearing silver jewelry.

他是谁呀？
潘瓦能桑遮瓦能章说：
“他就是省腊省丽扎美恩散木直，
他居住在能朵阴地方，
他生活的地方，
生长着松盘布山藤。”

Who was he?
Hpan Wa Ningsang Chye Wa Ningchyang replied:
“He is Sinlap Sinli Jamoi Asam Maji.
He lives in Ningto,
Where grow the vine of Sumhpan Pasham.”

远古，
瓦囊能退拉的创造，
能星能锐木占的繁衍，
生下了一个大石盖，
有了一个大石洞。
这是做什么的呀？
潘瓦能桑遮瓦能章说：
“等将来有了凶死的，
就埋在这个地方。”

In remote antiquity,
The creation by Wa-nang Ninghtoi La
And the multiplication by Ningsin Numroi Majan
Made a huge stone cover
And a big stone cave.
What were these for?
Hpan Wa Ningsang Chye Wa Ningchyang replied:
“In the future, those who die in violence
Will be buried here.”

远古，
瓦囊能退拉的创造，
能星能锐木占的繁衍，
有了大张着嘴，
砍自己的腿，
割自己肉的。

In remote antiquity,
The creation by Wa-nang Ninghtoi La
And the multiplication by Ningsin Numroi Majan
Bore creatures who opened their mouths,
Cut their own legs
And their flesh.

他们是谁呀？	Who were they?
潘瓦能桑遮瓦能章说：	Hpan Wa Ningsang Chye Wa Ningchyang answered:
“他们是管大石洞、	“They are the ones in charge of the big cave
使用大石盖的	And can handle the huge stone cover.
凶死萨洼鬼①，	They are Sa-wa ghosts① who die in violence.
尖仍阿拉和尖仍木占②。”	They are called Tsen Ren Ala and Tsen Ren Majan②.”

远古，	In remote antiquity,
瓦囊能退拉的创造，	The creation by Wa-nang Ninghtoi La
能星能锐木占的繁衍，	And the multiplication by Ningsin Numroi Majan
生下了一个	Bore a creature
浑身沾鲜血的。	With blood all over him.
他是谁呀？	Who was he?
潘瓦能桑遮瓦能章说：	Hpan Wa Ningsang Chye Wa Ningchyang answered:
“他是主宰生命的	“He is Nat Jauhpa
智神热那诏帕鬼。	The Ghost of Wisdom,
他生活在木砣登绿	Who controls the destiny of all beings.
圣热乌鲁地方。	He lives in a place called
他居住地方，	Majoi Dinglu Shing-ra Walu,
生长着贡技贡巴草。”	Where grow the grass of Hkungji Kumba.”

远古，	In remote antiquity,

① 萨洼鬼：指短命鬼。
② 尖仍阿拉和尖仍木占：指短命的一对男女鬼。

① Sa-wa ghost: a short-lived person's ghost.
② Tsen Ren Ala and Tsen Ren Majan: a couple who died young.

瓦囊能退拉的创造，	The creation by Wa-nang Ninghtoi La
能星能锐木占的繁衍，	And the multiplication by Ningsin Numroi Majan
生下了血块，	Bore a blood clot
有了血团。	And a blood ball.
他是什么呀？	What was it?
潘瓦能桑遮瓦能章说：	Hpan Wa Ningsang Chye Wa Ningchyang replied:
“他就是能通格努能日木杂杜①，	“It is Ninghtum Ganu Ning-ri Matsa Du①.
他居住在黑暗里，	It lives in the dark.
他生活在石洞中。”	It lives in a cave.”

远古，	In remote antiquity,
瓦囊能退拉的创造，	The creation by Wa-nang Ninghtoi La
能星能锐木占的繁衍，	And the multiplication by Ningsin Numroi Majan
生下了像雾	Bore a creature
又像水的。	Who was like mist and water.
他是什么呀？	Who was he?
潘瓦能桑遮瓦能章说：	Hpan Wa Ningsang Chye Wa Ningchyang replied:
“这是凶残鬼	“He is Ningtum Share Ning-ri Matse,
能通诗热能日木接，	A ferocious ghost
他生活在皮松统地方。”	Who lives in Hpri Sumhtong.”

① 能通格努能日木杂杜：传说中很会诅咒的鬼。

① Ninghtum Ganu Ning-ri Matsa Du: a ghost who likes cursing.

远古，	In remote antiquity,
瓦囊能退拉的创造，	The creation by Wa-nang Ninghtoi La
能星能锐木占的繁衍，	And the multiplication by Ningsin Numroi Majan
生下了神弓，	Produced holy bows
有了神箭；	And holy arrows,
生下了神刀，	Holy knives
有了神锤；	And holy hammers,
生下了神风，	Holy wind
有了神火；	And holy fire,
生下了神蛇，	Holy snakes
有了神水。	And holy water.
谁来使用这些兵器呢？	Who would use these weapons?
潘瓦能桑遮瓦能章说：	Hpan Wa Ningsang Chye Wa Ningchyang answered:
“将来的凶狠天神	“Mado Shinlang Jahka Ninghprang,
木夺神浪直卡能旁，	The God of War,
将使用这些兵器。”	Will use these weapons in the future.”

远古，	In remote antiquity,
瓦囊能退拉的创造，	The creation by Wa-nang Ninghtoi La
能星能锐木占的繁衍，	And the multiplication by Ningsin Numroi Majan
生下了一个	Bore a creature
能使水干涸，	Who could make the water dry up
会叫山摇动的。	And the mountains quake.
这是什么呀？	Who was it?

潘瓦能桑遮瓦能章说：	Hpan Wa Ningsang Chye Wa Ningchyang said:
“这是战神木夺神浪	“It is the holy snake to be commanded by
将来使用的神蛇。”	Mado Shinlang, the God of War in the future.”

远古，	In remote antiquity,
瓦囊能退拉的创造，	The creation by Wa-nang Ninghtoi La
能星能锐木占的繁衍，	And the multiplication by Ningsin Numroi Majan
生下了一个	Bore a creature
身躯像巨石，	Whose body was like a huge rock,
眼睛像黑果的。	Whose eyes were like black fruits.
他是谁呀？	Who was he?
潘瓦能桑遮瓦能章说：	Hpan Wa Ningsang Chye Wa Ningchyang answered:
“这就是使用兵器和神蛇的战神，	“He is Mado Shinlang Jahka Ninghprang, the God of War
木夺神浪直卡能旁。	Who uses the weapons and commanded the holy snake.
他生活在直套文仁地方。	He lives in Jahtau Wunrim.
将来出征打仗时，	In the future when marching to war, we will
就在圆场的中柱祭献他。	Offer sacrifices to him at the center pillar of the square.
木夺神浪生活的地方直套文仁地方已有了，	The place Jahtau Wunrim has been created for Mado Shinlang,
他就去生活在那里，	So he just went over to live there
去居住在那里！”	And stayed there!”

远古，	In remote antiquity,

瓦囊能退拉的创造，
能星能锐木占的繁衍，
生下了一对
还在娘胎里
就不停地摇摆的，
他们是谁呀？
潘瓦能桑遮瓦能章说：
“雄的叫尹暖拉，
是百兽的父神；
雌的叫给冠木占，
是百兽的母神。”

The creation by Wa-nang Ninghtoi La
And the multiplication by Ningsin Numroi Majan
Bore a pair of creatures,
Who kept shaking
In their mother's womb.
Who were they?
Hpan Wa Ningsang Chye Wa Ningchyang said:
"The male was called Yinnon La,
The Father God of Animals.
The female was Krikron Majan,
The Mother God of Animals."

四、尹暖拉和给冠木占的创造繁衍

Ⅳ. Creation and Multiplication by Yinnon La and Krikron Majan

远古，
尹暖拉的创造，
给冠木占的繁衍，
生下了一对
有着尖嘴、
长着长尾的。
他们是谁呀？

In remote antiquity,
The creation by Yinnon La
And the multiplication by Krikron Majan
Bore a pair of creatures,
Who had beaks
And long tails.
Who were they?

潘瓦能桑遮瓦能章说：
“他们是鼠的祖先，
雌的叫尤子格努，
雄的叫尤巷木杜。”

Hpan Wa Ningsang Chye Wa Ningchyang answered:
“They are the ancestors of rats.
The female is named Yu Tsi Ganu.
The male is named Yu Gang Madu.”

远古，
尹暖拉的创造，
给冠木占的繁衍，
生下了一对
身上长着刺的。
他们是谁呀？
潘瓦能桑遮瓦能章说：
“他们是刺猬的祖先，
雌的叫阿独格努，
雄的叫冬西木杜。”

In remote antiquity,
The creation by Yinnon La
And the multiplication by Krikron Majan
Bore a pair of creatures
With thorns all over them.
Who were they?
Hpan Wa Ningsang Chye Wa Ningchyang replied:
“They are the ancestors of the hedgehogs.
The female is called Adu Ganu.
The male is called Dumsi Madu.”

远古，
尹暖拉的创造，
给冠木占的繁衍，
生下了一对
浑身都是绿色，
身躯细长的。
他们是谁呀？
潘瓦能桑遮瓦能章说：

In remote antiquity,
The creation by Yinnon La
And the multiplication by Krikron Majan
Bore a pair of creatures,
Who were green all over
And had thin long bodies.
Who were they?
Hpan Wa Ningsang Chye Wa Ningchyang said:

“他们是草类的祖先，	“They are the ancestors of grass.
雌的叫曾都格努，	The female is Tsingdu Ganu.
雄的叫曾满木杜。”	The male is Tsingman Madu.”
远古，	In remote antiquity,
尹暖拉的创造，	The creation by Yinnon La
给冠木占的繁衍，	And the multiplication by Krikron Majan
生下了一对	Bore a pair of creatures,
摇着尾巴，	Wagging their tails,
长满花纹的。	And having patterns all over their sides.
他们是谁呀？	Who were they?
潘瓦能桑遮瓦能章说：	Hpan Wa Ningsang Chye Wa Ningchyang answered:
“他们是豹类的祖先，	“They are the ancestors of the panthers.
雌的叫电帮木占，	The female is Tengpang Majan.
雄的叫电帮拉。	The male is Tengpang La.
远古，	In remote antiquity,
尹暖拉的创造，	The creation by Yinnon La
给冠木占的繁衍，	And the multiplication by Krikron Majan
生下了一对	Bore a couple of creatures
长着薄翅、	With thin wings
带着毒针的。	And poisonous stings.
他们是谁呀？	Who were they?
潘瓦能桑遮瓦能章说：	Hpan Wa Ningsang Chye Wa Ningchyang answered:

“他们是蜂类的祖先，	“They are the ancestors of the bees.
雌的叫申东格努木占，	The female is Shintung Ganu Majan.
雄的叫申干木杜拉。”	The male is Shingam Madu La.”
蜂类生活的草坡有了，	There were grassy slopes for bees to live
蜂类居住的山包也有了。	And there were hills for them to stay.
潘瓦能桑遮瓦能章对蜂类的祖先说：	Hpan Wa Ningsang Chye Wa Ningchyang told the ancestors of the bees,
“到你们生活的草坡去吧，	“Go and live on the grassy slopes.
到你们居住的山包去吧。”	Go and stay on the hills.”

远古，	In remote antiquity,
尹暖拉的创造，	The creation by Yinnon La
给冠木占的繁衍，	And the multiplication by Krikron Majan
生下了一对	Bore a pair of creatures
长着鳞、	With scales
生着鳃的。	And gills.
他们是谁呀？	Who were they?
潘瓦能桑遮瓦能章说：	Hpan Wa Ningsang Chye Wa Ningchyang answered:
“他们是鱼类的祖先，	“They are the ancestors of the fishes.
雄的叫乌圆拉，	The male is Wuyon La.
雌的叫乌圆木占。”	The female is Wunyen Majan.”

远古，	In remote antiquity,
尹暖拉的创造，	The creation by Yinnon La

给冠木占的繁衍，	And the multiplication by Krikron Majan
生下了一对，	Bore a couple of creatures,
尤亚拉和尤斑木占。	Yuya La and Yuban Majan.
他们是谁呀？	Who were they?
潘瓦能桑遮瓦能章说：	Hpan Wa Ningsang Chye Wa Ningchyang said:
“他们是木若鬼类的祖先。”	“They are the ancestors of Ghost Maros.”

远古，	In remote antiquity,
尹暖拉的创造，	The creation by Yinnon La
给冠木占的繁衍，	And the multiplication by Krikron Majan,
该创造的创造了，	They created all the creatures they could;
该生的都生下了，	They multiplied all the living beings they could.
一个消失在天边，	One disappeared in the Sky.
一个安息在地沿。	The other rested on the Earth.

远古，	In remote antiquity,
瓦囊能退拉的创造，	The creation by Wa-nang Ninghtoi La
能星能锐木占的繁衍，	And the multiplication by Ningsin Numroi Majan
生下了神杈，	Produced the holy branch
有了巨柱；	And the huge pillar;
生下了九拃[①]长的针，	Produced a nine-arm-span-long[①] needle
有了九拃长的线；	And a nine-span-long thread;

① 九拃：这里不是指实际长度，而是指很长的意思。

① A nine-arm-span-long: Here it doesn't refer to the actual length, but means it is very long.

生下了拱山的竹盖文腊①，	Bore Jugai Wunla① who could dig into the mountains,
有了穿山的大蟒；	And the python that could go through the mountains,
生下了圆圆的大蒸笼。	And a big round steamer.
它们是做什么的呀？	What could they do?
潘瓦能桑遮瓦能章说：	Hpan Wa Ningsang Chye Wa Ningchyang said:
“等到了将来，	“In the future,
它们都会有自己的用处。”	They will all be useful.”
远古，	In remote antiquity,
天要往下沉，	The Sky sank,
地要往上升。	And the Earth rose.
它们要贴到一起。	They would stick together.
用神杈往上一撑，	Propped up by the the holy branch,
天不再往下沉；	The Sky would no longer sink.
用巨柱往下一抵，	Pressed down by the huge pillar,
地不再往上升。	The Earth would no longer rise.
远古，	In remote antiquity,
天裂开了，	The Sky cracked open,
地也被竹盖文腊拱开了，	And the Earth was split open by Jugai Wunla.
用九拃长的针，	With the nine-arm-span-long needle
用九拃长的线，	And the nine-arm-span-long thread,

① 竹盖文腊：传说中一种能穿山拱地的动物。

① Jugai Wunla: a legendary animal that can go through the mountains and dig into the Earth.

缝好了裂开的天；	The cracked Sky was mended.
正在拱地的竹盖文腊，	Jugai Wunla who was digging into the Earth
也被穿山的巨蟒吞吃了。	Was swallowed by the python going through the mountain.
远古，	In remote antiquity,
瓦囊能退拉的创造，	The creation by Wa-nang Ninghtoi La
能星能锐木占的繁衍，	And the multiplication by Ningsin Numroi Majan
生下灰色的一团。	Bore a gray mass.
这是什么呀？	What was it?
潘瓦能桑遮瓦能章说：	Hpan Wa Ningsang Chye Wa Ningchyang answered:
“这是坚硬的石头。”	“This is a hard rock.”
坚硬的石头说，	The hard rock said
它要张嘴说话，	It wanted to open its mouth to speak,
它要生脚走路。	And to have feet to walk.
用九拿长的铁链，	With nine-arm-span-long shackles
捆住了石头，	The rock was bound,
石头才没有张嘴，	So that it didn't open its mouth
石头才没有走路。	Or start to walk.
远古，	In remote antiquity,
瓦囊能退拉的创造，	The creation by Wa-nang Ninghtoi La
能星能锐木占的繁衍，	And the multiplication by Ningsin Numroi Majan
生下了一对	Bore a pair of creatures,

还在娘胎里	Who could shake their heads
就会摇头；	In the womb,
还没有出生，	And keep on shaking
就会晃动的。	Before birth.
男的生殖器像舂棒，	The genitals of the male were like a pestle,
女的生殖器像簸箕。	And the genitals of the female were like a dustpan.
他们是谁呀？	Who were they?
潘瓦能桑遮瓦能章说：	Hpan Wa Ningsang Chye Wa Ningchyang answered:
“男的叫彭干支伦，	“The male is named Hpunggam Chyanun,
女的叫木占威纯。”	And the female is named Majan Woishun.”
瓦囊能退拉觉得生够了，	Wa-nang Ninghtoi La felt that he had created everything.
能星能锐木占感到活够了，	Ningsin Numroi Majan felt she had lived long enough.
瓦囊能退拉安息在山顶，	Wa-nang Ninghtoi La rested on the mountain top,
他在山顶发出亮光，	Where he gave off light.
所以黎明从山顶开始；	That is why dawn starts from the mountain top.
能星能锐木占安息在山洼，	Ningsin Numroi Majan rested in the valley,
她在山洼里引出黑暗，	Where she caused darkness.
所以夜幕从山洼里开始。	Thus night starts from the valley.

五、尤亚拉和尤斑木占的创造繁衍

V. Creation and Multiplication by Yuya La and Yuban Majan

远古，
尤亚拉的创造，
尤斑木占的繁衍，
生下了木若干荣歪。
他是干什么的呀？
潘瓦能桑遮瓦能章说：
“他是发生仇杀时
祭献的木若神，
他住在木直崩昆戛瓦兰。”

In remote antiquity,
The creation by Yuya La
And the multiplication by Yuban Majan
Gave birth to Marong Gam Rumwai.
What could he do?
Hpan Wa Ningsang Chye Wa Ningchyang replied:
“He is the Ghost Maro to whom sacrifices must be offered
When revenge killing is taking place.
He lives on Mount Maji Bunghkum Ga Wa Lam.”

远古，
尤亚拉的创造，
尤斑木占的繁衍，
生下了木若弄荣拐。
他是干什么的呀？
潘瓦能桑遮瓦能章说：
“这是将来战争停止时，

In remote antiquity,
The creation by Yuya La
And the multiplication by Yuban Majan
Gave birth to Maro Nong Rumkoi.
What could he do?
Hpan Wa Ningsang Chye Wa Ningchyang replied:
“He is the Peace Ghost Maro, to whom sacrifices

祭献的和平木若神，	Must be offered when in the future the war ends.
他居住在戛昂肯带木章敢卖地方。	He lives in Gaang Hkindai Machyang Gatmai."

远古，	In remote antiquity,
尤亚拉的创造，	The creation by Yuya La
尤斑木占的繁衍，	And the multiplication by Yuban Majan
生下了壤敖木若。	Bore Ra-ngau Maro.
他是干什么的呀？	What could he do?
潘瓦能桑遮瓦能章说：	Hpan Wa Ningsang Chye Wa Ningchyang replied:
"这是将来的铁匠	"He is the Ghost Maro
祭献的木若神，	To whom the future blacksmiths offer sacrifices.
他住在火炉旁。"	He lives by the stove."

远古，	In remote antiquity,
尤亚拉的创造，	The creation by Yuya La
尤斑木占的繁衍，	And the multiplication by Yuban Majan
生下了能独木若。	Bore Ningdu Maro.
他是干什么的呀？	What could he do?
潘瓦能桑遮瓦能章说：	Hpan Wa Ningsang Chye Wa Ningchyang said:
"这是将来发生战争，	"When in the future the war takes place,
赎回俘虏时，	And when the captives are redeemed,
祭献的木若鬼，	He is the Ghost Maro to whom sacrifices must be be offered.
他住在能独诗贡山。"	

	He lives on Mount Ningdu Shagong."
远古，	In remote antiquity,
尤亚拉的创造，	The creation by Yuya La
尤斑木占的繁衍，	And the multiplication by Yuban Majan
生下了星来当木若。	Bore Sinlai Tang Maro.
他是干什么的呀？	What could he do?
潘瓦能桑遮瓦能章说：	Hpan Wa Ningsang Chye Wa Ningchyang said:
“他是将来举行目瑙时，	"When the Manau ritual is held in the future,
祭献的木若神，	He is the one to whom sacrifices must be offered.
他住在星来诗贡山。”	He lives on Mount Sinlai Shagong."
远古，	In remote antiquity,
尤亚拉的创造，	The creation by Yuya La
尤斑木占的繁衍，	And the multiplication by Yuban Majan
生下了能占木若。	Bore Ningjap Maro.
他是干什么的呀？	What could he do?
潘瓦能桑遮瓦能章说：	Hpan Wa Ningsang Chye Wa Ningchyang answered:
“他是将来房子被烧时	"When the house is burnt in the future,
祭献的木若神，	He is the one to whom sacrifices must be offered.
他居住在能占诗贡山。	He lives on Mount Ningjap Shagong.
远古，	In remote antiquity,
尤亚拉的创造，	The creation by Yuya La

尤斑木占的繁衍，	And the multiplication by Yuban Majan
生下了来仲木若。	Bore Laijum Maro.
他是干什么的呀？	What could he do?
潘瓦能桑遮瓦能章说：	Hpan Wa Ningsang Chye Wa Ningchyang said:
“他是将来的歌手	“He is the Ghost Maro
祭献的木若神，	To whom future singers offer sacrifices.
他住在屋檐下。”	He lives under the roof. ”

远古，	In remote antiquity,
尤亚拉的创造，	The creation by Yuya La
尤斑木占的繁衍，	And the multiplication by Yuban Majan
生下了陶直木若。	Bore Htauji Maro.
他是干什么的呀？	What could he do?
潘瓦能桑遮瓦能章说：	Hpan Wa Ningsang Chye Wa Ningchyang answered:
“他是将来的巫师	“He is the Ghost Maro
祭献的木若神，	To whom future wizard offer sacrifices.
他住在陶直纯陶哦昆地方。”	He lives in Htauji Shun Htaunga Hkun.”

远古，	In remote antiquity,
尤亚拉的创造，	The creation by Yuya La
尤斑木占的繁衍，	And the multiplication by Yuban Majan
生下了肯庄木若。	Bore Hkringjong Maro.
他是干什么的呀？	What could he do?
潘瓦能桑遮瓦能章说：	Hpan Wa Ningsang Chye Wa Ningchyang answered:

“他是将来的祭师	“He is the Ghost Maro,
祭献的木若神，	To whom future priests offer sacrifices.
他居住在陶直纯陶哦昆地方。”	He lives in Htauji Shun.”
远古，	In remote antiquity,
尤亚拉的创造，	The creation by Yuya La
尤斑木占的繁衍，	And the multiplication by Yuban Majan
生下了卜卦木若。	Bore the diviner Maro.
他是干什么的呀？	What could he do?
潘瓦能桑遮瓦能章说：	Hpan Wa Ningsang Chye Wa Ningchyang said:
“他是将来卜卦的	“He is the Ghost Maro
祭献的木若神，	To whom future diviners offer sacrifices.
他住在文伦诗贡文浪文蒙地方。”	He lives on Mount Wunlut Shagong Wunlang Wunmong.”
远古，	In remote antiquity,
尤亚拉的创造，	The creation by Yuya La
尤斑木占的繁衍，	And the multiplication by Yuban Majan
生下了斋力木若。	Bore Jaili Maro.
他是干什么的呀？	What could he do?
潘瓦能桑遮瓦能章说：	Hpan Wa Ningsang Chye Wa Ningchyang said:
“这是将来吟诵‘斋瓦’时	“He is the Ghost Maro to whom sacrifices must be offered
祭献的木若神，	When Jaiwa is chanted in the future.

他居住在能然瓦洋地方。”	He lives in Ning-ran Wayang."
远古，	In remote antiquity,
尤亚拉的创造，	The creation by Yuya La
尤斑木占的繁衍，	And the multiplication by Yuban Majan
生下了瑙双木若。	Bore Nau Shong Maro.
他是干什么的呀？	What could he do?
潘瓦能桑遮瓦能章说：	Hpan Wa Ningsang Chye Wa Ningchyang answered:
“他是将来目瑙的领舞者	"He is the Ghost Maro
祭献的木若神，	To whom future lead dancers of Manau offer sacrifices.
他住在寨旁。”	He lives by the stockade."
远古，	In remote antiquity,
尤亚拉的创造，	The creation by Yuya La
尤斑木占的繁衍，	And the multiplication by Yuban Majan
生下了帕知木若。	Bore Hpaji Maro.
他是干什么的呀？	What could he do?
潘瓦能桑遮瓦能章说：	Hpan Wa Ningsang Chye Wa Ningchyang answered:
“他是将来有知识的智者	"He is the Ghost Maro
祭献的木若神，	To whom future wise men offer sacrifices.
他住在帕知诗贡帕然文蒙地方。”	He lives on Mount Hpaji Shagong Hparat Wunmong."
远古，	In remote antiquity,

尤亚拉的创造，
尤斑木占的繁衍，
生下了扎力木若。
他是干什么的呀？
潘瓦能桑遮瓦能章说：
“他是将来经商的人
祭献的木若神，
他住在做生意的路上。”

The creation by Yuya La
And the multiplication by Yuban Majan
Bore Jali Maro.
Who was he?
Hpan Wa Ningsang Chye Wa Ningchyang said:
“He is the Ghost Maro
To whom future businessmen offer sacrifices.
He lives on the road to business.”

远古，
尤亚拉的创造，
尤斑木占的繁衍，
生下了恩胆木若。
他是干什么的呀？
潘瓦能桑遮瓦能章说：
“他是将来丰收的年成
祭献的木若神，
他住在山洼和石洞里。”

In remote antiquity,
The creation by Yuya La
And the multiplication by Yuban Majan
Bore Ntam Maro.
What could he do?
Hpan Wa Ningsang Chye Wa Ningchyang said:
“He is the Ghost Maro to whom sacrifices must be offered
For bumper harvests in the future.
He lives in the valley and the cave.”

远古，
尤亚拉的创造，
尤斑木占的繁衍，
生下了地吨木若。
他是干什么的呀？

In remote antiquity,
The creation by Yuya La
And the multiplication by Yuban Majan
Bore Di Dun Maro.
What could he do?

潘瓦能桑遮瓦能章说：	Hpan Wa Ningsang Chye Wa Ningchyang answered:
“他是将来的煮饭者	“He is the Ghost Maro
祭献的木若神，	To whom future cooks offer sacrifices.
他住在火塘边。”	He lives by the fireplace.”

远古，	In remote antiquity,
尤亚拉的创造，	The creation by Yuya La
尤斑木占的繁衍，	And the multiplication by Yuban Majan
生下了布木若。	Bore Bu Maro.
他是干什么的呀？	What could he do?
潘瓦能桑遮瓦能章说：	Hpan Wa Ningsang Chye Wa Ningchyang replied:
“他是将来举行婚礼时	“He is the Ghost Maro to whom sacrifices must be offered
祭献的木若神，	When a marriage ceremony is held in the future.
他住在礼篮中[①]。”	He lives in the hampers[①].”

远古，	In remote antiquity,
尤亚拉的创造，	The creation by Yuya La
尤斑木占的繁衍，	And the multiplication by Yuban Majan
生下了锐翁木若。	Bore Roi Ong Maro.
他是干什么的呀？	What could he do?
潘瓦能桑遮瓦能章说：	Hpan Wa Ningsang Chye Wa Ningchyang replied:
“他是将来谷子丰收时	“He is the Ghost Maro to whom sacrifices must be offered

① 礼篮：姑娘出嫁时，娘家装礼的竹篮。

① Hampers: When a girl is married, her parents put the gifts in this kind of bamboo basket.

祭献的木若神，	When in the future there is a bumper millet harvest.
他住在田地边。”	He lives in the fields."
远古，	In remote antiquity,
尤亚拉的创造，	The creation by Yuya La
尤斑木占的繁衍，	And the multiplication by Yuban Majan
生下了达吨木若。	Bore Da Dun Maro.
他是干什么的呀？	What could he do?
潘瓦能桑遮瓦能章说：	Hpan Wa Ningsang Chye Wa Ningchyang replied:
“他是将来纺织的人	"He is the Ghost Maro
祭献的木若神，	To whom future weavers offer sacifices.
他住在纺织的地方。”	He lives in the place of textiles."
远古，	In remote antiquity,
尤亚拉的创造，	The creation by Yuya La
尤斑木占的繁衍，	And the multiplication by Yuban Majan
生下了窝越木若。	Bore Oi Yang Maro.
他是干什么的呀？	What could he do?
潘瓦能桑遮瓦能章说：	Hpan Wa Ningsang Chye Wa Ningchyang replied:
“他是将来会唱山歌的人	"He is the Ghost Maro
祭献的木若神，	To whom future folk singers offer sacrifices.
他住在迈丽枯能东昆地方。”	He lives in the Mali Hku Numdung Hkun River area."
远古，	In remote antiquity,

尤亚拉的创造，
尤斑木占的繁衍，
生下了如直木若。
他是谁呀？
潘瓦能桑遮瓦能章说：
“他是将来串姑娘惹祸时
祭献的木若神，
他住在草丛里。”

The creation by Yuya La
And the multiplication by Yuban Majan
Bore Ruji Maro.
Who was he?
Hpan Wa Ningsang Chye Wa Ningchyang replied:
“He is the Ghost Maro to whom sacrifices must be offered
When in the future young lovers get into trouble.
He lives in the tall grass.”

远古，
尤亚拉该造的创造够了，
尤斑木占该生的生完了。

In remote antiquity,
Yuya La created everything he could,
Yuban Majan bore everything in her capacity.

附记：

以上提到的各种鬼神，有善鬼，也有恶鬼，但都得按不同的种类、不同的场合、不同的方式祭献他们，以求善鬼的帮助和恶鬼的躲避。在对各种鬼的追根溯源中，最后都源从这里。

Excursus:

The Ghosts mentioned above can be divided into the kind ghosts and the evil ones. However, they should all be offered sacrifices based on different kinds, on different occasions and in different ways. Thus, people can get the help of kind ghosts and avoid being harmed by evil ghosts. This is the original resource that the different kinds of ghosts can be traced back to.

六、彭干支伦和木占威纯的创造和繁衍 Ⅵ. Creation by Hpunggam Chyanun and Multiplication by Majan Woishun

远古，	In remote antiquity,
彭干支伦的创造，	The creation by Hpunggam Chyanun
木占威纯的繁衍，	And the multiplication by Majan Woishun
生下了旋风，	Produced the tornado
有了微风。	And the breeze.
它们是做什么的呀？	What could they do?
潘瓦能桑遮瓦能章说：	Hpan Wa Ningsang Chye Wa Ningchyang answered:
“等将来有了新的天，	“In the future there will be a new Sky
等将来有了新的地，	And there will be a new Earth.
新的天不够晴朗，	When the new Sky is not clear enough,
新的地不够干硬，	And the new Earth is not dry and hard enough,
让旋风去使天晴朗，	The tornado will clear the Sky,
让微风去使地干硬。”	And the breeze will dry the Earth.”
远古，	In remote antiquity,
彭干支伦的创造，	The creation by Hpunggam Chyanun
木占威纯的繁衍，	And the multiplication by Majan Woishun
生下了夜间的雾，	Produced the night fog

有了早晨的露。
它们是做什么的呀？
潘瓦能桑遮瓦能章说：
“等将来有了新的天，
等将来有了新的地，
天上飞满了灰，
地上布满了尘，
让雾洗尽天上的灰，
让露除去地上的尘。”

And the morning dew.
What could they do?
Hpan Wa Ningsang Chye Wa Ningchyang answered:
“In the future there will be a new Sky,
And there will be a new Earth.
When the Sky is full of ash,
And the Earth is covered with dust,
The fog will clean the ash in the Sky,
And the dew would remove the dust on the Earth.”

远古，
彭干支伦的创造，
木占威纯的繁衍，
生下了蓝蓝的一片，
有了竹笆一样的一块。
这是什么呀？
潘瓦能桑遮瓦能章说：
“这就是新的天，
这就是新的地。”

In remote antiquity,
The creation by Hpunggam Chyanun
And the multiplication by Majan Woishun
Produced a blue expanse,
And a patch like a bamboo fence.
What were they?
Hpan Wa Ningsang Chye Wa Ningchyang answered:
“They are the new Sky
And the new Earth.”

远古，
新的天有了，
新的地有了，
新的天不够晴朗，

In remote antiquity,
There were the new Sky,
And the new Earth.
The new Sky was not clear enough,

新的地不够干硬，	And the new Earth was not dry and hard enough.
让旋风在天上吹，	They let the tornado blow in the Sky,
让微风在地上吹，	And the breeze blow on the Earth,
新的天晴朗了，	Then the new Sky was clear,
新的地干硬了。	And the new Earth was dry and hard.
远古，	In remote antiquity,
新的天有了，	There were the new Sky,
新的地有了，	And the new Earth.
新的天飞满了灰，	There was lots of ash flying in the Sky,
新的地布满了尘，	And lots of dust covering the Earth.
让雾洗尽天上的灰，	The fog cleaned the ash in the Sky,
让露除去地上的尘，	And the dew removed the dust on the Earth.
天上的灰洗尽了，	The ash was cleaned away
地上的尘除去了。	And the dust was removed.
远古，	In remote antiquity,
彭干支伦的创造，	The creation by Hpunggam Chyanun
木占威纯的繁衍，	And the multiplication by Majan Woishun
生下了沉重的巨石。	Produced a heavy rock.
巨石是做什么的呀？	What was the rock used for?
潘瓦能桑遮瓦能章说：	Hpan Wa Ningsang Chye Wa Ningchyang replied:
“把巨石放到大地上，	“Put the rock on the Earth,
新的地会更坚实，	And the new Earth

新的地会更稳固。	Will be firm and solid."
远古，	In remote antiquity,
彭干支伦的创造，	The creation by Hpunggam Chyanun
木占威纯的繁衍，	And the multiplication by Majan Woishun
生下了长绳，	Made a long rope
有了粗索。	And a big cord.
它们是做什么的呀？	What were they used for?
潘瓦能桑遮瓦能章说：	Hpan Wa Ningsang Chye Wa Ningchyang replied:
"这是捆巨石的绳，	"This is the rope to bind the rock.
这是拴巨石的索，	This is the cord to tie up the rock.
只有稳住了巨石，	Only if the rock is held still,
才能稳住新的大地。"	Will the new Earth be stable."
远古，	In remote antiquity,
彭干支伦的创造，	The creation by Hpunggam Chyanun
木占威纯的繁衍，	And the multiplication by Majan Woishun
生下了勒木崩顶地方。	Produced the place of Lamun Pungding .
这是做什么的地方呀？	What could be done there?
潘瓦能桑遮瓦能章说：	Hpan Wa Ningsang Chye Wa Ningchyang replied:
"这是将来他自己	"This is the place
生活居住的地方。"	Where he himself will live in the future."
远古，	In remote antiquity,

彭干支伦的创造，
木占威纯的繁衍，
生下了戛昂阿崩山，
山上有一把铁交椅。
这是做什么的地方呀？
潘瓦能桑遮瓦能章说：
“这是将来宁贯督
生活居住的地方。”

The creation by Hpunggam Chyanun
And the multiplication by Majan Woishun
Produced Mount Gaang Abum,
Where there was an iron chair.
What could be done there?
Hpan Wa Ningsang Chye Wa Ningchyang replied:
“This is the place where N-gon Du
Will stay and live in the future.”

远古，
彭干支伦的创造，
木占威纯的繁衍，
生下了崩乃诏帕山。
这是做什么的山呀？
潘瓦能桑遮瓦能章说：
“这是将来德如贡散木干贡潘王子
生活居住的地方。”

In remote antiquity,
The creation by Hpunggam Chyanun
And the multiplication by Majan Woishun
Produced Mount Bumnoi Chyauhpa.
What could be done there?
Hpan Wa Ningsang Chye Wa Ningchyang replied:
“This is the place Prince Daru Gumsan Magam Gumhpan
Will stay and live in the future.”

远古，
彭干支伦的创造，
木占威纯的繁衍，
生下了木佐崩极山。
这是做什么的山呀？

In remote antiquity,
The creation by Hpunggam Chyanun
And the multiplication by Majan Woishun
Produced Mount Matso Punggyi.
What could be done there?

潘瓦能桑遮瓦能章说：	Hpan Wa Ningsang Chye Wa Ningchyang replied:
“这是将来的天王	“This is the place where Matso Maulam,
木佐毛兰生活居住的地方。”	The King of the Sky of the future, will stay and live.”

远古，	In remote antiquity,
彭干支伦的创造，	The creation by Hpunggam Chyanun
木占威纯的繁衍，	And the multiplication by Majan Woishun
生下了阿拜崩朗格巴山。	Produced Mount Apai Bumlang Gaba.
这是做什么的山呀？	What could be done there?
潘瓦能桑遮瓦能章说：	Hpan Wa Ningsang Chye Wa Ningchyang replied:
“这是将来的天神	“This is the place
木佐肯万诺木努	Where Matso Hkringwan No Munu, a god of the future,
生活居住的地方。”	Will stay and live in the future.”

远古，	In remote antiquity,
彭干支伦的创造，	The creation by Hpunggam Chyanun
木占威纯的繁衍，	And the multiplication by Majan Woishun
生下了木几争若歪地方。	Produced the place Makyit Zingro Wai.
这是做什么的地方呀？	What could be done there?
潘瓦能桑遮瓦能章说：	Hpan Wa Ningsang Chye Wa Ningchyang replied:
“这是将来的天神	“This is the place
木佐苏瓦朋农	Where Matso Sut Wa Hpungnung, a god of the future,
生活居住的地方。”	Will stay and live in the future.”

远古，	In remote antiquity,
彭干支伦的创造，	The creation by Hpunggam Chyanun
木占威纯的繁衍，	And the multiplication by Majan Woishun
生下了木佐郭勒扎地方。	Produced the place Matso Golaja.
这是什么地方呀？	What could be done there?
潘瓦能桑遮瓦能章说：	Hpan Wa Ningsang Chye Wa Ningchyang replied:
“这是将来的天神，	“This is the place
木佐志胜热	Where Matso Ji Shing-ra, a god of the future,
生活居住的地方。”	Will stay and live.”

远古，	In remote antiquity,
彭干支伦的创造，	The creation by Hpunggam Chyanun
木占威纯的繁衍，	And the multiplication by Majan Woishun
生下了诗兰顶西星能兰台约丁地方。	Produced the place Sharat Dingsi Sing Ninglam Htaiyo Ting.
这是什么地方呀？	What could be done there?
潘瓦能桑遮瓦能章说：	Hpan Wa Ningsang Chye Wa Ningchyang replied:
“这是将来的太阳神	“This is the place
占瓦能桑文布颇朗	Where Jan Wa Ningsang Wunbu Hpro-nang,
生活居住的地方。”	The Sun God of the future, will stay and live.”

远古，	In remote antiquity,
彭干支伦的创造，	The creation by Hpunggam Chyanun
木占威纯的繁衍，	And the multiplication by Majan Woishun

生下了乌蒙诗贡山。
这是什么地方呀？
潘瓦能桑遮瓦能章说：
“这是将来的天神
木夺格努直卡杜
生活居住的地方。”

Produced Mount Wumung Shagong.
What could be done there?
Hpan Wa Ningsang Chye Wa Ningchyang replied:
“This is the place
Where Mado Ganu Jahka Du, a god of the future,
Will stay and live.”

远古，
彭干支伦的创造，
木占威纯的繁衍，
生下了阿苏贡顶阿干栽类[1]地方。
这是什么地方呀？
潘瓦能桑遮瓦能章说：
“这是将来的天神
颇干杜正塔扎占能桑
生活居住的地方。”

In remote antiquity,
The creation by Hpunggam Chyanun
And the multiplication by Majan Woishun
Produced the place Asut Kumding Agan Tsailui.
What could be done there?
Hpan Wa Ningsang Chye Wa Ningchyang replied:
“This is the place
Where Hpro-gam Du Jinghta Jan Ningsang, a god of the future,
Will stay and live.”

远古，
彭干支伦的创造，
木占威纯的繁衍，
生下了卡木劳石芽革松崩浪

In remote antiquity,
The creation by Hpunggam Chyanun
And the multiplication by Majan Woishun
Produced the place Hka Malau Shaya Kasung Bumlang

---

[1] 阿苏贡顶阿干栽类：地名。

革巴地方。	Gabam.
这是什么地方呀?	What could be done there?
潘瓦能桑遮瓦能章说:	Hpan Wa Ningsang Chye Wa Ningchyang replied:
“这是将来的彩虹神	“This is the place
麻星格努麻羊格者豪昆杜	Where Masing Ganu Mayang Kajat Hkauhkun Du,
生活居住的地方。”	The Rainbow God of the future , will stay and live.”
远古,	In remote antiquity,
彭干支伦的创造,	The creation by Hpunggam Chyanun
木占威纯的繁衍,	And the multiplication by Majan Woishun
生下了一块	Bore a place
圆圆的像篾盘的地方。	Shaped like a bamboo plate.
这是什么地方呀?	What kind of the place was it?
潘瓦能桑遮瓦能章说:	Hpan Wa Ningsang Chye Wa Ningchyang replied:
“这是将来的天药	“This is Lamu Wunhte Ga Thing-ye,
木夺格努直卡杜	Where Mado Ganu Jahka Du, a heavenly herb,
生长的勒木文铁戛腾越地方。”	Will grow in the future.”
远古,	In remote antiquity,
彭干支伦的创造,	The creation by Hpunggam Chyanun
木占威纯的繁衍,	And the multiplication by Majan Woishun
生下了一对	Bore a pair of creatures
长着绿叶,	With green leaves
有着树枝的。	And branches.

他们是谁呀？
潘瓦能桑遮瓦能章说：
“男的是登顶根石帮，
女的是星星退木宽[①]。
他们生活的地方
生长着天药。”

Who were they?
Hpan Wa Ningsang Chye Wa Ningchyang replied:
"The male is Ding Ding Kring Shabrang,
The female is Sing Sing Htoi Mahkon[①].
In the place where they live
Grow heavenly herbs."

七、登顶根石帮和星星退木宽的创造繁衍

VII. Creation by Ding Ding Kring Shabrang and Multiplication by Sing Sing Htoi Mahkon

远古，
登顶根石帮的创造，
星星退木宽的繁衍，
生下了登旷日波拉，
有了登旷日波木占。
登顶根石帮对他们说：
“登旷日波拉呀，
登旷日波木占，
这里的天药，
你们栽培吧，

In remote antiquity,
The creation by Ding Ding Kring Shabrang
And the multiplication by Sing Sing Htoi Mahkon
Bore Dinghkong Rihpro La,
And Dinghkong Rihpro Majan.
Ding Ding Kring Shabrang said to them:
"Dinghkong Rihpro La and
Dinghkong Rihpro Majan,
These are heavenly herbs.
Plant them

① 登顶根石帮、星星退木宽：传说中管理天上神药的一对少男少女。

① Ding Ding Kring Shabrang and Sing Sing Htoi Mahkon: a boy and a girl who took care of heavenly herbs.

你们管理吧。"	And take care of them."

八、登旷日波拉和登旷日波木占的繁衍

Ⅷ. Creation by Dinghkong Rihpro La and Multiplication by Dinghkong Rihpro Majan

远古，	In remote antiquity,
登旷日波拉的创造，	The creation by Dinghkong Rihpro La
登旷日波木占的繁衍，	And the multiplication by Dinghkong Rihpro Majan
生下了圣灵乐索，	Bore Shinglim Lasho
有了圣断波翁。	And Shington Hpro Ong.
他们是做什么的呀？	What would they do?
潘瓦能桑遮瓦能章说：	Hpan Wa Ningsang Chye Wa Ningchyang said:
"他们将继续栽培天药，	"They will continue to plant heavenly herbs.
他们将跟着管理天药。	They will continue to take care of heavenly herbs.

远古，	In remote antiquity,
登旷日波拉的创造，	The creation by Dinghkong Rihpro La
登旷日波木占的繁衍，	And the multiplication by Dinghkong Rihpro Majan
生下了莱谷莱岗地方。	Produced the place Laigu Laigang.
这是什么地方呀？	What kind of place was it?
潘瓦能桑遮瓦能章说：	Hpan Wa Ningsang Chye Wa Ningchyang said:
"他是不成功的巫师	"It is the place

根利根翁根桑根浪	Where Ginli-gin-um Ginsang Ginlang,
生活居住的地方。”	An unsuccessful wizard, stays and lives."
远古，	In remote antiquity,
登旷日波拉的创造，	The creation by Dinghkong Rihpro La
登旷日波木占的繁衍，	And the multiplication by Dinghkong Rihpro Majan
生下了苦勒斑浪能善。	Bore Hku Lapau Lang Ningshan.
他是做什么的呀？	What was he?
潘瓦能桑遮瓦能章说：	Hpan Wa Ningsang Chye Wa Ningchyang said:
“他是不成功的巫师。”	"He is an unsuccessful wizard."
远古，	In remote antiquity,
登旷日波拉的创造，	The creation by Dinghkong Rihpro La
登旷日波木占的繁衍，	And the multiplication by Dinghkong Rihpro Majan
生下了勒旦勒中瓦。	Bore Ladan Lachyung Wa.
他是做什么的呢？	What was he?
潘瓦能桑遮瓦能章说：	Hpan Wa Ningsang Chye Wa Ningchyang said:
“他是将来的巫师。”	"He is the wizard of the future."
远古，	In remote antiquity,
彭干支伦，	Hpunggam Chyanun
木占威纯，	And Majan Woishun
力量耗尽了，	Exhausted their strength
生命衰竭了，	And wore away.

不能创造了，	They could no longer go on with their creation
不能生育了。	And their multiplication.
衰老的彭干支伦	The aging Hpunggam Chyanun
想要返老还童，	Wanted to rejuvenate himself,
来到瓦洋呆冒旁地方，	And came to the place Wayang Tai Mau Hpang
改变了自己衰老的面貌，	And changed his old face
包上崭新的包头，	By wearing a brand-new head decoration.
变得年轻了；	Then he became young again.
衰老的木占威纯，	The aging Majan Woishun
想要返老还童，	Wanted to rejuvenate herself,
来到瓦洋呆冒旁地方，	And came to the place Wayang Tai Mau Hpang
改变了自己衰老的面貌，	And changed her old face
穿上美丽的筒裙，	By dressing in a beautiful straight skirt.
变得年轻了。	Then she became young again.
远古，	In remote antiquity,
彭干支伦，	Hpunggam Chyanun
木占威纯，	And Majan Woishun
第一次返老还童，	Rejuvenated themselves for the first time.
又能创造了，	They could continue their creation
又能繁衍了。	And multiplication now.
远古，	In remote antiquity,

彭干支伦的创造，
木占威纯的繁衍，
生下了割脐带的刀，
有了锋利的斧头；
生下了尖尖的叉子，
有了敷肚脐的金粉；
生下了洗孩子的金槽，
有了洗孩子的清水；
生下了女性生殖器，
有了男性生殖器；
生下了性欲药，
有了润滑油。
这些是做什么的呀？
潘瓦能桑遮瓦能章说：
“等将来创造人的时候，
这些都会有用处。”

The creation by Hpunggam Chyanun
And the multiplication by Majan Woishun
Produced a knife for cutting the umbilical cord
And a sharp axe,
A sharp fork and the gold powder
That was applied to the umbilical cord,
The golden sink and the clean water
To bathe babies,
The female genitals
And the male genitals,
The love potion
And the lubricating oil.
What were these for?
Hpan Wa Ningsang Chye Wa Ningchyang said:
“In the future when human beings are created,
These will be used.”

远古，
彭干支伦的创造，
木占威纯的繁衍，
生下了天王木佐毛浪。
潘瓦能桑遮瓦能章
给他接了生，
用刀隔断了他的脐带，

In remote antiquity,
The creation by Hpunggam Chyanun
And the multiplication by Majan Woishun
Bore Matso Maulam, the King of the Sky.
Hpan Wa Ningsang Chye Wa Ningchyang
Delivered him.
He used the knife to cut the umbilical cord

又在肚脐上敷上金粉，	And applied the gold powder to the wound.
又给他取了名字。	He also gave him a name.
他生活的木佐崩吉能藏崩旦	He lived in Matso Punggui Ningtsang Pungdam,
地方，	Where grew big green trees.
生长着大青树。	

远古，	In remote antiquity,
彭干支伦的创造，	The creation by Hpunggam Chyanun
木占威纯的繁衍，	And the multiplication by Majan Woishun
生下了天神木佐肯万诺木努。	Bore God Matso Hkringwan No Munu.
潘瓦能桑遮瓦能章	Hpan Wa Ningsang Chye Wa Ningchyang
给他接了生，	Delivered him.
用刀隔断了他的脐带，	He cut the umbilical cord with a knife
又在肚脐上敷上金粉，	And applied the gold powder to the wound.
又给他取了名字。	He also gave him a name.
他生活的阿拜崩朗格巴地方，	He lived in Apai Bumlang Gaba,
生长着黄果树。	Where grew yellow fruit trees.

远古，	In remote antiquity,
彭干支伦的创造，	The creation by Hpunggam Chyanun
木占威纯的繁衍，	And the multiplication by Majan Woishun
生下了天神木佐苏瓦朋农	Bore God Matso Sut Wa Hpungnung Ningtsang Gan
能藏干龙孔。	Lunghkrung.
潘瓦能桑遮瓦能章	Hpan Wa Ningsang Chye Wa Ningchyang

给他接了生，
用刀隔断了他的脐带，
又在肚脐上敷上金粉，
又给他取了名字。
他生活的木几曾若外支考同巴摆地方，
生长着大青树。

Delivered him.
He used the knife to cut the umbilical cord
And applied the gold powder to the wound.
He also gave him a name.
He lived in Makyit Zing-ri Wai Chyahkrau Htumpa Pai,
Where grew big green trees.

远古，
彭干支伦的创造，
木占威纯的繁衍，
生下了天神木佐志胜热。
潘瓦能桑遮瓦能章
给他接了生，
用刀割断了他的脐带，
又在肚脐上敷上金粉，
又给他取了名字。
他生活的木佐志胜热能藏荣塔地方，
生长着大青树。

In remote antiquity,
The creation by Hpunggam Chyanun
And the multiplication by Majan Woishun
Bore God Matso Ji Shingra.
Hpan Wa Ningsang Chye Wa Ningchyang
Delivered him.
He used the knife to cut the umbilical cord
And applied the gold powder to the wound.
He also gave him a name.
He lived in Matso Ji Shingra Ningtsang Rumhta,
Where grew big green trees.

远古，
彭干支伦的创造，
木占威纯的繁衍，

In remote antiquity,
The creation by Hpunggam Chyanun
And the multiplication by Majan Woishun

生下了太阳神	Bore Jan Wa Ningsang Wunbu Hpronang,
占瓦能桑文布颇朗。	The Sun God.
潘瓦能桑遮瓦能章	Hpan Wa Ningsang Chye Wa Ningchyang
给他接了生，	Delivered him.
用刀割断了他的脐带，	He used the knife to cut the umbilical cord,
又在肚脐上敷上金粉，	And applied the gold powder to the wound.
又给他取了名字。	He also gave him a name.
他生活的石然登西星能兰台约顶地方，	He lived in Sharat Dingsi Sing Ninglam Htaiyo Ting,
生长着大青树。	Where grew big green trees.

远古，	In remote antiquity,
彭干支伦的创造，	The creation by Hpunggam Chyanun
木占威纯的繁衍，	And the multiplication by Majan Woishun
生下了天神	Bore Mado Ganu Loi Leng Singgu Du,
木夺格努吕良省谷杜。	Another god.
潘瓦能桑遮瓦能章	Hpan Wa Ningsang Chye Wa Ningchyang
给他接了生，	Delivered him.
用刀割断了他的脐带，	He used the knife to cut the umbilical cord,
又在肚脐上敷上金粉，	And applied the gold powder to the wound.
又给他取了名字。	He also gave him a name.
他生活的乌蒙诗贡乌迈文蒙地方，	He lived in Wumung Shagong Wumai Wunmong,
生长着竹子。	Where grew bamboos.

远古，
彭干支伦的创造，
木占威纯的繁衍，
生下了木代天神 ①
颇干杜正塔扎占能桑。
潘瓦能桑遮瓦能章
给他接了生，
用刀割断了他的脐带，
又在肚脐上敷上金粉，
又给他取了名字。
他居住的苏贡顶阿干栽类地方，
生长着大青树。

In remote antiquity,
The creation by Hpunggam Chyanun
And the multiplication by Majan Woishun
Bore Hpro-gam Du Jinghta Ja Jan Ningsang,
God Madai①.
Hpan Wa Ningsang Chye Wa Ningchyang
Delivered him.
He used the knife to cut the umbilical cord,
And applied the gold powder to the wound.
He also gave him a name.
He lived in Sut Gumding Agan Tsailui,
Where grew big green trees.

远古，
彭干支伦的创造，
木占威纯的繁衍，
生下了天神
木星格努木羊格遮考昆杜。
潘瓦能桑遮瓦能章
给他接了生，

In remote antiquity,
The creation by Hpunggam Chyanun
And the multiplication by Majan Woishun
Bore Masing Ganu Mayang Gajet Hkau Hkun Du,
Another god.
Hpan Wa Ningsang Chye Wa Ningchyang
Delivered him.

① 木代天神：景颇族中最高级别的神，须官家才能祭献。

① God Madai: the god with the highest position for the Jingpo people. Only the royal court had the right to offer sacrifices to him.

用刀割断了他的脐带，	He used the knife to cut the umbilical cord,
又在肚脐上敷上金粉，	And applied the gold powder to the wound.
又给他取了名字。	He also gave him a name.
他居住的卡木老石芽革松崩浪格巴地方，	He lived in Hka Malau Shaya Kasung Bumlang Gabam,
生长着芭蕉树。	Where grew banana trees.

九、天神的儿女两兄妹 Ⅸ. The Son and the Daughter of God

远古，	In remote antiquity,
天神的儿女，	God had two children.
男的叫能戈玛能桑，	The male was called Ninggo Ma Ningsang.
女的叫木佐玛诗依，	The female was called Matso Ma Shayi.
他们天天生活在一起，	They stayed together every day,
他们时时不相离，	And never separated for one minute.
他们相爱了。	They fell in love.
能戈玛能桑	Ninggo Ma Ningsang
给木佐玛诗依	Gave Matso Ma Shayi
送了几拿长的腰带，	A several-arm-span-long[1] belt,
送了刻着花纹的口弦筒；	And a jaw harp engraved with patterns.

① Several-arm-span-long: Here it means“very long”. —Translators’note.

木佐玛诗依
给能戈玛能桑
送了绣花的腰带。
他们生下了一个孩子，
他们把孩子送到森林里，
那里生出了杰通藤，
那里长出了杰三树。
远古，
潘瓦能桑遮瓦能章说：
“替我给万物取名的潘格来出生了，
代我给万事解难的遮能代有了，
他们是占瓦能桑和木夺直卡。
从现在起，
你们就给万物取名，
给万事解难吧！”
他回勒门崩顶地方去了，
临走时留下话说：
“等将来出现了，
没有脖子没有头，
像冬瓜一样的东西，
不会取名，

Matso Ma Shayi
Gave Ninggo Ma Ningsang
An embroidered belt.
They bore a kid,
And sent him into a forest,
Where grew the gyep htong vines
And the gyep san trees.
In remote antiquity,
Hpan Wa Ningsang Chye Wa Ningchyang said:
“Hpan Galai who helps me name all creatures was born.
Chye Ningtai who solves all problems for me was born.
They are Jan Wa Ningsang and Mado Jahka.
From now on,
You'll give creatures names,
And solve all problems!”
He returned to Mount Lamun Pungding.
Before his departure he left some words:
“In the future when there is a thing
Without a neck and a head,
And looking like a white gourd,
And if you cannot give him a name,
And cannot explain it,
Just meet me at Mount Lamun Pungding.
I will give him a name,

不会解释时，	And solve the problem for you."
就到勒门崩顶山来叫我，	
我给他取名，	
我给他解难。"	
远古，	In remote antiquity,
彭干支伦，	Hpunggam Chyanun
木占威纯，	And Majan Woishun
生命衰竭了，	Wore away
力量耗尽了。	And exhausted their strength.
衰老的彭干支伦，	The aging Hpunggam Chyanun
想要返老还童，	Wanted to rejuvenate himself.
来到瓦洋呆冒旁地方，	He came to Wayang Tai Mau Hpang,
改变了自己的容貌，	And changed his own face
包上崭新包头，	By putting on a brand-new head decoration.
变得年轻了；	He became young again.
衰老的木占威纯，	The aging Majan Woishun
想要返老还童，	Wanted to rejuvenate herself.
来到瓦洋呆冒旁地方，	She came to Wayang Tai Mau Hpang,
改变了自己的面貌，	Changed her face,
穿上美丽的筒裙，	Put on a beautiful straight skirt
变得年轻了。	And became young again.
远古，	In remote antiquity,

彭干支伦，	Hpunggam Chyanun
木占威纯，	And Majan Woishun
第二次返老还童，	Rejuvenated themselves for the second time.
变得年轻了，	They became young,
又能创造了，	And could go on with their creation
又能繁衍了。	And multiplication.
远古，	In remote antiquity,
彭干支伦的创造，	The creation by Hpunggam Chyanun
木占威纯的繁衍，	And the multiplication by Majan Woishun
生下了顶着羽冠、	Bore a creature with a feathered crest
戴着羽帽的。	And a feathered hat.
他是谁呀？	Who was he?
潘格来遮能代说：	Hpan Galai Chye Ningtai answered:
“他就是将来	“He is God Tsingdu Madai[1],
富人不理、	Whom in the future the rich would ignore
穷人祭献的宗都木代神[1]。	And to whom only the poor would offer sacrifices.
远古，	In remote antiquity,
彭干支伦的创造，	The creation by Hpunggam Chyanun
木占威纯的繁衍，	And the multiplication by Majan Woishun
生下了顶着铁冠、	Bore a creature with an iron crest

① 宗都木代神：传说是穷人祭献的神。穷人祭献这种神后就会变得富有起来。

① Tsingdu Madai: a legendary god to whom the poor offered sacrifices so that they could become rich.

戴着铁帽的。	And an iron hat.
他是谁呀？	Who was he?
潘格来遮能代说：	Hpan Galai Chye Ningtai answered:
“这是老大日旺干[1]，	“He is God Madai to whom Rawang[1] Gam,
祭献的木代神。”	The eldest brother, offered sacrifices.”
远古，	In remote antiquity,
彭干支伦的创造，	The creation by Hpunggam Chyanun
本占威纯的繁衍，	And the multiplication by Majan Woishun
生下了顶着铁冠，	Bore a creature with an iron crest
戴着铁帽的。	And an iron hat.
他是谁呀？	Who was he?
潘格来遮能代说：	Hpan Galai Chye Ningtai answered:
“这是老二农弄省举[2]	“He is God Madai to whom
祭献的木代神。”	Nong Nong Singgyi[2], the second brother, offered sacrifices.”
远古，	In remote antiquity,
彭干支伦的创造，	The creation by Hpunggam Chyanun
木占威纯的繁衍，	And the multiplication by Majan Woishun
生下了顶着大肚冠，	Bore a creature with a belly-like crest

① 日旺：传说是景颇族的一个支系。
② 农弄省举：传说中景颇族的一个支系。

① Rawang: a branch of the Jingpo people.
② Nung Nong Singgyi: a branch of the Jingpo people in legend.

戴着大肚帽的。	And a belly-like hat.
他是谁呀？	Who was he?
潘格来遮能代说：	Hpan Galai Chye Ningtai answered:
“他是老三木如腊皮①	“He is God Madai to whom
祭献的木代神。	Maru La Hpri①, the third brother, offered sacrifices.
他居住的地方，	He lives in the place
长满了金竹。”	Full of golden bamboos.”

远古，	In remote antiquity,
彭干支伦的创造，	The creation by Hpunggam Chyanun
木占威纯的繁衍，	And the multiplication by Majan Woishun
生下了戴着扁帽、	Bore a creature
缠着丝绸的。	Wearing a flat hat and silk cloth.
他是谁呀？	Who was he?
潘格来遮能代说：	Hpan Galai Chye Ningtai answered:
“他是老四贡氏都曼②	“He is God Madai to whom Gumdi Tu Man②,
以泼水的形式来祭献的木代神。”	The fourth brother, offered sacrifices by splashing water.”

远古，	In remote antiquity,
彭干支伦的创造，	The creation by Hpunggam Chyanun

① 木如腊皮：景颇族的一个支系。
② 贡氏都曼：传说中氐羌的部落，是傣族的先民。

① Maru La Hpri: a branch of the Jingpo people in legend.
② Gumdi Tu Man: in legend, a tribe of the Di-Qiang ethnic group, the ancestors of the Dai people.

木占威纯的繁衍，	And the multiplication by Majan Woishun
生下了顶着扁帽、	Bore a creature with a flat hat
戴着金冠的。	And a golden crest.
他是谁呀？	Who was he?
潘格来遮能代说：	Hpan Galai Chye Ningtai answered:
“他是老五掸当贡秧[①]	“He is God Madai to whom
祭献的木代神。”	Sam Tang Kum-yang[①], the fifth brother, offered sacrifices.”
远古，	In remote antiquity,
彭干支伦的创造，	The creation by Hpunggam Chyanun
木占威纯的繁衍，	And the multiplication by Majan Woishun
生下了顶着羽冠、	Bore a creature with a feathered crest
戴着羽帽的。	And a feathered hat.
他是谁呀？	Who was he?
潘格来遮能代说：	Hpan Galai Chye Ningtai answered:
“他是老六蚌拥瓦景颇[②]	“He is God Madai to whom
祭献的木代神。”	Pong Yong Wa Jinghpo[②], the sixth brother, offered sacrifices.”
远古，	In remote antiquity,

① 掸当贡秧：传说是缅甸掸族的先民。
② 蚌拥瓦景颇：传说是缅甸傣族的先民。

① Sam Tang Kum-yang: In legend, the ancestors of the Shan in Myanmar.
② Pong Yong Wa Jinghpo: This refers to the ancestors of the Jingpo people in Myanmar.

彭干支伦的创造，	The creation by Hpunggam Chyanun
木占威纯的繁衍，	And the multiplication by Majan Woishun
生下了顶着铁冠、	Bore a creature with an iron crest
戴着铜帽的。	And a copper hat.
他是谁呀？	Who was he?
潘格来遮能代说：	Hpan Galai Chye Ningtai answered:
“他是老七直黎瓦康康[①]	“He is God Madai to whom
祭献的木代神。”	Jili Wa Hkang Hkang[①], the seventh brother, offered sacrifices.”

远古，	In remote antiquity,
彭干支伦的创造，	The creation by Hpunggam Chyanun
木占威纯的繁衍，	And the multiplication by Majan Woishun
生下了顶着扁帽，	Bore a creature with a flat hat
戴着金冠的。	And a golden crest.
他是谁呀？	Who was he?
潘格来遮能代说：	Hpan Galai Chye Ningtai answered:
“他是老八蒙嫩瓦锐藏[②]	“He was God Madai to whom
祭献的木代神。	Mungnun Wa Roiza[②], the eighth brother, offered sacrifices.

① 直黎瓦康康：传说是缅甸的钦族。
② 蒙嫩瓦锐藏：传说中的藏族。

① Jili Wa Hkang Hkang: In legend, this refers to the Qin in Myanmar.
② Mungnun Wa Roiza: In legend, this refers to the Tibetan.

远古，	In remote antiquity,
彭干支伦的创造，	The creation by Hpunggam Chyanun
木占威纯的繁衍，	And the multiplication by Majan Woishun
生下了顶着铁冠，	Bore a creature with an iron crest
戴着铜帽的。	And a copper hat.
他是谁呀？	Who was he?
潘格来遮能代说：	Hpan Galai Chye Ningtai answered:
“他是老九缅瓦木干[①]	“He was God Madai to whom
祭献的木代神。”	Myen Wa Ma Gam[①], the ninth brother, offered sacrifices.”
远古，	In remote antiquity,
彭干支伦的创造，	The creation by Hpunggam Chyanun
木占威纯的繁衍，	And the multiplication by Majan Woishun
生下了顶着毡帽、	Bore a creature
缠着丝绸的。	Wearing a felt hat and silk.
他是谁呀？	Who was he?
潘格来遮能代说：	Hpan Galai Chye Ningtai answered:
“他是倒数老大迷瓦瓦汤瓦[②]	“He is God Madai to whom Miwa Wa Htang Wa[②],
祭献的木代神。”	The youngest brother, offered sacrifices.”
远古，	In remote antiquity,

① 缅瓦木干：传说中的缅族。
② 迷瓦瓦汤瓦：据说是汉族第一个酋长商汤。

① Myen Wa Ma Gam: In legend, this refers to the Bamar.
② Miwa Wa Htang Wa: In legend, this refers to Tang of Shang, the first chief of the Han people.

彭干支伦的创造，	The creation by Hpunggam Chyanun
木占威纯的繁衍，	And the multiplication by Majan Woishun
生下了顶着扁帽、	Bore a creature with a flat hat
戴着铁冠的。	And an iron crest.
他是谁呀？	Who was he?
潘格来遮能代说：	Hpan Galai Chye Ningtai answered:
“他是倒数老二蒙岭蒙旁[①]	“He is God Madai to whom Mungling Munghpang[①],
祭献的木代神。”	The last but one brother, offered sacrifices.”
远古，	In remote antiquity,
彭干支伦的创造，	The creation by Hpunggam Chyanun
木占威纯的繁衍，	And the multiplication by Majan Woishun
生下了塌着眼皮，	Bore a creature with drooped eyelids
长着短腿的。	And short legs.
他是谁呀？	Who was he?
潘格来遮能代说：	Hpan Galai Chye Ningtai answered:
“他是将来出征时	“He is God Shingditb, to whom
祭献的石狄神[②]。	Sacrifices will be offered when we go to war.
他居住在勒目狄扩阿戛恩官地方	He lives in Lamu Dihkro Aga N-got,
	Where grow the tender Jabu trees.”

① 蒙岭蒙旁：传说中的蒙古族。

② 石狄神：打仗出征时官家祭献的神。

① Mungling Munghpang: In legend, this refers to the Mongolian people.

② God Shingdit: The god to whom sacrifices would be offered when the royal court went to war.

那里生长着支布嫩树。”

远古，
彭干支伦的创造，
木占威纯的繁衍，
生下了塌眼皮、
长着短腿的。
她是谁呀？
潘格来遮能代说：
“她是守村护寨的木租神。
将来抵抗敌人时
就要杀牛祭献她；
她生活的地方，
生长着格东树。”

In remote antiquity,
The creation by Hpunggam Chyanun
And the multiplication by Majan Woishun
Bore a creature with drooped eyelids
And short legs.
Who was she?
Hpan Galai Chye Ningtai answered:
“She is Goddess Matsu,
Who is responsible for guarding the village.
In the future when resisting the enemy,
We will sacrifice oxen to her.
Where she lives, gadum trees grow.”

远古，
彭干支伦，
木占威纯，
力量耗尽了，
生命衰竭了，
不能创造了，
不能繁衍了。
衰老的彭干支伦，
想要返老还童，

In remote antiquity,
Hpunggam Chyanun
And Majan Woishun
Exhausted their strength
And wore away.
They couldn't continue their creation
And multiplication.
The aging Hpunggam Chyanun
Wanted to rejuvenate himself.

来到瓦洋呆冒旁地方，	He came to Wayang Tai Mau Hpang
改变了自己衰老的面貌，	And changed his face
包上崭新的包头，	With a brand-new head decoration.
变得年轻了；	Then he became young.
衰老的木占威纯，	The aging Majan Woishun
想要返老还童，	Wanted to rejuvenate herself.
来到瓦洋呆冒旁地方，	She came to Wayang Tai Mau Hpang,
改变了自己衰老的面貌，	Changed her face,
穿上美丽的筒裙，	And dressed in a beautiful straight skirt.
变得年轻了。	Then she became young.
远古，	In remote antiquity,
彭干支伦，	Hpunggam Chyanun
木占威纯，	And Majan Woishun
第三次返老还童，	Rejuvenated themselves for the third time.
变得年轻了，	Young again,
又能创造了，	They could continue their creation
又能繁衍了。	And multiplication again.
远古，	In remote antiquity,
彭干支伦的创造，	The creation by Hpunggam Chyanun
木占威纯的繁衍，	And multiplication by Majan Woishun
生下了金水槽，	Produced a golden ditch
有了银水槽。	And a silver ditch.

这是做什么的呀？
潘格来遮能代说：
“等将来有了迈里开江，
等将来有了恩迈开江[①]，
迈里开江从金水槽上流，
恩迈开江从银水槽上淌。”

What were they used for?
Hpan Galai Chye Ningtai said:
“When in the future there are the Mali Hka River
And the Nmai Hka River[①],
The Mali Hka River will flow through the golden ditch,
The Nmai Hka River will run through the silver ditch.”

附记：

在这部景颇族史诗中，有的地名，虽然今天还能对得上，但不一定指今天的地方。因为据说景颇人在向南迁徙途中，有这样一个习惯，即到了任何地方都要按原来住过的地方的名称给新地方起名称，如江、河、山等。所以，文中提到的恩迈开江和迈里开江，不 定是今天的这两条江。

Excursus:

The rivers in this epic may not be the ones with the same names today. When the Jingpo people migrated south, they often named new places, such as mountains and rivers, after those they had left behind.

---

① 迈里开江、恩迈开江：两江均在缅甸境内，地处缅甸西北部。两江之间的地方景颇语为“卡苦戛”即汉语中的江心坡，传说是景颇族的发祥地之一。

① Nmai Hka River and Mali Hka River: The two rivers are located in the northwest of Myanmar. The area between the two rivers is called “Hka Hku Ga” in Jingpo language, which means “the area between the rivers”. It is said that this area is one of the birthplaces of the Jingpo people.

远古，	In remote antiquity,
彭干支伦的创造，	The creation by Hpunggam Chyanun
木占威纯的繁衍，	And the multiplication by Majan Woishun
生下了一背篓金块，	Produced a pack basket of gold bullions
有了一背篓银块，	And a pack basket of silver bullions.
这是做什么的呀？	What were they for?
潘格来遮能代说：	Hpan Galai Chye Ningtai said:
“金块给迈里开江，	“The gold bullions are for the Mali Hka River.
银块给恩迈开江。”	The silver bullions are for the Nmai Hka River.”

远古，	In remote antiquity,
彭干支伦的创造，	The creation by Hpunggam Chyanun
木占威纯的繁衍，	And the multiplication by Majan Woishun
生出三十只金水桶，	Produced thirty gold buckets
有了三十只银水桶。	And thirty silver buckets.
它们是做什么的呀？	What were they used for?
潘格来遮能代说：	Hpan Galai Chye Ningtai said:
“将来用金水桶量迈里开江，	“In the future the gold buckets will be used to measure the Mali Hka River,
将来用银水桶量恩迈开江”。	And the silver buckets would be used to measure the Nmai Hka River.”

远古，	In remote antiquity,

彭干支伦的创造，
木占威纯的繁衍，
生下了一个大石头，
石头下有一个水源。
这是什么地方呀？
潘格来遮能代说：
“这是恩迈开江的源头，
这是迈里开江的开端。”

The creation by Hpunggam Chyanun
And the multiplication by Majan Woishun
Bore a huge rock.
Under it was a water source.
What kind of place was it?
Hpan Galai Chye Ningtai said:
“This is the source of the Nmai Hka River
And the beginning of the Mali Hka River.”

远古，
彭干支伦的创造，
木占威纯的繁衍，
生下了抱着会漏掉，
背着会消失的。
这是什么呀？
潘格来遮能代说：
“这就是恩迈开江水，
这就是迈里开江水。”

In remote antiquity,
The creation by Hpunggam Chyanun
And the multiplication by Majan Woishun
Bore something that would leak out when it was held,
And would disappear when it was carried.
What was it?
Hpan Galai Chye Ningtai said:
“This is the water of the Nmai Hka River,
And that is the water of the Mali Hka River.”

远古，
彭干支伦的创造，
木占威纯的繁衍，
生下了会冒烟，
会发热的。

In remote antiquity,
The creation by Hpunggam Chyanun
And the multiplication by Majan Woishun
Bore something that could produce smoke
And heat.

这是什么呀？
潘格来遮能代说：
“这是将来人们使用的火。”

What was it?
Hpan Galai Chye Ningtai said:
“This is the fire that people will use in the future.”

远古，
彭干支伦的创造，
木占威纯的繁衍，
生下了分管各类事物的女神。
她们分管些什么呀？
潘格来遮能代说：
“木苦努申兰木占，
是分管音乐的女神。
她有一副甜美的嗓子；
木龙贡东努木占，
是分管人体运动的女神，
她会给人们解除疲劳；
阿旁星桑旁木占，
是分管记忆的女神，
她会提醒歌手的记忆；
戛惹努松尊尊木占，
是分管烹饪的女神，
她会教人们做好吃的饭菜；
帕知能力努木占，

In remote antiquity,
The creation by Hpunggam Chyanun
And the multiplication by Majan Woishun
Bore the goddesses in charge of all things.
What kind of things were they responsible for?
Hpan Galai Chye Ningtai said:
“Mahku Nu Shinglam Majan,
The Goddess in charge of music,
Has a sweet voice.
Malug Kungdung Nu Majan,
The Goddess in charge of body movements,
Will relieve our fatigue.
Ahpang Sin Seng Hpang Majan,
The Goddess in charge of memory,
Will recover the memories of singers.
Kara Nu Sing Tsun Tut Majan,
The Goddess in charge of cooking,
Will teach the people to cook delicious dishes.
Hpajia Ningli Nu Majan,
The Goddess in charge of knowledge,

是分管知识的女神，
她会给人们以智慧。
她们生活的地方，
生长着好多，
让人精神清爽的茶叶。”

Will endow people with wisdom.
In the places where they live
Grow a lot of tea
That can make people feel refreshed.”

远古，
彭干支伦的创造，
木占威纯的繁衍，
生下了松炯拉，
有了松姜木占。
他们是干什么的呀？
潘格来遮能代说：
“松炯拉是树的父神，
松姜木占是树的母神，
他们将背着简帕，
他们将装着树籽，
把树种播遍高山，
把树籽撒满坝子。”

In remote antiquity,
The creation by Hpunggam Chyanun
And the multiplication by Majan Woishun
Bore Sumkyung La
And Sumkyung Majan.
What could they do?
Hpan Galai Chye Ningtai said:
“Sumkyung La is the father of trees.
Sumkyung Majan is the mother of trees.
They will carry a satchel
Fill with tree seeds.
They will plant the seeds
All over the mountains and the valleys.”

远古，
彭干支伦的创造，
木占威纯的繁衍，
生下了洁白

In remote antiquity,
The creation by Hpunggam Chyanun
And the multiplication by Majan Woishun
Bore something white

又带咸味的。 And salty.
这是什么呀？ What was it?
潘格来遮能代说： Hpan Galai Chye Ningtai said:
“她就是盐的母亲 “She is Sumsu Loihkam Majan,
松素吕坎木占。 The Mother of Salt.
她生活的地方， Where she lives,
生长着格塔树。” Gahta trees grow.”

十、松素吕坎木占 X. Sumsu Loihkam Majan

远古， In remote antiquity,
盐的母亲 The dishes cooked by Sumsu Loihkam Majan,
松素吕坎木占做的菜， The Mother of salt,
又香又可口， Were delicious,
儿子们做的菜， While the dishes cooked by her sons
又淡又不好吃， Tasted mild and yucky.
儿子们觉得很奇怪， So they were curious.
母亲做菜时， When Mother cooked,
儿子们便悄悄地扒在篱笆上看， The sons secretly leaned on the fence
And watched Mother cooking.
只见母亲， They saw Mother kept dropping her sweat
不断地把身上的汗水， Into the cooking pot.

滴进锅里，
儿子们愤怒了，
儿子们生气了，
把母亲赶出了家门外。
松素吕坎木占，
她是多么的伤心，
来到屋檐下，
流下了许多泪水，
在浸透她泪水的地方，
飞来了许多蜜蜂。

They were furious
And annoyed,
And drove their Mother out of home.
Sumsu Loihkam Majan, the Mother,
Was so heart-broken.
She stood under the roof,
Shedding lots of tears.
The spot soaked with her tears
Attracted many bees.

松素吕坎木占
她又来到了野外，
在她撒过尿的地方，
喷出了温泉，
山林里的野象、野猪，
豪猪、野牛，
都到这里来饮水。

Sumsu Loihkam Majan
Came to the wilderness.
A hot spring erupted from the spot
Soaked by her urine,
And wild elephants, wild boars,
Porcupines, and bison
All came here to drink water.

松素吕坎木占，
她又来到如旺山，
在那里滴下了泪水，
又撒下了尿，
那里出现了如旺盐坑。

Sumsu Loihkam Majan
Came to Mount Ruwang.
On it she dropped her tears
And pissed.
Thus the Ruwang salt pit came into being.

松素吕坎木占	Sumsu Loihkam Majan
她又来到蚌景颇山，	Came to Mount Pong Jinghpo.
在那里滴下了泪水，	On it she dropped her tears
撒下了尿，	And urinated.
那里有了蚌景颇盐坑。	Thus the Pong Jinghpo salt pit came into being.
松素吕坎木占，	Sumsu Loihkam Majan
来到江的下游，	Came to the lower reach of the river
安息在了西方，	And rested in the west.
在她安息的地方，	In the place where she rested
有了宽广的盐海。	Appeared the wide Salt Sea.
远古，	In remote antiquity,
彭干支伦的创造，	The creation by Hpunggam Chyanun
木占威纯的繁衍，	And the multiplication by Majan Woishun
生下了梯木梯拉，	Bore Htip Mahti La
有了梯木梯木占。	And Htip Mahti Majan.
他们是干什么的呀？	What could they do?
潘格来遮能代说：	Hpan Galai Chye Ningtai answered:
“他们生下的儿女们，	“The children they bore
将给人们传播各种技艺。	Will spread all kinds of skills to people.

十一、梯木梯拉和梯木梯木占的创造繁衍

XI. Creation and Multiplication by Htip Mahti La and Htip Mahti Majan

远古，	In remote antiquity,
梯木梯拉的创造，	The creation by Htip Mahti La
梯木梯木占的繁衍，	And the multiplication by Htip Mahti Majan
生下了老大。	Bore the eldest son.
他是做什么的呀？	What did he do?
潘格来遮能代说：	Hpan Galai Chye Ningtai answered:
“他懂得历史知识，	“He knows history
他最先吟颂‘斋瓦’。”	And is the first to chant ‘Jaiwa’.”
远古，	In remote antiquity,
梯木梯拉的创造，	The creation by Htip Mahti La
梯木梯木占的繁衍，	And the multiplication by Htip Mahti Majan
生下了老二。	Bore the second son.
他是做什么的呀？	What did he do?
潘格来遮能代说：	Hpan Galai Chye Ningtai answered:
“他最先懂得吟颂祭词，	“He is the first to know how to chant sacrificial songs.
他的名字叫木兰能如准德布。”	His name was Malan Ningru Jun Dabu.”

远古，	In remote antiquity,
梯木梯拉的创造，	The creation by Htip Mahti La
梯木梯木占的繁衍，	And the multiplication by Htip Mahti Majan
生下了老三。	Bore the third son.
他是做什么的呀？	What did he do?
潘格来遮能代说：	Hpan Galai Chye Ningtai answered:
“他是最先的祭师肯庄，	“He is Hkringjong, the earliest priest.
他的名字叫木东权腊桑。”	His name is Madum Hkyeng La-sang.”
远古，	In remote antiquity,
梯木梯拉的创造，	The creation by Htip Mahti La,
梯木梯木占的繁衍，	And the multiplication by Htip Mahti Majan,
生下了老四。	Bore the fourth son.
他是做什么的呀？	What did he do?
潘格来遮能代说：	Hpan Galai Chye Ningtai answered:
“他是最先管礼宾的盆龙，	“He is Hpunlum, the first protocol officer.
他的名字叫阿杜德旺。”	His name is Adu Dawang.”
远古，	In remote antiquity,
梯木梯拉的创造，	The creation by Htip Mahti La
梯木梯木占的繁衍，	And the multiplication by Htip Mahti Majan
生下了老五。	Bore the fifth son.
他是做什么的呀？	What did he do?

潘格来遮能代说：	Hpan Galai Chye Ningtai answered:
“他是最先会卜卦的能外，	“He is Ningwot, the first diviner.
他的名字叫温伦瓦温郎。”	His name is Wunlut Wa Wunlang.”
远古，	In remote antiquity,
梯木梯拉的创造，	The creation by Htip Mahti La
梯木梯木占的繁衍，	And the multiplication by Htip Mahti Majan
生下了老六。	Bore the sixth son.
他是做什么的呀？	What did he do?
潘格来遮能代说：	Hpan Galai Chye Ningtai answered:
“他是最先能说会唱，	“He is the first orator and singer.
他的名字叫布蒙瓦。”	His name is Pamung Wa.”
远古，	In remote antiquity,
梯木梯拉的创造，	The creation by Htip Mahti La
梯木梯木占的繁衍，	And the multiplication by Htip Mahti Majan
生下了老七。	Bore the seventh son.
他是做什么的呀？	What did he do?
潘格来遮能代说：	Hpan Galai Chye Ningtai answered:
“他最先会打铁，	“He is the first blacksmith.
他的名字叫能东瓦。”	His name is Ningdut Wa.”
远古，	In remote antiquity,
梯木梯拉的创造，	The creation by Htip Mahti La

梯木梯木占的繁衍，
生下了老八。
他是做什么的呀？
潘格来遮能代说：
“他最先懂得文字，
他最先具备知识。”

And the multiplication by Htip Mahti Majan
Bore the eighth son.
What did he do?
Hpan Galai Chye Ningtai answered:
“He is the first to know written words.
And the first to acquire knowledge.”

远古，
梯木梯拉的创造，
梯木梯木占的繁衍，
生下了老九。
他是做什么的呀？
潘格来遮能代说：
“他最先会做生意。”

In remote antiquity,
The creation by Htip Mahti La,
And the multiplication by Htip Mahti Majan,
Bore the ninth son.
What did he do?
Hpan Galai Chye Ningtai answered:
“He is the first to do business.”

远古，
梯木梯拉的创造，
梯木梯木占的繁衍，
生下了老十。
他是做什么的呀？
潘格来遮能代说：
“他最先懂得生育，
他的名字叫汤瓦。”

In remote antiquity,
The creation by Htip Mahti La
And the multiplication by Htip Mahti Majan
Bore the tenth son.
What did he do?
Hpan Galai Chye Ningtai answered:
“He is the first to know reproductive knowledge.
His name is Nhtang Wa.”

远古，	In remote antiquity,
梯木梯拉的创造，	The creation by Htip Mahti La
梯木梯木占的繁衍，	And the multiplication by Htip Mahti Majan
生下了第十一个。	Bore the eleventh son.
他是做什么的呀？	What did he do?
潘格来遮能代说：	Hpan Galai Chye Ningtai answered:
“他最先懂得畜牧。”	“He is the first to know how to raise livestock.”
远古，	In remote antiquity,
梯木梯拉的创造，	The creation by Htip Mahti La
梯木梯木占的繁衍，	And the multiplication by Htip Mahti Majan
生下了女的老大	Bore the eldest daughter.
她是做什么的呀？	What did she do?
潘格来遮能代说：	Hpan Galai Chye Ningtai answered:
“她最先懂得出嫁。”	“She is the first to marry off.”
远古，	In remote antiquity,
梯木梯拉的创造，	The creation by Htip Mahti La
梯木梯木占的繁衍，	And the multiplication by Htip Mahti Majan
生下了女的老二。	Bore the second daughter.
她是做什么的呀？	What did she do?
潘格来遮能代说：	Hpan Galai Chye Ningtai answered:
“她最先懂得烧火，	“She is the first to know how to light a fire
她最先懂得煮饭。”	And cook a meal.”

远古，
梯木梯拉的创造，
梯木梯木占的繁衍，
生下了女的老三。
她是做什么的呀？
潘格来遮能代说：
“她最先懂得耕种，
她最先懂得收获。”

In remote antiquity,
The creation by Htip Mahti La
And the multiplication by Htip Mahti Majan
Bore the third daughter.
What did she do?
Hpan Galai Chye Ningtai answered:
“She is the first to know
How to cultivate the Earth and gather in crops.”

远古，
梯木梯拉的创造，
梯木梯木占的繁衍，
生下了女的老四。
她是做什么的呀？
潘格来遮能代说：
“她最先认识文字，
她最先具备知识。”

In remote antiquity,
The creation by Htip Mahti La
And the multiplication by Htip Mahti Majan
Bore the fourth daughter.
What did she do?
Hpan Galai Chye Ningtai answered:
“She is the first to know how to read and write
And the first to acquire knowledge.”

远古，
梯木梯拉的创造，
梯木梯木占的繁衍，
生下了女的老五。
她是做什么的呀？

In remote antiquity,
The creation by Htip Mahti La
And the multiplication by Htip Mahti Majan
Bore the fifth daughter.
What did she do?

潘格来遮能代说：	Hpan Galai Chye Ningtai answered:
“她最先懂得爱情，	“She is the first to know love
她最先会唱山歌。”	And the first to sing mountain songs.”
远古，	In remote antiquity,
梯木梯拉的创造，	The creation by Htip Mahti La
梯木梯木占的繁衍，	And the multiplication by Htip Mahti Majan
生下了女的老六。	Bore the sixth daughter.
她是做什么的呀？	What did she do?
潘格来遮能代说：	Hpan Galai Chye Ningtai answered:
“她最先会用金钱。	“She is the first to know how to use money
她最先会做生意。”	And the first to know how to do business.”
远古，	In remote antiquity,
梯木梯拉的创造，	The creation by Htip Mahti La
梯木梯木占的繁衍，	And the multiplication by Htip Mahti Majan
生下了女的老七。	Bore the seventh daughter.
她是做什么的呀？	What did she do?
潘格来遮能代说：	Hpan Galai Chye Ningtai answered:
“她最先知道怀孕，	“She is the first to know how to conceive
她最先懂得生育。”	And give birth.”
远古，	In remote antiquity,
梯木梯拉的创造，	The creation by Htip Mahti La

梯木梯木占的繁衍，	And the multiplication by Htip Mahti Majan
生下了女的老八。	Bore the eighth daughter.
她是做什么的呀？	What did she do?
潘格来遮能代说：	Hpan Galai Chye Ningtai answered:
“她最先知道迎送，	“She is the first to have good manners,
她最先懂得礼宾。”	And the first to know how to treat guests appropriately.”
远古，	In remote antiquity,
梯木梯拉的创造，	The creation by Htip Mahti La
梯木梯木占的繁衍，	And the multiplication by Htip Mahti Majan
生下了女的老九。	Bore the ninth daughter.
她是做什么的呀？	What did she do?
潘格来遮能代说：	Hpan Galai Chye Ningtai answered:
“她最先懂得纺线，	“She is the first
她最先知道织布。”	To know spinning and weaving.”
远古，	In remote antiquity,
梯木梯拉的创造，	The creation by Htip Mahti La
梯木梯木占的繁衍，	And the multiplication by Htip Mahti Majan
生下了女的老十。	Bore the tenth daughter.
她是做什么的呀？	What did she do?
潘格来遮能代说：	Hpan Galai Chye Ningtai answered:
“她最先懂得养猪，	“She is the first to know how to raise pigs
她最先知道喂鸡。”	And to feed chickens.”

远古，	In remote antiquity,
梯木梯拉的创造，	The creation by Htip Mahti La
梯木梯木占的繁衍，	And the multiplication by Htip Mahti Majan
生下了女的第十一个。	Bore the eleventh daughter.
她是做什么的呀？	What did she do?
潘格来遮能代说：	Hpan Galai Chye Ningtai answered:
"她最先会做酒药，	"She is the first to know
她最先会酿酒。"	How to make yeast and wine."
远古，	In remote antiquity,
彭干支伦的创造，	The creation by Hpunggam Chyanun
木占威纯的繁衍，	And the multiplication by Majan Woishun
生下了盛代权阿拉，	Bore Shingtai Hkyen Ala
有了盛代权木占。	And Shingtai Hkyen Majan.
它们是做什么的呀？	What did they do?
潘格来遮能代说：	Hpan Galai Chye Ningtai said:
"它们是蚕的祖先，	"They were the ancestors of the silkworms.
它们生活的地方，	In the place where they live
生长着桑树。"	Grow many mulberry trees."
远古，	In remote antiquity,
彭干支伦的创造，	The creation by Hpunggam Chyanun
木占威纯的繁衍，	And the multiplication by Majan Woishun

生下了阿嫩格努，
有了登然木独。
它们是做什么的呀？
潘格来遮能代说：
“它们是绵羊的祖先，
它们生活的地方，
生长着羊耳朵树。”

Bore Anut Ganu
And Ting-ra Madu.
What did they do?
Hpan Galai Chye Ningtai said:
“They are the ancestors of sheep.
In the place where they live
Grow many lamb-ear trees.”

远古，
彭干支伦的创造，
木占威纯的繁衍，
生下了扁嘴巴的鸭，
有了长脖子的鹅。
它们是做什么的呀？
潘格来遮能代说：
“它们将守护王宫，
它们生活的地方，
生长着槟榔树。”

In remote antiquity,
The creation by Hpunggam Chyanun
And the multiplication by Majan Woishun
Bore the duck with a flat mouth
And the goose with a long neck.
What could they do?
Hpan Galai Chye Ningtai said:
“They will guard the palace.
In the place where they live
Grow many areca nut trees.”

远古，
彭干支伦的创造，
木占威纯的繁衍，
生下了神刀，
有了神箭；

In remote antiquity,
The creation by Hpunggam Chyanun
And the multiplication by Majan Woishun
Bore holy knives
And the arrows of God,

生下了敲天的大锤，
有了打地的铁砧；
生下了量天的标杆，
有了丈地的绳索；
生下了泥块，
有了土团。
这些是做什么的呀？
潘格来遮能代说：
“等将来宁贯督施瓦囊贡努
打造天地时，
会用到它们。”

The sledge hammer with which to pound the Sky
And the iron anvil on which to strike the Earth,
The range pole to measure the Sky
And the rope to measure the Earth,
The clod and the clay mass.
What could they do?
Hpan Galai Chye Ningtai said:
“When N-gon Du Shawa Nang Kumnu
Creates the Sky and the Earth,
They will be used.”

远古，
彭干支伦，
木占威纯，
力量耗尽了，
生命衰竭了，
不能创造了，
不能繁衍了。
衰老的彭干支伦，
想要返老还童，
来到瓦洋呆冒旁地方，
改变了自己衰老的面貌，
包上崭新的包头，

In remote antiquity,
Hpunggam Chyanun
And Majan Woishun
Exhausted their strength
And wore away.
They could no longer go on
With their creation and multiplication.
The aging Hpunggam Chyanun
Wanted to rejuvenate himself.
He came to Wayang Tai Mau Hpang,
And changed his old face
With a brand-new head decoration.

变得年轻了；	Then he became young.
衰老的枯威纯，	The aging Majan Woishun
想要返老还童，	Wanted to rejuvenate herself.
来到瓦洋呆冒旁地方，	She came to Wayang Tai Man Hpang
改变了自己衰老的面貌，	And changed her face
穿上美丽的筒裙，	By wearing a beautiful straight skirt.
变得年轻了。	She became young again.
远古，	In remote antiquity,
彭干支伦，	Hpunggam Chyanun
木占威纯，	And Majan Woishun
第四次返老还童，	Rejuvenated themselves for the fourth time.
变得年轻了，	Young again,
又能创造了，	They could continue
又能繁衍了。	Their creation and multiplication.
远古，	In remote antiquity,
彭干支伦的创造，	The creation by Hpunggam Chyanun
木占威纯的繁衍，	And the multiplication by Majan Woishun
生下了老大。	Bore the eldest son.
他是谁呀？	Who was he?
潘格来遮能代说：	Hpan Galai Chye Ningtai said:
“他叫诗瓦鹏，	“He is Shawa Hpung.
他生活的地方，	In the place where he lives

生长着诗贡乌仍树。”	Grow the Shagong Wuring trees.”
远古，	In remote antiquity,
彭干支伦的创造，	The creation by Hpunggam Chyanun
木占威纯的繁衍，	And the multiplication by Majan Woishun
生下了老二。	Bore the second son.
他是谁呀？	Who was he?
潘格来遮能代说：	Hpan Galai Chye Ningtai said:
“他叫顶如鹏，	“He is Dingru Hpung.
他生活的地方，	In the place where he lives
生长着诗贡昂麻藤①。”	Grow the Shagong Angma①.”
远古，	In remote antiquity,
彭干支伦的创造，	The creation by Hpunggam Chyanun
木占威纯的繁衍，	And the multiplication by Majan Woishun
生下了老三。	Bore the third son.
他是谁呀？	Who was he?
潘格来遮能代说：	Hpan Galai Chye Ningtai said:
“他叫登纳鹏，	“He is Dingna Hpung.
他生活的地方，	In the place he lives,
生长着真专②。”	Grow Chyingjon②.”

① 诗贡昂麻藤：传说中的一种藤子。
② 真专：一种可以吃的植物。

① Shagong Angma: a kind of vine in Jingpo legend.
② Chyingjon: an edible plant.

远古，	In remote antiquity,
彭干支伦的创造，	The creation by Hpunggam Chyanun
木占威纯的繁衍，	And the multiplication by Majan Woishun
生下了老四。	Bore the fourth son.
他是谁呀？	Who was he?
潘格来遮能代说：	Hpan Galai Chye Ningtai said:
“他叫迷地东，	“He is Myidi Tung.
将来打造天地时，	In the creation of the new Sky and the new Earth in the future,
他要扛九尺长的斧头。”	He will carry a 9-foot-long axe.”

远古，	In remote antiquity,
彭干支伦的创造，	The creation by Hpunggam Chyanun
木占威纯的繁衍，	And the multiplication by Majan Woishun
生下了老五。	Bore the fifth son.
他是谁呀？	Who was he?
潘格来遮能代说：	Hpan Galai Chye Ningtai said:
“他叫纳旁鹏，	“He is Na-hpang Hpung.
将来打造天地时，	In the creation of the new Sky and the new Earth in the future,
他要扛巨大石柜，	He will carry a huge stone box
他要扛九尺斧头。”	And a 9-foot-long axe.”

远古，
彭干支伦的创造，
木占威纯的繁衍，
生下了老六。
他是谁呀？
潘格来遮能代说：
“他叫诗亚当伢，
将来打造天地时，
他将带能射过九座山的弓，
他给宁贯督当卫士。”

In remote antiquity,
The creation by Hpunggam Chyanun
And the multiplication by Majan Woishun
Bore the sixth son.
Who was he?
Hpan Galai Chye Ningtai said:
“He is Shi-ya Dang-ya.
In the creation of the new Sky and the new Earth in the future,
He will carry a bow that could shoot over nine mountains.
He will serve N-gon Du as a guard.”

远古，
彭干支伦的创造，
木占威纯的繁衍，
生下了老七。
他是谁呀？
潘格来遮能代说：
“他叫穆达东文，
将来打造天地时，
他拿着神剑给宁贯督当卫士。”

In remote antiquity,
The creation by Hpunggam Chyanun
And the multiplication by Majan Woishun
Bore the seventh son.
Who was he?
Hpan Galai Chye Ningtai said:
“He is Mada Dungngut.
In the creation of the new Sky and the new Earth in the future,
He will serve N-gon Du as a guard with a holy sword.”

远古，

In remote antiquity,

彭干支伦的创造，	The creation by Hpunggam Chyanun
木占威纯的繁衍，	And the multiplication by Majan Woishun
生下了一个	Bore a giant.
母亲生他时	When his mother gave birth to him,
拉断了背带、	She broke the brace
蹬断了竹桩的巨人。	And the bamboo stake.
他是谁呀？	Who was he?
潘格来遮能代说：	Hpan Galai Chye Ningtai said:
“他就是将来的创世英雄宁贯督施瓦囊贡努[1]。”	“He is N-gon Du Shawa Nang Kumnu[1], Hero of the Creation.”

远古，	In remote antiquity,
潘格来遮能代，	Hpan Galai Chye Ningtai
对宁贯督说：	Said to N-gon Du:
“宁贯督呀，	“N-gon Du,
跟你打天的英雄有了，	There are heroes to create the Sky,
跟你造地的勇士也有了；	And warriors to make the Earth with you;

① 宁贯督：景颇族传说中打天造地的英雄。他打造了天地，给各种家禽家畜取了名。景颇族娶媳妇结婚时穿草棚的习惯据说就是从他开始的。同时他又是景颇族的第一个官。直到后来如骑马，收取宁冠（如官租、官职等特权）据说也是从他开始的。

① N-gon Du: In the legend of the Jingpo ethnic group, he is the hero who created the Sky and the Earth. Then, he named the poultry and livestock. The custom that when the Jingpo people got married, the newlyweds would pass through the straw hut began from him. Meanwhile, he was the first official from the Jingpo ethnic group. It is said that he started horse riding and the N-gon collecting tribute (the privilege of getting money from official land rent and from official positions).

你带的神弓有了，	There is the bow for you to carry
你挎的神刀也有了；	And the knife for you to hold;
你敲天的大锤有了，	There is the sledge hammer for you to beat the Sky
你打地的铁砧也有了；	And the anvil for you to strike the Earth;
你量天的标杆有了，	There is the range pole for you to measure the Sky
你丈地的绳索也有了；	And the rope for you to measure the Earth;
你用的泥块有了，	There is the clod
你要的土团也有了。	And the clay for you to use.
到你的戛昂崩山①，	You should go to Mount Gaang Bum①
坐你的铁交椅吧。”	And sit in the leading chair of power."
远古，	In remote antiquity,
彭干支伦的创造，	The creation by Hpunggam Chyanun
木占威纯的繁衍，	And the multiplication by Majan Woishun
生下了宁贯督的妹妹，	Bore the sister of N-gon Du.
她叫什么呀？	What was her name?
潘格来遮能代说：	Hpan Galai Chye Ningtai said:
“她的名字叫波南文布。”	"Her name is Hpro Nang Wunbu."
远古，	In remote antiquity,

① 戛昂崩山：戛昂，景颇语意为中央、中原，戛昂山是景颇族传说中群山中央的一座，也是景颇族的发祥地之一。

① Mount Gaang Bum: Gaang refers to the center in the Jingpo language. Mount Gaang Bum is located in the center of all the mountains. It is also one of the origins of the Jingpo people.

彭干支伦的创造，	The creation by Hpunggam Chyanun
木占威纯的繁衍，	And the multiplication by Majan Woishun
生下了还在娘胎里	Bore creatures
就不停地翻滚；	Who rolled over in the womb,
还没有生出	And moved a lot
就到处冲撞的。	Before they were born.
它们是谁呀？	Who were they?
潘格来遮能代说：	Hpan Galai Chye Ningtai answered:
“它们是畜类的祖先，	“They are Wureng La and Ting Tang Majan,
乌仁拉和丁当木占。”	The ancestors of livestock.”

十二、乌仁拉和丁当木占的创造繁衍 XII. Creation by Wureng La and Multiplication by Ting Tang Majan

远古，	In remote antiquity,
乌仁拉的创造，	The creation by Wureng La
丁当木占的繁衍，	And the multiplication by Ting Tang Majan
生下了会扒地找食的。	Bore creatures
这是什么呀？	That could paw the ground for food.
潘格来遮能代说：	What were these?
“它们是星松拉星松木占，	Hpan Galai Chye Ningtai answered:
它们是鸡的祖先，	“They are Sik Sok La Sik Sok Majan,

它们生活的地方，	The ancestors of chickens.
生长着星松树。”	In the place where they live grow Sik Sok trees.”
远古，	In remote antiquity,
乌仁拉的创造，	The creation by Wureng La
丁当木占的繁衍，	And the multiplication by Ting Tang Majan
生下了长着长嘴巴的。	Bore creatures with a long snout.
这是什么呀？	What were these?
潘格来遮能代说：	Hpan Galai Chye Ningtai answered:
“它们是梯托拉和梯托木占，	“They are Htik Htok La and Htik Htok Majan,
它们是猪的祖先，	The ancestors of pigs.
它们生活的地方	In the place where they live
生长着芭蕉树。”	Grow banana trees.”
远古，	In remote antiquity,
乌仁拉的创造，	The creation by Wureng La
丁当木占的繁衍，	And the multiplication by Ting Tang Majan
生下了长着胡子的，	Bore creatures with some goatees.
这是什么呀？	What were they?
潘格来遮能代说：	Hpan Galai Chye Ningtai answered:
“它们是能背拉和能权木占，	“They are Ningboi La and Ninghyen Majan,
它们是羊的祖先，	The ancestors of goats.
它们生活的地方	In the place where they live

生长着拜南[1]树。”	Grow Bainam[1] trees.”
远古，	In remote antiquity,
乌仁拉的创造，	The creation by Wureng La
丁当木占的繁衍。	And the multiplication by Ting Tang Majan
生下了长着浓毛的。	Bore creatures with thick hair.
这是什么呀？	What were they?
潘格来遮能代说：	Hpan Galai Chye Ningtai answered:
“它们是乌智拉和乌卡木占，	“They are Wujik La and Wuhkak Majan,
它们是狗的祖先，	The ancestors of dogs.
它们生活的地方	In the place where they live
生长着鱼腥草。”	Grow the Houttuynia Cordatas.”
远古，	In remote antiquity,
乌仁拉的创造，	The creation by Wureng La
丁当木占的繁衍，	And the multiplication by Ting Tang Majan
生下了长着鬃毛的。	Bore creatures with mane.
它们是谁呀？	What were they?
潘格来遮能代说：	Hpan Galai Chye Ningtai answered:
“它们是东达拉和东达木占，	“They are Duk Dak La and Duk Dak Majan,
它们是马的祖先，	The ancestors of horses.
它们生活的地方，	In the place where they live
生长着贡然木渣藤。”	Grow Gumra Machya vines.”

① 拜南：景颇语，指山羊。

① Bainam：It means “goat” in Jingpo language.

远古，	In remote antiquity,
乌仁拉的创造，	The creation by Wureng La
丁当木占的繁衍，	And the multiplication by Ting Tang Majan
生下了脚大角尖的。	Bore creatures with big feet and sharp horns.
它们是什么呀？	What were they?
潘格来遮能代说：	Hpan Galai Chye Ningtai answered:
“它们是水牛的祖先，	“They are the ancestors of buffalos.
它们生活的地方，	In the place where they live
生长着那丁然树。”	Grow Ting-ra trees.”

远古，	In remote antiquity,
乌仁拉的创造，	The creation by Wureng La
丁当木占的繁衍，	And the multiplication by Ting Tang Majan
生下了长着弯角的。	Bore creatures with bent horns.
它们是谁呀？	What were they?
潘格来遮能代说：	Hpan Galai Chye Ningtai answered:
“它们是乌刚拉和乌刚木占，	“They are Wugang La and Wugang Majan,
它们是牦牛的祖先，	The ancestors of yaks.
它们生活的地方，	In the place where they live
生长着牛藤子树。”	Grow cattle vine trees.”

远古，	In remote antiquity,
乌仁拉的创造，	The creation by Wureng La

丁当木占的繁衍，	And the multiplication by Ting Tang Majan
生下了还在娘胎里	Bore creatures that branch out and sprout
就抽枝发芽的，	In their mother's womb.
它们是谁呀？	What were they?
潘格来遮能代说：	Hpan Galai Chye Ningtai answered:
“它们是五谷的祖先。	"They are Yunji La and Yunnang Majan,
尹知拉和尹囊木占。”	The ancestors of the five grains."

十三、尹知拉和尹囊木占的创造和繁衍 / XIII. Creation by Yunji La and Multiplication by Yunnang Majan

远古，	In remote antiquity,
尹知拉的创造，	The creation by Yunji La
尹囊木占的繁衍，	And the multiplication by Yunnang Majan
生下了枝枝杈杈的。	Bore a creature with twiggy bushes.
这是什么呀？	What was it?
潘格来遮能代说：	Hpan Galai Chye Ningtai said:
“它就是祖格努藏都鬼，	"It is Ghost Tsu Ganu Tsang Du.
将来丰收的年成，	In the bumper harvest years in the future,
要用酒献它，	It will be offered wine,
要用肉祭它。	And meat as sacrifices.
它居住在竹林里，	It lives in the bamboo forests.

它生活的地方，	In the place where he lives
长着挤代若树。”	Grow Tsu Daijo trees."
远古，	In remote antiquity,
尹知拉的创造，	The creation by Yunji La
尹囊木占的繁衍，	And the multiplication by Yunnang Majan
生下了枝枝杈杈的。	Bore a creature with twiggy bushes.
它是谁呀？	Who was it?
潘格来遮能代说：	Hpan Galai Chye Ningtai said:
“它是饿鬼足勒蒙藏南崩，	"It is the hungry ghost Tsu Lamung Tsam Nampum.
将来人们吃喝前，	Before each meal in the future,
要先把饭菜扔给它，	People will throw some food to him.
它生活在村寨旁。”	It lived by the village."
远古，	In remote antiquity,
尹知拉的创造，	The creation by Yunji La
尹囊木占的繁衍，	And the multiplication by Yunnang Majan
生下了白谷，	Bore white rice
有了红谷；	And red rice,
生下了地谷，	Mountain rice
有了田谷；	And field rice,
生下了绿谷，	Green rice
有了矮谷；	And short rice;
生下了山地黑谷，	Black mountain rice

有了山地绿谷；	And green mountain rice,
生下了热带绿谷，	Tropical green rice
有了热带芦谷。	And tropical reed rice,
生下了小红米，	Red millet
有了粟米；	And corn,
生下了狗尾巴米，	Dog-tailed rice
有了高粱；	And sorghum,
生下了芦谷米，	Bore reed rice
有了苞谷；	And maize,
生下了大黄豆，	Big soya beans
有了小黄豆；	And small soya beans,
生下了白芝麻，	White sesame
有了黑芝麻。	And black sesame,
生下了冬瓜，	Wax gourds
有了南瓜；	And pumpkins,
生下了松棚芋[①]，	Sumhpong taros
有了浪东芋；	And Langdong taros,
生下了能刚芋，	Ninggang taros
有了艿腊芋；	And Naila taros,
生下了艿顶芋，	Naiding taros
有了艿洋芋；	And Naiyang taros,
生下了乌云芋，	Wuyun taros

① 松鹏芋：芋头的一种，这里和以下各种芋头均是音译。

有了能如芋；	And Numru taros
生下了红薯，	Sweet potatoes
有了银桶山药；	And silver-bucket yams,
生下了韭菜，	Leeks
有了苤菜；	And pie orchids,
生下了薄荷，	Peppermint
有了茄子。	And eggplant.
远古，	In remote antiquity,
尹知拉的创造，	The creation by Yunji La
尹囊木占的繁衍，	And the multiplication by Yunnang Majan
生下了一个	Bore a creature
没有脖子没有脚，	Without a neck or feet,
像冬瓜一样的东西。	Looking like a wax gourd.
这是什么呀？	What was it?
潘格来遮能代说：	Hpan Galai Chye Ningtai
“不知道该怎样取名，	Failed to name it,
也不知道怎样解释。”	Or to describe it.
远古，	In remote antiquity,
潘瓦能桑遮瓦能章说：	Hpan Wa Ningsang Chye Wa Ningchyang said:
“等将来生下了	“When in the future you cannot
没有脖子没有脚，	Name and describe a creature
像冬瓜一样的东西，	Without a neck or feet,

不知道怎样取名，
不知道怎样解释时，
就到勒门崩顶山去找我。”
按潘瓦能桑遮瓦能章留下的话，
潘格来遮能代，
来到勒门崩顶山，
找到了潘瓦能桑遮瓦能章。

Looking like a wax gourd,
Just go to Mount Lamun Pungding for me.”
Remembering the words
Left by Hpan Wa Ningsang Chye Wa Ningchyang,
Hpan Galai Chye Ningdai
Came to Mount Lamun Pungding
And found him.

潘瓦能桑遮瓦能章
带着斧头，
拿着长刀；
带着女性生殖器，
拿着男性生殖器，
带着性欲药，
拿着铃铛[①]；
带着润滑药，
拿着生育药，
从勒门崩顶山赶来了。

Hpan Wa Ningsang Chye Wa Ningchyang
Came over from Mount Lamun Pungding,
Carrying with him an axe,
A sword,
Female genitals,
Male genitals,
A love potion,
Some bells[①],
some lubricant
And fertility drugs.

潘瓦能桑遮瓦能章
用长刀和斧头，
把没有脖子没有脚，

Hpan Wa Ningsang Chye Wa Ningchyang
Cut the thing looking like a wax gourd
And having no neck and no feet

① 铃铛：指睾丸。

① The bells: Here they refer to the testicles.

像冬瓜一样的东西，	Into two halves
剖成两半，	With his sword and axe,
右半是德如贡散，	The right half being Daru Gumsan
左半是木干贡潘，	And the left half being Magam Gumhpan.
他要让他们，	He would turn them
变成将来的人类。	Into future human beings.

黑黑的头发有了，	Dark hair was formed,
呼吸的鼻子安上了；	And the nose for breathing was added;
看东西的眼睛有了，	The eyes for seeing were formed,
听声音的耳朵安上了；	And the ears for hearing were added;
说话的嘴巴有了，	The mouth for speaking was formed,
吃饭的舌头安上了；	And the tongue for eating was added;
呼喊的喉咙有了，	The throat for shouting was formed,
胸膛乳房安上了；	And the breasts on the chest were added;
脊骨有了，	The spine was formed,
肩膀安上了；	And the shoulders were added;
左手有了，	The left hand
右手安上了；	And the right hand were added;
左脚有了，	The left foot
右脚安上了；	And the right foot were added;
圆圆的屁股有了，	The round hips were formed,
两腿间的阴沟通了；	And the groin between the legs took shape;
全身的骨齐了，	The skeleton was completed

全身的肉满了；	With flesh filled in;
心肝有了，	The heart and liver were formed,
肠肚也有了。	And intestines and stomach were added.
左边放上男性生殖器，	The male genitals were added on the left half
右边安上女性生殖器，	And the female genitals on the right half.
给男人装上生育药，	The man was provided with fertility drugs
给女人安上润滑油，	While the woman was provided with lubricant.
因为男人要出远门，	Since the man would go on a trip,
性欲药只涂在	The love potion was applied
男人生殖器的顶端；	To the tip of his genitals.
因为女人守在家，	Since the woman would stay at home,
性欲药涂满了	The love potion was applied
女人的生殖器，	all over her genitals.
所以男人的性欲	So men's sexual desire
走不到楼梯口，	doesn't last long,
女性的性欲	While women's sexual desire
能延续半个早上。	Lasts a hundred times longer.
人是做好了，	The creation of human beings was completed,
但还不会动，	But they couldn't move.
潘瓦能桑遮瓦能章	Hpan Wa Ningsang Chye Wa Ningchyang
叫来了盆南腿能桑，	Asked Hpunnam Htoi Ningsan
给德如贡散吹了口气，	To breathe on Daru Gumsan,

德如贡散会动了；	And he could move.
给木干贡潘吹一口气，	Then he breathed on Magam Gumhpan,
木干贡潘会呼吸了。	And she could breathe.
潘瓦能桑遮瓦能章	Hpan Wa Ningsang Chye Wa Ningchyang
对他们说：	Said to them:
“德如贡散呀，	“Daru Gumsan
木干贡潘，	And Magam Gumhpan,
将来宁贯督打天造地，	When N-gon Du creates the world in the future,
量天的标杆会打着你们，	The range pole for measuring the Sky may hit you;
大地的绳索会碰着你们，	The rope for measuring the Earth may hurt you.
你们先躲到勒木卢酸地方，	You can hide yourselves in Lamu Lupson,
将来再来接你们。”	And I will come to bring you back later.”
远古	In remote antiquity,
彭干支伦的创造，	The creation by Hpunggam Chyanun
木占威纯的繁衍，	And the multiplication by Majan Woishun
生下了枯瓦贡哦，	Led to the birth of Hku Wa Gong O
胜热瓦贡扎。	And Shing Re Wa Gong Ja.
远古，	In ancient time,
潘瓦能桑遮瓦能章	Hpan Wa Ningsang Chye Wa Ningchyang
对彭干支伦、	Said to Hpunggam Chyanun
木占威纯说：	And Majan Woishun:

“彭干支伦呀，	“Hpunggam Chyanun
木占威纯，	And Majan Woishun,
该你们创造的都创造了，	You have created all you could,
该你们繁衍的都繁衍了，	And have multiplied all you could.
停止创造吧，	Now stop your creation
停止繁衍吧。”	And your multiplication.”
远古，	In remote antiquity,
彭干支伦，	Hpunggam Chyanun
木占威纯，	And Majan Woishun
生命衰竭了，	Wore away
力量耗尽了，	And exhausted their strength.
不能创造了，	They could no longer continue
不能繁衍了。	Their creation and their multiplication.
远古，	In remote antiquity,
彭干支伦，	After Hpunggam Chyanun
木占威纯，	And Majan Woishun
他们咽气后，	Breathed their last,
从他们的嘴里	An auspicious wind
生出一股祥风。	Floated out of their mouths.
在落着他们的皮的地方，	In the place where their skin fell,
长出了绿绿的青草；	Green grass grew.
在落着他们骨头的地方，	In the place where their bones fell,

有了铁块铁片；	Pieces of iron were found.
在落着他们脑汁的地方，	In the place where their brains dropped,
有了银坑；	A silver pit was formed.
在落着他们头盖骨的地方，	In the place where their skulls fell,
有了一块块玉；	Pieces of jade were formed.
在落着他们牙齿的地方，	In the place where their teeth fell,
有了瓷器；	Porcelain was found.
在落着他们心脏的地方，	In the place where their hearts fell,
有了金坑；	A gold pit was formed.
在落着他们肠子的地方，	In the place where their guts fell,
有了长长的项链；	A long necklace was found.
在落着他们肚子的地方，	In the place where their belly fell,
长出了给支树[1]；	Kaji trees[1] grew.
在落着他们粪便的地方，	In the place where their feces fell
长出了各种蔬菜。	All kinds of vegetables grew.
远古，	In remote antiquity,
彭干支伦、	After Hpunggam Chyanun
木占威纯，	And Majan Woishun
他们咽气后，	Breathed their last,
猴子吃了他们的肉，	Monkeys ate their flesh.
擦过嘴的地方，	In the place where they wiped their muzzles,

① 给支树：给支即项链；给支树也就是可以做成项链的树。

① Kaji trees: Kaji means necklace, so Kaji trees refer to the trees which can be used to make necklaces.

长出了勒山菌，	Lashap mushrooms
生出了木岭菌；	And maling mushrooms grew.
野猪吃了他们的肉，	Wild boars ate their flesh,
擦过嘴的地方，	And in the place where they wiped their snouts,
长出了野猪菌；	Wild boar mushrooms grew.
马鹿吃了他们的肉，	Red deer ate their flesh,
擦过嘴的地方，	And in the place where they wiped their muzzles,
长出了奶浆菌；	Lactarius volemuses grew.
老熊吃了他们的肉，	Bears ate their flesh,
擦过嘴的地方，	And in the place where they wiped their muzzles,
长出了熊掌菌；	Bear-paw mushrooms grew.
犀鸟吃了他们的肉，	Toucans ate their flesh,
擦过嘴的地方，	And in the place where they wiped their beaks,
长出了秋菌；	Autumn mushrooms grew.
勒弄省瓦鸟吃了他们的肉，	Lanung Sinwa birds ate their flesh,
擦过嘴的地方，	And in the place where they wiped their beaks,
长出了白蘑菇；	White mushrooms grew.
乌都鸟吃了他们的肉，	Utu birds ate their flesh,
擦过嘴的地方，	And in the place where they wiped their beaks,
长出了香菇；	Fragrant mushrooms grew.
老鹰吃了他们的肉，	Eagles ate their flesh
擦过嘴的地方，	And in the place where they wiped their beaks,
长出了老鹰菌；	Eagle mushrooms grew.
花头鸟吃了他们的肉，	Plum-headed birds ate their flesh,

擦过嘴的地方，	And in the place where they wiped their beaks,
长出了花头菌；	Plum-headed mushrooms grew.
白鹇鸡吃了他们的肉，	White pheasants ate their flesh,
擦过嘴的地方，	And in the place where they wiped their beaks,
长出了蛮底线菌；	Mat Tisen mushrooms grew.
乌公鸡吃了他们的肉，	Black-boned roosters ate their flesh,
擦过嘴的地方，	And in the place where they wiped their beaks,
长出了星星菌；	Star mushrooms grew.
竹鸡吃了他们的肉，	Bamboo partridges ate their flesh,
擦过嘴的地方，	And in the place where they wiped their beaks,
长出了给仙菌；	Kasen mushrooms grew.
竹风子鸟吃了他们的肉，	Kawa Tsi birds ate their flesh,
擦过嘴的地方，	And in the place where they wiped their beaks,
长出了竹蘑菇；	Bamboo mushrooms grew.
鬼吃了他们的肉，	Ghosts ate their flesh,
擦过嘴的地方，	And in the place where they wiped their mouths,
长出了鬼菌；	Ghost mushrooms grew.
蛇吃了他们的肉，	Snakes ate their flesh,
擦过嘴的地方，	And in the place where they wiped their mouths,
长出了蛇蘑菇；	Snake mushrooms grew.
蜗牛吃了他们的肉，	Snails ate their flesh,
擦过嘴的地方，	And in the place where they wiped their mouths,
长出了木耳；	Agarics grew.
直八鸟吃了他们的肉，	Chyaba birds ate their flesh,

擦过嘴的地方，	And in the place where they wiped their beaks,
长出了香菇；	Fragrant mushrooms grew.
最后剩下的一块肉，	The last piece of flesh
变成泥蛋菌。	Became mud-egg mushrooms.

十四、江、河的起源　XIV. The Origins of the Rivers

远古，	In remote antiquity,
潘瓦能桑遮瓦能章	Hpan Wa Ningsang Chye Wa Ningchyang
拿着金水桶，	Came to the foot of the rock
带着银水桶，	With a gold bucket
来到石块下，	And a silver bucket.
用金水桶和银水桶	With the help of the two buckets,
引出了迈里开江，	He made a channel for the Mali Hka River.
再倒进三十桶金子，	He poured thirty buckets of gold
再倒进四十桶银子，	And forty buckets of silver into it.
她就是老大迈里囊果[1]。	Then Mali Nang Ko[1], the eldest river, came into being.
远古，	In remote antiquity,
潘瓦能桑遮瓦能章	Hpan Wa Ningsang Chye Wa Ningchyang

① 这里是按顺序给江河取名，就如给兄弟姐妹按大小取名一样。

① The rivers were given the names like brothers and sisters, from the eldest to the youngest.

拿着金水桶，	Came to the foot of the rock
带着银水桶，	With the gold bucket
来到石块下，	And the silver bucket.
用金水桶和银水桶	With the help of the two buckets,
引出了恩迈开江，	He made a channel for the Nmai Hka River.
再倒进三十桶金子，	He poured thirty buckets of gold
再倒进四十桶银子，	And forty buckets of silver into it.
她就是老二恩迈囊鲁。	Then Nmai Nang Lu, the second river, came into being.
远古，	In remote antiquity,
潘瓦能桑遮瓦能章	Hpan Wa Ningsang Chye Wa Ningchyang
拿着金水桶，	Came to the foot of the rock
带着银水桶，	With the gold bucket
来到石块下，	And the silver bucket.
用金水桶和银水桶	With the help of the two buckets,
引出了打洛江，	He made a channel for the Talau River.
再倒进三十桶金子，	He poured thirty buckets of gold
再倒进四十桶银子，	And forty buckets of silver into it.
她就是老三打洛囊锐。	Then Talau Nang Roi, the third river, came into being.
远古，	In remote antiquity,
潘瓦能桑遮瓦能章	Hpan Wa Ningsang Chye Wa Ningchyang
拿着金水桶，	Came to the foot of the rock
带着银水桶，	With the gold bucket

来到石块下，
用金水桶和银水桶
引出了德壁江，
再倒进三十桶金子，
再倒进四十桶银子，
她就是老四德壁囊途。

And the silver bucket.
With the help of the two buckets,
He made a channel for the Dabyi River.
He poured thirty buckets of gold
And forty buckets of silver into it.
Then Dabyi Nhtu, the fourth river, came into being.

远古，
潘瓦能桑遮瓦能章
拿着金水桶，
带着银水桶，
来到石块下，
用金水桶和银水桶
引出了萨空江①，
再倒进三十桶金子，
再倒进四十桶银子，
她就是老五萨空囊阶。

In remote antiquity,
Hpan Wa Ningsang Chye Wa Ningchyang
Came to the foot of the rock
With the gold bucket
And the silver bucket.
With the help of the two buckets,
He made a channel for the Sahkung① River.
He poured thirty buckets of gold
And forty buckets of silver into it.
Then Sahkung Nang Kai, the fifth river, came into being.

远古，
潘瓦能桑遮瓦能章
拿着金水桶，
带着银水桶，

In remote antiquity,
Hpan Wa Ningsang Chye Wa Ningchyang
Came to the foot of the rock
With the gold bucket

① 萨空江：景颇语指怒江。

① Sahkung River: It refers to Nu River in the Jingpo language.

来到石块下，	And the silver bucket.
用金水桶和银水桶	With the help of the two buckets,
引出了德荣德旺江，	He made a channel for the Tarung Tawang River.
再倒进三十桶金子，	He poured thirty buckets of gold
再倒进四十桶银子，	And forty buckets of silver into it.
她就是老六德荣德旺。	Then Tarung Tawang, the sixth river, came into being.
远古，	In remote antiquity,
潘瓦能桑遮瓦能章	Hpan Wa Ningsang Chye Wa Ningchyang
拿着金水桶，	Came to the foot of the rock
带着银水桶，	With the gold bucket
来到石块下，	And the silver bucket.
用金水桶和银水桶	With the help of the two buckets,
引出了德云江，	He made a channel for the Dayun River.
再倒进三十桶金子，	He poured thirty buckets of gold
再倒进四十桶银子，	And forty buckets of silver into it.
她就是老七德云江。	Then the Dayun River, the seventh river, came into being.
远古，	In remote antiquity,
潘瓦能桑遮瓦能章	Hpan Wa Ningsang Chye Wa Ningchyang
拿着金水桶，	Came to the foot of the rock
带着银水桶，	With the gold bucket
来到石块下，	And the silver bucket.
用金水桶和银水桶，	With the help of the two buckets,

引出了泉水、小溪。	He made a channel for springs and streams.
远古，	In remote antiquity,
潘瓦能桑遮瓦能章	Hpan Wa Ningsang Chye Wa Ningchyang
拿着金水桶，	Came to the foot of the rock
带着银水桶，	With the gold bucket
来到石块下，	And the silver bucket.
用金水桶和银水桶，	With the help of the two buckets,
引出了四条江，	He created four big rivers
引出了三条河。	And three small rivers,
江河汇成了宽广的海洋。	Which merged into a vast ocean.
远古，	In remote antiquity,
潘瓦能桑遮瓦能章	Hpan Wa Ningsang Chye Wa Ningchyang
拿着金水桶，	Came to the foot of the rock
带着银水桶，	With the gold bucket
来到石块下，	And the silver bucket.
用金水桶和银水桶，	With the help of the two buckets,
把水洒向了天空，	He sprinkled water into the Sky.
等将来有了不讲理的恶人，	When in the future there were unreasonable people,
就让它变成暴雨，	The water would become rainstorms
惩罚骗子和恶人。	To punish the cheats and villains.
远古，	In remote antiquity,

迈里开江囊果	Nang Ko, the Mali Hka River, said to
对妹妹恩迈开江说：	Her younger sister, the Nmai Hka River:
“妹妹囊鲁呀，	“Nang Lu, my dear sister,
我的身体不如你，	I am in poor health
我的力气没你的大，	And not as strong as you.
我不能翻山越岭，	I cannot go up hill and down dale,
我只能走平路。	But move on a flat road.
你身体比我强，	You are stronger than me
力气比我大，	And in good health.
你能吃苦耐劳，	You can bear hardships
你能翻山越岭，	And tramp over the mountains.
你就从木如山走，	So would you climb Mount Maru
让我们在莱量山下相会吧！”	And meet me at the foot of Mount Laileng!”
听了姐姐的话，	Hearing her elder sister's words,
恩迈开江囊鲁	Nang Lu, the Nmai Hka River,
接过潘瓦能桑遮瓦能章	Took over from Hpan Wa Ningsang Chye Wa Ningchyang
给的开山长刀，	The long sword
和穿山的长矛，	And the long spear.
用长刀劈开木如山，	She cut Mount Maru in two with the long sword,
用长柔穿过木如山，	Piercing through it.
拉着飞蛇的尾巴，	Then she came swiftly to the foot of Mount Laileng,
飞快地来到莱量山下，	Dragging the tale of a flying snake behind her.
没有等姐姐囊果，	

就独自往前走了。	From there, she moved on,
	Without waiting for her sister, Nang Ko.

迈里开江囊果，	Nang Ko, the Mali Hka River,
拉着蟒蛇的尾巴，	Moved forward slowly
沿着平坦的坝子，	On flat land,
缓慢地向前走着。	Dragging the tail of a python behind her.
当她来到莱量山下时，	When she arrived at the foot of Mount Laileng,
妹妹囊鲁已经走了，	Her younger sister had already gone.
她伤心地想：	She felt very sad, thinking:
本来约好在这里相会，	We had an agreement to meet here.
妹妹却先走了。	But she didn't wait for me.
迈里开江囊果想着，	Angry with her younger sister,
就赌气往回走了。	Nang Ko, the Mali Hka River, turned back.
来到平坦的恩贡果涌地方，	She came to the flat N-kong Ko-yong,
在那里徘徊起来。	Wandering up and down there.

木足肯瓦胜热诏刚懂萨[①]	Mazup Hkringwa Shing-ra Chyauka Dumsa[①],
站在高高的岩石上，	Standing on a high rock,
大声地对姐妹俩说：	Shouted loudly at the sisters:

① 木足肯瓦胜热诏刚懂萨：传说是潘瓦能桑遮瓦能章之后的全知全能，即潘格来遮能代，在这里他换了另一个名。

① Mazup Hkringwa Shing-ra Chyauka Dumsa: another name for Hpan Galai Chye Ningtai, the omniscient and omnipotent God after Hpan Wa Ningsang Chye Wa Ningchyang.

“迈里开江囊果呀，	“Mali Hka River
恩迈开江囊鲁，	And Nmai Hka River,
你们是亲姐妹，	You are sibling sisters.
你们不应该各走各。”	You should not go your separate ways.”
木足肯瓦胜热诏刚懂萨说完，	After these words,
拿出金块，	Mazup Hkringwa Shing-ra Chyauka Dumsa
拿出金砂；	Took out gold bullion,
拿出金席子，	Gold sand,
拿出银链子，	A golden mat,
拿出绿毯子；	A silver chain,
拿出一把水芹菜，	A green blanket,
拿出一把芦苇草，	A handful of water celeries,
拿出一棵金水柳，	A handful of reeds,
送给了姐妹俩。	And a gold water willow,
听了木足肯瓦胜热诏刚懂萨	And gave them all to the two sisters.
的话，	With Mazup Hkringwa Shing-ra Chyauka Dumsa's words
拿着他送的礼物，	in mind,
姐妹俩手拉着手，	The two sisters took the gifts
顺着平坦的坝子，	And went ahead along the flat road
一起向前走了。	Hand in hand.

附记：

序歌中除了阳神能万拉和阴神能斑木占，其他诸

Excursus:

Except the male deity Nengwam La and the female deity Ningpan Majan, the other deities in the “Prologue” are

神后来都没有出现，演唱者对他们的来龙去脉也未解释过，这里是按演唱的内容翻译的。

not mentioned later in this book, and the chanter did not provide us with their origins. We just recorded what the chanter sang.

第二章 平整天地

Canto 2 Leveling the Sky and the Earth

一、宁贯督打天造地 Ⅰ. N-gon Du Shaping the Earth and the Sky

远古，	In remote antiquity,
在戛昂阿崩地方，	In a place named Mount Gaang Abum,
招齐了打天下的英雄，	Gathered heroes to create the world,
整地的勇士，	Warriors to shape the Earth,
勇敢的前锋，	Brave pioneers
剽悍的后卫。	And doughty guards.
打天的英雄，	Heroes who would create the Sky,
举起了神刀，	Lifted holy knives,
整地的勇士，	And warriors who would create the Earth
拿起了神锤。	Swung holy hammers.
跟着宁贯督，	Following N-gon Du,
开始了打天造地。	They started to create the world.
前面是打天的英雄，	In the front were the heroes who would create the Sky,
后面是整地的勇士，	Followed by the warriors who would shape the Earth.
敲天的大锤举起了，	Sledgehammers to beat the Sky were lifted,
打地的铁砧支好了，	Iron anvils were mounted,
量天的标杆竖起了，	Poles to measure the Sky were set up,
丈地的绳索扯开了。	And ropes to map the Earth were disengaged.

远古，
宁贯督率领打天造地的队伍，
翻过高山，
越过平坝，
用标杆去量天，
用绳索去丈地，
一锤打到迈里开江岸，
一锤打到恩迈开江边，
热旺松康山打好了，
热旺松康山造好了，
再铺上土块泥团，
土壤肥沃了，
土地湿润了，
庄稼可以生长了。

In remote antiquity,
N-gon Du led the team to create the world,
Riding over mountains,
Crossing plains,
Measuring the Sky with poles,
And mapping the Earth with ropes.
One swing of the hammer hit the banks of the Mali Hka River,
And another swing hit the banks of the Nmai Hka River.
The Mount Rawang Sumhkang was created;
The Mount Rawang Sumhkang was built.
With layers of soil and mud pies,
The land became fertile,
The land became moist,
And crops could be planted.

远古，
宁贯督率领打天造地的队伍，
翻过高山，
越过平坝，
打好了热旺松康山，
又开始打侬山。

In remote antiquity,
N-gon Du led the team to create the world,
Riding over mountains,
And crossing plains.
After creating the Mount Rawang Sumhkang,
They started to carve the Mount Nung.
They measured the Sky with poles,

用标杆去量天，
用绳索去丈地，
一锤打到迈里开江岸，
一锤打到恩迈开江边，
依山打好了，
依山造好了，
再铺上土块泥团，
土壤肥沃了，
土地湿润了，
庄稼可以生长了。

And mapped the Earth with ropes.
One swing of the hammer hit the banks of the Mali Hka River;
Another swing hit the banks of the Nmai Hka River.
The Mount Nung was created;
The Mount Nung was built.
With layers of soil and mud pies,
The land became fertile,
The land became moist,
And crops could be planted.

远古，
宁贯督率领打天造地的队伍，
翻过高山，
越过平坝，
打好了依山，
又开始打贡氏山。
用标杆去量天，
用绳索去丈地，
一锤打到迈里开江岸，
一锤打到恩迈开江边，
贡氏山打好了。
贡氏山造好了，
再铺上土块泥团，

In remote antiquity,
N-gon Du led the team to create the world,
Riding over mountains,
And crossing plains.
After creating the Mount Nung,
Starting to carve the Mount Gumdi.
They measured the Sky with poles,
And mapped the Earth with ropes.
One swing of the hammer hit the banks of the Mali Hka River;
Another swing hit the banks of the Nmai Hka River.
The Mount Gumdi was created;
The Mount Gumdi was built.

土壤肥沃了，
土地湿润了，
庄稼可以生长了。

With layers of soil and mud pies,
The land became fertile,
The land became moist,
And crops could be planted.

远古，
宁贯督率领打天造地的队伍，
翻过高山，
越过平坝，
打好了贡氏山，
又开始打掸诗贡山。
用标杆去量天，
用绳索去丈地，
一锤打到迈里开江岸，
一锤打到恩迈开江边，
掸诗贡山打好了，
掸诗贡山造好了，
再铺上土块泥团，
土壤肥沃了，
土地湿润了，
庄稼可以生长了。

In remote antiquity,
N-gon Du led the team to create the world,
Riding over mountains,
And crossing plains.
After creating Mount Gumdi,
They started to carve the Mount Sam Shagong.
They measured the Sky with poles,
And mapped the Earth with ropes.
One swing of the hammer hit the banks of the Mali Hka
River;
Another swing hit the banks of the Nmai Hka River.
The Mount Sam Shagong was created,
The Mount Sam Shagong was built,
With layers of soil and mud pies,
The land became fertile;
The land became moist.
And crops could be planted.

远古，

In remote antiquity,

宁贯督率领打天造地的队伍，	N-gon Du led the team to create the world,
翻过高山，	Riding over mountains,
越过平坝，	And crossing plains.
打好了掸诗贡山，	After creating Mount Sam Shagong,
又开始打蚌景颇山。	They started to carve Mount Pong Jinghpo.
用标杆去量天，	They measured the Sky with poles,
用绳索去丈地，	And mapped the Earth with ropes.
一锤打到迈里开江岸，	One swing of the hammer hit the banks of the Mali Hka River;
一锤打到恩迈开江边，	Another swing hit the banks of the Nmai Hka River.
蚌景颇山打好了，	The Mount Pong Jinghpo was created;
蚌景颇山造好了，	The Mount Pong Jinghpo was built.
再铺上土块泥团，	With layers of soil and mud pies,
土壤肥沃了，	The land became fertile,
土地湿润了，	The land became moist,
庄稼可以生长了。	And crops could be planted.

远古，	In remote antiquity,
宁贯督率领打天造地的队伍，	N-gon Du led the team to create the world,
翻过高山，	Overriding mountains
越过平坝，	And crossing plains.
打好了蚌景颇山，	After creating the Mount Pong Jinghpo,
又开始打直黎山。	They started to carve the Mount Jili.
用标杆去量天，	They measured the Sky with poles,

用绳索去丈地，
一锤打到迈里开江岸，
一锤打到恩迈开江边，
直黎山打好了，
直黎山造好了，
再铺上土块泥团，
土壤肥沃了，
土地湿润了，
庄稼可以生长了。

And mapped the Earth with ropes.
One swing of the hammer hit the banks of the Mali Hka River;
Another swing hit the banks of the Nmai Hka River.
The Mount Jili was created;
The Mount Jili was built.
With layers of soil and mud pies,
The land became fertile,
The land became moist,
And crops could be planted.

远古，
宁贯督率领打天造地的队伍，
翻过了高山，
越过了平坝，
打好了直黎山，
又开始打蒙嫩锐藏山。
用标杆去量天，
用绳索去丈地，
一锤打到迈里开江岸，
一锤打到恩迈开江边，
蒙嫩锐藏山打好了，
蒙嫩锐藏山造好了，
再铺上土块泥团，

In remote antiquity,
N-gon Du led the team to create the world,
Overriding mountains
And crossing plains.
After creating Mount Jili,
They started to carve Mount Mungnun Roiza.
They measured the Sky with poles,
And mapped the Earth with ropes.
One swing of hammer hit the banks of the Mali Hka River;
Another swing hit the banks of the Nmai Hka River.
The Mount Mungnun Roiza was created;
The Mount Mungnun Roiza was built.

土壤肥沃了，
土地湿润了，
庄稼可以生长了。

With layers of soil and mud pies,
The land became fertile,
The land became moist,
And crops could be planted.

远古，
宁贯督率领打天造地的队伍，
翻过高山，
越过平坝，
打好了蒙嫩锐藏山，
又开始打缅诗贡山，
用标杆去量天，
用绳索去丈地，
一锤打到迈里开江岸，
一锤打到恩迈开江边，
缅诗贡山打好了，
缅诗贡山造好了，
再铺上土块泥团，
土壤肥沃了，
土地湿润了，
庄稼可以生长了。

In remote antiquity,
N-gon Du led the team to create the world,
Overriding mountains
And crossing plains.
After creating the Mount Mungnun Roiza,
They started to carve Mount Myen Shagong.
They measured the Sky with poles,
And mapped the Earth with ropes.
One swing of the hammer hit the banks of the Mali Hka River;
Another swing hit the banks of the Nmai Hka River.
Mount Myen Shagong was created;
Mount Myen Shagong was built.
With layers of soil and mud pies,
The land became fertile,
The land became moist,
And crops could be planted.

远古，

In remote antiquity,

宁贯督率领打天造地的队伍，	N-gon Du led the team to create the world,
翻过高山，	Riding over mountains,
越过平坝，	And crossing plains.
打好了缅诗贡山，	After creating Mount Myen Shagong,
又开始打密瓦诗贡山[1]。	They started to carve Mount Miwa Shagong[1].
用标杆去量天，	They measured the Sky with poles,
用绳索去丈地，	And mapped the Earth with ropes.
一锤打到迈里开江岸，	One swing of the hammer hit the banks of the Mali Hka River;
一锤打到恩迈开江边，	Another swing hit the banks of the Nmai Hka River.
密瓦诗贡山打好了，	Mount Miwa Shagong was created;
密瓦诗贡山造好了，	Mount Miwa Shagong was built.
再铺上土块泥团，	With layers of soil and mud pies,
土壤肥沃了，	The land became fertile,
土地湿润了，	The land became moist,
庄稼可以生长了。	And crops could be planted.

远古，	In remote antiquity,
宁贯督率领打天造地的队伍，	N-gon Du led the team to create the world,
翻过高山，	Overriding mountains,
越过平坝，	And crossing plains.
打好了密瓦诗贡山，	After creating Mount Miwa Shagong ,

① 密瓦：指汉族，是景颇人对汉族的称呼。

① Miwa: It is the term used by the Jingpo people to refer to the Han people.

又开始打蒙岭蒙旁山，
用标杆去量天，
用绳索去丈地，
一锤打到迈里开江岸，
一锤打到恩迈开江边，
蒙岭蒙旁山打好了，
蒙岭蒙旁山造好了，
再铺上土块泥团，
土壤肥沃了，
土地湿润了，
庄稼可以生长了。

They started to carve Mount Mungling Munghpang.
They measured the Sky with poles,
And mapped the Earth with ropes.
One swing of the hammer hit the banks of the Mali Hka River;
Another swing hit the banks of the Nmai Hka River,
Mount Mungling Munghpang was created;
Mount Mungling Munghpang was built.
With layers of soil and mud pies,
The land became fertile;
The land became moist.
And crops could be planted.

远古，
宁贯督率领打天造地的队伍，
翻过高山，
越过平坝，
在勒章松坎瑙然地方，
杀了石牛，
宰了石猪，
跳起目瑙舞[1]，

In remote antiquity,
N-gon Du led the team to create the world,
Riding over mountains,
And crossing plains.
In a place named Lachyang Sumhkran Naura,
They killed the stone ox
And slew the stone pig.
They performed the Manau Dance[1]

① 目瑙舞：这是景颇族中有重大事件时举行的大型舞蹈，它按事件的不同性质又分为不同的种类。

① The Manau Dance: It is a set of dance routines performed when events of importance for the Jingpo people take place. It can be further categorized according to different nature of the events.

庆贺打好的高山，
造好的平坝。
并在洛芒龙布地方，
建成了宏伟的王宫。

To celebrate the mountains created
And plains built.
In a place named Lo-myang Lungpu,
They built a magnificent palace.

远古，
为了给子孙留下美好的传说，
为了给未来留下永恒的记忆，
为了继续打天造地的事业，
为了过江去打木如山，
宁贯督率领打天造地的队伍，
翻过高山，
越过平坝，
来到恩迈开江边，
准备修一座过江的石桥。

In remote antiquity,
In order to leave behind a great legend for future generations,
In order to create everlasting memories for the future,
In order to continue the great course of creating the
　　world,
And in order to build Mount Maru across the river,
N-gon Du led his team,
Riding over mountains
And crossing plains,
To the banks of the Nmai Hka River,
Preparing to build a bridge to cross the river.

就在这个时候，
子朗能对鸟
飞来对宁贯督说：
“宁贯督呀，
你家里的独妹妹死了，
你快快回去吧。”

Right then,
The Zanang Ningdui bird
Flew over and said to N-gon Du,
“N-gon Du,
Your only sister is dying.
Hurry home.”

宁贯督回答说：	N-gon Du replied,
“鸟的尾巴掉了，	“If the tail of a bird falls off,
又会长出新的，	Another one will grow.
妹妹死了呀，	If little sister dies,
又会有替代的。”	Another will take her place.”
子朗能对鸟	The Zanang Ningdui bird
飞来对宁贯督说：	Flew over and said to N-gon Du,
“宁贯督呀，	“N-gon Du,
你的母亲不在了，	Your mother is gone.
快快回去吧。”	Hurry home.”
宁贯督回答说：	N-gon Du replied,
“鸟的尾巴掉了，	“If the tail of a bird falls off,
又会长出新的，	Another one will grow.
母亲不在了，	If mother dies,
还会有替代的。”	Another will take her place.”
子朗能对鸟	The Zanang Ningdui bird
飞来对宁贯督说：	Flew over and said to N-gon Du again,
“宁贯督呀，	“N-gon Du,
你的父亲去世了，	Your father has passed away.
你快快回去吧。”	Hurry home.”

宁贯督回答说：	N-gon Du replied,
“鸟的尾巴掉了，	“If the tail of a bird falls off,
又会长出新的。	Another one will grow.
父亲去世了，	If father dies,
再没有替代的。”	No one will take his place.”
听说父亲去世了，	Hearing that his father had passed away,
宁贯督是多么的悲伤，	How upset N-gon Du was!
抽出长刀。	He drew out his machete,
把正在修造的石桥，	Hacking the bridge that was being built
砍入了恩迈开江，	Into the Nmai Hka River.
又挥刀一砍，	Another swing of his machete
把高大的给松崩山	Split mighty Mount Kasung
砍成了两半，	Into two halves.
丢下的敲天的大锤，	The sledgehammer he dropped
推倒的打地的铁砧，	And the iron anvil he knocked over
变成了诗东崩岭山；	Turned into Mount Shatung Bangling.
掉下的量天的标杆，	The pole for measuring the Sky fell down,
变成了深深的峡谷；	And turned into a deep canyon.
留下的丈地的绳索	The rope for mapping the Earth was left behind
变成了汹涌的激流。	And turned into fierce torrents.
因为石桥没有修成，	Because the stone bridge was not finished,
打天造地的队伍	The creation team

没有渡过恩迈开江，	Did not cross the Nmai Hka River,
也没有打造木如山。	And did not carve Mount Maru.
宁贯督从恩迈开江，	Leaving the Nmai Hka River,
回到戛昂王宫，	N-gon Du returned to the Gaang Palace.
独妹妹不见了，	His only sister was gone,
母亲不在了，	His mother was gone, too,
父亲也去世了，	And his father passed away,
留下他孤孤单单的，	He was left alone and lonely
没有人跟他说话。	With no one to talk to.
宁贯督流着泪喊道，	N-gon Du cried out in tears,
“父亲，彭干支伦呀，	“Father Hpunggam Chyanun,
母亲木占威纯，	Mother Majan Woishun,
你们为什么不见我，	Why do you leave stealthily,
就悄悄地走了。”	Without seeing me?”
从遥远的地方，	N-gon Du heard faint echoes
宁贯督听到隐隐约约的回声。	From far away.
宁贯督又说：	N-gon Du spoke again,
“父亲彭干支伦呀，	“Father Hpunggam Chyanun,
你没有给儿子留下话，	You have not left me any words.
你不能离开我。”	You cannot leave me.”

在遥远的天空，
传来了彭干支伦的声音：
“儿子宁贯督呀
记住我留下的话吧，
将来的日子，
你沿着野象的足迹，
找到野象安息的地方，
你就会得到无限的财富。”

宁贯督说：
“父亲彭干支伦呀，
母亲木占威纯，
你们生下了我，
没吃过我打的松鼠①，
你们养育了我，
没吃过我晒的干鱼，
你们不能离开我。”

彭干支伦说：
“儿子宁贯督呀，
我已经到了天上，

From the Sky far away,
There came the voice of Hpunggam Chyanun,
“My son N-gon Du,
Remember my words
That in the coming days,
You shall follow the tracks of wild elephants
To locate where they rest in peace.
Then you will harvest
Countless treasures.”

N-gon Du said,
“Father Hpunggam Chyanun
And Mother Majan Woishun,
You gave birth to me,
Yet have not enjoyed the squirrels① I hunted;
You raised me,
Yet have not tasted the fish I dried.
You cannot leave me.”

Hpunggam Chyanun said,
“Son N-gon Du,
I am already in heaven

① 松鼠：景颇族用的祭献物之一。

① Squirrel: It is an offering used by the Jingpo people.

和你的哥哥们在一起，	With your older brothers.
在今后的日子，	In the coming days,
你祭献太阳神时，	When you make offerings to the Sun God,
我就能吃到你的松鼠，	I can enjoy your squirrels,
我就能享用你的干鱼。”	And I can taste your dried fish."

木占威纯说：	Majan Woishun said,
“儿子宁贯督呀，	"Son N-gon Du,
我已经到了地下，	I already lie beneath the ground
和你的独妹妹在一起，	With your only little sister.
在今后的日子，	In the coming days,
你祭献石狄和水土神时，	When you make offerings to the God Shingdit and the God of Water and Soil,
我就能吃到你的松鼠，	I can enjoy your squirrels,
我就能享用你的干鱼①。”	And I can taste your dried fish①."

宁贯督说：	N-gon Du said,
“父亲彭干支伦呀，	"Father Hpunggam Chyanun
母亲木占威纯，	And Mother Majan Woishun,
我还想和父亲在一起，	I want to be with father
我还想吃母亲的乳汁。”	And drink mother's milk."

① 干鱼：至今景颇族祭献祖先时拿干鱼当祭品。

① Dried fish: The Jingpo people nowadays still use dried fish as offerings.

木占威纯说：	Majan Woishun said,
“儿子宁贯督呀，	“Son N-gon Du,
母亲的乳汁，	Mother's milk has been sprinkled
已洒在大地上，	Across the Earth.
在洒着乳汁的地方，	Where the milk is sprinkled,
会长出木挤龙东酒药草，	Matsi Luptung yeast herbs will grow,
会生出诗旺迷木荣酒药草；	Shawa Myit Marung yeast herbs will grow,
会长出木挤勒盘酒药草，	Matsi Lahpat yeast herbs will grow,
会生长出拾旺迷敢酒药草；	Shawang Myit Gat yeast herbs will grow,
会长出木挤勒摆酒药草，	Matsi Lapai Ahkai yeast herbs will grow,
会生出拾旺迷台酒药草。	Shawa Myit Htai yeast herbs will grow,
会长出叔努勒菠菜，	Shanu Lapom Ahkai herbs will grow,
会生出木瓦叶菜；	Hka-bau Pot Ahkai herbs will grow,
会长出卡包波菜，	Lapu Pot Ahkai herbs will grow,
会生出勒布波菜，	Muwa Lap Ahkai herbs will grow,
会长出克戛能买菜；	Hkaka Ningmai Ahkai herbs will grow,
会生出木岭诗南菜。	Maling Shanam Ahkai herbs will grow,
会长出甘蔗，	Sugarcane will grow,
会长出芭蕉树，	Banana plants will grow,
会生出菠萝树，	Pineapple trees will grow,
会长出牛肚子果树。	And jackfruit trees will grow.
你将来用酒药草，	You will use those yeast herbs
酿出甜甜的水酒，	To brew sweet wine.
你将来吃到美味的蔬菜，	The tasty vegetables you'll eat

你将来尝到好吃的水果，	And the delicious fruit you'll taste
你就吃到了母亲的乳汁。”	Are your mother's milk."
彭干支伦说：	Hpunggam Chyanun said,
“儿子宁贯督呀，	"Son N-gon Du,
将来的日子，	In the coming days,
你听到雷响，	When you hear thunder roar
看见闪电，	And see lightning strike,
就该想到，	You shall realize that
父亲还没有离开你。”	Father has not left you yet."
木占威纯说：	Majan Woishun said,
“儿子宁贯督呀，	"Son N-gon Du,
我虽然住在地下，	Though I live beneath the ground,
也会常来看望你，	I will visit you frequently.
当山摇地动时①，	When mountains shake and the Earth quivers①,
你就大声喊，	You shall shout loudly:
知道了，	I have seen you,
听到了，	I have heard you.
大地就不再摇晃了。”	Then the Earth shall stop quaking."

① 山摇地动：这里指地震，过去景颇族人认为地震是由于木占威纯从地下来看儿子宁贯督造成的，所以地一震，就喊“听到了，知道了”，他们认为这样可以减轻地震。

① Mountains shake and the Earth quivers: It refers to earthquake in this particular context. The Jingpo people used to think that an earthquake was the result of Majan Woishun visiting her son from underneath the ground. Thus in case of an earthquake, they would shout "I have heard you and I have seen you", believing that the intensity of the earthquake would then be diminished.

二、特荣特热拉撒树种

Ⅱ. Htarum Htarai La Scattering Tree Seeds

远古，
特荣特热拉
从松炯拉和松姜木占那里，
背上树种，
带上草籽，
开始撒树种了，
开始播草籽了。

In remote antiquity,
Htarum Htarai La
Brought tree seeds
And grass seeds
From Sumkyung La
And Sumkyang Majan,
And started to scatter them.

特荣特热拉
背上树种，
带上草籽，
来到热旺松康山，
撒下了树种，
播下了草籽。
这边撒到迈里开江岸，
那边播到恩迈开江边。
热旺松康山上，
长出了千种树，
生出了万种草，

Htarum Htarai La,
Carrying tree seeds on his back
And bringing grass seeds with him,
Came to Mount Rawang Sumhkang.
He scattered the tree seeds
And sowed the grass seeds
Along the banks of the Mali Hka River over here,
And the banks of the Nmai Hka River over there.
On Mount Rawang Sumhkang ,
Numerous types of trees grew,
And countless kinds of grass came up.

这边绿到迈里开江岸，	The greenness reached the banks of the Mali Hka River.
那边绿到恩迈开江边。	The greenness touched the banks of the Nmai Hka River.

远古，	In remote antiquity,
特荣特热拉	Htarum Htarai La,
背上树种，	Carrying tree seeds on his back
带上草籽，	And bringing grass seeds with him,
从热旺松康山，	Left Mount Rawang Sumhkang
又来到了侬山，	And reached Mount Nung .
撒下树种，	He scattered the tree seeds
播下草籽，	And sowed the grass seeds
这边撒到迈里开江岸，	Along the banks of the Mali Hka River over here,
那边播到恩迈开江边。	And the banks of the Nmai Hka River over there.
侬山上，	On Mount Nung ,
长出了千种树，	Numerous types of trees grew
生出了万种草，	And countless kinds of grass came up.
这边绿到迈里开江岸，	The greenness reached the banks of the Mali Hka River.
那边绿到恩迈开江边。	The greenness touched the banks of the Nmai Hka River.

远古，	In remote antiquity,
特荣特热拉	Htarum Htarai La,
背上树种，	Carrying tree seeds on his back
带上草籽，	And bringing grass seeds with him,
从侬山，	Left Mount Nung

又来到贡氏山，	And came to Mount Gumdi .
撒下了树种，	He scattered the tree seeds
播下了草籽。	And sowed the grass seeds
这边撒到迈里开江岸，	Along the banks of the Mali Hka River over here,
那边播到恩迈开江边。	And the banks of the Nmai Hka River over there.
贡氏山上，	On Mount Gumdi ,
长出了千种树，	Numerous types of trees grew
生出了万种草，	And countless kinds of grass came up.
这边绿到迈里开江岸，	The greenness reached the banks of the Mali Hka River.
那边绿到恩迈开江边。	The greenness touched the banks of the Nmai Hka River.

远古，	In remote antiquity,
特荣特热拉	Htarum Htarai La,
背上树种，	Carrying tree seeds on his back
带上树籽，	And bringing grass seeds with him,
从贡氏山，	Left Mount Gumdi
又来到了掸山，	And came to Mount Sam.
撒下了树种，	He scattered the tree seeds
播下了草籽。	And sowed the grass seeds
这边撒到迈里开江岸，	Along the banks of the Mali Hka River over here,
那边播到恩迈开江边。	And the banks of the Nmai Hka River over there.
掸山上，	On Mount Sam,
长出了千种树，	Numerous types of trees grew
生出了万种草，	And countless kinds of grass came up.

这边绿到迈里开江岸， The greenness reached the banks of the Mali Hka River.
那边绿到恩迈开江边。 The greenness touched the banks of the Nmai Hka River.

远古， In remote antiquity,
特荣特热拉 Htarum Htarai La,
背上树种， Carrying tree seeds on his back
带上草籽， And bringing grass seeds with him,
从撣山， Left Mount Sam
又来到了蚌景颇山。 And came to Mount Pong Jinghpo.
撒下了树种， He scattered the tree seeds
播下了草籽。 And sowed the grass seeds
这边撒到迈里开江岸， Along the banks of the Mali Hka River over here,
那边播到恩迈开江边。 And the banks of the Nmai Hka River over there.
蚌景颇山上， On Mount Pong Jinghpo,
长出了千种树， Numerous types of trees grew
生出了万种草， And countless kinds of grass came up.
这边绿到迈里开江岸， The greenness reached the banks of the Mali Hka River.
那边绿到恩迈开江边。 The greenness touched the banks of the Nmai Hka River.

远古， In remote antiquity,
特荣特热拉 Htarum Htarai La,
背上树种， Carrying tree seeds on his back
带上草籽， And bringing grass seeds with him,
从蚌景颇山， Left Mount Pong Jinghpo

又来到了直黎山，	And came to Mount Jili.
撒下了树种，	He scattered the tree seeds
播下了草籽。	And sowed the grass seeds
这边撒到迈里开江岸，	Along the banks of the Mali Hka River over here,
那边播到恩迈开江边。	And the banks of the Nmai Hka River over there.
直黎山上，	On Mount Jili,
长出了千种树，	Numerous types of trees grew
生出了万种草，	And countless kinds of grass came up.
这边绿到迈里开江岸，	The greenness reached the banks of the Mali Hka River.
那边绿到恩迈开江边。	The greenness touched the banks of the Nmai Hka River.

远古，	In remote antiquity,
特荣特热拉	Htarum Htarai La,
背上树种，	Carrying tree seeds on his back
带上草籽，	And bringing grass seeds with him,
从直黎山，	Left Mount Jili
又来到蒙嫩锐藏山，	And came to Mount Mungnun Roiza.
撒下了树种，	He scattered the tree seeds
播下了草籽。	And sowed the grass seeds
这边撒到迈里开江岸，	Along the banks of the Mali Hka River over here,
那边播到恩迈开江边。	And the banks of the Nmai Hka River over there.
锐藏山上，	On Mount Mungnun Roiza,
长出了千种树，	Numerous types of trees grew
生出了万种草，	And countless kinds of grass came up.

这边绿到迈里开江岸，	The greenness reached the banks of the Mali Hka River.
那边绿到恩迈开江边。	The greenness touched the banks of the Nmai Hka River.
远古，	In remote antiquity,
特荣特热拉	Htarum Htarai La,
背上树种，	Carrying tree seeds on his back
带上草籽，	And bringing grass seeds with him,
从锐藏山，	Left Mount Mungnun Roiza
又来到了缅山，	And came to Mount Myen.
撒下了树种，	He scattered the tree seeds
播下了草籽。	And sowed the grass seeds
这边撒到迈里开江岸，	Along the banks of the Mali Hka River over here,
那边播到恩迈开江边。	And the banks of the Nmai Hka River over there.
缅山上，	On Mount Myen,
长出了千种树，	Numerous types of trees grew
生出了万种草，	And countless kinds of grass came up.
这边绿到迈里开江岸，	The greenness reached the banks of the Mali Hka River.
那边绿到恩迈开江边。	The greenness touched the banks of the Nmai Hka River.
远古，	In remote antiquity,
特荣特热拉	Htarum Htarai La,
背上树种，	Carrying tree seeds on his back
带上草籽，	And bringing grass seeds with him,
从缅山，	Left Mount Myen

又来到了密瓦山，	And came to Mount Miwa.
撒下了树种，	He scattered the tree seeds
播下了草籽。	And sowed the grass seeds
这边撒到迈里开江岸，	Along the banks of the Mali Hka River over here,
那边播到恩迈开江边。	And the banks of the Nmai Hka River over there.
密瓦山上，	On Mount Miwa,
长出了千种树，	Numerous types of trees grew
生出了万种草，	And countless kinds of grass came up.
这边绿到迈里开江岸，	The greenness reached the banks of the Mali Hka River.
那边绿到恩迈开江边。	The greenness touched the banks of the Nmai Hka River.

远古，	In remote antiquity,
特荣特热拉	Htarum Htarai La,
背上树种，	Carrying tree seeds on his back
带上草籽，	And bringing grass seeds with him,
从密瓦山，	Left Mount Miwa
又来到了蒙岭蒙旁山，	And came to Mount Mungling Munghpang.
撒下了树种，	He scattered the tree seeds
播下了草籽。	And sowed the grass seeds
这边撒到迈里开江岸，	Along the banks of the Mali Hka River over here,
那边播到恩迈开江边。	And the banks of the Nmai Hka River over there.
蒙旁山上，	On Mount Mungling Munghpang,
长出了千种树，	Numerous types of trees grew
生出了万种草，	And countless kinds of grass came up.

这边绿到迈里开江岸，	The greenness reached the banks of the Mali Hka River.
那边绿到恩迈开江边。	The greenness touched the banks of the Nmai Hka River.
远古，	In remote antiquity,
特荣特热拉	Htarum Htarai La,
背上树种，	Carrying tree seeds on his back
带上草籽，	And bringing grass seeds with him,
从这山到那山，	Traveled from mountain to mountain
撒下了树种，	To scatter tree seeds
播下了草籽。	And sow grass seeds
这边撒到迈里开江岸，	Along the banks of the Mali Hka River over here,
那边播到恩迈开江边。	And the banks of the Nmai Hka River over there.
辽阔的大地上，	Across the vast Earth,
长出了千种树，	Numerous types of trees grew
生出了万种草，	And countless kinds of grass came up.
这边绿到迈里开江岸，	The greenness reached the banks of the Mali Hka River.
那边绿到恩迈开江边。	The greenness touched the banks of the Nmai Hka River.
千座高山好看了，	Hundreds of mountains were now delightful
万个坝子美丽了。	And thousands of plains became appealing.

三、燕子巡视大地　Ⅲ. Swallow Touring the World

远古，	In remote antiquity,
潘瓦能桑遮瓦能章，	Hpan Wa Ningsang Chye Wa Ningchyang
对燕子说过：	Said to the swallow,
“燕子呀，	“Swallow,
等将来有了新的天，	When there is a new Sky,
等将来有了新的地，	And when there is a new Earth,
你就飞出石洞，	You will fly out of the stone cave,
离开你生活的地方，	Leaving the place you have lived in,
去巡视新的天，	To tour the new Sky
去巡视新的地。”	And to tour the new Earth.”
新的天有了，	There came the new Sky;
新的地有了，	There came the new Earth.
按潘瓦能桑遮瓦能章	Following the words of
留下的话，	Hpan Wa Ningsang Chye Wa Ningchyang,
燕子飞出了石洞，	The swallow flew out of the stone cave,
离开它生活的地方，	Leaving where it had lived,
开始巡视新的天，	And started to tour the new Sky
开始巡视新的地。	And tour the new Earth.

顺着迈里开江飞，	Flying along the Mali Hka River,
沿着恩迈开江翔，	Hovering over the Nmai Hka River,
燕子飞到了热旺松康山。	The swallow flew over to Mount Rawang Sumhkang .
热旺松康山更高了，	Mount Rawang Sumhkang became higher,
热旺松康坝更宽了，	And the Rawang Sumhkang Plain became vaster.
热旺松康山望不到顶啦，	Mount Rawang Sumhkang was too high to see the top,
热旺松康坝走不到边了。	And the Rawang Sumhkang Plain was too vast to walk across.

顺着迈里开江飞，	Flying along the Mali Hka River,
沿着恩迈开江翔，	Hovering over the Nmai Hka River,
燕子从热旺松康山，	The swallow left Mount Rawang Sumhkang,
又飞到了侬山。	And flew over to Mount Nung .
侬山更高了，	Mount Nung became higher,
侬坝更宽了，	And the Nung Plain became vaster.
侬山望不到顶啦，	Mount Nung was too high to see the top,
侬坝走不到边了。	And the Nung Plain was too vast to walk across.

顺着迈里开江飞，	Flying along the Mali Hka River,
沿着恩迈开江翔，	Hovering over the Nmai Hka River,
燕子从侬山，	The swallow left Mount Nung
又飞到了贡氏山。	And flew over to Mount Gumdi .
贡氏山更高了，	Mount Gumdi became higher,

贡氏坝更宽了；	And the Gumdi Plain became vaster.
贡氏山望不到顶啦，	Mount Gumdi was too high to see the top,
贡氏坝走不到边了。	And the Gumdi Plain was too vast to walk across.
顺着迈里开江飞，	Flying along the Mali Hka River,
沿着恩迈开江翔，	Hovering over the Nmai Hka River,
燕子从贡氏山，	The swallow left Mount Gumdi,
又飞到了掸山。	And flew over to Mount Sam.
掸山更高了，	Mount Sam became higher,
掸坝更宽了，	And the Sam Plain became vaster.
掸山望不到顶啦，	Mount Sam was too high to see the top,
掸坝走不到边了。	And the Sam Plain was too vast to walk across.
顺着迈里开江飞，	Flying along the Mali Hka River,
沿着恩迈开江翔，	Hovering over the Nmai Hka River,
燕子从掸山，	The swallow left Mount Sam,
又飞到了蚌景颇山，	And flew over to Mount Pong Jinghpo.
蚌景颇山更高了，	Mount Pong Jinghpo became higher,
蚌景颇坝更宽了，	And the Pong Jinghpo Plain became vaster.
蚌景颇山望不到顶啦，	Mount Pong Jinghpo was too high to see the top,
蚌景颇坝走不到边了。	And the Pong Jinghpo Plain was too vast to walk across.
顺着迈里开江飞，	Flying along the Mali Hka River,
沿着恩迈开江翔，	Circling over the Nmai Hka River,

燕子从蚌景颇山，	The swallow left Mount Pong Jinghpo
又飞到了直黎山。	And flew over to Mount Jili.
直黎山更高了，	Mount Jili became higher,
直黎坝更宽了，	And the Jili Plain became vaster.
直黎山望不到顶啦，	Mount Jili was too high to see the top,
直黎坝走不到边了。	And the Jili Plain was too vast to walk across.

顺着迈里开江飞，	Flying along the Mali Hka River,
沿着恩迈开江翔，	Hovering over the Nmai Hka River,
燕子从直黎山，	The swallow left Mount Jili,
又飞到了锐藏山，	And flew over to Mount Mungnun Roiza.
锐藏山更高了，	Mount Mungnun Roiza became higher,
锐藏坝更宽了，	And the Mungnun Roiza Plain became vaster.
锐藏山望不到顶啦，	Mount Mungnun Roiza was too high to see the top,
锐藏坝走不到边了。	And the Mungnun Roiza Plain was too vast to walk across.

顺着迈里开江飞，	Flying along the Mali Hka River,
沿着恩迈开江翔，	Hovering over the Nmai Hka River,
燕子从锐藏山，	The swallow left Mount Mungnun Roiza,
又飞到了缅山。	And flew over to Mount Myen.
缅山更高了，	Mount Myen became higher,
缅坝更宽了，	And the Myen Plain became vaster.
缅山望不到顶啦，	Mount Myen was too high to see the top,

缅坝走不到边了。	And the Myen Plain was too vast to walk across.
顺着迈里开江飞，	Flying along the Mali Hka River,
沿着恩迈开江翔，	Hovering the Nmai Hka River,
燕子从缅山，	The swallow left Mount Myen,
又飞到了密瓦山。	And flew over to Mount Miwa.
密瓦山更高了，	Mount Miwa became higher,
密瓦坝更宽了，	And the Miwa Plain became vaster.
密瓦山望不到顶啦，	Mount Miwa was too high to see the top,
密瓦坝走不到边了。	And the Miwa Plain was too vast to walk across.
顺着迈里开江飞，	Flying along the Mali Hka River,
沿着恩迈开江翔，	Hovering over the Nmai Hka River,
燕子从密瓦山，	The swallow left Mount Miwa,
又飞到了蒙岭蒙旁山。	And flew over to Mount Mungling Munghpang.
蒙岭山更高了，	Mount Mungling Munghpang became higher,
蒙旁坝更宽了，	And the Mungling Munghpang Plain became vaster.
蒙岭山望不到顶啦，	Mount Mungling Munghpang was too high to see the top,
蒙旁坝走不到边了。	And the Mungling Munghpang Plain was too vast to walk across.
顺着迈里开江飞，	Flying along the Mali Hka River,
沿着恩迈开江翔，	Hovering over the Nmai Hka River,

燕子从这山飞到那山，	The swallow flew from mountain to mountain.
天更宽了，	The Sky became more extensive,
地更广了。	And the Earth became more spacious.

四、鸟类扒平大地　Ⅳ. Birds Leveling the Earth

远古，	In remote antiquity,
潘瓦能桑遮瓦能章	Hpan Wa Ningsang Chye Wa Ningchyang
对鸟类说过：	Said to the birds,
“等将来有了新的天，	“Birds,
鸟类们呀，	When there is a new Sky,
等将来有了新的地，	And when there is a new Earth,
你们就飞出石洞，	You will fly out of the stone cave,
离开你们生活的地方，	Leaving the place you have lived in,
就飞向开空，	To soar in the Sky
去扒平大地吧。”	And to level the Earth.”

新的天有了，	Then came the new Sky;
新的地有了，	Then came the new Earth.
按潘瓦能桑遮瓦能章	Following the words of
留下的话，	Hpan Wa Ningsang Chye Wa Ningchyang,
鸟类飞出了石洞，	The birds flew out of the stone cave,

离开它们生活的地方，	Leaving where they had lived,
飞向天空，	Flying towards the Sky
扒平大地去了。	And starting to level the Earth.
鸟类飞到热旺松康山，	The birds flew to
从迈里开江岸，	Mount Rawang Sumhkang ,
扒到恩迈开江边。	And leveled all the Earth
东边扒平了，	From the banks of the Mali Hka River
西边扒好了；	To the banks of the Nmai Hka River,
南边扒平了，	From east to west,
北边扒好了；	From north to south.
热旺松康山整齐了，	Mount Rawang Sumhkang looked smooth,
热旺松康坝平坦了。	And the Rawang Sumhkang Plain became level.
扒好了热旺松康山，	Having shaped Mount Rawang Sumhkang ,
鸟类又飞到了依山，	The birds flew over
从迈里开江岸，	To Mount Nung,
扒到恩迈开江边。	And leveled all the Earth
东边扒平了，	From the banks of the Mali Hka River
西边扒好了；	To the banks of the Nmai Hka River,
南边扒平了，	From east to west,
北边扒好了；	From north to south.
依山整齐了，	Mount Nung looked smooth,
依坝平坦了。	And the Nung Plain became level.

扒好了侬山，	Having shaped Mount Nung,
鸟类又飞到了贡氏山，	The birds flew over
从迈里开江岸，	To Mount Gumdi,
扒到恩迈开江边。	And leveled all the Earth
东边扒平了，	From the banks of the Mali Hka River
西边扒好了；	To the banks of the Nmai Hka River,
南边扒平了，	From east to west,
北边扒好了；	From north to south.
贡氏山整齐了，	Mount Gumdi looked smooth,
贡氏坝平坦了。	And the Gumdi Plain became level.

扒好了贡氏山，	Having shaped Mount Gumdi,
鸟类又飞到了搾山，	The birds flew over
从迈里开江岸，	To Mount Sam,
扒到恩迈开江边。	And leveled all the Earth
东边扒平了，	From the banks of the Mali Hka River
西边扒好了；	To the banks of the Nmai Hka River,
南边扒平了，	From east to west,
北边扒好了；	From north to south.
搾山整齐了，	Mount Sam looked smooth,
搾坝平坦了。	And the Sam Plain became level.

扒好了搾山，	Having shaped Mount Sam,

鸟类又飞到了蚌景颇山，	The birds flew over
从迈里开江岸，	To Mount Pong Jinghpo,
扒到恩迈开江边，	And leveled all the Earth
东边扒平了，	From the banks of the Mali Hka River
西边扒好了；	To the banks of the Nmai Hka River,
南边扒平了，	From east to west,
北边扒好了；	From north to south.
蚌景颇山整齐了，	Mount Pong Jinghpo looked smooth,
蚌景颇坝平坦了。	And the Pong Jinghpo Plain became level.
扒好了蚌景颇山，	Having shaped Mount Pong Jinghpo,
鸟类又飞到了直黎山，	The birds flew over
从迈里开江岸，	To Mount Jili,
扒到恩迈开江边。	And leveled all the Earth
东边扒平了，	From the banks of the Mali Hka River
西边扒好了；	To the banks of the Nmai Hka River,
南边扒平了，	From east to west,
北边扒好了；	From north to south.
直黎山整齐了，	Mount Jili looked smooth,
直黎坝平坦了。	And the Jili Plain became level.
扒好了直黎山，	Having shaped Mount Jili,
鸟类又飞到了缅山。	The birds flew over
从迈里开江岸，	To Mount Myen,

扒到恩迈开江边。	And leveled all the Earth
东边扒平了，	From the banks of the Mali Hka River
西边扒好了；	To the banks of the Nmai Hka River,
南边扒平了，	From east to west,
北边扒好了；	From north to south.
缅山整齐了，	Mount Myen looked smooth,
缅坝平坦了。	And the Myen Plain became level.

扒好了缅山，	Having shaped Mount Myen,
鸟类又飞到了密瓦山，	The birds flew over
从迈里开江岸，	To Mount Miwa,
扒到恩迈开江边。	And leveled all the Earth
东边扒平了，	From the banks of the Mali Hka River
西边扒好了；	To the banks of the Nmai Hka River,
南边扒平了，	From east to west,
北边扒好了；	From north to south.
密瓦山整齐了，	Mount Miwa looked smooth,
密瓦坝平坦了。	And the Miwa Plain became level.

扒好了密瓦山，	Having shaped Mount Miwa,
鸟类又飞到了蒙岭蒙旁山，	The birds flew over
从迈里开江岸，	To Mount Mungling Munghpang,
扒到恩迈开江边。	And leveled all the Earth
东边扒平了，	From the banks of the Mali Hka River

西边扒好了；	To the banks of the Nmai Hka River,
南边扒平了，	From east to west,
北边扒好了；	From north to south.
蒙岭山整齐了，	Mount Mungling Munghpang looked smooth,
蒙旁坝平坦了。	And the Mungling Munghpang Plain became level.
鸟类从这山扒到那山，	The birds leveled the Earth from mountain to mountain.
千座高山整齐了，	Hundreds of them became smooth,
万个坝子平坦了，	And thousands of plains were made flat.
新的天更宽了，	The new Sky was stretched,
新的地更广了。	And the new Earth was extended.

五、宁贯督与妹妹　V. N-gon Du and His Younger Sister

远古，	In remote antiquity,
宁贯督和妹妹颇囊文布，	N-gon Du and his younger sister Hpronang Wunbu
白天在一起，	Stayed together during the day
晚上不分离，	And did not part during the night.
他们像一对山雀，	They were like a pair of titmice,
飞出飞进。	Flying in and out together.
他们是兄妹俩，	They were brother and sister.
怎么能像夫妻在一起，	How could they be together

远近的人们，
开始议论这件事。

听到人们的议论，
颇囊文布脸红了，
颇囊文布害羞了。
她心里想：
再也不能留在王宫
和宁贯督在一起了，
只有到遥远的赛如山，
远远地离开宁贯督。

善良的颇囊文布，
还未走出王宫，
王宫里的猫对她说：
“颇囊文布呀，
你要到赛如山，
让我跟你一起去吧，
你一个人路上太冷清，
我会像伙伴一样陪着你。”
颇囊文布说：
“好心的猫呀，
你不能跟我去，
王宫需要你守，

Like husband and wife?
People near and far started to talk about it.

Hearing the gossip,
Hpronang Wunbu blushed;
Hpronang Wunbu was embarrassed.
She thought that
She could no longer stay in the palace
And be with N-gon Du.
She could only go to Mount Sairu far away
And stay away from N-gon Du.

Kind-hearted Hpronang Wunbu
Had not yet left the palace
When the cat in the palace told her,
“Hpronang Wunbu,
If you are going to Mount Sairu,
Let me go with you,
Or you will be lonely on the way.
Like a friend I will accompany you.”
Hpronang Wunbu said,
“Kind cat,
You cannot go with me.
The palace needs your guarding;

王宫需要你护。”	The palace needs your protection.”
颇囊文布说完，	With that, Hpronang Wunbu
给猫留下了好看的花纹。	Left the cat with beautiful patterns.

颇囊文布告别了猫	She waved goodbye to the cat
来到了王宫的门坎，	And came to the threshold of the palace.
守门狗对她说：	The watch dog there said to her,
“颇囊文布呀，	“Hpronang Wunbu,
你要到赛如山，	If you are going to Mount Sairu,
让我跟你去吧，	Let me go with you.
路上遇上猛兽，	If there is any beast on the way,
我会尽力保护你。”	I will try my best to protect you.”
颇囊文布说：	Hpronang Wunbu said,
“好心的狗呀，	“Kind dog,
你不能跟我去，	You cannot go with me.
王宫需要你守，	The palace needs your guarding;
王宫需要你护。”	The palace needs your protection.”
颇囊文布说完，	With that, Hpronang Wunbu
给狗留下了细密的绒毛。	Left the dog with soft fur.

颇囊文布告别了狗	She waved goodbye to the dog
来到鸡圈旁，	And came to the chicken pen.
鸡圈里的公鸡对她说：	The rooster in the pen said to her,
“颇囊文布呀，	“Hpronang Wunbu,

你要到赛如山，	If you are going to Mount Sairu,
让我跟你去吧，	Let me go with you.
我会呼唤太阳，	I can call the sun to rise and shine
赶走路上的黑暗。”	To dismiss the darkness on the way."
颇囊文布说：	Hpronang Wunbu said,
“好心的公鸡呀，	"Kind rooster,
你不能和我去，	You cannot go with me.
王宫的太阳，	The sun over the palace
需要你呼唤。”	Needs your calling."
颇囊文布说完，	With that, Hpronang Wunbu
给公鸡留下了五彩的羽毛。	Left the rooster with colorful feathers.

颇囊文布告别了公鸡	She waved goodbye to the rooster
来到场院上，	And came to the yard.
场院上的猪对她说：	The pig in the yard said to her,
“颇囊文布呀，	"Hpronang Wunbu,
你要到赛如山，	If you are going to Mount Sairu,
让我跟你去吧，	Let me go with you.
你走的路不平坦，	The path you follow is not smooth,
我会用嘴拱平它。”	Yet I can clear it with my nose."
颇囊文布说：	Hpronang Wunbu said,
“好心的猪呀，	"Kind pig,
你不能和我去，	You cannot go with me.
你留在王宫，	You will stay in the palace

王子需要你。”	For the prince needs you."
颇囊文布说完，	With that, Hpronang Wunbu
给猪留下了一对大耳朵。	Left the pig with a pair of big ears.
颇囊文布告别了猪	Hpronang Wunbu waved goodbye to the pig
来到牛圈边，	And came to the barn.
牛圈里的牛对她说：	The ox said to her,
“颇囊文布呀，	"Hpronang Wunbu,
你要到赛如山，	If you are going to Mount Sairu,
让我跟你去吧，	Let me go with you.
我会为你踏平路，	I will make the road smooth for you;
我能为你负重物。”	I will bear the load for you."
颇囊文布说：	Hpronang Wunbu said,
“好心的牛呀，	"Kind ox,
你要为王宫种地，	You must do the farm work for the palace;
你要为王子出力。”	You must work hard for the prince."
颇囊文布说完，	With that, Hpronang Wunbu
给牛留下了一对弯角。	Left the ox with a pair of curving horns.
颇囊文布告别了牛	Hpronang Wunbu waved goodbye to the ox
来到马圈旁，	And came to the stable.
马圈里的马对她说：	The horse in the stable said to her,
“颇囊文布呀，	"Hpronang Wunbu,
你要到赛如山，	If you are going to Mount Sairu,

让我跟你一起去，	Let me go with you.
你骑到我身上，	You ride on my back
比风还要快。”	And will be faster than the wind.”
颇囊文布说：	Hpronang Wunbu said,
“好心的马呀，	“Kind horse,
你不能跟我去，	You cannot go with me.
你是宁贯督的坐骑，	You are the ride of N-gon Du.
你不能丢下他。”	You cannot leave him behind.”
颇囊文布说完，	With that, Hpronang Wunbu
给马留下了长长的鬃毛。	Left the horse with a long mane.
颇囊文布	Hpronang Wunbu
来到王宫外，	Came out of the palace
生下了一个	And there she gave birth to
像鸡蛋一样的东西，	An egg-like object.
独自一个人，	Alone, she went to
到遥远的赛如山去了。	Mount Sairu far away.
从鸡蛋一样的东西里	From the egg-like object
生出了一只鹰，	Broke out an eagle.
它是什么鹰呀？	What kind of eagle was it?
潘瓦能桑遮瓦能章说：	Hpan Wa Ningsang Chye Wa Ningchyang said,
“它是一只造美的神鹰，	“It is a sacred eagle who can create beauty.
它飞到哪里，	Wherever it flies,

哪里就会变得美丽。”	It will bring beauty.”
潘瓦能桑遮瓦能章	Hpan Wa Ningsang Chye Wa Ningchyang
对造美神鹰说：	Said to the beauty-creating sacred eagle,
“造美神鹰呀，	“Beauty-creating sacred eagle,
张开你的翅膀，	Spread your wings
去美化高山吧，	To beautify the mountains
去美化平坝吧。”	And the plains.”
造美的神鹰	The beauty-creating sacred eagle
飞到热旺松康，	Flew to Mount Rawang Sumhkang .
这边飞到迈里开江岸，	It flew to the banks of the Mali Hka River over here
那边飞到恩迈开江边。	And the banks of the Nmai Hka River over there.
东边的花开了，	The flowers in the east bloomed;
西边的树绿了；	The trees in the west turned green.
南边的花开了，	The flowers in the south bloomed;
北边的树绿了；	The trees in the north turned green.
热旺松康山好看了，	Mount Rawang Sumhkang were now delightful,
热旺松康坝美丽了。	And the Rawang Sumhkang Plain became appealing.
造美的神鹰	The beauty-creating sacred eagle
从热旺松康山	Flew from Mount Rawang Sumhkang
飞到了侬山，	To Mount Nung.
这边飞到迈里开江岸，	It flew to the banks of the Mali Hka River over here

那边飞到恩迈开江边。
东边的花开了，
西边的树绿了；
南边的花开了，
北边的树绿了；
依山好看了，
依坝美丽了。

And the banks of the Nmai Hka River over there.
The flowers in the east bloomed;
The trees in the west turned green.
The flowers in the south bloomed;
The trees in the north turned green.
Mount Nung were now delightful,
And the Nung Sumhkang Plain became appealing.

造美的神鹰
从依山
飞到了贡氏山，
这边飞到迈里开江岸，
那边飞到恩迈开江边。
东边的花开了，
西边的树绿了；
南边的花开了，
北边的树绿了；
贡氏山好看了，
贡氏坝美丽了。

The beauty-creating sacred eagle
Flew from Mount Nung
To Mount Gumdi.
It flew to the banks of the Mali Hka River over here
And the banks of the Nmai Hka River over there.
The flowers in the east bloomed;
The trees in the west turned green.
The flowers in the south bloomed;
The trees in the north turned green.
Mount Gumdi were now delishtful,
And the Gumdi Plain became appealing.

造美的神鹰
从贡氏山
飞到了撣山，
这边飞到迈里开江岸，

The beauty-creating sacred eagle
Flew from Mount Gumdi
To Mount Sam.
It flew to the banks of the Mali Hka River over here

那边飞到恩迈开江边。	And the banks of the Nmai Hka River over there.
东边的花开了，	The flowers in the east bloomed;
西边的树绿了；	The trees in the west turned green.
南边的花开了，	The flowers in the south bloomed;
北边的树绿了；	The trees in the north turned green.
掸山好看了，	Mount Sam were now delightful,
掸坝美丽了。	And the Sam Plain became appealing.
造美的神鹰	The beauty-creating sacred eagle
从掸山	Flew from Mount Sam
飞到蚌景颇山，	To Mount Pong Jinghpo.
这边飞到迈里开江岸，	It flew to the banks of the Mali Hka River over here
那边飞到恩迈开江边。	And the banks of the Nmai Hka River over there.
东边的花开了，	The flowers in the east bloomed;
西边的树绿了；	The trees in the west turned green.
南边的花开了，	The flowers in the south bloomed;
北边的树绿了；	The trees in the north turned green.
蚌景颇山好看了，	Mount Pong Jinghpo were now delightful,
蚌景颇坝美丽了。	And the Pong Jinghpo Plain became appealing.
造美的神鹰	The beauty-creating sacred eagle
从蚌景颇山	Flew from Mount Pong Jinghpo
飞到了直黎山，	To Mount Jili.
这边飞到迈里开江岸，	It flew to the banks of the Mali Hka River over here

那边飞到恩迈开江边。	And the banks of the Nmai Hka River over there.
东边的花开了，	The flowers in the east bloomed;
西边的树绿了；	The trees in the west turned green.
南边的花开了，	The flowers in the south bloomed;
北边的树绿了；	The trees in the north turned green.
直黎山好看了，	Mount Jili were now delightful,
直黎坝美丽了。	And the Jili Plain became appealing.
造美的神鹰	The beauty-creating sacred eagle
从直黎山	Flew from Mount Jili
飞到了缅山，	To Mount Myen.
这边飞到迈里开江岸，	It flew to the banks of the Mali Hka River over here
那边飞到恩迈开江边。	And the banks of the Nmai Hka River over there.
东边的花开了，	The flowers in the east bloomed;
西边的树绿了；	The trees in the west turned green.
南边的花开了，	The flowers in the south bloomed;
北边的树绿了；	The trees in the north turned green.
缅山好看了，	Mount Myen were now delightful,
缅坝美丽了。	And the Myen Plain became appealing.
造美的神鹰	The beauty-creating sacred eagle
从缅山	Flew from Mount Myen
飞到了密瓦山，	To Mount Miwa.
这边飞到迈里开江岸，	It flew to the banks of the Mali Hka River over here

那边飞到恩迈开江边。	And the banks of the Nmai Hka River over there.
东边的花开了，	The flowers in the east bloomed;
西边的树绿了；	The trees in the west turned green.
南边的花开了，	The flowers in the south bloomed;
北边的树绿了；	The trees in the north turned green.
密瓦山好看了，	Mount Miwa were now delightful,
密瓦坝美丽了。	And the Miwa Plain became appealing.
造美的神鹰	The beauty-creating sacred eagle
从密瓦山	Flew from Mount Miwa
飞到了蒙岭蒙旁山，	To Mount Mungling Munghpang.
这边飞到迈里开江岸，	It flew to the banks of the Mali Hka River over here
那边飞到恩迈开江边。	And the banks of the Nmai Hka River over there.
东边的花开了，	The flowers in the east bloomed;
西边的树绿了；	The trees in the west turned green.
南边的花开了，	The flowers in the south bloomed;
北边的树绿了；	The trees in the north turned green.
蒙岭山好看了，	Mount Mungling Munghpang was now delightful,
蒙旁坝美丽了。	And the Mungling Munghpang Plain became appealing.
远古，	In remote antiquity,
造美的神鹰	The beauty-creating sacred eagle
完成了自己的使命，	Accomplished its mission.
向着西方飞去，	It flew to the west,

在英格兰地方	And in a place named the Inggalan
永远地安息了。	Rested in peace forever.
所以那里的人们	Therefore people there
肤色是白的。	Had fair complexions;
神鹰没有飞到的地方，	Where the eagle did not reach,
人们的肤色是黑的。	The skin tone of the people was dark.
神鹰咽气时，	When the eagle breathed its last breath,
从它的喉咙里，	From its throat,
生出了一股黑风；	Came a gust of dark wind;
从它的嘴里，	From its mouth,
生出了甜草，	Sweet grass came into being,
长出了芦苇；	And reeds came into leaf;
从它的嗓子，	From its throat,
生出了席草，	Mat grass came into being;
从它的羽冠，	From its crest,
长出了鸡冠花；	Cockscomb flowers came into blossom;
从它的头颅，	From its head,
生出了药筒葫芦；	Bottle gourds came into being;
从它的脖颈，	From its neck,
长出了水飘葫芦；	Water hyacinth came into leaf;
从它的羽毛，	From its feathers,
生出了牛梳子藤；	Comb vines came into being;
从它的翅膀，	From its wings,

长出了弯果藤；	Curved fruit vines came into leaf;
从它的屁股，	From its bottom,
生出了女子藤；	Ladies' vine came into being;
从它的脊梁，	From its spine,
长出了金竹；	Golden bamboo came into leaf;
从它的脚杆，	From its ankles,
长出了直杆树；	Pole trees came into being;
从它的爪子，	From its claws,
长出了鹰爪刺；	Talon thorns came into leaf;
从它的肋巴骨，	From its ribs,
生出了茅草；	Thatch came into being;
从它的血管，	From its veins,
长出了苏木树；	Logwood trees came into leaf;
从它的心，	From its heart,
长出了马藤树；	Horse vine trees came into being;
从它的肚子，	From its stomach,
长出了地老瓜藤。	Leguminosae vines came into leaf.

第三章 洪水

Canto 3 The Flood

一、宁贯督发洪水

Ⅰ. N-gon Du Started the Flood

远古，
百姓拥戴宁贯督，
人民敬重宁贯督。
美味的官腿[①]，
只献给宁贯督；
无偿的官工[②]，
只给宁贯督出；
如山的官谷[③]，

In remote antiquity,
People respected N-gon Du
And the general public honored him.
Delicious meat tribute[①]
Was offered only to N-gon Du;
Free labor tribute[②]
Was offered only to N-gon Du;
Mountains of grain tribute[③]

① 官腿：景颇族社会官家享有一定的特权，官腿就是其中的一项，即辖下的百姓打猎或宰杀牲畜时，都得向官家交纳一条后腿。景颇语中也称“宁贯”，据传说宁贯督是景颇族的第一代官，交纳腿是从他那里开始的。

② 官工：官家的特权之一，即每年辖下的百姓都得给官家出一定的无偿劳动力。

③ 官谷：官家的特权之一，每年的收获季节，辖下的百姓都得向官家交纳一定数量的谷物。

① Meat tribute: Jingpo officials enjoyed certain privileges and meat tribute was one of them. When common people under their jurisdiction hunted or slaughtered livestock, they were required to hand in one hind leg to the royal family. It is also termed "N-gon" in Jingpo language as it is said that N-gon Du represented the first generation of court officials among the Jingpo people and the tradition started with him.

② Labor tribute: It was a privilege enjoyed by court officials. Common people under their jurisdiction must offer them a certain amount of free labor on a yearly basis.

③ Grain tribute: It was a privilege enjoyed by court officials. Common people under their jurisdiction were required to hand in a certain proportion of grain during harvest season.

只交给宁贯督。	Were paid only to N-gon Du.
宁贯督的哥哥	The nine sons of
诗瓦鹏的九个儿子，	N-gon Du's brother Shawa Hpung
看着眼红了，	They became jealous
想着嫉妒了，	And covetous.
他们放出大话：	They made claims,
“叔叔宁贯督，	"Uncle N-gon Du,
美味的官腿，	Delicious meat tribute
他一个人享用；	Is enjoyed only by him,
无偿的官工，	Free labor tribute
只给他一个人出；	Is offered only to him,
如山的官谷，	Mountain-high piles of grain tribute
只交给他。	Are paid only to him.
我们不能就这样看着他，	We cannot stand aside and watch him.
我们要杀掉他。	We shall kill him.
至尊的官位，	The supreme position,
我们要坐；	We want to take.
美味的官腿，	Delicious meat tribute,
我们要享用；	We want to enjoy.
无偿的官工，	Free labor tribute,
要给我们做；	We want to receive.
如山的官谷，	Mountain-high piles of grain tribute,
我们要收。”	We want to collect."

宽厚的宁贯督
听了九兄弟的大话，
看了九兄弟的举动，
对勒顶勒庄拉① 说：
“勒顶勒庄拉呀，
我的侄子们不懂事，
你去劝劝他们，
叫他们不要乱说，
让他们不要乱动。”

Generous N-gon Du
Heard the nine brothers' talk,
And seeing what they had done,
Said to Ladin Lachyong La①,
"Ladin Lachyong La,
My nephews are acting immaturely.
You go and persuade them
Not to make irresponsible remarks
And not to take irresponsible actions."

勒顶勒庄拉
按宁贯督的吩咐，
对九兄弟说：
“九兄弟呀，
你们的叔叔宁贯督，
让我来劝你们，
叫你们不要乱说，
让你们不要乱动。”

Ladin Lachyong La,
Following the orders of N-gon Du,
Said to the nine brothers,
"Nine brothers,
Your Uncle N-gon Du
Asks me to persuade you
Not to make irresponsible remarks
And not to take irresponsible actions."

九兄弟回答说：
“我们是了不起的九兄弟，

The nine brothers answered,
"We are the amazing nine brothers,

① 勒顶勒庄拉：传说中宁贯督的使者，后来变成野猫。

① Ladin Lachyong La: an envoy of N-gon Du in the tales, who later turned into a wild cat.

叔叔宁贯督算什么，	Who does Uncle N-gon Du think he is?
官腿我们要享用，	It should be us who will enjoy delicious meat tribute,
官工要给我们出，	It should be us who will receive free labor tribute,
官谷要由我们收，	It should be us who will collect grain tribute.
我们要挖他的眼睛，	We will gouge out his eyes
断他的腿。"	And break his legs."
勒顶勒庄拉	Ladin Lachyong La
给宁贯督回话：	Reported to N-gon Du,
"尊敬的宁贯督呀，	"Honorable N-gon Du,
九兄弟不听我的劝告，	The nine brothers choose to dismiss my advice.
他们执意要官夺位，	They are determined to take the supreme position.
还说要挖你的眼睛，	They also threaten to dig out your eyes
断你的腿。"	And break your legs."
宽厚的宁贯督	Generous N-gon Du
对勒顶勒庄拉说：	Said to Ladin Lachyong La,
"勒顶勒庄拉呀，	"Ladin Lachyong La,
你再去劝劝他们吧。	You go and try to persuade them again.
如果他们再不听，	If they still do not listen,
我就要用太阳烧他们。"	I will burn them with the sun."
勒顶勒庄拉	Ladin Lachyong La
又对九兄弟说：	Said to the nine brothers again,

“九兄弟呀，	“Nine brothers,
你们还是听听劝告吧，	Follow my advice.
如果你们再不听，	Should you choose to dismiss it again,
你们的叔叔宁贯督，	Your Uncle N-gon Du
就要用太阳烧你们。”	Will burn you with the sun.”
九兄弟回答说：	The nine brothers answered,
“让太阳来吧，	“Let the sun come.
我们是了不起的九兄弟，	We are the amazing nine brothers.
我们就像九条河，	We are like nine rivers.
太阳不够我们当火烤，	The sun is not even qualified to be our furnace,
太阳晒着还嫌冷。”	And we still feel cold even when the sun is burning.”
勒顶勒庄拉	Ladin Lachyong La
给宁贯督回话：	Reported to N-gon Du,
“尊敬的宁贯督呀，	“Honorable N-gon Du,
九兄弟还是不听劝告。	The nine brothers still choose to dismiss my advice.
说太阳不够他们当火烤，	They say that the sun is not qualified to be their furnace,
说太阳晒着还嫌冷。”	And that they still feel cold even when the sun is burning.”
宽厚的宁贯督，	Generous N-gon Du
对勒顶勒庄拉说：	Said to Ladin Lachyong La,
“勒顶勒庄拉呀，	“Ladin Lachyong La,
你再去劝劝他们吧，	You go and try to persuade them again.

如果他们不听，	If they still dismiss your advice,
就要用大风刮他们。”	I will blow them away with a gale.”
勒顶勒庄拉	Ladin Lachyong La
又对九兄弟说：	Said to the nine brothers again,
“九兄弟呀，	“Nine brothers,
你们还是听听劝告吧，	Follow my advice.
如果你们再不听，	Should you choose to dismiss it again,
你们的叔叔宁贯督，	Your Uncle N-gon Du
就要让大风刮你们。”	Will blow you away with a gale.”
九兄弟回答说：	The nine brothers answered,
“让大风快来吧，	“Let the gale come.
我们是了不起的九兄弟，	We are the amazing nine brothers.
我们像九座山，	We are like nine mountains.
狂风刮不走，	The gale won't blow us away
暴风吹不动。”	And a gust won't move us a bit.”
勒顶勒庄拉	Ladin Lachyong La
给宁贯督回话说：	Reported to N-gon Du,
“尊敬的宁贯督呀，	“Honorable N-gon Du,
九兄弟还是不听劝告，	The nine brothers still choose to dismiss my advice.
说他们像九座山，	They say that they are like nine mountains.
狂风刮不走，	The gale won't blow them away

暴风吹不动。”	And a gust won't move them a bit."
宽厚的宁贯督	Generous N-gon Du
对勒顶勒庄拉说：	Said to Ladin Lachyong La,
“勒顶勒庄拉呀，	"Ladin Lachyong La,
你再去劝劝他们吧，	You go and try to persuade them again.
如果他们再不听，	If they still do not listen,
就要用暴雨淋他们。”	I will drench them with a rainstorm."
勒顶勒庄拉	Ladin Lachyong La
又对九兄弟说：	Said to the nine brothers again,
“九兄弟呀，	"Nine brothers,
你们还是听听劝告吧，	Follow my advice.
如果你们再不听，	Should you choose to dismiss it again,
你们的叔叔宁贯督，	Your Uncle N-gon Du
就要用暴雨淋你们。”	Will drench you with a rainstorm."
九兄弟回答说：	The nine brothers answered,
“让暴雨来吧，	"Let the rainstorm come.
我们是了不起的九兄弟，	We are the amazing nine brothers.
我们正想冲身子，	We happen to want to take a shower,
只怕暴雨淋不湿身子。”	And we are afraid the rainstorm won't even make us wet."
勒顶勒庄拉	Ladin Lachyong La

给宁贯督回话说：	Reported to N-gon Du,
“尊敬的宁贯督呀，	“Honorable N-gon Du,
九兄弟还是不听劝告，	The nine brothers still choose to dismiss my advice.
说暴雨来了，	They say that if the rainstorm comes,
他们正好冲身子，	It is perfect for them to take a shower.
只怕暴雨淋不湿身子。”	They are worried the rainstorm won't even make them wet.”

宽厚的宁贯督	Generous N-gon Du
对勒顶勒庄拉说：	Said to Ladin Lachyong La,
“勒顶勒庄拉呀，	“Ladin Lachyong La,
你再去劝劝他们吧，	You go and persuade them again.
这是最后一次了，	This is my ultimatum,
如果他们再不听，	If they still dismiss it,
我就要发洪水淹他们了。”	I will start a flood to drown them.”

勒顶勒庄拉	Ladin Lachyong La
又对九兄弟说：	Said to the nine brothers again,
“九兄弟啊，	“Nine brothers,
你们还是听听劝告吧，	Follow my advice.
这是最后一次了，	This will be the ultimatum.
如果你们再不听，	Should you choose to dismiss it again,
你们的叔叔宁贯督，	Your Uncle N-gon Du
就要发洪水了。”	Will start a flood.”

九兄弟回答说：
“让洪水快来吧，
我们是了不起的九兄弟，
我们的嘴巴像山洞，
我们的肚子像峡谷，
洪水来了呀，
还不够我们喝下肚。”

The nine brothers answered,
“Let the flood come.
We are the amazing nine brothers.
Our mouths are like caves,
And our stomachs like valleys.
When the flood comes,
It will not be enough to quench our thirst.”

勒顶勒庄拉，
给宁贯督回话说：
“尊敬的宁贯督呀，
九兄弟还是不听劝告，
说他们的嘴巴像山洞，
他们的肚子像峡谷，
洪水来了，
还不够他们喝下肚。”

Ladin Lachyong La
Reported to N-gon Du,
“Honorable N-gon Du,
The nine brothers still choose to dismiss my advice.
They say that their mouths are like caves,
And their stomachs are like valleys.
When the flood comes,
It will not be enough to quench their thirst.”

听了勒顶勒庄拉的话，
宁贯督愤怒了，
宁贯督再也忍不住了。
他要发洪水，
惩罚九兄弟。

Hearing the words of Ladin Lachyong La,
N-gon Du’s rage roared.
N-gon Du could no longer control himself.
He was going to start a flood
To punish the nine brothers.

宁贯督的儿女[①]说：	N-gon Du's son and daughter[①] said,
“父亲宁贯督呀，	"Father N-gon Du,
你要发洪水，	If you start a flood,
到处都会变成汪洋，	Every place will turn into an ocean.
让我们到哪里住，	Where shall we stay,
叫我们往哪里藏？”	And where shall we hide?"
宁贯督对儿女说：	N-gon Du said to his son and daughter,
“孩子俩呀，	"My two children,
你们不用害怕，	You need not panic
你们不用担心，	And you need not worry.
我已做好木鼓船，	I have made a wooden drum-shaped boat.
洪水涨得多高，	However high the water level rises,
木鼓船也会漂得多高，	The wooden drum-shaped boat will rise with it.
你们躲在里面，	You'll hide inside it,
洪水淹不着，	The flood won't drown you,
大雨漏不进。”	And the rain won't seep in."
勒顶勒庄拉，	Ladin Lachyong La
也来对宁贯督说：	Also came to N-gon Du and said,

① 宁贯督的儿女：传说“宁贯督与他的妹妹颇囊文布生下了一男一女两兄妹，两兄妹又结成了一对夫妻。

① N-gon Du's son and daughter: It is said that N-gon Du and his younger sister Hpronang Wunbu had an elder son and a younger daughter together. The brother and sister were married.

"尊敬的宁贯督呀，
你发了洪水，
到处都会成为汪洋，
让我到哪里住，
叫我往哪里藏？"

"Honorable N-gon Du,
If you start a flood,
Every place will turn into an ocean.
Where shall I stay,
And where shall I hide?"

宁贯督对勒顶勒庄拉说：
"勒顶勒庄拉呀，
你就坐到木鼓船上面吧，
洪水涨得多高，
木鼓船也会漂得多高。"

N-gon Du replied,
"Ladin Lachyong La,
You shall come and stay in the wooden drum-shaped boat.
However high the water level rises,
The wooden drum-shaped boat will rise with it."

照宁贯督说的话，
兄妹俩钻进了木鼓船，
里面放着吃食，
装着九根针，
关着九只鸡。
勒顶勒庄拉，
也坐到了木鼓船上面，
木鼓船已经盖紧，
就等着洪水的到来。

Following the words of N-gon Du,
The brother and sister climbed into the wooden drum-shaped boat,
Where food was laid,
Nine needles were placed,
And nine chickens were caged.
Ladin Lachyong La
Sat on the top of the boat,
Which was securely sealed,
And waited for the arrival of the flood.

宁贯督推倒大山，	N-gon Du toppled mountains
堵住了所有的江河，	To clog all the rivers,
宁贯督砍开巨石，	And cut giant stones in half
挡住了所有的峡谷，	To block all valleys.
宁贯督让天神降下了暴雨。	He asked God for a downpour of rain.
天上的雨水涨起来了，	The rain fell heavily from above,
江河里的水漫起来了，	And the water in the rivers started to brim over.
宁贯督离开了戛昂阿崩山，	N-gon Du left Mount Gaang Abum
到赛如石贡山[①]去了。	And went to Mount Sairu Shagong[①].
过了一百四十天，	After one hundred and forty days,
见不着一块坝子，	He neither saw a single patch of plain,
看不到一座高山了，	Nor laid eyes on any mountain.
整个大地，	The entire Earth
都成了水的世界。	Became a world of water.
潘格来遮能代想，	Hpan Galai Chye Ningdai wondered,
只有水的世界，	In a world where there was only water,
人类就无法生存，	People could not survive.
只有将洪水撤退，	Only when the floodwater receded
人类才能继续繁衍。	Could humanity continue to reproduce.

① 赛如石贡山：据传说是高原上的大山，是宁贯督的独妹居住的地方。宁贯督到赛如石贡山，主要是躲避洪水。

① Mount Sairu Shagong: It is said to be a huge mountain on the plateau where the only younger sister of N-Gon Du lived alone. He traveled there mainly to seek shelter from the flood.

潘格来遮能代	Hpan Galai Chye Ningdai
派出大力神	Sent the God of Strength
诗仁诗牙贡木戛拉，	Named Sharing Shaya Kong Magra La
让他撤退洪水。	To drain the floodwater.
大力神打了一锤，	The God of Strength swung his hammer once,
堵在江河上的大山，	And the mountains clogging the rivers
马上被打开了；	Were smashed immediately.
大力神射了一箭，	The God of Strength shot an arrow,
挡在峡谷上的巨石，	And the giant stones blocking valleys
瞬间被射穿了。	Were pierced by it.
江河流畅了，	Rivers ran smoothly,
峡谷疏通了，	Valleys were cleared,
洪水退去了，	The flood receded,
大地露面了，	And the Earth resurfaced.
但整个大地，	Yet the entire Earth
都成了一片白沙滩。	Became a large white beach.
木鼓船漂呀漂呀，	The wooden drum-shaped boat drifted on and on
一直漂了一百四十天	For one hundred and forty days
才停了下来，	Before it came to a stop.
木鼓船里的兄妹俩	The brother and sister inside it
不知道外面的世界	Did not know about the world outside.

就从木鼓里
放出一只鸡，
鸡被木鼓上的野猫吃掉了，
没有听到鸡的叫声，
认为洪水没有退去；
又从鼓缝里，
投出了一根针，
但还是听不到针的响声，
以为洪水还没有退去。
九只鸡放了八只，
九根针投了八根，
还是不知道
木鼓外面的世界。

From inside of the boat
They released a chicken,
Which was swallowed by a wild cat on the top of the boat.
They failed to hear its crowing
And thought the flood had not receded yet.
From the seams of the boat
They threw out a needle,
But still did not hear the sound it made
And thought the flood had not receded.
They released eight out of the nine chickens
And threw out eight out of the nine needles.
Yet still they failed to know about
The world outside the wooden drum-shaped boat.

最后一只鸡放出去了，
听到鸡在说：
“可怜的兄妹呀，
洪水退去了，
大山出头了，
平坝露面了，
快快出来吧。”

The last chicken was released.
They heard it saying,
“Poor brother and sister,
The flood has receded,
Mountains have resurfaced,
Plains have emerged.
Hurry outside.”

最后一根针投出来了，

The last needle was thrown out,

听到了针头
碰到了沙滩的声音，
兄妹俩才知道，
洪水真的退去了。
兄妹俩走出木鼓船，
见到外面是茫茫的沙滩，
山上没有一棵树，
地上没有一根草，
兄妹俩不知如何走，
兄妹俩不知该找谁。

兄妹俩手拉着手，
为寻找居住的地方，
为寻找懂事的大人，
不停地找着，
不停地走着，
终于看到沙滩上，
有一行野猫的脚印。

兄妹俩沿着野猫的脚印
走了九十九天，
找了九十九夜。
遇到了丁热纯老人[①]。

And they heard the sound
Of it landing on the beach.
The brother and sister then realized that
The flood had indeed receded.
They stepped out of the boat
And saw the vast beach outside.
There were no trees on the mountains
And no grass on the ground.
The brother and sister did not know
Where to go or whom to look for.

Hand in hand, the brother and sister
Looked for a place to stay
And looked for knowledgeable adults.
Walking on and on,
Searching non-stop,
Finally on the beach they saw
A set of paw prints from a wild cat.

Following the paw prints of the wild cat,
The brother and sister walked for ninety-nine days
And searched for ninety-nine days.
Then they met an old man named Ting-ra Shun Dingla[①].

① 丁热纯老人：传说中吃人的妖怪。

① Ting-ra Shun Dingla: an ogre in the tales.

丁热纯老人问：	Ting-ra Shun Dingla asked,
“可怜的孩子呵，	“Poor children,
你们从哪里来，	Where are you from,
你们到哪里去，	Where are you going,
你们是哪家的，	Who are your parents
你们是什么姓？”	And what is your family name?”
兄妹俩回答说：	The brother and sister replied,
“我们是宁贯督的孩子，	“We are children of N-gon Du.
野猫的脚印，	The paw prints of a wild cat
把我们带到这里，	Led us here.
我们不知道回家的路，	We do not know our way back home,
我们不知道父母在哪里，	And we do not know where our parents are.
好心的老人呵，	Kind-hearted old man,
你就收留我们吧。”	Please take us in.”
丁热纯老人说：	Ting-ra Shun Dingla said,
“可怜的孩子呵，	“Poor children,
你们不用担心，	You need not panic;
你们不用害怕，	You need not worry.
你们跟我在一起，	Stay with me
这里就是你们的家。	And this will be your home.
你们先睡觉，	You two go to sleep
我去接水来，	While I will fetch some water

给你们煮饭。”	To cook for you.”
丁热纯老人拿着竹筒，	Ting-ra Shun Dingla held a bamboo tube,
边接水边对水说：	Saying to the water while fetching it,
“水呀，水呀，	“Water, water,
快快地流吧，	Run fast.
快快地满吧，	Fill the tube fast.
我要煮孩子的肉，	I want to boil the meat of the children;
我要吃孩子的心。”	I want to eat the hearts of the children.”
可怜的兄妹俩，	The poor brother and sister,
听到丁热纯老人的话，	Hearing the words of Ting-ra Shun Dingla,
知道他是吃人的妖精，	Realized he was a man-eating monster.
便又沿着野猫的脚印，	They fled quickly,
赶快逃走了。	Following the paw prints from the wild cat.
翻过九十九座高山，	Surmounting ninety-nine high mountains
越过九十九个平坝，	And crossing ninety-nine smooth plains,
兄妹两人，	The brother and sister
遇到了吴枯昆老人。	Ran across an old man named Uhku Hkun,
吴枯昆老人问他们：	Who asked them,
“可怜的孩子呵，	“Poor children,
你们从哪里来，	Where are you from,
你们到哪里去，	Where are you going,
你们是哪家的，	Who are your parents

你们是什么姓？”	And what is your family name?”
兄妹俩回答说：	The brother and sister replied,
“我们是宁贯督的孩子，	“We are children of N-gon Du.
野猫的脚印，	The paw prints of a wild cat
把我们引到这里，	Led us here.
我们不知道回家的路，	We do not know our way back home,
我们不知道父母在哪里，	And we do not know where our parents are.
有个妖精老人，	There was an old monster,
要煮我们的肉，	Who wanted to cook us
要吃我们的心，	And eat our hearts.
好心的爷爷呀，	Kind grandpa,
救救我们吧。	Please help us.
好心的老人呵，	Kind-hearted sir,
你就收留我们吧。”	please take us in.”
吴枯昆老人说：	Uhku Hkun said,
“可怜的孩子呀，	“Poor children,
你们不用担心，	You need not panic;
你们不用害怕，	You need not worry.
和我在一起，	Stay with me
你们会平安，	And you will be safe.
你们先去找柴来，	You two go and fetch some firewood.
我接水煮饭给你们。”	I will collect some water to cook for you.”

吴枯昆老人拿着竹筒，	Uhku Hkun held a bamboo tube,
边接水边对水说：	Saying to the water while fetching it,
“水呀，水呀，	“Water, water,
快快地流呀，	Run fast.
快快地淌吧，	Flow fast.
两个孩子饿坏了，	The two children are starving.
我要煮饭给他们。”	I want to cook for them.”
兄妹俩听到老人的话，	Hearing the words of the old man,
知道他是个好人。	The brother and sister knew he was a good man.
兄妹俩还没有喘口气，	The brother and sister had not caught a breath
兄妹俩还没有吃上饭，	Or put food in their mouths
就听到呼呼地怪叫，	When they heard bawing and squalling.
妖精老人追来了。	The old ogre was catching up.
吴枯昆老人说：	Uhku Hkun said,
“孩子们呀，	“Children,
你们不用慌，	You need not panic.
爷爷我会想办法。	Grandpa will come up with an idea.
你们带上沙和水，	You bring sand and water
你们带上响铃果。	And the bell-ringing fruit with you
藏到门头上。	And hide above the door.
当你们听到我喊，	When you hear me shout

天呀地呀时，	'Oh Sky! Oh Earth!'
你们就泼下水，	You pour the water,
撒下沙，	Throw the sand,
摇响响铃果。"	And ring the bell-ringing fruit."
兄妹俩按老人的吩咐	Just when they hid above the door
刚刚藏到门头上，	As the old man told them to,
露出獠牙的妖精	The ogre, with its fangs out,
吐着白沫追到了，	Arrived, foaming at the mouth.
来到吴枯昆老人门前，	It came to the door of Uhku Hkun
大吼大叫道：	And shouted loudly,
"吴枯昆老人我问你，	"Uhku Hkun, I ask you,
可看见两个孩子？	Do you see two children?
我要煮他们的肉，	I will cook them.
我要吃他们的心。"	I will eat their hearts."
吴枯昆老人说：	Uhku Hkun said,
"我整天守在家，	"I have stayed home all day,
不知道外面的事，	And do not know what's going on outside.
你说的两个孩子，	The two children you talk about,
我没有见过。"	I have not seen them."
妖精老人说：	The old ogre said,
"我沿着他们的脚印，	"I have followed their footsteps here.

才追到这里，	Their footsteps
他们的脚印，	Cross your threshold.
进了你的门，	How could you say
怎么说不知道，	You do not know
怎么说没有见，	And you have not seen them?
如果真是那样，	If that is the case indeed,
我就要进门来搜找。”	I am coming in to search."
吴枯昆老人说：	Uhku Hkun said,
“你不信我的话，	"If you do not believe me,
硬要跨进我的门，	And cross my threshold against my will,
天神就会惩罚你。	God will punish you.
老天呀！	Oh Sky!
大地呀！	Oh Earth!
惩罚妖精吧。”	Punish the orge!"
吴枯昆老人刚喊完，	Immediately,
沙子落下了，	Sand fell down,
雨水降下了，	Rain poured down,
雷声也响起了。	And thunder roared.
凶狠的妖精，	The fierce orge,
以为天神在惩罚他，	Believing it was God punishing him,
风一样地逃走了。	Fled faster than the wind.

在吴枯昆老人的家里，	In the house of Uhku Hkun,
兄妹俩一天天地长大，	The brother and sister grew up day by day.
为了让他们繁衍后代，	In order to let them reproduce,
吴枯昆老人，	Uhku Hkun came up with an idea.
想了一个办法，	He asked them to collect firewood every day.
每天让他们去找柴。	Firewood collected from this mountain
这山的柴找来了，	Was not satisfactory to Uhku Hkun.
吴枯昆老人不满意，	Firewood brought from another mountain
那山的柴背来了，	Did not make him happy, either.
吴枯昆老人不合心，	The brother and sister had no other option
兄妹俩没有办法，	And fetched the last kind of firewood.
最后找来的柴，	Crackling while burning,
烧起来会剥剥直炸，	The hydrochloric acid trees
不能做柴的盐酸树，	Could not be used as firewood.
吴枯昆老人却满意了。	But Uhku Hkun was satisfied.

寒冷的夜晚，	On cold nights,
兄妹俩盖着芭蕉叶，	The brother and sister slept beside the fireplace
同睡在火塘边。	With banana leaves as covers.
火塘里的盐酸树，	The hydrochloric acid tree in the fireplace
烧得剥剥直炸，	Crackled while burning.
火星子四处乱飞。	Sparks flew around.
他们互相拍打着火星，	They patted each other to put out the sparks.
火星拍掉了，	Sparks extinguished,

兄妹两人，	The brother and sister
却从此相爱了。	Fell in love.
兄妹俩成了夫妻，	They became husband and wife.
他们生下了一个小孩，	They had a baby.
每一个白天，	Everyday, during the daytime,
他们都出门去干活，	They went out to work,
留下吴枯昆老人，	And left Uhku Hkun behind
在家带孩子。	To take care of the baby at home.
有一天兄妹俩出门后，	One day, after the brother and sister left,
孩子整天不停地哭，	The baby would not stop crying.
吴枯昆老人说：	Uhku Hkun said,
“孩子呀，	“Baby,
你不要哭了，	If you cry no more,
我就给你烧干巴。”	I will cook dried meat for you.”
孩子还是哭，	The baby continued to wail.
吴枯昆老人说：	Uhku Hkun said,
“孩子呀，	“Baby,
你不要哭了，	If you cry no more,
我就要给你烧鱼吃。”	I will cook fish for you.”
孩子还是不停地哭，	The baby still cried.
吴枯昆老人生气了：	Uhku Hkun became angry,

“给你什么也不要，	“You would not take whatever I offered.
还是不停地哭，	You cry and cry.
还是不停地叫，	You scream and scream.
我要把你剁碎，	I will chop you to pieces
撒到九岔路口上。”	And throw them at the crossroad of Mount Sairu.”
孩子不哭了，	The baby stopped crying;
孩子不叫了，	The baby stopped screaming.
吴枯昆老人拿起长刀，	Uhku Hkun cut out the baby's heart
取下孩子的心，	With a long machete.
其余的剁成碎肉，	He chopped the body of the baby into pieces,
用芭蕉叶包成九包，	Wrapped them with banana leaves into nine packs,
放到九岔路口上。	And put them at the crossroad of Mount Sairu.
把留下的心，	The heart was made into
煮成一锅稀饭，	A pot of porridge,
炖在火塘旁。	Stewing beside the fireplace.
兄妹俩晚上回到家，	The brother and sister came home in the evening.
听不到孩子的笑声，	Not hearing the giggling of the baby,
见不到孩子的身影，	And not seeing the baby,
急得忙问老人说：	They asked the old man anxiously,
“爷爷呀，	“Grandpa,
进门听不到孩子叫，	We are burning with anxiety
我们心里急得焦，	Because we can't hear the sound of the baby.

我们的孩子在哪里，	Where is our baby?
先让我们看看吧。”	Please let us see it at first."
吴枯昆老人说：	Uhku Hkun said,
“你们别着急，	"You need not worry;
你们别心焦，	You need not panic.
火塘边炖着稀饭，	There is porridge stewing by the fireplace.
吃饱了再看孩子吧。”	You can see the baby after eating."
兄妹俩吃完了稀饭，	After finishing the porridge,
揭开床上的毯子，	The brother and sister lifted the blanket on the bed.
见床上只有一根木头，	There was only a wood chunk on it
却不见孩子的身影。	With no sign of the baby.
兄妹俩哭着说：	The brother and sister cried,
“爷爷呀，	"Grandpa,
石头不会变成牛，	Stones won't turn into cattle;
孩子不会变木头，	Children won't turn into wood.
我们的孩子在哪里，	Where is our baby?
你快告诉我们吧。”	Please tell us! Now!"
吴枯昆老人说：	Uhku Hkun said,
“你们的孩子，	"Your baby
变成了红红的碎肉，	Has been made into red mince.
就在九岔路口，	At the crossroad of Mount Sairu,

你们去看吧。”

You can go and see.”

听了吴枯昆老人的话，
兄妹俩来到九岔路口，
只见一块块碎肉，
变成了一个个孩子，
他们的脸上，
带着红红的血迹，
他们的身上，
都带着伤痕。

Hearing this,
They came to the crossroad of Mount Sairu
And saw pieces of mince
Turn into children.
On their faces,
There were red blood traces.
On their bodies,
There were injuries.

兄妹俩对他们说：
“孩子们呀，
你们的父亲来了，
你们的母亲来了，
跟我们回家吧。”

The brother and sister said to them,
“Children,
Your father is here;
Your mother is here.
Come home with us.”

听到兄妹俩的话，
孩子们惊恐地说：
“你们吃了我们的心，
不再是我们的父母。
你们快走吧，
我们怕你们。”
孩子们说完

Hearing these words,
The children said in horror,
“You ate our hearts,
You are no longer our parents.
Hurry away,
We are scared of you.”
Having said that,

就拼命地逃走了。	The children rushed away.
顺着地上的脚印，	Following the footsteps on the ground,
兄妹俩要找回孩子们，	The brother and sister tried to get their children back.
追到酸杷果树下，	They came to a sour fruit tree
看到酸杷果树下，	And saw cuts on the trunk
有孩子们砍下的刀痕，	Made by the children.
刀痕上流下的树浆，	The tree sap that had flowed from the cuts
已结成红色的硬块，	Had turned into hard red lumps.
想着孩子们已经走远，	Thinking the children had gone far away,
兄妹俩放慢了脚步。	They slowed down their pace.
追到芭蕉树下，	Coming to a banana forest,
看见孩子们砍倒的芭蕉树，	They saw a banana tree
芭蕉桩的心子，	Cut down by the children.
已伸出了一大截，	A new tree had grown out of the stump.
想着孩子们已经走远，	Thinking the children had gone far away,
兄妹俩放慢了脚步。	They slowed down their pace.
追到太阳宫时，	Coming to the Palace of the Sun,
孩子们已关上了大门，	They saw that
兄妹俩进不了门，	The children had closed its gate.
请蜗牛来帮了忙。	So they asked a snail for help.
蜗牛把身上的黏液	The snail painted its slime

涂到太阳宫的大门脚，	On the foot of the gate.
轻轻地一推，	Pushing lightly,
太阳宫的大门打开了。	The gate opened.
兄妹俩走进太阳宫，	They entered the Palace of the Sun
对孩子们说：	And said to the children,
“孩子们呀，	“Children,
你们的父亲来了，	Your father is here;
你们的母亲来了。	Your mother is here.
跟我们回去吧。”	Come home with us.”
孩子们听到他们俩的声音，	The children, hearing their voices,
惊恐地说：	Said in horror,
“你们吃过我们的心，	“You ate our hearts,
不再是我们的父母。”	You are no longer our parents.”
孩子们说完，	With that,
逃出了太阳宫，	They fled out of the Palace of the Sun
关上了太阳宫的门。	And closed the gate behind them.
兄妹俩出不了门，	The brother and sister could not get out
只好留在太阳宫，	And had to stay in the Palace of the Sun.
在太阳宫里，	In the Palace of the Sun,
他们生下了一个女孩。	They had a girl.
女孩长大后，	When the girl grew up,

就对父母说：	She said to her parents,
“亲亲的父亲呀，	“My dear father,
亲亲的母亲，	My dear mother,
我一个人多冷清，	How lonely I am.
我一个人多寂寞，	How deserted I feel!
难道我没有姐姐，	Don't I have sisters?
难道我没有哥哥？”	Don't I have brothers?”
兄妹俩回答说：	The brother and sister replied,
“可怜的孩子呀，	“Poor child,
你有好多的姐姐，	You have many sisters,
也有好多的哥哥，	And many brothers as well.
但他们都生活在大地上。”	Yet they all live on the Earth.”
女孩子又说：	The girl said again,
“亲亲的父亲呀，	“My dear father,
亲亲的母亲，	My dear mother,
我也要到大地上，	I want to go to the Earth
和哥哥姐姐在一起。”	To be with my brothers and sisters.”
兄妹俩回答说：	The brother and sister replied,
“可怜的孩子呀，	“Poor child,
你长得太漂亮，	You are too pretty;
你生得太好看，	You look too beautiful.

还没有到大地，	Before you can see the Earth
还没有见着你的哥哥姐姐，	And your brothers and sisters,
你就会在半路，	You will be snatched away
被格兰瓦娶走。”	By Kalan Wa as his bride.”
女孩子不听父母的话，	The girl did not listen
还是要到大地上，	And insisted on going to the Earth
找自己的哥哥，	To look for her brothers
找自己的姐姐。	And sisters.
她路过格兰寨时，	On her way through the Kalan Village,
被格兰瓦娶走了，	Kalan Wa married her and took her away.
她没有见到哥哥，	She did not meet her brothers,
也没有见到姐姐。	Nor did she see her sisters.
女孩和格兰瓦，	The girl and Kalan Wa
一个月生一个孩子，	Had a baby every month.
格兰寨兴旺了，	The Kalan Village became prosperous.
格兰寨热闹了。	The Kalan Village became lively.
远古，	In remote antiquity,
有个打鱼人，	There was a fisherman,
名叫木如乌英，	Whose name was Maru Wu-ing.
他每次打鱼，	Every time he went fishing,
都要经过格兰寨，	He had to pass the Kalan Village.
每当打着鱼，	When he caught fish

回家煮吃后，	And ate them at home,
肚子就会疼，	He suffered a stomachache
肚子就会胀，	And flatulence.
他便在心里想：	He thought to himself,
一定是格兰寨的枇杷鬼①，	It must be the Pipa ghost① from Kalan Village
缠着了他。	Haunting him.
木如乌英	Maru Wu-ing
找到了带兵的勒史塔那②，	Found Commander Lashi Hta-nya②
让他带上人马	And asked him to bring his troops
去烧杀格兰寨，	To slaughter and burn down the Kalan Village.
事先他们约好，	They made a deal beforehand that
格兰寨的人，	No one from the Kalan Village
一个也不能留；	Would live,
格兰寨的东西，	And nothing in it
一样也不能要。	Would be taken.
勒史塔那带着人马	Lashi Hta-nya led his troops
冲进了格兰寨，	Charging into Kalan Village,
格兰寨被杀尽了，	Which experienced slaughter

① 枇杷鬼：鬼的一种。是长头发、长指甲的美貌女性鬼，缠着人会生病。

② 勒史塔那：传说是带兵打仗的武官。

① Pipa ghost: a female ghost with long hair and nails of beauty. Those haunted would become sick.

② Lashi Hta-nya: a military officer commanding troops.

格兰寨被烧光了，	And witnessed flames.
快要离开时，	When he was about to leave,
勒史塔那看到一个女孩，	Lashi Hta-nya saw a girl,
长得真好看，	With stunning beauty,
他不忍心杀死她，	Whom he did not have the heart to kill.
便悄悄地把她藏到筒帕里。	Secretly, he hid her in a satchel.
勒史塔那带回的女孩，	The girl brought back by Lashi Hta-nya
越看越好看，	Became increasingly gorgeous
越长越美丽。	And looked increasingly attractive.
让她去守谷地，	Her work was to look after the millet field,
她守的谷地，	And sparrows did not dare
山雀不敢来，	To come close it because she was there.
女孩的漂亮，	The beauty of the girl
邻居们眼红了；	Made the neighbors green-eyed.
女孩的能干，	The competence of the girl
邻居们嫉妒了。	Made the neighbors jealous.
他们对勒史塔那说：	They said to Lashi Hta-nya,
“勒史塔那呀，	“Lashi Hta-nya,
你的女俘虏	Your female captive
没有守谷地，	Did not go to watch the millet field.
你地里的谷子	The millet in your field

快被山雀吃完了。”	Is almost eaten up by sparrows.”
听了邻居的话，	Hearing that,
勒史塔那生气了，	Lashi Hta-nya became angry.
他捡起棍子	He picked up a wooden stick
就去找小女孩。	And went to look for the girl.
他来到谷地边，	Arriving at the millet field,
听到女孩，	He heard the girl
用忧伤的比浪①声，	Telling him her grievance
向勒史塔那	With the sad sound of the bilang①:
诉说心中的委屈：	“Lashi Hta-nya,
“勒史塔那拉呀，	Do not believe your neighbors.
你别听信邻居的话，	Not a single grain
我守的谷子，	Of the millet under my watch
山雀一粒也没吃，	Has been eaten by sparrows.
谷地上的谷子，	Not a single grain
一颗也没少，	Of the millet in the field is lost.
如果你不信，	If you do not believe me,
你仔细看吧。”	Go and see for yourself.”
勒史塔那	Lashi Hta-nya
走进谷地里，	Walked into the millet field,

① 比浪：一种用谷秆做成的乐器。

① The bilang: a musical instrument made from grain straws.

见地里的谷子	And saw the millet in the field
一粒也没少，	Was not missing a single grain.
便对女孩说，	He then asked the girl,
“孩子呀，	“Kid,
在格兰寨，	In the Kalan Village,
你的父亲种什么，	What does your father plant?
你的母亲吃什么？”	What does your mother eat?”
女孩回答说：	The girl replied,
“勒史塔那拉呀，	“Lashi Hta-nya,
在格兰寨，	In the Kalan Village,
我的父亲种诗兰叶①，	My father plants Shalap plants①.
我的母亲吃诗兰叶。”	My mother eats Shalap leaves.”
听了女孩的话，	Hearing that,
勒史塔那心里想：	Lashi Hta-nya thought to himself,
女孩说的诗兰叶，	“The Shalap leaves mentioned by the girl
也许是一种灵药。	Must be an elixir.
她吃了这种灵药，	Because she has eaten it,
山雀才不敢飞到谷地里，	Sparrows do not dare to fly into the millet field.

① 诗兰叶：一种草本植物，叶宽约三指，正面有花纹，多生于低洼潮湿处，景颇人过去认为是鬼吃的东西，所以祭鬼时常用此叶。

① Shalap plant: a herbaceous plant with leaves of approximately 3–4 millimeters in width and a pattern on the front. The plant is usually found in low-lying damp places. The Jingpo people used to think it was food for ghosts, thus it was commonly used when offering sacrifice to ghosts.

我如果娶了她，
一定会有好福气。

If I marry her,
I will be blessed with good fortune."

勒史塔那娶了女孩，
他们生了许多孩子，
他们生的孩子，
生一个活一个，
而前妻的孩子，
生一个死一个，

Lashi Hta-nya married the girl
And they had numerous children.
Every one of their children
Survived after birth.
However, the children of his first wife
All died after birth.

前妻悲伤地哭着说：
"勒史塔那拉呀，
我种的不是麻芋，
所以会腐烂掉；
你的俘虏妻子，
她种的是麻芋，
所以越种越发。"
听了前妻的话，
勒史塔那领悟到，
原来后妻有枇杷鬼。
勒史塔那越想越后悔，
越想越害怕，
他想离开她。
拿定了主意，

His first wife wailed in sorrow,
"Lashi Hta-nya,
What I have planted is not taro.
That's why it rots.
Your captive wife,
What she has planted is taro.
It grows as time goes."
Hearing these words,
Lashi Hta-nya realized that
His second wife was possessed by the Pipa ghost.
The more he thought about it,
The more he regretted it,
And the more he was scared.
He was determined to leave her.

勒史塔那对后妻说：	Lashi Hta-nya said to his second wife,
“让我们带着孩子	“Let's take the children
到羌河那边去吧，	To the other side of the Qiang River
那里土地肥沃，	Where the Earth is fertile
那里日子好过。”	And life will be comfortable.”
后妻同意了，	His second wife agreed,
和勒史塔那带上孩子，	And they took the children
来到羌河的那边，	To the other side of the Qiang River,
在那里砍了地，	Where they cleared a patch of Earth
又种上庄稼。	And planted crops.
留下吃的和用的，	Leaving behind food and necessities,
勒史塔那	Lashi Hta-nya
又回到了河这边，	Came back to this side of the Qiang River
并砍断了羌河上的桥，	And cut down the bridge over it.
后妻和她的孩子们，	His second wife and the children
再也不能回到河这边。	Could not return to this side anymore.

二、迎接宁贯督　Ⅱ. Welcoming N-gon Du

远古，	In remote antiquity,
发了洪水后，	Since the start of the flood,

宁贯督住在赛如石贡山。	N-gon Du had been living on Mount Sairu Shagong.
大地上的人们，	People of the Earth,
因为没有王子，	Without their prince,
天下不稳定，	Lived in an unstable world;
人心不安宁。	Lived in a troubled world.
大地上的人们，	The people of the Earth
商量着接回宁贯督，	Talked about welcoming N-gon Du back
但不知派谁去。	But did not know whom to send to speak for them.

鸡的祖先，	The ancestors of chickens,
西所拉和西所木占说：	Sik Sok La and Sik Sok Majan said,
“让我们去吧，	“Let us do it.
我们会接回宁贯督。”	We will bring N-gon Du back.”
西所拉和西所木占	Sik Sok La and Sik Sok Majan
离开了戛昂王宫，	Left the Gaang Palace
来到赛如山，	For Mount Sairu
找到了宁贯督。	And found N-gon Du.
他们对宁贯督说：	They said to him,
“宁贯督呀，	“N-gon Du,
你离开戛昂王宫后，	Since you left the Gaang Palace,
天下不稳定，	The world has been unstable
人心不安宁，	And the people have been troubled.
你跟我们回去吧。”	Please come back with us.”

宁贯督回答说：	N-gon Du replied,
“回是要回去的，	“I will come back sooner or later,
但不知大地上的人们	But I don’t know how you are addressed
怎样称呼你们？”	By the people of the Earth?”
西所拉和西所木占说：	Sik Sok La and Sik Sok Majan said,
“大地上的人们	“The people of the Earth
叫我们西所拉和西所木占。”	Call us Sik Sok La and Sik Sok Majan.”
宁贯督对它们说：	N-gon Du said to them,
“你们的名字，	“Your names
不该叫西所拉和西所木占，	Should not be Sik Sok La and Sik Sok Majan.
我另给你们取一个名字，	I will give you another name.
就叫你们鸡吧。	I will call you chicken.
你们不能骑，	You cannot be ridden.
你们不能背，	You cannot carry things on your backs.
你们还是先回去，	Why don’t you return
去守着戛昂王宫吧。”	And guard the Gaang Palace?”
鸡离开了赛如山，	The chickens left Mount Sairu
回到戛昂王宫。	And returned to the Gaang Palace.
大地上的人们问：	The people of the Earth asked them,
“你们到了赛如山，	“You’ve been to Mount Sairu,
怎么没有接回宁贯督？”	But why haven’t you brought back N-gon Du?”
鸡回答说：	The chickens replied,

“宁贯督说了，	“N-gon Du said that
他是要回来的，	He was coming back,
但我们不能骑，	But because we cannot be ridden
也不能背，	Or carry things on our backs,
他让我们先回来守王宫。”	He told us to come back first to guard the royal palace.”

大地上的人们，	The people of the Earth
又商量接宁贯督，	Talked about welcoming N-gon Du back again,
但不知派谁去。	But they did not know whom to send.
猪的祖先，	The ancestors of the pig,
梯脱拉和梯脱木占说：	Htik Htok La and Htik Htok Majan said,
“让我们到赛如山，	“Let us do it.
我们会接回宁贯督。”	We will bring N-gon Du back.”

梯脱拉和梯脱木占	Htik Htok La and Htik Htok Majan
离开了戛昂王宫，	Left the Gaang Palace
来到赛如山，	And went to Mount Sairu.
找到了宁贯督，	They found N-gon Du
对宁贯督说，	And said to him,
“宁贯督呀，	“N-gon Du,
你离开戛昂王宫后，	Since you left the Gaang Palace
天下不稳定，	The world has been unstable
人心不安宁，	And the people have been troubled.
你跟我们回去吧。”	Please come back with us.”

宁贯督回答说：	N-gon Du replied,
“回是要回去的，	“I will come back sooner or later,
但不知大地上的人们	But I don’t know how you are addressed
怎样称呼你们？”	By the people of the Earth?”
梯脱拉和梯脱木占说：	Htik Htok La and Htik Htok Majan said,
“大地上的人们	“The people of the Earth
叫我们梯脱拉和梯脱木占。”	Call us Htik Htok La and Htik Htok Majan.”
宁贯督说：	N-gon Du said to them,
“你们的名字，	“Your names
不该叫梯脱拉和梯脱木占，	Should not be Htik Htok La and Htik Htok Majan.
我另给你们取一个名字，	I will give you another name.
就叫你们猪吧。	I will call you pig.
你们不能骑，	You cannot be ridden.
你们不能背，	You cannot carry things on your backs.
你们还是先回去，	Why don’t you return
守着王宫吧。”	And guard the Gaang Palace?”
猪离开了赛如山，	The pigs left Mount Sairu
回到戛昂王宫，	And returned to the Gaang Palace.
人们问猪说：	The people asked them,
“你们到了赛如山，	“You’ve been to Mount Sairu,
怎么没接回宁贯督？”	But why haven’t you brought back N-gon Du?”

猪回答说：	The pigs replied,
“宁贯督说了，	“N-gon Du said that
他是要回来的，	He was coming back,
但我们不能骑，	But because we cannot be ridden
也不能背，	Or carry things on our backs.
让我们先回来守王宫。”	He told us to come back first to guard the royal palace.”
大地上的人们，	The people of the Earth
又商量接宁贯督，	Talked about welcoming N-gon Du back again,
但不知派谁去。	But they did not know whom to send.
山羊的祖先，	The ancestors of goats,
空康拉和空康木占说：	Hkruk Hkrak La and Hkruk Hkrak Majan, said,
“让我们到赛如山，	“Let us do it.
我们接回宁贯督。”	We will bring N-gon Du back.”
空康拉和空康木占	Hkruk Hkrak La and Hkruk Hkrak Majan
离开戛昂王宫，	Left the Gaang Palace
来到赛如山，	And went to Mount Sairu.
找到了宁贯督，	They found N-gon Du,
对宁贯督说：	And said to him,
“宁贯督呀，	“N-gon Du,
你离开戛昂王宫后，	Since you left the Gaang Palace
天下不稳定，	The world has been unstable
人心不安宁，	And the people have been troubled.

你跟我们回去吧。”	Please come back with us.”
宁贯督回答说：	N-gon Du replied,
“回是要回去的，	“I will come back sooner or later,
但不知大地上的人们	But I don’t know how you are addressed
怎样称呼你们？”	By the people of the Earth?”
空康拉和空康木占说：	Hkruk Hkrak La and Hkruk Hkrak Majan said,
“大地上的人们	“The people of the Earth
叫我们空康拉和空康木占。”	Call us Hkruk Hkrak La and Hkruk Hkrak Majan.”
宁贯督说：	N-gon Du said to them,
“你们的名字，	“Your names should not be
不该叫空康拉和空康木占，	Hkruk Hkrak La and Hkruk Hkrak Majan.
我另给你们取一个名字，	I will give you another name.
就叫你们山羊吧。	I will call you goat.
你们不能骑，	You cannot be ridden.
你们不能背，	You cannot carry things on your backs.
你们还是先回去，	Why don’t you return
守着王宫吧。”	And guard the Gaang Palace?”
山羊离开了赛如山，	The goats left Mount Sairu
回到戛昂王宫，	And returned to the Gaang Palace.
大地上的人们问：	The people of the Earth asked the goats,
“你们到了赛如山，	“You’ve been to Mount Sairu,

怎么没有接回宁贯督？”

But why haven't you brought back N-gon Du?"

山羊回答说：
“宁贯督说了，
他是要回来的，
但我们不能骑，
也不能背，
他让我们先回来守王宫。”

The goats replied,
"N-gon Du said that
He was coming back,
But because we cannot be ridden
Or carry things on our backs,
He told us to come back first to guard the royal palace."

大地上的人们，
又商量接宁贯督，
但不知派谁去。
狗的祖先，
乌直拉和乌刚木占说：
“让我们到赛如山，
我们会接回宁贯督。”

The people of the Earth
Talked about welcoming N-gon Du back again,
But they did not know whom to send.
The ancestors of dogs,
Wujik La and Wugak Majan, said,
"Let us do it.
We will bring N-gon Du back."

乌直拉和乌刚木占
离开戛昂王宫，
来到赛如山，
找到了宁贯督，
对宁贯督说：
“宁贯督呀，
你离开戛昂王宫后，

Wujik La and Wugak Majan
Left the Gaang Palace
And went to Mount Sairu.
They found N-gon Du
And said to him,
"N-gon Du,
Since you left the Gaang Palace

天下不稳定，	The world has been unstable
人心不安宁，	And the people have been troubled.
你跟我们回去吧。”	Please come back with us."
宁贯督回答说，	N-gon Du replied,
“回是要回去的，	"I will come back sooner or later,
但不知地上的人们，	But I don't know how you are addressed
怎样称呼你们？”	By people of the Earth?"
乌直拉和乌刚木占说：	Wujik La and Wugak Majan said,
“大地上的人们	"The people of the Earth
叫我们乌直拉和乌刚木占。”	Call us Wujik La and Wugak Majan."
宁贯督说：	N-gon Du said to them,
“你们的名字，	"Your names
不该叫乌直拉和乌刚木占，	Should not be Wujik La and Wugak Majan.
我另给你们取一个名字，	I will give you another name.
就叫你们狗吧。	I will call you dog.
你们不能骑，	You cannot be ridden.
你们不能背，	You cannot carry things on your backs.
你们还是先回去，	Why don't you return
守着王宫吧。”	And guard the Gaang Palace?"
狗离开赛如山，	The dogs left Mount Sairu
回到戛昂王宫，	And returned to the Gaang Palace.

大地上的人们问：	The people of the Earth asked them,
“你们到了赛如山，	“You've been to Mount Sairu,
怎么没接回宁贯督？”	But why haven't you brought back N-gon Du?”
狗回答说：	The dogs replied,
“宁贯督说了，	“N-gon Du said that
他是要回来的，	He was coming back,
但我们不能骑，	But because we cannot be ridden,
也不能背，	And neither can we carry things on our backs,
他让我们先回来守王宫。”	He told us to come back first to guard the royal palace.”
大地上的人们，	The people of the Earth
又商量接宁贯督，	Talked about welcoming N-gon Du back again,
但不知派谁去。	But they did not know whom to send.
黄牛的祖先，	The ancestors of cattle,
盆邦拉和盆邦木占说：	Hputbyang La and Hputbyang Majan said,
“让我们到赛如山，	“Let us do it.
我们会接回宁贯督。”	We will bring N-gon Du back.”
盆邦拉和盆邦木占	Hputbyang La and Hputbyang Majan
离开戛昂王宫，	Left the Gaang Palace
来到赛如山，	And went to Mount Sairu.
找到了宁贯督，	They found N-gon Du
对宁贯督说：	And said to him,

“宁贯督呀，	“N-gon Du,
你离开戛昂王宫后，	Since you left the Gaang Palace
天下不稳定，	The world has been unstable
人心不安宁，	And the people have been troubled.
你跟我们回去吧。”	Please come back with us.”
宁贯督回答说：	N-gon Du replied,
“回是要回去的，	“I will come back sooner or later,
但不知大地上人们	But I don't know how you are addressed
怎样称呼你们？”	By the people of the Earth?”
盆邦拉和盆邦木占说：	Hputbyang La and Hputbyang Majan said,
“大地上的人们	“The people of the Earth
叫我们盆邦拉和盆邦木占。”	Call us Hputbyang La and Hputbyang Majan.”
宁贯督说：	N-gon Du said to them,
“你们的名字，	“Your names should not be
不该叫盆邦拉和盆邦木占，	Hputbyang La and Hputbyang Majan.
我另给你们取一个名字，	I will give you another name.
就叫你们黄牛吧。	I will call you cattle.
你们不能骑，	You cannot be ridden.
你们不能背，	You cannot carry things on your backs.
你们还是先回去，	Why don't you return
守着王宫吧。”	And guard the Gaang Palace?”

黄牛离开赛如山，	The cattle left Mount Sairu
回到了戛昂王宫，	And returned to the Gaang Palace.
大地上的人们问：	The people of the Earth asked them,
“你们到了赛如山，	“You’ve been to Mount Sairu,
怎么没接回宁贯督？”	But why haven’t you brought back N-gon Du?”
黄牛回答说：	The cattle replied,
“宁贯督说了，	“N-gon Du said that
他是要回来的，	He was coming back,
但我们不能骑，	But because we cannot be ridden,
也不能背，	And neither can we carry things on our backs,
他让我们先回来守王宫。”	He told us to come back first to guard the royal palace.”

大地上的人们，	The people of the Earth
又商量接宁贯督，	Talked about welcoming N-gon Du back again,
但不知派谁去。	But they did not know whom to send.
水牛的祖先，	The ancestors of water buffalos,
乌崩拉和乌邦木占说：	Wubung La and Wubang Majan, said,
“让我们到赛如山，	“Let us do it.
我们会接回宁贯督。”	We will bring N-gon Du back.”

乌崩拉和乌邦木占，	Wubung La and Wubang Majan
离开戛昂王宫，	Left the Gaang Palace
来到赛如山，	And went to Mount Sairu.
找到了宁贯督，	They found N-gon Du

对宁贯督说：	And said to him,
“宁贯督呀，	“N-gon Du,
你离开戛昂王宫后，	Since you left the Gaang Palace
天下不稳定，	The world has been unstable
人心不安宁，	And the people have been troubled.
你跟我们回去吧。”	Please come back with us.”
宁贯督回答说：	N-gon Du replied,
“回是要回去的，	“I will come back sooner or later,
但不知大地上的人们	But I don’t know how you are addressed
怎样称呼你们？”	By the people of the Earth?”
乌崩拉和乌邦木占说：	Wubung La and Wubang Majan said,
“大地上的人们	“The people of the Earth,
叫我们乌崩拉和乌邦木占。”	Call us Wubung La and Wubang Majan.”
宁贯督说：	N-gon Du said to them,
“你们的名字，	“Your names should not be
不该叫乌崩拉和乌崩木占，	Wubung La and Wubang Majan.
我另给你们取一个名字，	I will give you another name.
就叫你们水牛吧。	I will call you water buffalo.
你们不能骑，	You cannot be ridden.
你们不能背，	You cannot carry things on your backs.
你们还是先回去，	Why don’t you return
守着王宫吧。”	And guard the Gaang Palace?”

水牛离开赛如山，　The water buffalos left Mount Sairu
回到戛昂王宫，　And returned to the Gaang Palace.
大地上的人们问：　The people of the Earth asked the water buffalos,
“你们到了赛如山，　“You’ve been to Mount Sairu,
怎么没有接回宁贯督？”　But why haven’t you brought back N-gon Du?”
水牛回答说：　The water buffalos replied,
“宁贯督说了，　“N-gon Du said that
他是要回来的，　He was coming back,
但我们不能骑，　But because we cannot be ridden
也不能背，　And neither can we carry things on our backs,
他让我们先回来守王宫。”　He told us to come back first to guard the royal palace.”

大地上的人们，　The people of the Earth
又商量接宁贯督，　Talked about welcoming N-gon Du back again,
但不知派谁去。　But they did not know whom to send.
牦牛的祖先，　The ancestors of yaks,
乌冈拉和乌冈木占说：　Wugang La and Wugang Majan, said,
“让我们到赛如山，　“Let us do it.
我们会接回宁贯督。”　We will bring N-gon Du back.”

乌冈拉和乌冈木占　Wugang La and Wugang Majan
离开戛昂王宫，　Left the Gaang Palace
来到赛如山，　And went to Mount Sairu.

找到了宁贯督，	They found N-gon Du
对宁贯督说：	And said to him,
“宁贯督呀，	“N-gon Du,
你离开戛昂王宫后，	Since you left the Gaang Palace
天下不稳定，	The world has been unstable
人心不安宁，	And the people have been troubled.
你跟我们回去吧。”	Please come back with us.”
宁贯督回答说：	N-gon Du replied,
“回是要回去的，	“I will come back sooner or later,
但不知大地上的人们	But I don’t know how you are addressed
怎样称呼你们？”	By the people of the Earth?”
乌冈拉和乌冈木占说：	Wugang La and Wugang Majan said,
“大地上的人们	“The people of the Earth
叫我们乌冈拉和乌冈木占。”	Call us Wugang La and Wugang Majan.”
宁贯督说：	N-gon Du said to them,
“你们的名字，	“Your names should not be
不该叫乌冈拉和乌冈木占，	Wugang La and Wugang Majan.
我另给你们取一个名字，	I will give you another name.
就叫你们牦牛吧。	I will call you yak.
你们不能骑，	You cannot be ridden.
你们不能背，	You cannot carry things on your backs.
你们还是先回去，	Why don’t you return

守着王宫吧。”	And guard the Gaang Palace?”
牦牛离开赛如山，	The yaks left Mount Sairu
回到戛昂王宫，	And returned to the Gaang Palace.
大地上的人们问：	The people of the Earth asked them,
“你们到了赛如山，	“You've been to Mount Sairu,
怎么没有接回宁贯督？”	But why haven't you brought back N-gon Du?”
牦牛回答说：	The yaks replied,
“宁贯督说了，	“N-gon Du said that
他是要回来的，	He was coming back,
但我们不能骑，	But because we cannot be ridden
也不能背，	And neither can we carry things on our backs,
他让我们先回来守王宫。”	He told us to come back first to guard the royal palace.”
大地上的人们，	The people of the Earth
又商量接宁贯督，	Talked about welcoming N-gon Du back again,
但不知派谁去。	But they did not know whom to send.
马的祖先，	The ancestors of horses,
冬达拉和冬达木占说：	Duk Dak La and Duk Dak Majan, said,
“我们能背，	“We can carry things on our backs
我们能骑。	And we can be ridden.
让我们到赛如山，	Let us to go to Mount Sairu.
我们会接回宁贯督。”	We will bring N-gon Du back.”

冬达拉和冬达木占	Duk Dak La and Duk Dak Majan
离开了戛昂王宫，	Left the Gaang Palace
来到赛如山，	And went to Mount Sairu.
找到了宁贯督，	They found N-gon Du
对宁贯督说：	And said to him,
“宁贯督呀，	“N-gon Du,
你离开戛昂王宫后，	Since you left the Gaang Palace
天下不稳定，	The world has been troubled
人心不安宁，	And the people have been anxious.
你跟我们回去吧。”	Please come back with us.”
宁贯督回答说：	N-gon Du replied,
“回是要回去的，	“I will come back sooner or later,
但不知大地上的人们	But I don’t know how you are addressed
怎样称呼你们？”	By the people of the Earth?”
冬达拉和冬达木占说：	Duk Dak La and Duk Dak Majan said,
“大地上的人们	“The people of the Earth
叫我们冬达拉和冬达木占。”	Call us Duk Dak La and Duk Dak Majan.”
宁贯督说：	N-gon Du said to them,
“你们的名字，	“Your names should not be
不该叫冬达拉和冬达木占，	Duk Dak La and Duk Dak Majan.
我另给你们取一个名字，	I will give you another name.
就叫你们马吧。	I will call you horse.

你们能骑，	You can be ridden.
你们能背，	You can carry things on your backs.
我就骑着你们回王宫吧。”	I will ride you to return to the Royal Palace.”
吃到赛如山的草，	Eating the grass of Mount Sairu
饮了赛如山的水，	And drinking its water,
马能负重了，	The horses can carry heavy burdens
马能远行了，	And travel far.
宁贯督骑着马①，	N-gon Du returned to the Gaang Palace①
回到了戛昂王宫。	On horseback.
远古，	In remote antiquity,
发洪水的时候，	When the flood came,
蛮横的九兄弟，	The nine bullying brothers
躲到了乌崩山，	Hid on Mount Wubung.
洪水退去后，	When the flood receded,
他们又回到大地上，	They returned to the Earth
继续在人间作乱。	And resumed their atrocities.
看见九兄弟	Seeing the nine brothers
还是这样无理，	Being unreasonably troublesome,

① 宁贯督骑着马：过去景颇族官员出门有骑马的规矩，据传说就源于宁贯督骑着马从赛如山回到大地。

① In old times, Jingpo officials usually went out on horseback, a custom initiated by N-gon Du.

宁贯督心里想，	N-gon Du thought that
要想天下稳定，	The nine brothers must be eliminated
要想人心安宁，	So that the people could live peacefully
先得除掉九兄弟。	In a stable world.
宁贯督想好主意，	Having a plan set, N-gon Du
请来了九兄弟。	Invited the nine brothers over.
他一手拿着见旺菌[1]，	He held a mushroom in one hand
一手提着大官刀，	And a large machete in the other.
对九兄弟说："侄子们呀，	He said to the nine brothers, "My nephews,
我们不能再斗气，	We should fight no more.
我们不能再对立，	We should be antagonistic no more.
吃下这见旺菌，	Let's share the mushroom
我们就和好吧。"	And make up with each other."
听了宁贯督的话，	Hearing that,
九兄弟相信了。	The nine brothers believed him.
宁贯督拿起人官刀	N-gon Du lifted the large machete
开始削见旺菌，	And started to cut the mushroom into two halves.
九兄弟吃刀那边的，	N-gon Du ate one half,
宁贯督吃刀这边的，	And the nine brothers ate the other half,
刀的那面涂着孔雀胆，	Which was poisoned with peacock gall

[1] 见旺菌：传说是一种可以吃的菌子。

九兄弟吃了见旺菌，　　On the other side of the machete.
一下就死了八个，　　Eight of the nine brothers died immediately.
最后剩下老五，　　The surviving one was the fifth brother,
名叫乌崩当山。　　Whose name was Wubung Tang Shan.

百姓们恨死了九兄弟，　　The people loathed the nine brothers.
把乌崩当山　　They took Wubung Tang Shan
带到下鱼笼的地方，　　To where fish traps were placed under water.
贪心的乌崩当山　　Greedy Wubung Tang Shan,
看着鱼笼里活蹦乱跳的鱼，　　Seeing fish jumping in the traps,
再也收不住自己的手　　Could not hold back his hands.
当他进水取鱼时，　　When he went into the water to catch the fish,
百姓们锋利的长刀，　　People beheaded him
砍下了他的头颅。　　With sharp long machetes.
九兄弟死光了，　　Now that all the nine brothers
九兄弟灭绝了，　　Were eliminated,
天下稳定了，　　The world was stable
人心安宁了。　　And the people were peaceful.

宁贯督带着百姓，　　N-gon Du and his people
建成了罗芒王宫，　　Built the Lo-myang Palace,
盖起了勒章王宫，　　Constructed the Lachyang Palace,
建成了松康王宫，　　Built the Sumhkran Palace,
盖好了荣布王宫。　　And constructed the Rongput Palace.

东面有了王宫，
西面有了王宫，
南面有了王宫，
北面也有了王宫。

There was a palace in the east.
There was a palace in the west.
There was a palace in the south.
There was a palace in the north, too.

三、迎接德如贡散

Ⅲ. Welcoming Daru Gumsan

远古，
彭干支伦和木占威纯
生下了德如贡散，
他将帮助王子，
他将管理王业，
因为宁贯督打造天地，
怕量天的标杆打着他，
怕丈地的绳索碰着他，
潘格来遮能代
把他送到勒木卢酸天宫。

In remote antiquity,
Hpunggam Chyanun and Majan Woishun
Gave birth to Daru Gumsan.
He would help the prince;
He would manage the kingdom.
While N-gon Du was creating the world,
He was worried the pole measuring the Sky would hit him
And the rope mapping the Earth would hurt him.
So Hpan Galai Chye Ningdai
Sent him to Lamu Lupson, the heavenly palace.

由于没有德如贡散，
无人帮助王子，
无人管理王业，

Without Daru Gumsan,
There was no one to help the prince
And no one to manage the kingdom.

王位不巩固，	The throne was not solid
天下不兴旺。	And the world was not prosperous.
大地上的人们，	The people of the Earth
商量去接德如贡散，	Discussed welcoming Daru Gumsan back,
但不知派谁去。	But they did not know whom to send.
鸡出来说：	A chicken stood out and said,
“让我到天宫去，	“Let me go to the heavenly palace
我会接回德如贡散。”	And I will bring Daru Gumsan back.”
鸡离开戛昂王宫，	The chicken left the Gaang Palace,
顺着云路走，	Following the road of the clouds,
沿着风路飞，	Flying along the path of the wind,
来到了天宫，	And arriving at the heavenly palace
德如贡散问它说：	Daru Gumsan asked it,
“你是谁呀，	“Who are you?
你来做什么？”	What are you doing here?”
鸡回答说：	The chicken answered,
“我是大地上的鸡，	“I am a chicken from the Earth.
我来接你回大地。	I am here to welcome you back.
德如贡散呀，	Daru Gumsan,
因为没有你，	Because you are away,
无人帮助王子，	No one helps the prince;
无人管理王业，	No one manages the kingdom.

王位不巩固，　The throne is not consolidated.
天下不兴旺，　The world is not prosperous.
你就跟我回大地吧。”　Come back to the Earth with me please.”

德如贡散说：　Daru Gumsan said,
“鸡呀，　“Chicken,
我是要回去的，　I will be back sooner or later,
但你的脚太细，　But your legs are too slim
翅膀太软，　And your wings too soft
驮不动我，　To carry me
也背不动我。　On your back.
你还是先回去，　Why don't you go back
让驮得动我、　And send someone who can carry me
背得动我的来接吧。”　To pick me up?”
德如贡散说完，　Daru Gumsan said this
破开了鸡脚爪，　And cut open the feet of the chicken.
鸡从此才有了扒食的爪。　Thus chickens have paws to pick out food.

鸡回到戛昂王宫，　The chicken went back to the Gaang Palace
大地上的人们问：　And the people of the Earth asked,
“你到了天宫，　“You've been to the heavenly palace,
怎么没接回德如贡散？”　Why haven't you brought back Daru Gumsan?”
鸡回答说：　The chicken answered,
“德如贡散说，　“Daru Gumsan said that

我的脚太细，	My legs are too slim
翅膀太软，	And the wings too soft
驮不动他，	To carry him.
分开了我的脚爪，	He split my feet
让驮得动他、	And asked us to send someone who can carry him
也背得动他的去接他。”	And support him to pick him up."
大地上的人们，	The people of the Earth
又商量去接德如贡散，	Discussed welcoming Daru Gumsan back again,
但不知派谁去。	But did not know whom to send.
猪出来说：	The pig stood out and said,
“让我到天宫去，	"Let me go to the heavenly palace
我会接回德如贡散。”	And I will bring Daru Gumsan back."
猪离开戛昂王宫，	The pig left the Gaang Palace,
顺着云路走，	Following the road of the clouds,
沿着风路去，	Flying along the path of the wind,
来到了天宫，	And arriving at the heavenly palace
德如贡散问它说：	Daru Gumsan asked it,
“你是谁呀，	"Who are you?
你来做什么？”	What are you doing here?"
猪回答说：	The pig answered,
“我是大地上的猪，	"I am a pig from the Earth.

我来接你回大地，	I am here to welcome you back.
德如贡散呀，	Daru Gumsan,
因为没有你，	Because you are away,
无人帮助王子，	No one helps the prince;
无人管理王业，	No one manages the kingdom.
王位不巩固，	The throne is not consolidated.
天下不兴旺，	The world is not prosperous.
你就跟我回大地吧。”	Come back to the Earth with me please.”
德如贡散说：	Daru Gumsan said,
“猪呀，	“Pig,
我是要回去的，	I will be back sooner or later,
但你的脚太短，	But your legs are too short
力气太小，	And the strength too weak
驮不动我，	To carry me
也背不动我。	On your back.
你还是先回去，	Why don't you go back
让驮得动我、	And send someone who can carry me
背得动我的来接吧。”	To pick me up?”
德如贡散说完，	Daru Gumsan said this
给猪分开了脚蹄，	And cut open the feet of the pig.
猪从此有了分开的蹄子。	Thus pigs have split hooves ever after.
猪回到戛昂王宫，	The pig went back to the Gaang Palace

大地上的人们问：
“你到了天宫，
怎么没接回德如贡散？”
猪回答说：
“德如贡散说，
我的脚太短，
力气太小，
驮不动他，
他分开了我的蹄子，
让背得动他、
也驮得动他的去接他。”

And the people of the Earth asked,
“You’ve been to the heavenly palace,
Why haven’t you brought Daru Gumsan back?”
The pig answered,
“Daru Gumsan said that
My legs are too short
And the strength too weak
To carry him.
He split my feet
And asked us to send someone
Who can carry him to pick him up.”

大地上的人们，
又商量去接德如贡散，
但不知派谁去。
山羊出来说：
“让我到天宫去，
我会接回德如贡散。”

The people of the Earth
Discussed welcoming Daru Gumsan back again,
But did not know whom to send.
The goat stood out and said,
“Let me go to the heavenly palace
And I will bring Daru Gumsan back.”

山羊离开戛昂王宫，
顺着云路走，
沿着风路去，
来到了天宫，
德如贡散问它说：

The goat left the Gaang Palace,
Following the road of the clouds,
Flying along the path of the wind,
And arriving at the heavenly palace
Daru Gumsan asked it,

“你是谁呀，	“Who are you?
你来做什么？”	What are you doing here?”
山羊回答说：	The goat answered,
“我是大地上的山羊，	“I am a goat from the Earth.
我来接你回大地，	I am here to welcome you back.
德如贡散呀，	Daru Gumsan,
因为没有你，	Because you are away,
无人帮助王子，	No one helps the prince,
无人管理王业，	And no one manages the kingdom.
王位不巩固，	The throne is not consolidated,
天下不兴旺，	And the world is not prosperous.
你就跟我回大地吧。”	Come back to the Earth with me please.”
德如贡散说：	Daru Gumsan said,
“山羊呀，	“Goat,
我是要回去的，	I will be back sooner or later,
但你的脚太细，	But your legs are too slim
力气太小，	And the strength too weak
驮不动我，	To carry me
也背不动我。	On your back.
你还是先回去，	Why don’t you go back
让驮得动我，	And send someone who can carry me
背得动我的来接吧。”	To pick me up?”

德如贡散说完，	Daru Gumsan said this
分开了山羊的脚蹄，	And cut open the feet of the goat.
从此山羊才有了分开的脚蹄。	Thus goats have split paws ever after.
山羊回到戛昂王宫，	The goat went back to the Gaang Palace
大地上的人们问：	And the people of the Earth asked,
"你到了天宫，	"You've been to the heavenly palace,
怎么没接回德如贡散？"	Why haven't you brought Daru Gumsan?"
山羊回答说：	The goat answered,
"德如贡散说：	"Daru Gumsan said
"我的脚太细，	My legs are too slim
力气太小，	And strength too weak
驮不动他，	To carry him
也背不动他。	On my back.
他分开了我的脚蹄，	He split my feet
让驮得动他、	And asked us to send someone
也背得动他的去接他。"	Who can carry him to pick him up."
大地上的人们，	The people of the Earth
又商量接德如贡散，	Discussed welcoming Daru Gumsan back again,
但不知派谁去。	But did not know whom to send.
狗出来说：	The dog stood out and said,
"让我到天宫去，	"Let me go to the heavenly palace

我会接回德如贡散。”	And I will bring Daru Gumsan back.”
狗离开戛昂王宫，	The dog left the Gaang Palace,
顺着云路走，	Following the road of the clouds,
沿着风路去，	Flying along the path of the wind,
来到了天宫，	And arriving at the heavenly palace
德如贡散问它说：	Daru Gumsan asked it,
“你是谁呀，	“Who are you?
你来做什么？”	What are you doing here?”
狗回答说：	The dog answered,
“我是大地上的狗，	“I am a dog from the Earth.
我来接你回大地，	I am here to welcome you back.
德如贡散呀，	Daru Gumsan,
因为没有你，	Because you are away,
无人帮助王子，	No one helps the prince,
无人管理王业，	And no one manages the kingdom.
王位不巩固，	The throne is not consolidated.
天下不兴旺，	The world is not prosperous.
你就跟我回去吧。”	Come back to the Earth with me please.”
德如贡散说：	Daru Gumsan said,
“狗呀，	“Dog,
我是要回去的，	I will be back sooner or later,

但你的脚太细，	But your legs are too slim
力气太小，	And the strength too weak
驮不动我，	To carry me
也背不动我，	On your back.
你还是先回去，	Why don't you go back
让驮得动我、	And send someone who can carry me
背得动我的来接吧。”	To pick me up?"
德如贡说完，	Daru Gumsan said this
给狗分开了脚掌，	And cut open the feet of the dog.
狗从此才有了分开的脚掌。	Thus dogs have split paws ever after.
狗回到戛昂王宫，	The dog went back to the Gaang Palace
大地上的人们问：	And the people of the Earth asked,
“你到了天宫，	"You've been to the heavenly palace,
怎么没有接回德如贡散？”	Why haven't you brought Daru Gumsan back?"
狗回答说：	The dog answered,
“德如贡散说，	"Daru Gumsan said that
我的脚太细，	My legs are too slim
力气太小，	And the strength too weak
驮不动他，	To carry him
也背不动他，	On my back.
他分开了我的脚掌，	He split my feet
让驮得动他、	And asked us to send someone

也背得动他的去接他。”	Who can carry him to pick him up."
大地上的人们，	The people of the Earth
又商量接德如贡散，	Discussed welcoming Daru Gumsan back again,
但不知派谁去。	But did not know whom to send.
黄牛出来说：	The ox stood out and said,
“让我到天宫去，	"Let me go to the heavenly palace
我会接回德如贡散。”	And I will bring Daru Gumsan back."
黄牛离开戛昂王宫，	The ox left the Gaang Palace,
顺着云路走，	Following the road of the clouds,
沿着风路去，	Flying along the path of the wind,
来到了天宫，	And arriving at the heavenly palace
德如贡散问它说：	Daru Gumsan asked it,
“你是谁呀，	"Who are you?
你来做什么？”	What are you doing here?"
黄牛回答说：	The ox answered,
“我是大地上的黄牛，	"I am an ox from the Earth.
我来接你回大地。	I am here to welcome you back.
德如贡散呀，	Daru Gumsan,
因为没有你，	Because you are away,
无人帮助王子，	No one helps the prince;
无人管理王业，	No one manages the kingdom.

王位不巩固，	The throne is not consolidated.
天下不兴旺，	The world is not prosperous.
你就跟我回大地吧。”	Come back to the Earth with me please."
德如贡散说：	Daru Gumsan said,
“黄牛呀，	"Ox,
我是要回去的，	I will be back sooner or later,
但你的角太尖，	But your horns are too sharp
腰太粗，	And the back too large
驮不动我，	To carry me
也背不动我。	On your back.
你还是先回去，	Why don't you go back
让驮得动我、	And send someone who can carry me
也背得动我的来接吧。”	To pick me up?"
德如贡散说完，	Daru Gumsan said this
给黄牛分开了脚蹄，	And cut open the feet of the ox.
黄牛从此才有了分开的脚蹄。	Thus oxen have split hooves ever after.
黄牛回到戛昂王宫，	The ox went back to the Gaang Palace
大地上的人们问：	And the people of the Earth asked,
“你到了天宫，	"You've been to heavenly palace,
怎么没接回德如贡散？”	Why haven't you brought Daru Gumsan back?"
黄牛回答说：	The ox answered,

“德如贡散说，	“Daru Gumsan said that
我的角太尖，	My horns are too sharp
腰太粗，	And the back too large
驮不动他，	To carry him.
他分开了我的脚蹄，	He split my feet
让驮得动他、	And asked us to send someone
也背得动他的去接他。”	Who can carry him to pick him up.”

大地上的人们，	The people of the Earth
又商量去接德如贡散，	Discussed welcoming Daru Gumsan back again,
但不知派谁去。	But did not know whom to send.
水牛出来说：	The water buffalo stood out and said,
“让我到天宫去，	“Let me go to the heavenly palace
我会接回德如贡散。”	And I will bring Daru Gumsan back.”

水牛离开戞昂王宫，	The water buffalo left the Gaang Palace,
顺着云路走，	Following the road of the clouds,
沿着风路去，	Flying along the path of the wind,
来到了天宫，	And arriving at the heavenly palace
德如贡散问它说：	Daru Gumsan asked it,
“你是谁呀，	“Who are you?
你来做什么？”	What are you doing here?”

水牛回答说：	The water buffalo answered,

“我是大地上的水牛，
我来接你回大地，
德如贡散呀，
因为没有你，
无人帮助王子，
无人管理王业，
王位不巩固，
天下不兴旺，
你就跟我回大地吧。”

“I am a water buffalo from the Earth.
I am here to welcome you back.
Daru Gumsan,
Because you are away,
No one helps the prince,
No one manages the kingdom.
The throne is not consolidated.
The world is not prosperous.
Come back to the Earth with me please.”

德如贡散说：
“水牛呀，
我是要回去的，
但你的角太尖，
腰太粗，
驮不动我，
也背不动我。
你还是先回去，
让驮得动我、
背得动我的来接我。”
德如贡散说完，
给水牛分开了脚蹄，
水牛从此才有了分开的脚蹄。

Daru Gumsan said,
“Water buffalo,
I will be back sooner or later,
But your horns are too sharp
And the back too large
To carry me
On your back.
Why don’t you go back
And send someone who can carry me
To pick me up?”
Daru Gumsan said this
And cut open the hooves of the buffalo.
Thus water buffaloes have split hooves ever after.

水牛回到戛昂王宫，	The water buffalo went back to the Gaang Palace
大地上的人们问：	And the people of the Earth asked,
“你到了天宫，	“You've been to the heavenly palace,
怎么没有接回德如贡散？”	Why haven't you brought Daru Gumsan back?”
水牛回答说：	The water buffalo answered,
“德如贡散说，	“Daru Gumsan said that
我的角太尖，	My horns are too sharp
腰太粗，	And the back too large
驮不动他，	To carry him
也背不动他，	On my back.
他分开我的脚蹄，	He split my hooves
让驮得动他、	And asked me to send someone
也背得动他的去接他。”	Who can carry him to pick him up.”
大地上的人们，	The people of the Earth
又商量去接德如贡散，	Discussed welcoming Daru Gumsan back again,
但不知派谁去。	But did not know whom to send
牦牛出来说：	The yak stood out and said,
“让我到天宫，	“Let me go to the heavenly palace
我会接回德如贡散。”	And I will bring Daru Gumsan back.”
牦牛离开戛昂王宫，	The yak left the Gaang Palace,
顺着云路走，	Following the road of the clouds,

沿着风路去，	Flying along the path of the wind,
来到了天宫，	And arriving at the heavenly palace
德如贡散问它说：	Daru Gumsan asked it,
“你是谁呀，	“Who are you?
你来做什么？”	What are you doing here?”

牦牛回答说：	The yak answered,
“我是大地上的牦牛，	“I am a yak from the Earth.
我来接你回大地。	I am here to welcome you back.
德如贡散呀，	Daru Gumsan,
因为没有你，	Because you are away,
无人帮助王子，	No one helps the prince;
无人管理王业，	No one manages the kingdom.
王位不巩固，	The throne is not consolidated.
天下不兴旺，	The world is not prosperous.
你就跟我回大地吧。”	Come back to the Earth with me please.”

德如贡散说：	Daru Gumsan said,
“牦牛呀，	“Yak,
我是要回去的，	I will be back sooner or later,
但你的角太尖，	But your horns are too sharp
腰太粗，	And the back too large
驮不动我，	To carry me
也背不动我。	On your back.

你还是先回去，	Why don't you go back
让驮得动我、	And send someone who can carry me
背得动我的来接我。”	To pick me up?"
德如贡散说完，	Daru Gumsan said this
给牦牛分开了脚蹄，	And cut open the hooves of the yak.
牦牛从此才有了分开的脚蹄。	Thus yaks have split hooves ever after.
牦牛回到戛昂王宫，	The yak went back to the Gaang Palace
大地上的人们问：	And the people of the Earth asked,
“你到了天宫，	"You've been to the heavenly palace,
怎么没接回德如贡散？”	Why haven't you brought Daru Gumsan back?"
牦牛回答说：	The yak answered,
“德如贡散说，	"Daru Gumsan said that
我的角太尖，	My horns are too sharp
腰太粗，	And the back too large
驮不动他，	To carry him.
他分开了我的脚蹄，	He split my hooves
让驮得动他、	And asked us to send someone
也背得动他的去接他。”	Who can carry him to pick him up."
大地上的人们，	The people of the Earth
又商量去接德如贡散，	Discussed welcoming Daru Gumsan back again,
但不知派谁去。	But did not know whom to send.

马出来说：	The horse stood out and said,
“让我到天宫去，	“Let me go to the heavenly palace
我会接回德如贡散。”	And I will bring Daru Gumsan back.”
马离开戛昂王宫，	The horse left the Gaang Palace,
顺着云路走，	Following the road of the clouds,
沿着风路去，	Flying along the path of the wind,
来到了天宫，	And arriving at the heavenly palace
德如贡散问它说：	Daru Gumsan asked it,
“你是谁呀，	“Who are you?
你来做什么？”	What are you doing here?”
马回答说：	The horse answered,
“我是大地上的马，	“I am a horse from the Earth.
我来接你回大地，	I am here to welcome you back.
德如贡散呀，	Daru Gumsan,
因为没有你，	Because you are away,
无人帮助王子，	No one helps the prince;
无人管理王业，	No one manages the kingdom.
王位不巩固，	The throne is not consolidated.
天下不兴旺，	The world is not prosperous.
你就跟我回大地吧。”	Come back to the Earth with me please.”
德如贡散说：	Daru Gumsan said,

"马呀，
我是要回去的，
你的力气大，
脚也快，
驮得动我，
也背得动我。
我就骑着你回去。"

"Horse,
I will be back sooner or later.
You are strong
And fast,
And able to carry me and
Bear my weight.
I will ride you back."

马吃了天宫的草，
马饮了天宫的水，
马能负重了，
马能远行了，
德如贡散
翻身骑上马，
离开了勒木卢酸天宫，
回到了大地上。

Because the horse ate the grass
And drank the water of the heavenly palace.
It was able to carry a heavy load
And to travel afar.
Daru Gumsan
Mounted the horse,
Left Lamu Lupson, the heavenly palace,
And returned to the Earth.

德如贡散，
回到戛昂王宫，
行使王子职权，
管理天下大业，
王位巩固了，
天下兴旺了。

Daru Gumsan
Returned to the Gaang Palace.
He took the role of the prince
And managed the empire.
The throne was consolidated,
And the world was prosperous.

四、德如朋（宁贯督的大哥）

Ⅳ. Daru Hpung (eldest brother of N-gon Du)

远古，	In remote antiquity,
德如朋对孩子们说：	Daru Hpung said to his children,
“孩子们呀，	“Children,
我想吃鲜鱼，	I would like some fresh fish.
你们去堵水捉鱼吧，	Why don’t you go block the water and catch fish?
等你们堵好水，	Once you have blocked the water,
我会来下鱼药。”	I will come and scatter fish poison.”
德如朋的孩子们，	The children of Daru Hpung,
照父亲说的话，	Following the words of their father,
来到河里堵好水。	Came to the river to block the water.
德如朋吃了闹鱼药，	Daru Hpung took the fish poison
来到堵水的地方，	And came to where they were blocking the water
拉下了大便。	And emptied his bowels.
德如朋的孩子们，	The children of Daru Hpung
见上游的水面上，	Saw the waste of their father
漂来了父亲的粪便，	Floating down from upstream of the river.

都气愤地说：	They all said angrily,
“今天的力气，	“Today our efforts
算是白花了，	Are totally wasted.
父亲这样对我们，	Father treats us like this.
只有把他赶走。”	We have no choice but drive him away.”
德如朋的孩子们，	Thus the children of Daru Hpung
赶走了德如朋。	Drove him away.
到了深夜里，	Late at night,
德如朋悄悄回到家边，	Daru Hpung came back near the house quietly
听到小儿子说：	And heard his youngest son saying,
“天这么黑，	“It’s pitch black.
父亲不知在哪里，	I wonder where father is
父亲不知怎样了。”	And how he is going.”
听了小儿子的话，	Hearing the words of his youngest son,
德如朋把小儿子，	Daru Hpung quietly called him
轻轻地唤到门外，	To come outside of the door,
对他嘱咐道：	He told the son,
“孩子呀，	“Child,
将来盖房子，	If you are going to build a house in the future
如果不会盖，	And do not know how to do it,
就看着我的骨架盖。	Take a look at my skeleton.
不知取木料的时候，	If you do not know when to cut wood

不知道盖房子的季节，	Or which season to build a house,
你就牢记住，	Just keep in mind,
谷子黄的时候砍木料，	Cut wood when the grain turns yellow
红木树花开的时候盖房子。”	And build houses when the redwood is in blossom."
德如朋给小儿子留下话后，	After Daru Hpung left his son this message,
就死在远方的峭壁上。	He died on a sheer cliff far away.
德如朋的妻子，	Daru Hpung's wife
通南珍木占，	Htingnam Chyen Majan
和女儿通南退木宽，	And his daughter Htingnam Htoi Mahkon,
背上饭包，	Carrying food bags
带上酒筒，	And taking wine cylinders,
到处寻找德如朋。	Looked for Daru Hpung everywhere.
她们来到河岔口，	They came to the crossing of two rivers.
母亲对女儿说：	The mother said to the daughter,
“孩子呀，	"Child,
你沿着诗能河寻，	You look for him along the Shaning River.
我顺着登谷河找，	I will look for him down the Dinggu River.
到了水源头，	We will meet again
我们再相会。”	At the source of the rivers."
照母亲说的话，	Following the words of her mother,
女儿顺着诗能河找，	The daughter started looking for along the Shaning River,
母亲沿着登谷河寻，	And the mother looked for him down the Dinggu River.

还没有到水源头，	Before they could reach the source,
女儿就饿死了，	The daughter was starved to death
母亲就累死了，	And the mother was exhausted to death.
她们都成了知了，	They both turned into cicadas,
在森林里互相呼喊。	Calling each other's name in the forest.
"努依，努依①"，	"Nu-yi, Nu-yi①"
这是女儿喊母亲的声音；	Was the sound of the daughter calling her mother.
"沙依，沙依②"，	"Sha-yi, Sha-yi②"
这是母亲喊女儿的声音。	Was the sound of the mother calling her daughter.
从此，森林里，	Thereafter in the forest,
有了努依知了，	There were Nu-yi cicadas
也有了沙依知了。	And Sha-yi cicadas.
在德如朋安息的地方，	From where Daru Hpung rested in peace
吹出了一阵阵疾风，	Came gusts of wind.
在落着他的头发的地方，	Where his hair fell
生出各种草；	Grew different varieties of grass.
在落着他的耳朵的地方，	Where his ears fell
长出了杜鹃花；	Grew bushes of azalea.
在落着他的眼睛的地方，	From where his eyes fell
开出了诺报花；	Nobao flowers bloomed.

① 努依：景颇语"妈呀"之意。
② 沙依：景颇语"儿呀"之意。

① Nu-yi: It means "mother" in the Jingpo language.
② Sha-yi: It means "son" in the Jingpo language.

在落着他的屁股的地方，	From where his hips fell
传出了季节鸟的叫声；	Came the sounds of seasonal birds.
在落着他的嘴的地方，	From where his mouth fell
传来了各种小鸟的声音。	Came the songs of various birds.
从此，大地上，	Thereafter on the Earth,
分出了不同的季节。	Different seasons took turns.

第四章　宁贯督娶亲

Canto 4　N-gon Du Getting Married

一、宁贯督寻找财富　Ⅰ. N-gon Du Seeking for Wealth

远古，	In remote antiquity,
很早很早的时候，	So remote from now,
宁贯督的父亲	N-gon Du's father Hpunggam Chyanun
就对儿子说过：	Said to his son,
“儿子宁贯督呀，	"My son N-gon Du,
将来的日子，	In the future days,
如果需要财产，	If you need any property,
如果需要宝物，	If you need any treasure,
沿着野象的足迹，	Track the footprints left by the wild elephant,
找到野象安息的地方，	Find the place where they fall and die,
就会得到无尽的财富。”	You'll get abundant wealth."
按父亲留下的话，	Following his father's instructions,
宁贯督寻找财富去了。	N-gon Du set out in search of wealth.
翻过高耸的山峰，	Climbing over the towering peaks,
越过宽阔的平坝，	Traveling across the broad plains,
不知道找了多少天，	For numerous days,
不知道走了多少夜，	For countless nights,
在野象生活的地方，	In the place where the wild elephant lived,

宁贯督找到了野象的足迹。	N-gon Du finally saw its footprints.
在目东顶聂顺地方[①]，	But, in the place named Madum Tingnye Shun[①],
森林神特蒙格努特杰杜，	Htamung Ganu Htagye Du, the Forest God,
用倒下的树干，	With fallen logs,
挡住了去路；	Blocked the way.
用掉下的树叶，	And with fallen leaves,
遮住了野象的脚印。	He covered the footprints of the wild elephant.
王子宁贯督，	Prince N-gon Du
真诚地对森林神说：	Sincerely said to the Forest God,
"特蒙格努特杰杜呀，	"Forest God Htamung Ganu Htagye Du,
你用象牙做夹子，	You can make clips out of ivory,
你用象耳做扇子，	You can make fans out of elephant ears,
请你不要挡住我的路，	So please don't stand in my way,
请你不要遮住野象的脚印。	Please don't cover the footprints of the wild elephant.
等我找到了野象，	When I find the wild elephant,
我会杀牛祭献你；	I'll kill oxen as an offering to you;
等找到了财富，	When I find the wealth,
我会用金银报答你。"	I shall reward you with gold and silver."
从森林里出来，	Coming out of the forest,

① 目东顶聂顺地方：地名，据传有森林有野象。

① It was a place where there were forest and wild elephants.

沿着野象的足迹，	Following the footprints of the wild elephant,
宁贯督继续寻找着。	N-gon Du kept looking round.
跨过深深的峡谷，	Traveling across the deep ravine,
渡过宽阔的江河，	Crossing the broad rivers,
宁贯督终于找到了	N-gon Du finally found the place
野象安息的地方。	Where the wild elephant died and rested.

挖开野象安息的地方，	Digging open the resting place of the wild elephant,
宁贯督得到了一头公猪，	N-gon Du found a boar.
他心里想：	He thought,
挖到公猪也好，	A boar would do,
把它送给哥哥塔瓦波汤。	I could give it to my elder brother Hta Hprohtang.

宁贯督继续挖着，	On and on dug N-gon Du,
又得到了一头公猪，	Another boar he found,
他心里想：	And he thought,
这一头送给哥哥占瓦能桑。	Well, I could give this one to my elder brother Jan Wa Ningsang.

宁贯督继续挖着，	N-gon Du continued digging.
又得到了一头公牛，	A bull he got this time.
他心里想：	He thought,
这一头送给哥哥颇干独真塔。	This bull would go to my elder brother Prince Hprogam Du Jinhta.

宁贯督继续挖着，	On and on N-gon Du kept digging.
在落着象牙的地方，	Where the elephant's teeth had dropped,
挖出了金齿银牙；	He dug up gold and silver teeth.
在落着象头的地方，	Where the elephant's head had dropped,
挖出了铓锣；	He dug out a gong.
在落着象脑的地方，	Where the elephant's brain had dropped,
挖出了银块；	He dug out silver pieces.
在落着象眼的地方，	Where the elephant's eyes had dropped,
挖出了格镝相[1]；	He dug out gold treasure.
在落着象耳的地方，	Where the elephant's ears had dropped,
挖出了大嘴锣；	He dug out a gong.
在落着象舌的地方，	Where the elephant's tongue had dropped,
挖出了琥珀；	He dug out amber.
在落着象唇的地方，	Where the elephant's lips had dropped,
挖出了铜器；	He dug out bronze ware.
在落着象鼻的地方，	Where the elephant's nose had dropped,
挖出了金条；	He dug out a gold bar.
在落着象皮的地方，	Where the elephant's skin had dropped,
挖出了龙袍衣和银披挂；	He dug out a golden imperial dragon robe and a silver cloak.
在落着象肩的地方，	Where the elephant's shoulders had dropped,
挖出了西搏肩尾巴[2]；	

① 格镝相：传说属财宝一类。
② 西搏肩尾巴：最早的一种枪。

在落着象骨的地方，
挖出了铁块；
在落着象心的地方，
挖出了铜块；
在落着象齿的地方，
挖出了瓷器；
在落着象胆的地方，
挖出了玉石；
在落着象肠的地方，
挖出了项链。

He dug out a gun.
Where the elephant's bones had dropped,
He dug out an iron piece.
Where the elephant's heart had dropped,
He dug out copper.
Where the elephant's jaws had dropped,
He dug out porcelain.
Where the elephant's gallbladder had dropped,
He dug out jade.
Where the elephant's intestines had dropped,
He dug out a necklace.

宁贯督继续往下挖：
从地底下，
挖出了猪，
钻出了羊，
顶出了黄牛，
撞出了水牛。

N-gon Du continued digging.
From under the ground
He dug out a pig,
He drilled out a goat,
He shouldered out an ox,
He struck out a water buffalo.

背着无数的财宝，
赶着成群的家畜，
王子宁贯督，
回到了戛昂王宫。

Carrying countless valuables,
Herding livestock in groups,
Prince N-gon Du
Finally returned to the Gaang Palace.

为了感谢父亲，	To show gratitude to his father,
为了报答母亲，	To pay thanks to his mother,
为了得到的财宝，	In return for the treasures and valuables,
宁贯督要杀牛祭献	N-gon Du intended to offer an ox
太阳神扎占能桑，	As a sacrifice to Ja Jan Ningsang, the Sun God.
还要举行盛大的目瑙。	He also planned to have a Manau Dance Festival.
宁贯督赶回的牛，	The oxen he herded back were left to graze
放牧在贡巴亚草地上，	On the Gong Ba Ya Pasture,
让人去牵时，	But none were seen
却一头也不见了，	When he sent a guy to get the oxen.
找牛的人，	The guy looking for the oxen
找到草丛中，	Searched in a bush
捉到了一只长尾巴鸟，	Only to find a long-tailed bird.
虽然找不到牛，	Still, he was happy,
仍然很高兴。	Though he found no ox.
因为没有牛，	Because no ox was found,
只好烧熟长尾巴鸟，	The bird was to be burned and cooked
招待远方来的客人。	To entertain the guests from afar.
他把长尾巴鸟，	N-gon Du placed the long-tailed bird
放到砧板上，	On the chopping block.
越剁肉越香，	The more chopping, the better flavor;
越剁肉越多，	The more chopping, the more meat.

所有的客人都吃够了，	Every guest ate to satisfaction
所有的客人都吃饱了。	And felt full.
长尾巴鸟的香味，	The good smell of the long-tailed bird
飘到了天空，	Wafted upward to heaven.
颇干独真塔占能桑，	Hprogam Du Jinghta Jan Ningsang
他心里在想：	Said to himself,
宁贯督举办目瑙舞，	"N-gon Du is holding a Manau Dance Festival,
怎么用鸟肉招待客人？	But why is he entertaining the guests with bird meat?
也许是因为没有牛。	It may be because he does not have an ox?"
颇干独真塔想着，	As Hprogam Du Jinghta Jan Ningsang was thinking,
包上一包牛角片，	He wrapped up a bag of horn slices
包上一包狗尾巴米，	And a bag of foxtail millet.
朝大地上丢去。	He scattered them downward on the Earth.
地上的两兄弟，	The two brothers on the Earth,
邓纳干和邓纳诺，	Dingna Gam and Dingna No,
看到天上掉下的东西，	Saw the bags dropped from heaven.
拾起来打开一看，	They picked them up and opened.
一包是牛角片，	Horn slices in one bag
一包是狗尾巴米。	And foxtail millet in the other.
狡猾的邓纳诺，	The cunning brother Dingna No
连忙对哥哥说：	Hastily said to his elder brother Dingna Gam,

“哥哥邓纳干呀，	“Brother Dingna Gam,
你去种牛角片吧，	You plant the horn slices,
我去种狗尾巴米。”	I grow the foxtail millet.”
老实的邓纳干，	The honest elder brother
听了弟弟的话，	Followed the suggestion.
回去砍了一块火地，	He cultivated a piece of slash-and-burn Earth.
种上了牛角片。	There he planted the horn slices.
贪心的邓纳诺，	Greedy Dingna No
打着自己的主意，	Had a secret idea.
也回去砍了一块火地，	He also slashed and burned a piece of Earth
种上了狗尾巴米。	Where he grew foxtail millet.
过了一段时间，	Some time had passed,
哥哥的火地里，	On the elder brother's Earth
冒出一对对牛角；	Pairs of horns were springing up;
弟弟的火地里，	On the younger brother's Earth
长出一棵棵狗尾巴米。	Weeds of foxtail millet were growing up.
邓纳诺问哥哥说：	Dingna No asked his elder brother,
“哥哥邓纳干呀，	“Brother Dingna Gam,
你的火地里，	What's going on
不知怎样了？”	In your field?”
邓纳干回答说：	Dingna Gam answered,
“弟弟呀，	“My brother,

我的火地里，	In my field
到处都发出了牛叫声。”	The lowing of oxen can be heard.”
邓纳干又问弟弟说：	Then Dingna Gam asked his brother,
“弟弟邓纳诺呀，	“My dear brother,
你的火地里，	What’s going on
不知怎样了？”	In your field?”
邓纳诺回答说：	Dingna No answered,
“哥哥呀，	“Dear brother,
我的火地里，	In my field
到处都长满了狗尾巴米的苗。”	Seedlings of foxtail millet grow.”
听了哥哥的话，	Hearing that,
邓纳诺心里想，	The younger brother Dingna No thought,
种的是牛角片，	“It was horns that he planted,
火地里怎么发出牛叫声。	How come there the lowing of oxen?”
他跑到哥哥的火地上，	He rushed to his brother’s Earth,
见火地上到处都是牛，	Where he saw herds and herds of oxen.
他看着眼红了，	He became jealous.
想着后悔了，	He felt regretful.
邓纳诺用白面粉，	He found some white flour,
把哥哥火地里的牛，	With which he changed all the oxen
全染成花白色。	Into white ones.

邓纳诺回到家，	When Dingna No returned home,
对哥哥邓纳干说：	He said to his brother,
“哥哥邓纳干呀，	“Brother Dingna Gam,
你火地里的牛，	Of all the oxen in your field,
黑的是你的，	The black ones are yours,
花白的是我的。”	But the white ones belong to me.”
听了弟弟的话，	Hearing what his brother said,
邓纳干来到火地边。	Dingna Gam went to his field.
只见火地里的牛，	Every ox in his sight in his field
全都变成了花白的。	Had turned white.
邓纳干惊呆了，	Dingna Gam was stunned.
邓纳干愤怒了；	Dingna Gam was enraged.
他对着苍天呼，	He cried out to heaven.
他向着大地喊。	He exhaled to the Earth.
天上降下了大雨，	Heavy rain fell from heaven.
天上落下了冰雹，	Hail dropped from the Sky.
大雨和冰雹，	The rain and the hail
冲掉了牛身上的染料，	Washed away the dye on the oxen.
牛又变成了黑色的。	All oxen were black again in colour.
贪心的邓纳诺，	Greedy Dingna No
没有骗到哥哥的牛，	Failed to turn his brother’s oxen into his.

又在嫂嫂睡着时，	He poured sticky wine
把又黏又稠的酒水，	Onto his sister-in-law's hair
泼到她的头发上，	While she was asleep,
使她的头发，	Turning it
结得一团一块的。	Into hair knots.
第二天早上，	The next morning,
邓纳诺对哥哥说，	Dingna No said to his brother,
“哥哥邓纳干呀，	“My brother,
嫂嫂的头发，	Sister-in-law's hair
结得一团一块的，	Has turned into hair blocks.
是被野鬼缠着了，	Because she has been haunted by wild ghosts.
你不能让她再出门，	You must not allow her to go outside.
你赶快杀牛祭鬼吧。”	You must kill your oxen as an offering to the ghosts.”
老实的邓纳干，	Following his brother's advice,
听了弟弟的话，	Honest Dingna Gam
一次就杀了四五头牛，	Killed four or five oxen
为自己的妻子祭鬼。	As a sacrifice to the ghosts haunting his wife.
可是祭了鬼，	However, though the sacrifice had been offered,
妻子的头发，	His wife's hair
还是一团一块的。	Was still twisted in blocks.
邓纳诺说：	Dingna No said,
“你得杀更多牛，	“You must kill more oxen

为嫂嫂祭鬼。”	As sacrifices to the ghosts.”
老实的邓纳干，	Following his brother's advice,
听了弟弟的话，	Honest Dingna Gam
又杀了一二十头牛，	Killed two dozen oxen
为自己的妻子祭鬼。	As sacrifices to the ghosts haunting his wife.
可祭了鬼，	However, though the sacrifice had been offered,
妻子的头发，	His wife's hair
还是一团一块的。	Was still twisted in blocks.
邓纳诺对哥哥说：	Dingna No said to his brother,
“哥哥邓纳干呀，	“My brother,
嫂嫂的头发，	Your wife's hair
还是一团一块的，	Is still twisted.
你还得杀更多的牛，	You must kill even more oxen
为嫂嫂祭鬼。”	As sacrifices to the ghosts.”
老实的邓纳干，	Honest Dingna Gam
又杀了更多的牛，	Killed more oxen
为自己的妻子祭鬼。	As sacrifices to the ghosts haunting his wife.
可妻子的头发，	However, his wife's hair
还是一团一块的。	Was still twisted in blocks.
牛一次比一次杀得多，	More oxen were killed each time
最后杀得只剩一头了，	Until there was only one left.
正要再杀时，	When the last ox was ready to be killed,

再也看不下去的长老们，	The elders, who could keep silent no longer,
出来说话了：	Spoke out,
“可怜的邓纳干呀，	“Poor Dingna Gam,
牛只剩一头了，	You have only one ox left.
以往杀牛时，	Every time you kill your oxen,
大妹妹蒙松占，	Your first younger sister Mungsong Jan
二妹妹蒙桑占，	And your second younger sister Mungsang Jan
都来吃过了，	Both came and shared the beef with you,
唯有最小的妹妹勒扎占，	While your youngest sister Laja Jan
她一次也没能来过，	Has never come.
今天杀最后的一头牛，	Today the last ox is to be killed,
一定要请她来。”	Your youngest sister must be invited.”
按长老们说的话，	Following the elders’ advice,
邓纳干把三个妹妹，	Dingna Gam invited
全都请来了。	All three of his sisters.
三妹勒扎占问嫂嫂：	The youngest sister inquired of her sister-in-law,
“亲亲的嫂嫂呀，	“Dear sister-in-law,
你生了什么病，	What disease are you suffering?
你觉得哪里疼。”	Where do you feel pain?”
嫂嫂回答说：	The sister-in-law answered,
“好心的三妹呀，	“My dear sister,
我没生什么病，	I am suffering from no disease

我哪里也不疼，	And I feel no pain,
只是我的头发，	Except that my hair
结得一团一块的，	Has turned into hair knots.
弟弟邓纳诺说，	Brother Dingna No said that
是被野鬼缠着了，	It is because wild ghosts have been haunting me.
可杀了那么多牛，	Though so many oxen have been killed
祭了那么多次，	And sacrificed to the ghosts,
头发还是一团一块的。”	My hair is still twisted in hair blocks.”
三妹勒扎占，	Hearing her sister-in-law’s answer,
听了嫂嫂的话	The youngest sister
见嫂嫂的头发，	Noticed her sister-in-law’s hair
结得一团一块的，	Tied in blocks
还散发出一股酒的气味，	And giving off an odour of wine.
她心里明白了一切，	She understood everything at once.
便把嫂嫂叫到屋外，	She asked her sister-in-law outside
用热水洗净了她的头发，	And helped wash her hair in warm water.
嫂嫂的头发，	Now her sister-in-law’s hair
变得又松又软了。	Returned to its springy soft appearance.
三妹勒扎占，	The youngest sister Laja Jan
对长老和众人说：	Said to the elders and others,
“尊敬的长老们呀，	“Respected elders,
远近的亲朋们，	Friends and relatives,

你们看看吧，	Look at my sister-in-law!
嫂嫂的头发，	Her hair
结得一块一块的，	Has turned into hair knots.
不是被野鬼缠着，	She is not haunted by wild ghosts
而是被别人的妒嫉鬼咬着了。”	But by someone's ghost of jealousy."

听勒扎占说完，	Hearing what Leja Jan said,
长老们说：	The elders gave their advice,
“邓纳干呀，	"Dingna Gam, Dingna No,
邓纳诺，	The last ox,
这最后一头牛，	If it is kept here,
如果留着它，	Will again bring out jealousy
心上的妒嫉鬼	And cause you two brothers to live in disharmony.
还会使你们不和睦，	You'd better give it away as a present
不如把它当作赠礼，	To one of your younger sisters."
送给你们的妹妹。”	The two brothers agreed
兄弟俩同意了，	But were not sure
但不知道送给谁。	Whom to give it to.
长老们说：	The elders said,
“送给大妹妹蒙松占，	"If it is given to your first younger sister Mungsong Jan,
牛不会兴旺，	The ox will not prosper,
也不会发展；	The ox will not thrive.
送给二妹蒙桑占，	If it is given to your second younger sister Mungsang Jan,

牛会变瘦，	The ox will grow thinner,
牛会变小；	The ox will become smaller.
只有送给三妹勒扎占，	Only when it is given to your youngest sister Laja Jan,
牛才会肥胖，	Can the ox grow strong
牛才会发展。”	And reproduce prosperously."
邓纳干按长老们的话，	Dingna Gam adopted the elder's suggestion
把牛当作赠礼，	And gave the ox as a present
送给了三妹勒扎占。	To his youngest sister Laja Jan.
三妹对众人说：	Laja Jan said to them,
“牛既然送给我，	"Since you give me the ox,
我就要牵走了，	I'll take it along with me.
等将来跳目瑙，	Later when you need to sacrifice an ox
需要杀牛时，	For the Manau Festival ceremony,
你们就跟着斋瓦们，	Come with Jaiwa priests,
背上金条，	Carrying gold sticks,
带上银条，	Bringing silver sticks,
到勒扎地方来牵牛吧。”	To the place named Laja."
勒扎占牵起牛，	Leading the ox,
回勒扎地方去了。	Laja Jan returned to her place in Laja.

二、宁贯督娶龙女 Ⅱ. N-gon Du Marrying Dragon Daughter

远古，	In remote antiquity,
宁贯督没有王后，	N-gon Du had no queen;
宁贯督没有妻子，	N-gon Du had no wife.
白天没有人跟他玩耍，	He had no one to play with during the day;
晚上没有人跟他做伴，	He had no one to accompany in the evening.
他想要找个王后，	He wanted to have a queen;
他想要娶个妻子。	He wanted to have a wife.
宁贯督的媒人	N-gon Du sent his matchmaker
到天上去求亲，	To heaven to seek a marriage alliance.
天上的木代督们问：	The Madai immortals in heaven asked,
“从地上来的是什么人，	“Who is that from the Earth?
要娶木代女的是哪一个？”	Who wants to marry a daughter of the Madai family?”
媒人回答说：	The matchmaker replied,
“勒目木代呀，	“Respected Lamu Madai,
我们是大地上的人，	We are humans from the Earth.
要娶木代女的是宁贯督。”	The one wanting to marry Madai’s daughter is N-gon Du.”

勒目木代督们说：	The Lamu Madai immortals asked,
“木代家和宁贯督，	“The Madai family and N-gon Du
同属于一个家族①，	Have the same blood origin①.
男的是兄弟，	Sons from the two families should be brothers;
女的是姐妹，	Daughters from the two families should be sisters.
他不能娶木代女，	He cannot marry a daughter of the Madai family;
木代女不能嫁给他。”	No Madai daughter can marry off to him.”
没有娶着木代女，	His plan to marry a Madai daughter failing,
宁贯督又让媒人，	N-gon Du asked his matchmaker,
带上乐队，	Along with a music band,
到别的地方去求亲。	To seek marriage alliance somewhere else.
悦耳的东巴吹响了，	The melodic dum-ba instrument was played,
欢乐的竹笛吹响了，	The pleasing flute was played.
前面是木鼓，	Led by the drummer,
后面是大镗，	Followed by the gong players,
求亲的队伍，	The team planning to take a bride back
翻过无数座高山。	Climbed over numerous mountains,

① 同属于一个家族：在景颇族的婚姻制度中，同属于一个家族和姓氏的男女之间，不能相互通婚。

① In Jingpo culture, if a man and a woman come from the same clan and have the same family name, they are not allowed to marry each other.

越过无数个平坝，	Crossed countless plains.
顺着迈里开江寻，	They looked along the Mali Hka River;
沿着恩迈开江找，	They searched along the Nmai Hka River.
美妙的乐曲，	The wonderful music
向西面飘散，	Wafted to the west.
迈里开江翻起了浪，	The waves in the Mali Hka River mounted up;
恩迈开江腾起了波，	The waves in the Nmai Hka River rose up.
水底的龙女，	The daughter of the Dragon King,
听到乐曲声，	Hearing the music,
来到水面问：	Swam to the water surface and asked,
"你们的歌声真好听，	"Your songs are beautiful;
你们的乐曲真动人，	Your music is touching.
你们来做什么？"	What are you doing here?"
媒人回答说：	The matchmaker replied,
"我们从戛昂王宫来，	"We come from Gaang Palace.
我们为王子找王后，	We are seeking a princess for our prince.
我们到这里来求亲。"	We come to this place to seek a marriage alliance."
听媒人说完，	Hearing the reply,
龙女害羞地回去了。	The daughter of the Dragon retreated out of shyness.
龙王又出来问：	The Dragon King asked,
"想做姑爷的是哪一个	"Who wants to be my son-in-law?
他的名字叫什么？"	What name does he inherit?"

媒人回答说：	The matchmaker replied,
“他是大地上的王子，	“He is the prince of the Earth.
他的第一个名字叫宁贯督。	N-gon Du is the first name of our prince.
尊敬的龙王呵，	Respected Dragon King,
请你也告诉我们，	Please tell us in turn
龙女的名字叫什么？”	What the name of your daughter is?”
龙王回答说：	The Dragon King said,
“你们听着吧，	“Listen, guys!
上面的叫宁贯督，	The one from the Earth is named N-gon Du,
下面的叫登滚囊勒布，	The one from the Sea is named Tinggun Nang Lapu.
第一个名字相称了①，	Their first names are well-inherited①;
第一个名字相配了。”	Their first names are well-matched.”
媒人又问道：	The matchmaker then asked,
“尊敬的龙王呀，	“Respected Dragon King,
王子的第二个名字	Gaang Pran Wan
就叫戛昂帮湾，	Is the second name of our prince.
请你告诉我们，	Would you please let us know
龙女的第二个名字叫什么？”	The second name of your daughter?”

① 名字相称相配：据传在景颇族远古的男婚女配中，男女之间先得两个名字相配，念起来相配，即顺口押韵。

① In the ancient Jingpo marriage custom,the precondition for a man and a woman to marry each other was that their first names should rhyme and sound melodious.

龙王回答说：	The Dragon King replied,
“你们听着吧，	“You guys listen!
第二个名字，	As for the second name,
上面的叫戛昂帮湾，	The one from the Earth is Gaang Pran Wan
下面的叫登滚囊木占，	The one from the Sea is Tinggun Nang Majan.
第二个名字相称了，	Their second names are well-inherited;
第二个名字相配了。”	Their second names are well-matched.”
媒人又问道：	The matchmaker again asked,
“尊敬的龙王呀，	“Respected Dragon King,
王子的第三个名字	Gaang Pran Wan La Wuren
就叫戛昂帮湾拉乌仁，	Is the third name of our prince.
请你告诉我们，	Would you please let us know
龙女的第三个名字叫什么？”	The third name of your daughter?”
龙王回答说：	The Dragon King replied,
“你们听着吧，	“You guys listen!
第三个名字，	As for the third name,
上面的叫戛昂帮湾拉乌仁，	The one from the Earth is Gaang Pran Wan La Wuren.
下面的叫布仁侬扎圣，	The one from the Sea is Baren Num Ja Shen.
第三个名字也相称了，	Their third names are well-inherited;
第三个名字也相配了。	Their third names are well-matched.
宁贯督可以做姑爷，	N-gon Du can be my son-in-law.

我的女儿可以嫁给他。”
My daughter can marry him.”

隆重的送亲仪式，
在耀眼的王宫里举行，
龙王的鱼虾百姓，
像过年一样欢乐。
龙王拿出无数的财宝，
给女儿做嫁妆，
又架起出水的桥，
愿女儿幸福，
祝女儿吉祥。

There was a grand seeing-off ceremony
In the brilliant palace.
King Dragon's subjects, such as fish and shrimp,
Were as happy as they were celebrating New Year's Day.
The Dragon King took out countless treasure
As gifts to his daughter.
He also set up a bridge stretching out of the Sea
To wish his daughter every happiness,
To wish his daughter every good fortune.

在戛昂王宫，
宁贯督和龙女扎圣
就要举行婚礼，
但龙女的脸上，
还带着龙的斑纹，
在龙女身上，
还有着龙的腥味。

Back in the Gaang Palace,
N-gon Du and Dragon Daughter Ja Shen
Would hold a wedding ceremony soon.
But Dragon Daughter
Still wore dragon streaks,
And her body
Still had the smell of a dragon.

宁贯督找来花椒叶，
蘸上圣洁的泉水，
为龙女扎圣洗礼。
洗礼后的龙女扎圣，

N-gon Du found some wild pepper leaves.
They were dipped into the holy spring
To bathe Dragon Daughter Ja Shen.
After washing, Dragon Daughter Ja Shen

脸上的斑纹褪了些，	Had fewer dapples on the face.
身上的腥味减了些，	And she had only a faint smell of the sea.
但斑纹还没有褪尽，	But still there remained some streaks;
腥味还没有消失。	There still remained some smell of the sea.
宁贯督又找来香果叶，	N-gon Du found some allspice leaves.
蘸上圣洁的泉水，	They were dipped into the holy spring
为龙女扎圣洗礼。	To bathe Dragon Daughter Ja Shen.
洗礼后的龙女扎圣，	After washing, Dragon Daughter Ja Shen
脸上的斑纹又褪了些，	Had even fewer streaks on the face.
身上的腥味又减了些，	And she had an even fainter smell of the sea.
但斑纹没有褪尽，	But still there remained some streaks;
腥味没有消失。	There still remained some smell of the sea.
宁贯督又找来茏菜，	N-gon Du found some leek leaves.
蘸上圣洁的泉水，	They were dipped into the holy spring
为龙女扎圣洗礼。	To bathe Dragon Daughter Ja Shen.
洗礼后的龙女扎圣，	After washing, Dragon Daughter Ja Shen
脸上的斑纹又褪了些，	Had even fewer streaks on the face.
身上的腥味又减了些，	And she had an even fainter smell of the sea,
但斑纹没有褪尽，	But still there remained some streaks,
腥味没有消失。	There still remained some smell of the sea.
宁贯督又找来生姜，	N-gon Du found some ginger.

蘸上圣洁的泉水，	They were dipped into the holy spring
为龙女扎圣洗礼。	To bathe Dragon Daughter Ja Shen.
洗礼后的龙女扎圣，	After washing, Dragon Daughter Ja Shen
脸上的斑纹又褪了些，	Had even fewer streaks on the face.
身上的腥味又减了些，	And she had an even fainter smell of the sea.
但斑纹没有褪尽，	But still there remained some streaks;
腥味没有消失。	There still remained some smell of the sea.

宁贯督又找来贡芝贡巴草[①]，	N-gon Du found some Hkungji Kumba grass[①].
蘸上圣洁的泉水，	They were dipped into the holy spring
为龙女扎圣洗礼。	To bathe Dragon Daughter Ja Shen.
洗礼后的龙女扎圣，	After washing, Dragon Daughter Ja Shen
脸上的斑纹褪尽了，	Had no more streaks on the face.
身上的腥味消失了。	And she had no more smell of the sea.
龙女扎圣更漂亮了，	Dragon Daughter became even more beautiful than before.
龙女扎圣更动人了，	Dragon Daughter was even more charming than before.
从此，宁贯督有了王后，	Ever since then, N-gon Du had a queen;
宁贯督有了妻子。	Ever since then, N-gon Du had a wife.

远古，	In remote antiquity,

① 贡芝贡巴草：一种长得较高的草，为景颇族举行婚礼“过草桥”仪式专用草。

① This was a tall grass used in the ritual of “Crossing the Grass Bridge” during a Jingpo wedding ceremony.

宁贯督和龙女扎圣，	N-gon Du and Dragon Daughter Ja Shen
生下了戛昂阿督王子。	Bore Prince Gaang Adu.
戛昂阿督王子成熟了，	Gaang Adu grew up.
该给他说谋了，	It was time to find a girl for him;
该给他娶亲了。	It was time for him to get married.
媒人出来说：	The matchmakers said,
“要给戛昂阿督王子成亲，	“To find a wife for Prince Gaang Adu,
就到天上找木代家，	We must go to the Madai family in the Sky.
虽然是同一个家族，	Though they come from the same clan,
但已经过了七代[1]。”	It is already after seven generations[1].”
背上金，	Taking gold,
带上银，	Carrying silver,
媒人来到天上，	The matchmakers went to the Sky
向木代督求亲。	And proposed a marriage alliance to the Madai family.
木代督问：	King Madai asked,
“想做姑爷的是哪一个，	“Who wants to be my son-in-law?
他的名字叫什么？”	What name does he inherit?”
媒人回答说：	The matchmakers replied,

① 七代：据传在久远的年代，景颇族的婚俗中，属于同一个家族和姓氏的，过了第七代才可以通婚。但从今天的情况看，不管过了几代，仍然不行。

① This used to be the requirement that a man and a woman from the same clan must meet if they wanted to marry each other. But today, no marriage should take place between a man and a woman from the same clan, no matter how many generations have passed.

“他就是地上的王子，	“He is the prince of the Earth.
他的名字叫戛昂阿督。”	His inherited name is Gaang Adu.”
木代督说：	King Madai said,
“他和木代家，	“He and the Madai family
同属于一个家族，	Actually belong to the same clan.
现在已经过了七代，	But seven generations have passed.
可以相娶了，	Now they can be a match;
可以相爱了，	They can be lovers.
但他们的名字不相称，	But unfortunately their names are not well-matched;
但他们的名字不相配。”	Their names are not corresponding to each other.”
媒人又问道：	The matchmakers then asked,
“尊敬的木代督呀，	“Respected King Madai,
请你告诉我们，	Would you please tell us
木代女的名字叫什么？”	The name of your daughter?”
木代督说：	King Madai said,
“你们听着吧，	“You guys listen!
我女儿的名字，	Lamu Num Hkon Tong is
叫勒木侬宽东。”	My daughter’s inherited name.”
媒人们回到地上想，	Back on the Earth, the matchmakers had a good idea.
王子和木代女，	If the names of our prince
名字不相称，	And King Madai’s daughter

名字不相配，	Are not well-matched,
我们就按木代女的名字，	We can rename our prince
给王子另取名，	To match the name of King Madai's daughter.
木代女叫勒木侬宽东，	Madai's daughter's name is Lamu Num Hkon Tong,
戞昂王子就叫扎容壮，	Then Prince Gaang will be renamed Ja Rumjong.
如果木代女叫勒木侬坡纳，	If Madai's daughter's name is Lamu Num Hpro Nga,
戞昂王子就叫扎瓦容扎。	Prince Gaang will be renamed Ja Wa Rumja!
媒人们按木代女的名字，	The matchmakers renamed their prince
给王子取好了名字，	To match Madai's daughter's name.
又背上金，	Again carrying gold
带上银，	And taking silver along,
来到了天宫，	They went to the heavenly palace
向木代督求亲。	To propose a marriage alliance to King Madai.
木代督问：	King Madai asked,
"要做姑爷的是哪一个，	"Who wants to be my son-in-law?
他的名字叫什么？"	What name does he inherit?"
媒人回答说：	The matchmakers replied,
"他是地上的王子	"He is the prince of the Earth.
他的名字叫作扎容壮。	Ja Rumjong is his name.
尊敬的木代督呵，	Respected King Madai,
请你告诉我们，	Please tell us in turn,
你的女儿叫什么？"	What's the name of your daughter?"

木代督说：	King Madai said,
“你们听着吧，	“Listen, guys!
你们的王子，	Your prince’s name
名字叫作扎容壮；	Is Ja Rumjong;
我的女儿，	My daughter’s name
名字叫勒木依宽东，	Is Lamu Num Hkon Tong.
第一个名字相称了，	Their first names are well-inherited;
第一个名字相配了，	Their first names are well-matched.
但还有第二个名字，	But there should be the second name.
不知道叫什么？”	What’s that? ”

媒人回答说：	The matchmakers then replied,
“我们的王子，	“Our prince’s second name
他的第二个名字，	Is Ja wa Rumja.
就叫扎瓦容扎。	Respected King Madai,
尊敬的木代督呀，	Would you please
请你告诉我们，	Let us know
你的女儿，	The second name
她的第二个名字叫什么？	Of your daughter?”

木代督说：	King Madai said,
“你们听着吧，	“You guys listen!
我的女儿，	My daughter’s second name

她的第二个名字，	Is Lamu Num Hpro Nga.
叫勒木侬坡纳。	Your prince's second name
你们的王子，	Is Ja Wa Rumja.
他的第二个名字，	Their second names
叫扎瓦容扎。	Are well-inherited.
第二个名字相称了，	Their second names
第二个名字相配了，	Are well-matched."
你们的王子可以做姑爷，	Your prince can be my son-in-law.
我的女儿可以嫁给他。	My daughter can marry him.
大地上的人们呵，	You guys from the Earth,
你们带着她走吧，	Take her away with you.
女儿的嫁妆，	As for dowry,
等你们举行目瑙时，	When you celebrate your Manau Festival,
我会亲自送来。	I'll bring it in person.
女儿的彩礼，	And as for the betrothal gifts,
等你们举行目瑙时，	When you celebrate your Manau Festival,
我会亲自来取。"	I'll come to get them in person."

媒人们带着木代女，	The matchmakers took the Madai Daughter
回到了戛昂王宫，	Back to the Gaang Palace.
戛昂王子扎容壮和勒木侬宽东，	The Prince of Gaang and the Madai Daughter
举行了盛大的婚礼，	Held a grand wedding.
从此，他们生活在一起。	Ever since then they led a happy life.

远古，
戛昂王子和木代女
生下了王子苏瓦木都。
苏瓦木都长大后，
娶了干占肯努，
苏瓦木都和干占肯努
生下了王子德如增利。
德如增利长大后，
娶了木干增梯，
德如增利和木干增梯
生下了王子木托贡央。
木托贡央长大后，
娶了登萨勒刚。

In remote antiquity,
The Prince of Gaang and the Daughter of Madai
Bore Prince Sut Wa Madu.
When Sut Wa Madu grew up,
He married Kan Jan Hkrungngu.
Sut Wa Madu and Kan Jan Hkrungngu
Bore Prince Daru Tsingli.
When Daru Tsingli grew up,
He married Magam Tsinghti.
Daru Tsingli and Magam Tsinghti
Bore Prince Mahto Kum-yang.
When Mahto Kum-yang grew up,
He married Tingsa Lakang.

木托贡央和登萨勒刚
生下了老大卓西纳，
他生活在肯度央扎昆地方；
生下了老二张木扎，
他生活在恩波瓦浪缺的地方；
生下了老三董木浪腊桑，
他生活在省连权枯地方；
生下了老四格仁都弯，

Mahto Kum-yang and Tingsa Lakang
Gave birth to their First son Jo Sana,
Who lived in a place called Hkindu Yang Ja-hkun.
They gave birth to their second son Chyang Maja,
Who lived in a valley called Npo Wlam Hkyet.
They gave birth to their third son Dung Malang La-sang,
Who lived in a river-bank area called Sinlen Hkey Hku.
They gave birth to their fourth son Gareng Tu Lot,
Who lived in a place called Adam Sumhpra Hkang.

他生活在阿旦松巴康地方；	They gave birth to their fifth son Pyengtang Tingsa,
生下了老五扁当登萨，	Who lived in a place called Mount Pyen Shagong.
他生活在扁诗贡山；	They gave birth to their sixth son A-nang Dumbu Yo Htung,
生下了老六阿囊动布约筒，	Who lived in a place called A-nang Ningdung Hkang.
他生活在阿囊能动康地方；	They gave birth to their seventh son Nding Tasan Hka,
生下了老七恩顶德散卡，	Who lived in a place called the Nding Kaya Hku River.
他生活在恩顶格芽地方；	They gave birth to their eighth son N-gyem Sabo Roi,
生下了老八恩建思波瑞，	Who lived in a place called N-gyem Sabo Hkang.
他生活在恩建思波康地方；	They gave birth to their ninth son Mashun Tingmai Kying,
生下了老九木舜顶迈金，	Who lived in a place called Mount Mashun Tingmai.
他生活在木舜顶迈诗贡地方。	
从此，大地上的人们，	Ever since then, people on the Earth
有了不同的姓氏。	Have their different family names.

远古，	In remote antiquity,
老大卓西纳家，	The eldest son Jo Sana
有了一个伙子。	Had a son,
老二张木扎家，	While the second eldest son Chyang Maja
有了一个姑娘。	Had a daughter.
卓西纳家的伙子，	Jo Sana's son married
娶了张木扎家的姑娘。	Chyang Maja's daughter.

老二张木扎家，	The second eldest son Chyang Maja

有了一个伙子。	Also had a son.
老三董木浪腊桑家，	And the third eldest son Dung Malang La-sang
有了一个姑娘。	Had a daughter.
张木扎家的伙子，	Chyang Maja's son married
娶了董木浪腊桑家的姑娘。	Dung Malang La-sang's daughter.
老三董木浪腊桑家，	The third eldest son Dung Malang La-sang
有了一个伙子。	Also had a son.
老四格仁都鸾家，	And the fourth eldest son Gareng Tu Lot
有了一个姑娘。	Had a daughter.
董木浪腊桑家的伙子，	Dung Malang La-sang's son married
娶了格仁都鸾家的姑娘。	Gareng Tu Lot's daughter.
老四格仁都鸾家，	The fourth eldest son Gareng Tu Lot
有了一个伙子。	Also had a son.
老五扁当登萨家，	And the fifth eldest son Pyengtang Tingsa
有了一个姑娘。	Had a daughter.
格仁都鸾家的伙子，	Gareng Tu Lot's son married
娶了扁当登萨家的姑娘。	Pyengtang Tingsa's daughter.
老六阿囊动布约筒家，	The sixth eldest son Anang Dumbu Yo Htung
有了一个小伙子。	Also had a son.
老七恩顶德散卡家，	And the seventh eldest son Nding Tasan Hka
有了一个姑娘。	Had a daughter.

阿囊动布约筒家的伙子，	Anang Dumbu Yo Htung's son married
娶了恩顶德散卡家的姑娘。	Nding Tasan Hka's daughter.
老七恩顶德散卡家，	The seventh eldest son Nding Tasan Hka
有了一个伙子。	Also had a son.
老八恩建思波瑞家，	And the eighth eldest son N-gyem Sabo Roi
有了一个姑娘。	Had a daughter.
恩顶德散卡家的儿子，	Nding Tasan Hka's son married
娶了恩建思波瑞家的姑娘。	N-gyem Sabo Roi's daughter.
老八恩建思波瑞家，	The eighth eldest son N-gyem Sabo Roi
有了一个伙子。	Also had a son.
老九木舜丁迈金家，	And the ninth and youngest son Mashun Tingmai Kying
有了一个姑娘。	Had a daughter.
恩建思波瑞家的小伙子，	N-gyem Sabo Roi's son married
娶了木舜丁迈金家的姑娘。	Mashun Tingmai Kying's daughter.
老九木舜丁迈金家，	The ninth and youngest son Mashun Tingmai Kying
有了一个伙子。	Also had a son,
老大卓西纳家，	While the eldest son Jo Sana
有了一个姑娘。	Also had a daughter.
木舜丁迈金家的伙子，	Mashun Tingmai Kying's son
娶了卓西纳家的姑娘。	Married Jo Sana's daughter.
从此，大地上的人们，	Ever since then, people on the Earth

知道了丈人种，	Have their own daughter-in-law families
知道了姑爷神。	As well as their own son-in-law families.
大地上的人们更繁衍了，	And ever since then,
更昌盛了。	People on the Earth have multiplied and become more prosperous.

远古，	In remote antiquity,
卓西纳和勒旺崩瓦木占，	Jo Sana and Lawang Bum Wa Majan
生下老大，	Gave birth to their eldest son,
名字叫热旺瓦松康木干；	Whose name was Rai-wang Wa Sum-Hkang Magam
生下了老二，	Then the couple gave birth to their second eldest son,
名字叫侬弄生举；	Whose name was Nung Nong Singgyi.
生下了老三，	Then the couple gave birth to their third eldest son,
名字叫木如瓦腊批；	Whose name was Ma-ru Wa La-hpri.
生下了老四，	Then the couple gave birth to their fourth son,
名字叫贡氏瓦都曼；	Whose name was Gumdi Wa Tu Mai.
生下了老五，	Then the couple gave birth to their fifth son,
名字叫押当贡央；	Whose name was Sam Tang Kum yang.
生下了老六，	Then they gave birth to their sixth son,
名字叫蚌拥瓦景颇；	Whose name was Pong Yong Wa Jinghpo.
生下了老七，	Then they gave birth to their seventh son,
名字叫直黎瓦康康；	Whose name was Jili Wa Hkang Hkang.
生下了老八，	Later the couple gave birth to their eighth son,
名字叫蒙嫩瓦锐藏；	Whose name was Mungnun Wa Roiza.

生下了老九，	Then they gave birth to their ninth son,
名字叫缅瓦；	Whose name was Myen Wa.
生下老十，	And then they gave birth to their tenth son,
名字叫迷瓦瓦汤瓦；	Whose name was Mi-wa Wa Htang-wa.
生下了第十一个，	Finally they gave birth to their eleventh son,
名字叫蒙岭蒙旁。	Whose name was Mungling Munghpang.
从此，大地上的人们，	Ever since then, people on the Earth
有了民族和支系。	Have ethnic groups and ethnic branches.

三、蚌拥瓦景颇的繁衍 Ⅲ. Pong Yong Wa Jinghpo's Mulplication

远古，	In remote antiquity,
蚌拥瓦景颇和占玛诗伊，	Pong Yong Wa Jinghpo and Jan Ma Sha-yi
生下了瓦切瓦松贡木干。	Gave birth to Wa Hkyet Wa Singgong Magam.
瓦切瓦松贡木干长大后，	When Wa Hkyet Wa Singgong Magam grew up,
娶了木贡格旁木占。	He married Magong Kabang Majan.
他们生下了老大，	And they two gave birth to their eldest son,
名字叫木日瓦贡扎木干，	Whose name was Marip Wa Kumja Magam,
他住在阿端省贡地方；	Who lived in a place called Aton Singgong.
生下了老二，	Then the couple gave birth to their second son,
名字叫勒佗瓦诺乱，	Whose name was Lahto Wa No Lon,
他住在诗界龙让地方；	Who lived in a place called Shakrai Lung-rang.

生下了老三，	Later the couple gave birth to their third eldest son,
名字叫勒排瓦腊壮[1]，	Whose name was Lahpai Wa La Jong[1],
他住在扎日瓦戛地方；	Who lived in a place called Ja Rawa Ga.
生下了老四，	Then the couple gave birth to their fourth son,
名字叫德散都壮，	Whose name was Tasan Tu Jong,
他住在直权文腊地方；	Who lived in a place called Chyahkyet Wunla.
生下了老五，	Then the couple gave birth to their fifth son,
名字叫木然瓦能尚，	Whose name was Maran Wa Ningshang,
他住在贡树贡瓦戛地方；	Who lived in a place called Gumshu GumWa Ga.
生下了老六，	Later the couple gave birth to their sixth son,
名字叫拥昆用甸，	Whose name was Yonghkum Yongdeng,
他住在恩胆莪洋地方；	Who lived in a place called N-dan Ngo-yang.
生下了老七，	Later the couple gave birth to their seventh son,
名字叫卡树卡莎，	Whose name was Hka-shu Hka-sha,
他住在卓芒卓康地方；	Who lived in a place called Jo-mang Jo-hkang.
生下了老八，	Then the couple gave birth to their eighth son,
名字叫盆南诺瑞，	Whose name was Hpunnam No Roi,
他住在迈里省谷地方；	Who lived in a place called Mali Singgu.
生下了老九，	Lastly the couple gave birth to their ninth son,
名字叫木高瓦金囊，	Whose name was Ma-gau Wa Kyingnang,
他住在木高金囊地方。	Who lived in a place called Ma-gau Kyingnang.
从此，在景颇族里	Ever since then, among the Jinghpo people,

① 勒排瓦腊壮：有些斋瓦和史书上称为都昆。

① He is also called Du Kum in some Jaiwa chants and historical records.

又有了不同的姓氏。 There emerge different family names.

远古， In remote antiquity,
木日瓦贡扎木干家， Marip Wa Kumja Magam
有了姑娘， Had a daughter;
勒佗瓦诺乱家， Lahto Wa No Lon
有了伙子， Had a son.
木日瓦贡扎木干家的姑娘， Marip Wa Kumja Magam's daughter
嫁给了勒佗瓦诺乱家的伙子。Married Lahto Wa No Lon's son.

勒佗瓦诺乱家， Lahto Wa No Lon
有了姑娘， Had a daughter
勒排瓦腊壮家， While Lahpai Wa La Jong
有了伙子， Had a son.
勒佗瓦诺乱家的姑娘， Lahto Wa No Lon's daughter
嫁给了勒排瓦腊壮的伙子。 Married Lahpai Wa La Jong's son.

勒排瓦腊壮家， Lahpai Wa La Jong
有了姑娘， Had a daughter,
德散都壮家， And Tasan Tu Jong
有了伙子， Had a son.
勒排瓦腊壮家的姑娘， Lahpai Wa La Jong's daughter
嫁给了德散都壮家的伙子。 Married Tasan Tu Jong's son.

德散都壮家，	Tasan Tu Jong
有了姑娘，	Had a daughter.
木然瓦能尚家，	Maran Wa Ningshang
有了伙子，	Had a son.
德散都壮家的姑娘，	Tasan Tu Jong's daughter
嫁给了木然瓦能尚家的伙子。	Married Maran Wa Ningshang's son.
木然瓦能尚家，	Maran Wa Ningshang
有了姑娘，	Had a daughter.
拥昆用甸家，	And Yonghkum Yongdeng
有了伙子，	Had a son.
木然瓦能尚家的姑娘，	Maran Wa Ningshang's daughter
嫁给了拥昆用甸家的伙子。	Married Yonghkum Yongdeng's son.
拥昆用甸家，	Yonghkum Yongdeng
有了姑娘，	Had a daughter
卡树卡莎家，	While Hka-shu Hka-sha
有了伙子，	Had a son.
拥昆用甸家的姑娘，	Yonghkum Yongdeng's daughter
嫁给了卡树卡莎家的伙子。	Married Hka-shu Hka-sha's son.
卡树卡莎家，	Hka-shu Hka-sha
有了姑娘，	Had a daughter
盆南诺瑞家，	While Hpunnam No Roi

有了伙子，	Had a son.
卡树卡莎家的姑娘，	Hka-shu Hka-sha's daugher
嫁给了盆南诺瑞家的伙子。	Married Hpunnam No Roi's son.
盆南诺瑞家，	Phunnam No Roi
有了姑娘，	Had a daughter,
木高瓦金囊家，	And Ma-gau Wa Kyingnang
有了伙子，	Had a son.
盆南诺瑞家的姑娘，	Phunnam No Roi's daughter
嫁给了木高瓦金囊家的伙子。	Married Ma-gau Wa Kyingnang's son.
木高瓦金囊家，	Ma-gau Wa Kyingnang
有了姑娘，	Had a daughter,
木日瓦贡扎瓦木干家，	And Marip Wa Kumja Magam
有了伙子，	Had a son.
木高瓦金囊家的姑娘，	Ma-gau Wa Kyingnang's daughter
嫁给了木日瓦贡扎木干家的伙子。	Married Marip Wa Kumja Magam's son.
从此，大地上的人们，	Ever since then, people on the Earth
知道了丈人种和姑爷种。	Have their fathers-in-law and sons-in-law.
大地上的人们更繁衍了，	They reproduce and multiply
更昌盛了。	And become more prosperous than ever before.

第五章　目瑙的来历

Canto 5　The Origin of the Manau Festival

一、天上的目瑙舞

远古，
有了新的天，
有了新的地，
谁先竖目瑙桩，
谁先跳目瑙舞？
太阳出来的地方先竖目瑙桩[1]，
月亮升起的地方先跳目瑙舞。

太阳出来的地方，
竖起了目瑙桩，
月亮升起的地方，

Ⅰ. Manau Dance in Heaven

In remote antiquity,
There emerged the new Sky;
There emerged the new Earth.
Which place should be the first to set up the Manau columns[1]?
Which place should be the first to hold the Manau Dance?
The Manau columns should first be set up in the place where the sun rose.
The Manau Dance should first be held in the place where the moon rose.

In the place where the sun rose
Were set up the Manau columns.
In the place where the moon rose

① 目瑙桩：跳目瑙时，立在舞场中央的四桩。分雌雄，所以也称雌雄牌。上面刻有太阳月亮的图案和传统文化、图腾舞蹈行进的路线纹，下面的两条线表示天地。

① Manau Columns: On the occasion of Manau Festival, in the centre of the arena are set up four vertical columns, on which the patterns of sun, moon, traditional cultural totems as well as dance routes. Across the four vertical columns there are two horizontal ones symbolizing heaven and earth.

围起了目瑙场。	Was created the Manau arena.
谁来当主持，	Who would be the host?
谁来当总管？	Who would be the chief inspector?
占瓦能桑说：	Jan Wa Ningsang said,
“我来当主持，	“I will be the host.
我来当总管。”	I will be the chief inspector.”
谁来当懂萨[①]，	Who would be the priest Dumsa?
谁来念祭辞？	Who would say the prayers?
占瓦能章说：	Jan Wa Ningchyang said,
“我来当懂萨，	“I will be the priest Dumsa.
我来念祭辞。”	I will say the prayers.”
谁来当斋瓦，	Who would be the Jaiwa chanter?
谁来吟颂辞？	Who would chant the lyrics?
颇干杜真塔说：	Hprogam Du Jinghta said,
“我来当斋瓦，	“I will be the Jaiwa chanter.
我来吟颂辞。”	I will chant the lyrics.”
谁来当领舞，	Who would be the leading dancer?
谁来当先导？	Who would lead the dance group?

① 懂萨：吟唱祭辞的神职人员，即麽陶。

木左志圣热说：	Matso Ji Shing-ra said,
“我来当领舞，	“I will be the leading dancer.
我来当先导。”	I will lead the dance group.”
谁来帮领舞，	Who would be the assistant to the leading dancer?
谁来助先导？	Who would assist the leading dancer?
木左瓦毛浪说：	Matso Wa Maulam said,
“我来帮领舞，	“I will be the assistant to the leading dancer.
我来助先导。”	I will assist the leading dancer.”
谁来管屠宰，	Who would be the butcher?
谁来管祭坛？	Who would be in charge of the sacrificial altar?
木左肯万诺木努说：	Matso Hkringwan No Munu said,
“我来管屠宰，	“I will be the butcher.
我来管祭坛。”	I will be in charge of the sacrificial altar.”
谁来管祭酒，	Who would be the alcohol server?
谁来当监督？	Who would serve as the inspector?
木夺直卡说：	Mado Jahka said,
“我来管祭酒，	“I will be the alcohol server.
我来当监督。”	I will serve as the inspector.”
目瑙桩竖好了，	Manau columns were set up;
目瑙场整好了，	A Manau arena was created.

该有的都有了，	Everything necessary was gathered;
该做的都做了，	Every preparation was done.
天上的目瑙舞，	The Manau dance in Heaven
就要开始了。	Was to begin.
潘格来遮能代	Hpan Galai Chye Ningtai asked
问目瑙主管说：	The chief inspector,
“你们跳目瑙，	“When you hold the Manau Dance,
你们献什么神，	What god are you going to sacrifice to?
你们祭什么祖？”	What ancestor are you going to offer the sacrifice to?”
主管回答说：	The chief inspector replied,
“天上的目瑙舞，	“To hold the Manau Dance in Heaven,
我们献金神，	We are going to sacrifice to God of Gold;
我们祭银神。”	We are going to offer the sacrifice to God of Silver.”
金神献过了，	God of Gold had been sacrificed to;
银神祭过了，	God of Silver had been offered the sacrifice.
天上的目瑙，	The Manau Dance in Heaven
在宽广的太阳宫，	Was solemnly undergoing
隆重地进行着。	In the grand Sun Palace.
前面是领舞，	Going ahead was the leading dancer,
后面是舞队，	Who was followed by the dancing group.

跳的热闹地跳着，	The dancers were dancing excitedly;
唱的高声地唱着，	The singers were singing loudly.
天上的目瑙舞，	The Manau Dance in Heaven
跳得多热闹，	Was a display of exciting dancing
唱得多欢乐。	As well as joyful singing.
目瑙舞跳过后，	After the Manau Dance,
主持目瑙的富有了，	The host of the Manau became rich;
主管目瑙的如意了。	The chief inspector of the Manau was satisfied.

二、鸟类的目瑙 Ⅱ. Manau Dance of the Birds

远古，	In remote antiquity,
鸟类参加了天上的目瑙，	Birds attended the Manau Dance Festival in Heaven.
返回大地时，	On their way back to Earth,
来到康星央枯地方，	In the place called Hkrang-sin Yang Hku,
那里有一棵黄果树，	They felt so happy
上面结满了熟透的黄果。	To have seen
百鸟看见了，	That there grew an orange tree
它们是多么高兴。	Bearing lots of ripe oranges.
支尼年鸟说：	The Chya Nnyi Nyet bird said,

“这么好吃的黄果，	“They are delicious oranges.
让我们围起来，	Let’s surround the tree
悄悄吃掉吧。”	And eat them all without being noticed.”
石介鸟说：	The Shakrai bird said,
“这么好的黄果，	“They are delicious oranges.
不能光我们吃掉，	We cannot eat them alone.
应该请来所有的鸟类，	Let’s invite all kinds of birds
共同把黄果分享。”	To share with us the oranges.”
胜独鸟说：	The Shingtu bird said,
“这么好看的黄果，	“They are such beautiful oranges.
就这样吃掉，	It’s pity for them
实在太可惜，	To just be eaten and gone.
我们不如学着太阳宫，	Why don’t we imitate the Sun Palace
请来所有的鸟类，	And invite all kinds of birds
举行一次目瑙，	To hold a great Manau event
再欢欢乐乐地吃黄果。”	Before eating the oranges.”
所有的鸟	All the birds present
都同意了胜独鸟的建议，	Agreed with the Shingtu bird.
请来了所有的鸟类，	They invited all the other kinds of birds.
在黄果树上，	They would hold a Manau event
就要举行鸟类的目瑙了。	In the orange tree.

谁来当主持，	Who would be the host?
谁来做总管？	Who would be the chief inspector?
胜独鸟说：	The Shingtu bird said,
“我来当主持，	“I will be the host.
我来做总管。”	I will be the chief inspector.”
谁来当斋瓦，	Who would be the Jaiwa chanter?
谁来吟颂辞？	Who would chant the lyrics?
鹦哥鸟说：	The parrot said,
“我来当斋瓦，	“I will be the Jaiwa chanter.
我来吟颂辞。”	I will chant the lyrics.”
直到今天，	Ever since then,
鹦哥鸟的声音	The voice of parrots
仍然是哦……哦格岛日[1]。	Sounds like chanting.
谁来当懂萨，	Who would be the priest Dumsa?
谁来当祭辞？	Who would say the prayers?
章脑鸟说：	The Chyang-ngau bird said,
“我来当懂萨，	“I will be the priest Dumsa.
我来念祭辞。”	I will say the prayers.”
直到今天，	Ever since then,

① 哦……哦格岛日：象声词，即吟唱辞的声音。

章脑鸟的声音	The voice of Chyang-ngau birds
仍然是章脑，章脑[1]。	Sounds lis praying.
谁来管屠宰，	Who would be the butcher?
谁来管祭坛？	Who would be in charge of the sacrificial altar?
登科鸟说：	The Ding-hkok bird said,
“我来管屠宰，	“I will be the butcher.
我来管祭坛。”	I will be in charge of the sacrificial altar.”
直到今天，	Ever since then,
登科鸟的声音	The voice of Ding-hkok birds
仍然是科科、科科[2]。	Sounds like chopping meat.
谁来当领舞，	Who would be the leading dancer?
谁来当先导？	Who would lead the dance group?
犀鸟说：	The hornbill said,
“我来当领舞，	“I will be the leading dancer.
我来当先导。”	I will lead the dance.”
犀鸟头太大，	But the hornbill's head was too big,
别的鸟不跟着它；	And no other birds would follow him.
犀鸟的声音太粗重，	The hornbill's voice was too harsh,
别的鸟不愿听。	And no other birds would like to hear it.

① 章脑：象声词，念祭辞的声音。
② 科科：象声词，指剁肉的声音。

犀鸟当不成领舞，	The hornbill could not be the leading dancer;
犀鸟当不成先导，	The hornbill could not lead the dance.
它又请求主持说：	He pleaded with the host,
“就算做不成领舞，	“Even though I cannot be the leading dancer,
就算当不成先导，	Even if I cannot lead the dance,
也在我的头上	Please leave a mark① as a memento
做一个纪念的记号①。”	On my head.”
按犀鸟的要求，	The hornbill's wish was realized.
犀鸟的样子	Ever since then, the image of the hornbill
被做成了领舞的头饰。	Has been the head ornament for the leading dancers.

谁又来当领舞，	Who would be the leading dancer?
谁又来当先导？	Who would lead the dance group?
孔雀说：	The peacock said,
“我来当领舞，	“I will be the leading dancer.
我来当先导。”	I will lead the dance.”

谁来帮领舞，	Who would be the assistant to the leading dancer?
谁来助先导？	Who would assist the leading dancer?

① 记号：直到今天，目瑙领舞的头罩是用犀鸟的头做装饰，据说就是当时由于犀鸟做不成领舞而安慰它的。

① Mark: Up to this day, the hoods worn by the Manau leading dancers are decorated with hornbill heads as a sign of comfort offered to that hornbill.

勒农省瓦鸟和苏梅银鸟说：	The Lanung Sinwa bird and Sumui Yit bird said,
“我们来当领舞，	“We will be the assistants to the leading dancer.
我们来做先导。”	We will assist the leading dancer.”

谁来平目瑙场，	Who would flatten the Manau arena?
谁来整目瑙场？	Who would level the Manau arena?
支边别鸟说：	The Chyabyen Bye bird said,
“我来平目瑙场，	“I will flatten the Manau arena.
我来整目瑙场。”	I will level the Manau arena.”

谁来管酒，	Who would be in charge of alcohol?
谁来斟酒？	Who would serve the alcohol to guests?
凰仙鸟说：	The phoenix said,
“我来管酒，	“I will take charge of alcohol.
我来斟酒。”	I will serve alcohol to guests.”
直到今天，	Ever since then,
凰仙鸟的声音	The singing of phoenixes
仍然是相相、仙仙①。	Sounds likc pouring alcohol.

谁来当监督，	Who would be the supervisor?
谁来管分工？	Who would supervise the division of work?
直灵鸟说：	The Jingling bird said,
“我来当监督，	“I will be the supervisor.

① 相相、仙仙：斟酒声。

我来管分工。 I will supervise the division of work."
直到今天， Ever since then,
直灵鸟的声音， The singing of Jingling birds
仍然是顶顶、顶顶①。 Sounds like saying "Hold on! Hold on!"

谁来管分， Who would take charge of the allotment?
谁来管发？ Who would take charge of the delivery?
松拾木丽拾鸟说： The Sumshi Mali Shi bird said,
"我来管分， "I will take charge of the allotment.
我来管发。" I will take charge of the delivery."
直到今天， Ever since then,
松拾木丽拾鸟的声音， The singing of the Sumshi Mali Shi bird
仍然是松拾木丽拾②。 Sounds like counting the numbers thirty and forty.

谁来烧火， Who would make a fire?
谁来煮饭？ Who would cook meals?
恩直支锐鸟说： The Nji Chyaroi bird said,
"我来烧火， "I will make a fire.
我来煮饭。" I will cook meals."
直到今天， Ever since then,
恩直支锐鸟的声音， The singing of the Nji Chyaroi bird

① 顶顶、顶顶：坚持、坚持之意。
② 松拾木丽拾：三十、四十之意。

仍然是老地木、老地木[1]。	Sounds like "Hurry up! Hurry up!"
谁去背水，	Who would fetch water?
谁去打水？	Who would carry water?
空代乌公鸟说：	The Hkumtai Ugum bird said,
"我去背水，	"I will fetch water.
我去打水。"	I will carry water."
直到今天，	Ever since then,
空代乌公鸟仍然是恩空、恩空[2]。	The singing of Hkumtai Ugum birds Sounds like the breath of exhaustion.
谁来泡酒，	Who would make the drink?
谁来捣酒？	Who would pour the drink?
盆牙种鸟说：	The Hpun-ya Jung bird said,
"我来泡酒，	"I will make the drink.
我来捣酒。"	I will pour the drink."
直到今天，	Since then, the singing of Hpun-ya Jung birds
盆牙种鸟仍然是布布、布布[3]。	Sounds like pouring the drink.
谁来舂碓，	Who would husk rice?

① 老地木、老地木：快做吧，快做吧之意。

② 恩空、恩空：指背水喘气的声音。

③ 布布、布布：指捣酒的声音。

谁来簸米？
恩梅曼突鸟说：
“我来舂碓，
我来簸米。”
直到今天，
恩梅曼突鸟的声音，
仍然是叶西鲁、叶西鲁[1]。

Who would separate the rice from the chaff?
The Nmoi Mam Htu bird said,
“I will husk rice.
I will fan off the chaff.”
And today,
The singing of Nmoi Mam Htu birds
Sounds like the work song for husking rice.

谁来扫目瑙场，
谁来收目瑙场？
坡总松鸟说：
“我来扫目瑙场，
我来收目瑙场。”

Who would clean up the Manau arena?
Who would tidy up the Manau arena?
The Hpotsong Sok bird said,
“I will clean up the Manau arena.
I will tidy up the Manau arena.”

谁来送垃圾，
谁来倒垃圾？
乌快鸟说：
“我来送垃圾，
我来倒垃圾。”

Who would dump the litter?
Who would empty the dustbin?
The Uhkoi bird said,
“I will dump the litter.
I will empty the dustbin.”

该有的都有了，
该做的都做了。

Everything was ready.
Every preparation was done.

① 叶西鲁、叶西鲁：舂米的号子声。

用树杆做目瑙桩，	Tree trunks were used to make Manau columns.
用树枝做横档，	Tree branches were used to make boards.
用树梢做舞场。	Tree tops were used to encircle the Manau arena.
所有的鸟都跳起来了，	All birds danced.
所有的鸟都唱起来了。	All birds sang.
它们是多高兴，	How happy they were.
它们是多欢乐。	How joyful they felt.
就在这个时候，	Just then,
苏瓦木都和能匡斋瓦贡东都卡	Sut Wa Madu and Ninghkong Jaiwa Gumtung Tu Hkra
来到了黄果树下，	Arrived at the orange tree.
看到了鸟类的目瑙舞。	Seeing the birds' Manau Dance,
他们便大声问：	They shouted,
“树上的是做什么的呀？”	"What are you doing up there?"
树上的鸟回答说：	The birds in the tree replied,
“我们到天上参加日瑙，	"We have attended the Manau Dance in Heaven,
来到这里看到满树的黄果，	And on the way back we see the orange tree with ripe oranges.
我们心里高兴，	We are so happy
就学着天上的太阳神，	That we imitate the Sun God
跳起了目瑙舞。”	And have our own Manau Dance."

苏瓦木都又问：	Sut Wa Madu asked,
“树上跳目瑙，	“You have a Manau Dance in the tree,
主持是谁呀？”	But who is the host?”
树上回答说：	The ones in the tree replied,
“主持是胜独鸟。”	“The host is the Shing Tu bird.”
胜独鸟又问：	Then the Shing Tu bird asked,
“树下的是谁呀？”	“Who is that under the tree?”
树下的回答说：	The one under the tree replied,
“听着吧，	“Hey listen!
树上的叫胜独鸟，	The one in the tree is named Shing Tu bird,
树下的叫苏瓦木都，	And the one under the tree is named Sut Wa Madu.
名字相称了，	Our names are well-matched.
名字相配了。”	Our names accord with each other's.”

树下又问道：	There was another question from under the tree,
“树上的目瑙斋瓦是谁呀？”	“Which one of you is the Jaiwa chanter?”
树上回答说：	There came the reply from in the tree,
“树上的目瑙斋瓦，	“The Jaiwa chanter here
是能哦吴然鸟。”	Is the Ningngon Ura bird.”
树上又问道：	And there was also another question from in the tree,
“树下的是谁呀？”	“Who is that under the tree?”
树下回答说：	The one under the tree replied,
“听着吧，	“Hey listen!
上面的斋瓦叫能哦吴然，	The Jaiwa chanter in the tree is named Ningngon Ura.

下面的斋瓦叫贡东都卡，	The Jaiwa chanter under the tree is named Gumtung Tu Hkra.
名字相称了，	Our names are well-matched.
名字相配了，	Our names accord with each other's.
树下的人们，	People living under trees
也能跳目瑙了。"	Can also hold a Manau Dance."

三、大地上的目瑙　Ⅲ. Manau Dance on the Earth

远古，	In remote antiquity,
苏瓦木都和干占肯努	Sut Wa Madu and Kan Jan Hkringngu
在黄果树下	Witnessed under the orange tree
看到了鸟类的目瑙，	The Manau danced by birds.
便学着鸟类的样子，	They therefore followed the birds,
也要举办目瑙。	And decided to hold a Manau event on the Earth.
苏瓦木都和干占肯努，	Sut Wa Madu and Kan Jan Hkringngu
他们举办的目瑙，	Decided to hold the Manau Dance
选在正月中旬[①]。	In the middle of Lunar January[①].

① 正月中旬：在农历正月十五。直到今天，景颇族的目瑙仍选在这个日子。

① Mid-January: It refers to the 15th day of January on the lunar calendar. Up to this day, Jingpo people's Manau Festival is celebrated on the same day.

吟颂辞的斋瓦有了，	They already had the Jaiwa chanter.
念祭辞的懂萨来了；	They already had the Dumsa prayer.
管祭坛的肯庄有了，	They also had the Hkinjong in charge of the altar.
泡酒的盆伦来了；	And then there came the drink-maker Hpunlum.
舂碓的有了，	They had the one to husk rice.
簸米的来了。	And there came the one to separate the rice from the chaff.
目瑙桩竖起了，	The Manau columns were erected;
目瑙档支好了，	The Manau boards were fastened;
舞场整好了，	The Manau arena was leveled;
祭坛设好了，	The altar was set up.
长长的木鼓敲响了，	The long drum was played;
圆圆的大铓敲响了。	The round gong was struck.
苏瓦木都和干占肯努，	The Manau event
他们举办的目瑙，	Held by Sut Wa Madu and Kan Jan Hkringngu
隆重又热闹。	Was a grand scene of bustle and excitement.
跳完目瑞舞后，	When the Manau was over,
苏瓦木都和干占肯努，	Sut Wa Madu and Kan Jan Hkringngu became rich,
白米吃不完了，	White rice was more than enough;
红米堆成山了，	Red rice was piled as high as a mountain;
鸡猪数不清了，	Chicken and pigs being too many to be counted;
牛马满山坡了；	Oxen and horses were scattered over the hillsides.

金银门开了，	Their door to gold and silver was opened;
繁衍路通了。	Their road to prosperity was paved.
远古，	In remote antiquity,
德如曾利和木干真梯，	There were Daru Tsingli and Magam Chyinghti,
看到苏瓦木都和干占肯努	Who personally experienced the Manau
举办的目瑙，	Held by Sut Wa Madu and Kan Jan Hkringngu.
学着他们的样子，	They wanted to follow them as an example
也要举办目瑙。	And hold a Manau event.
德如曾利和木干真梯	The Manau event
他们举办的目瑙，	Held by Daru Tsingli and Magam Chyinghti
也选在正月中旬。	Was also set in the middle of lunar January
吟颂辞的斋瓦有了，	They already had the Jaiwa chanter;
念祭辞的懂萨来了；	They already had the Dumsa prayer.
管祭坛的肯庄有了，	They also had the Hkinjong in charge of the altar.
泡酒的盆伦来了；	And then there came the drink-maker Hpunlum.
舂米的有了，	They had the one to husk rice.
簸米的来了。	And there came the one to separate the rice from the chaff.
目瑙桩竖起了，	The Monau columns were erected;
目瑙档支好了，	The Monau boards were fastened;
舞场整好了，	The Manau arena was leveled;

祭坛设好了，	The altar was set up.
长长的木鼓敲响了，	The long drum was played;
圆圆的大铓敲响了。	The round gong was struck.
德如曾利和木干真梯，	The Manau event
他们举办的目瑙	Held by Daru Tsingli and Magam Chyinghti
隆重又热闹。	Was a grand scene of bustle and excitement.
跳完目瑙舞后，	When the Manau Dance was over,
德如曾利和木干真梯。	Daru Tsingli and Magam Chyinghti became rich,
白米吃不完了，	White rice was more than enough;
红米堆成山了，	And red rice piled as high as a mountain;
鸡猪数不清了，	Chicken and pigs too many to be counted;
牛马满山坡了，	Oxen and horses scattered over the hillsides.
金银门开了，	Their door to gold and silver was opened;
繁衍路通了。	Their road to prosperity was paved.
远古，	In remote antiquity,
木托贡央和登萨勒刚，	There were Mahto Kum-yang and Tingsa Lakang
看到德如曾利和木干真梯	Who personally experienced the Manau
举办的目瑙，	Held by Daru Tsingli and Magam Chyinghti.
学着他们的样子，	They wanted to follow them as an example
也要举办目瑙。	And hold a Manau event.
木托贡央和登萨勒刚，	The Manau event

他们举办的目瑙，	Held by Mahto Kum-yang and Tingsa Lakang
也选在正月中旬。	Was also set for the middle of lunar January.
吟颂辞的斋瓦有了，	They already had the Jaiwa chanter;
念祭辞的懂萨来了；	They already had the Dumsa prayer.
管祭坛的肯庄有了，	They also had the Hkinjong in charge of the altar.
泡酒的盆伦来了；	And then there came the drink-maker Hpunlum.
舂碓的有了，	They had the one to husk rice.
簸米的来了。	And there came the one to fan off rice chaff.
目瑙桩竖起了，	The Manau columns were erected;
目瑙档支好了，	The Manau boards were fastened;
舞场整好了，	The Manau arena was leveled;
祭坛设好了，	The altar was set up.
长长的本鼓敲响了，	The long drum was played;
圆圆的大铓敲响了。	The round gong was struck.
木托贡央和登萨勒刚，	The Manau event
他们举办的目瑙	Held by Mu-tuo Gong-yang and Tingsa Lakang
隆重又热闹。	Was a grand scene of bustle and excitement.
跳完目瑙舞后，	When the Manau Dance was over,
木托贡央和登萨勒刚，	Mahto Kum-yang and Tingsa Lakang became rich,
白米吃不完了。	White rice was more than enough;
红米堆成山了，	Red rice piled as high as a mountain;
鸡猪数不清了，	Chicken and pigs too many to be counted;

牛马满山坡了，	Oxen and horses scattered over the hillsides.
金银门开了，	Their door to gold and silver was opened;
繁衍路通了。	Their road to prosperity was paved.

远古，	In remote antiquity,
瓦切瓦星贡木干和木贡格旁木占，	There were Wahkyet Wa Singgong Magam and Magong Kabang Majan,
看到木托贡央和登萨勒刚	Who personally experienced the Manau
举办的目瑙，	Held by Mahto Kum-yang and Tingsa Lakang.
学着他们的样子，	They wanted to follow them as an example
也要举办目瑙。	And hold a Manau event.

瓦切瓦星贡木干和木贡格旁木占，	The Manau event
他们举办的目瑙，	Held by Wahkyet Wa Singgong Magam and Magong Kabang Majan
也选在正月中旬。	Was also set for the middle of lunar January.
吟颂词的斋瓦有了，	They already had the Jaiwa chanter;
念祭词的懂萨来了；	They already had the Dumsa prayer.
管祭坛的肯庄有了，	They also had the Hkinjong in charge of the altar.
泡酒的盆伦来了；	And then there came the drink-maker Hpunlum.
舂碓的有了，	They had the one to husk rice.
簸米的来了。	And there came the one to separate the rice from the chaff.

目瑙桩竖起了，
目瑙档支好了，
舞场整好了，
祭坛设好了，
长长的本鼓敲响了，
圆圆的大铓敲响了。
瓦切瓦星贡木干和木贡格旁木占，
他们举办的目瑙，
隆重又热闹。

The Manau columns were erected;
The Manau boards were fastened.
The Manau arena was leveled;
The altar was set up.
The long drum was played;
The round gong was struck.
The Manau event
Held by Wahkyet Wa Singgong Magam and Magong Kabang Majan
Was a grand scene of bustle and excitement.

跳完目瑙舞后，
瓦切瓦星贡木干和木贡格旁木占，
白米吃不完了。
红米堆成山了，
鸡猪数不清了，
牛马满山坡了，
金银门开了，
繁衍路通了。

When the Manau was over,
Wahkyet Wa Singgong Magam and Magong Kabang Majan became rich,
White rice was more than enough;
Red rice piled as high as a mountain;
Chicken and pigs too many to be counted;
Oxen and horses scattered over the hillsides.
Their door to gold and silver was opened;
Their road to prosperity was paved.

四、牵目瑙牛

Ⅳ. Getting Manau Oxen

远古，	In remote antiquity,
勒扎占说过，	Laja Jan once said
等将来举办目瑙，	If people on the Earth held the Manau event but
如果没有牛，	Did not have an ox,
就让大斋瓦们	The Jaiwa chanters could
背上金，	Carry gold bars
带上银，	And shoulder silver straps
到勒扎地方来牵牛。	To get an ox from the place called Laja.
因为要举办目瑙，	Because they had decided to hold a Manau event,
没有牛宰杀，	But did not have an ox,
照勒扎占说过的话，	As what Laja Jan had said to them,
大斋瓦们，	The Jaiwa chanters,
背上金，	Carrying gold bars
带上银，	And shouldering silver straps,
到勒扎地方牵牛去了。	Set out for the place called Laja to get the ox.
牵牛的斋瓦们，	The Jaiwa chanters
从盆代央动身，	Set out on a journey from Hpuntai Yang.

从盆代央起步，	They left Hpuntai Yang
来到贡老格列地方，	And then arrived at a place called Gumlau Kale.
翻过了克度坡，	They climbed over the Hkritu Hill,
渡过了克度河，	Crossed the Hkritu River,
来到昔马恩康地方；	And then arrived at a place called Sama Nhkang.
又走过逃热缺地方，	Then they passed a place called Htaura Hkyet,
来到恩坎地方，	And arrived at a place called En-kan.
又走过格栗买贡地方，	Then they walked past a place called Kali Maikung,
来到了阿商牙地方。	And arrived at a place called Ashang Yang.
牵牛的斋瓦们，	The Jaiwa chanters
越过了德榜亚坝，	Traveled across the Dabak Yang Valley,
渡过了德榜河，	Crossed the Dabak Yang River,
来到德崩地方；	And then arrived at a place called Dabung.
翻过了帮布达山，	Then they climbed over Prang Bada Hill,
渡过了恩门河；	Crossed the Nmun Hka River.
走过了能祖岔路口，	They walked past a forked road called Ningtsu,
来到了农毛地方；	And arrived at a place called Ningmau.
渡过了恩缅足河，	Then they crossed over the Nmyen Zup River,
来到达诺渡口，	And arrived at a ferry called Dano.
来到黎坡央地方，	Next they arrived at a place called Lihpom Yang,
走过了木东盆端杜地方。	And then passed a place called Madong Hpunton Tu.
牵牛的斋瓦们，	The Jaiwa chanters

越过吕帕央坝，
走过了贡几能蓬地方；
来到木章玉东地方，
走过了肯纠吕坎木达地方；
来到杂坡玉然地方，
走过了阿杰原阿莲地方；
来到了能肯敢年都格瓦苦地方，
走过了张旁顶盆地方；
走到了恩奔格兰龙地方，
走过了木尚根尚地方，
来到了巴松当桑的地方。

Traveled across the Loihpra Yang Valley,
Passed a place called Kungkyi Ninghpung,
And then arrived at a place called Majang Yitdung.
They passed a place called Hkinkyu Loihkam Mada,
And arrived at a place called Zahpo Yitra.
They passed a place called Akyet Yan Alet
And arrived at a river called Ninghking Gatnem Tu Kawa Hku.
They passed a place called Janghpang Dinghput
And arrived at a place called Nbon Kalan Lup.
They passed a place called Mashang Kinshang
And arrived at a place called Basum Tangsang.

牵牛的斋瓦们，
来到巴松那荣地方，
走过了磨康诗达地方，
来到磨康地拉东地方；
走过了洛桑诗达地方；
越过荣纳勒央坝，
走过了孟凯同巴地方；
来到荣纳真康地方，
走过了相招真康地方，
来到桑拍瓦央地方，
走过了当拍杜歪地方。

The Jaiwa chanters
Arrived at a place called Basum Narong.
Then they passed a place called Mohkang Shada
And arrived at a place called Mohkang Di La Tong.
They passed a place called Loksak Shada;
They traveled through a valley called Rumna Layang.
They passed a place called Munghkai Htumpang
And arrived at a place called Rumna Chyinghkrang.
They passed a place called Sengchyau Jinghkang
And then arrived at a place called Samhpe Wayang.
And they passed a place called Tanghpe Du Wai.

牵牛的斋瓦们，	The Jaiwa chanters
渡过勒孔空木足河，	Crossed over the Lahkong Hkrum Mazup River.
走过了能荣格答地方；	They passed a place called Numrong Gadap
来到待歪荣达地方，	And then arrived at a place called Taiwai Rumda.
渡过了韦诗足河；	They crossed the Wuishi Zup River
翻过戛萨贡山，	And climbed over Mount Ga Za Kong.
走过了东苏荣地方；	They passed a place called Dumsu Rong
来到阿诗八戛都地方，	And arrived at a place called Ashi Bakka Tu.
穿过了能郭苦，	They crossed the Ningkrop River;
渡过石羊卡河，	They crossed the Shiyang Hka River.
翻过待扬木里山，	They travelled over Mount Taiyang Mali;
走过了恩兰兰阿戛地方，	They then passed a place called Nlan Lan Aga
来到恩伴伴阿戛地方。	And arrived at a place called Nban Ban Aga.

牵牛的斋瓦们，	The Jaiwa chanters
走过了勒伴旁阿戛地方，	Walked past a place called Laban Hpang Aga.
来到勒伴康戛地方，	And they arrived at a place called Laban Hkang Ga.
走过了播萨播年戛地方，	They passed a place called Popsa Popnyeng Ga.
来到了登卡坎地方，	And they arrived at a place called Dinghkra Hkrat.
走过了盆尼木谷地方，	They passed a place called Hpunnyi Magut
来到了恩龙木荣东地方，	And arrived at a place called Nlung Marong Tong.
走过了蒙冒诗瓦狄东地方，	They passed a place called Mungmau Shawa Ditong
来到了诗依东鼓布地方，	And arrived at a place called Shayi Tunggu Bu.

走到了勒波恩旁杜地方。	They then passed a place called Lahpo Nhprang Tu.
牵牛的斋瓦们，	The Jaiwa chanters
来到诗南恩旁杜地方，	Arrived at a place called Shanum Nhprang Tu.
走过了诗高康戛地方，	They passed a place called Shakau Hkang Ga
来到了勒肩康戛地方，	And arrived at a place called Lagyen Hkang Ga.
翻过了都途格东山；	They walked over a mountain called Mount Tu Htu Gadong;
翻过登戛格东山，	They traveled across a mountain called Mount Dingga Gadong.
翻过了瓦仁贡山；	They crossed over Mount Wa Ring Kong.
渡过德如底羊格坎渡口，	They crossed the Daru Tiyang Gahakan Ferry.
走过了勒帕等腊都地方，	They passed a place called Lahpa Dingla Tu.
来到阿明瓦洋地方，	They arrived at a place called Amyin Wayang.
走过了木饶诗达地方。	And later they passed a place called Marau Shada.
牵牛的斋瓦们，	The Jaiwa chanters
来到木唐尚地方，	Arrived at a place called Mahtang Shang.
走过了格纯孟拱地方；	They passed a place called Kashun Munggong
来到松浪康地方，	And arrived at a place called Sumlang Hkang.
走过了昔马康地方，	They passed a place called Sama Hkang.
翻过荣背崩山，	They crossed over Mount Rumboi Bum.
走过了瓦蒙旁地方，	They passed a place called Wamung Hpang
来到勒弄康地方，	And arrived at a place called Lalong Hkang.

漂过了勒弄朋英湖；	They boated across the Lalong Hpung-ing Lake.
渡过了兹廊兹囊卡河，	They crossed the Zakro Zanang Hka River.
走过了勒高荣达地方。	They then passed a place called Lagau Rumda.
牵牛的斋瓦们，	The Jaiwa chanters
来到龙康格热地方，	Arrived at a place called Lunghkrang Garet.
走过了狄玛洋地方；	They passed a place called Dima Yang
来到贡狄玉东地方，	And arrived at a place called Gumdi Yitdung.
走过了贡通玉然地方，	They passed a place called Gumhtong Yitra
来到肯志拴地方，	And arrived at a place called Hkinji Shon.
走过了戛昂玉东地方，	They passed a place called Gaang Yitdung
来到声然玉然地方，	And arrived at a place called Shing-ra Yitra.
走过了阿康阿浪东地方；	They traveled past a place called Ahkang Alang Tong.
来到木剂勒盘都戛地方，	They arrived at a place called Matsi Lahpat Tu Ga
走过了隐箭克坦崩都地方。	Then passed a place called Yintsen Hkridat Bong Tu.
牵牛的斋瓦们，	The Jaiwa chanters
来到朱日旺岔路口，	Arrived at a forked road called Ju Rawang.
翻过了吕卡贡山，	They crossed Mount Loihka Gong.
翻过跟萨都真康山，	They crossed Mount Kinsa Tu Jinghkang.
走过了昔南木然都戛地方，	They passed a place called Sanam Mara Tu Ga.
越过阿苏控制勒扎盆地，	They traveled over a basin called Asut Hkungji Laja.
来到东奔瓦洋地方，	And they finally arrived at a place called Tumbon Wayang.
斋瓦们高兴地唱道，	The Jaiwas joyfully chanted,

“哎啰，	“Gee!
要说好呀，	To mention the best place,
就数东奔瓦洋地方。	It must be Tumbon Wayang.
这里的姑娘，	Girls in this place have
身材多匀称，	Beautiful figures
容貌多迷人。	And charming faces.
要说平坦呀，	To mention the flattest place,
就数东奔瓦洋地方。	It must be Tumbon Wayang.
要说心好呀，	To mention the girls with kindest hearts,
就数这个地方的姑娘。”	It must be the girls in Tumbon Wayang.”

东奔瓦洋地方，	Tumbon Wayang
实在是太美好了，	Was such a beautiful place
牵牛的斋瓦们，	That the Jaiwa chanters
怕自己的魂留恋那里，	Feared that their souls would not leave.
又难过地唱道：	They then chanted sorrowfully,
“哎啰，	“Gee!
要说难在呀，	To mention the worst place,
就数东奔瓦洋地方；	It must be Tumbon Wayang.
要说难看呀，	To mention the most ugly place,
就数东奔瓦洋地方的姑娘；	It must be girls in Tumbon Wayang.
要说陡峭呀，	To mention the steepest place,
就数东奔瓦洋地方；	It must be Tumbon Wayang.
要说狠毒呀，	To mention the most savage girls,

就数东奔瓦洋地方的姑娘；	It must be those in Tumbon Wayang.
过路的出门人呀，	Travelers on a journey,
不要留恋这个地方。”	Do not linger in this place."
牵牛的斋瓦们唱完	Finishing their chanting songs,
又继续赶路了。	The Jaiwa chanters went on.

牵牛的斋瓦们，	The Jaiwa chanters went on with their journey.
渡过阿浪顶空格坎渡口，	They crossed the Alang Dinghkong Gahkan Ferry.
走过了盆总地方，	They passed a place called Hprut Zup.
来到盆崩颂地方，	They arrived at a place called Hprut Bungso
来到盆木顶，	And arrived at a place called Hprut Madim.
走过了盆栾盆端都地方；	They then passed a place called Hpunglong Hpunton Tu.
来到达光背哦诗牙地方，	They arrived at a place called Dagong Hkringngu Shaya.
走过了松斑浪勒枯夺戛地方；	They passed a place called Sumpran Lang Lahkru Do Ga
来到莱然旁戛地方，	And then arrived at a place called Laira Hpang Ga.
走过了木砒龙浪胜然龙坎地方；	They walked over Mount Majoi Lunglam Shing-ra Lunghkram.
来到胜然崩栓地方，	They arrived at a place called Shing-ra Bungshon
走过了木贡更旺胜然奔让地方。	And passed a place called Makum Ginwang Shing-ra Punrang.

牵牛的斋瓦们，	The Jaiwa chanters,
来到木贡更旺地方，	Arriving at the place called Makum Ginwang,
又高兴地唱道：	Again happily chanted,

“木贡更旺地方呀，	“The place Makum Ginwang
什么都有，	Enjoys everything.
样样都齐。	It possesses everything.
哎啰！	Gee!
在这个美好的地方呀，	In this beautiful place,
居住着古老的格仁家族，	There lives the legendary Gareng family.
这里生长着，	In this beautiful place,
最古老的红木树，	There grows old-aged red sandalwood;
还有最早的芭蕉树。	There are also the oldest banana trees.
在这里呀，	In this beautiful place,
有最古的瓦断竹子，	There are the most ancient bamboos;
有最早的勒坡腊波奔叶，	There are the most aged Lahpo Lat Hpobon leaves.
这里的树上，	In the trees of this place,
还生活着最早的长尾鸟。	There live the earliest long-tailed birds.
各种树木呀，	Here can be found
都能在这里找到，	Various kinds of trees.
各种小鸟呀，	Different kinds of birds
都生活在这个地方，	Live here.
这里这么美好，	This place is so beautiful.
怪不得年老的斋瓦，	No wonder our Jaiwa ancestors
常常会提到这个地方。”	Frequently mention this place.”
斋瓦们唱完，	Finishing their chanting of the song,
又继续上路了。	The Jaiwa chanters went on with their journey.

牵牛的斋瓦们，	The Jaiwa chanters
来到陛玛木炭都地方，	Arrived at a place called Byinma Mahtan Tu.
走过了轻么松格朵切地方；	They walked past a place called Hkying Mosung Gado Hkyet.
来到相断真康地方，	And they arrived at a place called Sengdong Jinghkang.
走过了龙让切苦地方；	They walked past the Lung-rang Hkyet Hku River
来到木光吕浪阿布地方，	And arrived at a place called Magong Loilang Abu.
走过了扎日瓦地方；	They then passed a place called Ja Rawa.
来到扎昆肯万地方，	They arrived at a place called Ja-hkun Hkringwan.
走过了达安星达地方；	They passed a place called Da-an Sindda.
来到波奔都直瓦苦地方，	They arrived at the Jawa Hku River.
走过了恩坎龙团地方。	And then they passed a place called Nhkap Lunghton.

牵牛的斋瓦们，	The Jaiwa chanters
来到木砬龙弄地方，	Arrived at a place called Majoi Lungnong.
走过了胜然贡东地方；	They walked past a place called Shing-ra Gongdong.
来到瓦浪吕浪都地方，	And they arrived at a place called Walang Loilang Du.
走过了木光贡仁阿布地方；	They then passed a place called Magong Kungren Abu.
来到戛苦达游地方，	They arrived at a place called Kahkru Dayu.
走过了尤当圆那当康地方，	They passed a place called Yudang Yan Nyadang Hkang.
来到勒耐能明迈戛地方；	They arrived at a place called Langai Ningmyin Mai Ga.
走过了格龙登空东地方，	And then they passed a place called Galung Dinghkong Tong.
来到木萨纳入都戛地方，	They arrived at a place called Masa Na-ru Tu Ga
走过了格顶荣石嫩戛地方。	And then passed a place called Gading Rumshi Nut Ga.

牵牛的斋瓦们，	The Jaiwa chanters
来到阿尼格当木戛贡让地方，	Arrived at a place called Anyip Gadang Maga Kunrang.
走过了崩酸腾然地方；	They walked past a place called Bungson Thing-ra.
来到崩块龙玛地方，	And they arrived at a place called Bunghkoi Lungma.
走过了崩速崩康戛地方；	They then walked past a place called Pungsu Punghkang Ga.
来到勐松盆路口，	They arrived at a crossing called Mungsung.
走过了勐桑岔路口；	Then they passed a forked road called Mungsang.
渡过木章河，	They crossed the Machyang Hka River.
走过了婆暖音旺地方；	They arrived at a place called Hpronon Yinwang.
来到真通浓波岔路口，	They arrived at a forked road called Chyinghtong Numbro.
走过勒扎官庙。	And then they passed a worship altar for Laja family.
翻过千座山，	Crossing thousands of mountains
越过万个坝，	And traveling over thousands of valleys,
牵牛的斋瓦们，	The Jaiwa chanters
终于来到了勒扎寨，	Finally arrived at the Laja Village.
找到了勒扎占，	They visited Laja Jan
开始讲牛价。	And began bargaining for the ox.
斋瓦们说：	The Jaiwa chanters said,
“勒扎占呀，	“Hello, Laja Jan.
按你曾经留下的话，	As what you have promised,
为了举办目瑙，	In order to hold a Manau event,
我们带着金，	We have brought along gold bars;

我们背着银，	We have brought along silver straps
到你这里牵牛，	In order to get the ox.
我们出一两银子，	We offer you fifty grams of silver.
你觉得怎么样？”	What do you say?
勒扎占说：	Laja Jan said,
“斋瓦们呀，	“Hi, Jaiwa chanters.
一两银子，	Fifty grams of silver is not enough
还买不着牛耳朵。”	Even for ox ears.”
斋瓦们又说：	The Jaiwa chanters then said,
“勒扎占呀，	“Well, Laja Jan.
我们出二两银子，	We offer one hundred grams of silver.
你觉得怎么样？”	And what do you say?”
勒扎占说：	Laja Jan said,
“斋瓦们呀，	“Well, Jaiwa chanters.
二两银子，	One hundred grams of silver is not enough
还买不着弯牛角。”	Even for ox horns.”
斋瓦们又说：	The Jaiwa chanters then said,
“勒扎占呀，	“Well, Laja Jan.
我们出三两银子，	We offer one hundred and fifty grams of silver.
你觉得怎么样？”	And what do you say?”
勒扎占说：	Laja Jan said,
“斋瓦们呀，	“Well, Jaiwa chanters.

三两银子，	One hundred and fifty grams of silver
还买不着牛腿。”	Is not enough even for ox legs."
斋瓦们又说：	The Jaiwa chanters then said,
“勒扎占呀，	"Well, Laja Jan.
我们出四两银子，	We offer two hundred grams of silver,
你觉得怎么样？”	And what do you say?"
勒扎占说：	Laja Jan said,
“斋瓦们呀，	"Well, Jaiwa chanters.
四两银子，	Two hundred grams of silver
还买不着半条牛。”	Is not enough for even half of the ox."
斋瓦们又说：	The Jaiwa chanters then said,
“勒扎占呀，	"Well, Laja Jan.
我们出五两银子，	We offer two hundred and fifty grams of silver.
你觉得怎么样？”	And what do you say?"
勒扎占说：	Laja Jan said,
“斋瓦们呀，	"Well, Jaiwa chanters.
五两银子，	Two hundred and fifty grams of silver
不是买牛价。”	Is not a price for an entire ox."
斋瓦们又说：	The Jaiwa chanters then said,
“勒扎占呀，	"Well, Laja Jan.
我们出六两银子，	We offer three hundred grams of silver.

你觉得怎么样？”	And what do you say?”
勒扎占说：	Laja Jan said,
“斋瓦们呀，	“Well, Jaiwa chanters.
六两银子，	With three hundred grams of silver
你们牵不走牛。”	You cannot take the ox away.”

斋瓦们又说：	The Jaiwa chanters then said,
“勒扎占呀，	“Well, Laja Jan.
我们出七两银子，	We offer three hundred and fifty grams of silver.
你觉得怎么样？”	And what do you say?”
勒扎占说：	Laja Jan said,
“斋瓦们呀，	“Well, Jaiwa chanters.
七两银子，	Three hundred and fifty grams of silver
还不到买牛价。”	Is not a good price for an ox.”

斋瓦们又说：	The Jaiwa chanters then said,
“勒扎占呀，	“Well, Laja Jan.
我们出八两银子，	We offer four hundred grams of silver.
你觉得怎么样？”	And what do you say?”
勒扎占说：	Laja Jan said,
“斋瓦们呀，	“Well, Jaiwa chanters.
八两银子，	Four hundred grams of silver.
你们再想想吧。”	You should give it a second thought.”

斋瓦们又说：	The Jaiwa chanters then said,
“勒扎占呀，	“Well, Laja Jan.
我们出九两银子，	We offer four hundred and fifty grams of silver.
你觉得怎么样？”	And what do you say?”
勒扎占说：	Laja Jan said,
“斋瓦们呀，	“Well, Jaiwa chanters.
九两银子，	Can you offer more than
你们还是再加一点吧。”	Four hundred and fifty grams of silver?”

斋瓦们又说：	The Jaiwa chanters then said,
“勒扎占呀，	“Well, Laja Jan.
我们出十两银子，	We offer five hundred grams of silver.
你觉得怎么样？”	And what do you say?”
勒扎占说：	Laja Jan said,
“斋瓦们呀，	“Well, Jaiwa chanters.
十两银子，	Five hundred grams of silver is OK.
你们可以找牛绳了。”	Find a rope for the ox.”

牵牛的斋瓦们，	The Jaiwa chanters
终于和勒扎占	Finally came to an agreement with Laja Jan
讲好了牛价钱，	On the price of the ox.
找到牛绳牵上牛，	They found a rope for the ox
又要动身了。	And got ready to return.

牵牛的斋瓦们，	The Jaiwa chanters
从勒扎寨动身，	Set out from Laja Village.
来到扎日瓦地方，	They arrived at a place called Ja Rawa.
走过了彭奔诗腊地方；	They walked past a place called Hpungpun Shala.
来到栽瑞阿戛地方，	And they arrived at a place called Tsairui Aga.
走过了栽奔阿官地方；	They then passed a place called Zaibon Akron.
来到支量盆郭地方，	They arrived at a crossing called Chyaleng Hpunggo.
走过了阿克都地方；	Then they passed a place called Ahkri Tu.
来到肯杂苦地方；	They arrived at the Hkinza Hku River.
走过了阿苦容洞地方，	And then they passed a place called Ahkrup Rumdung.
来到胜然洞彭地方。	They arrived at a place called Shing-ra Dumhpong.

牵牛的斋瓦们，	The Jaiwa chanters leading the ox
走过了胜然乃帕地方；	Walked past a place called Shing-ra Nai Hpra.
来到阿屯准瓦地方，	And they arrived at a place called Adum Jumwa.
走过了仁生排切地方；	They then passed a place called Rit Singhpai Hkyet.
来到腾乃当勒壮地方，	They arrived at a crossing called Htingnai Dang Lajong.
走过了都伦龙仁地方；	Then they passed a place called Tulum Lup-ring.
来到哦吕龙顶地方，	They arrived at a place called Nga Loi Lupding.
来到阿短星光戛地方，	And then they arrived at a place called Aton Singgong Ga.
走过了荣光圆荣旺木达地方；	They passed a place called Rumgong Yan Rumwang Mada.
来到阿贡木直鲁地方，	And then they arrived at a place called Ahkrung Machyit Lup.
走过了仲通圆真东阿戛地方。	And then they passed a place called Chyunghtong Yan Chyingdong Aga.

牵牛的斋瓦们，	The Jaiwa chanters leading the ox
来到东苏光当德如地方，	Arrived at a place called Dumsu Kongdang Daru.
走过了帕代都地方；	They walked past a place called Hpa-tai Tu.
来到盆甸温顿地方，	And they arrived at a place called Hpunteng Wudun.
走过了崩诗格鲁地方；	They then passed a place called Brungshi Galu.
来到肯弯阿官地方，	They arrived at a crossing called Hkringwon Akron.
走过了登内崩栓地方；	Then they passed a place called Dingnoi Bungshon.
来到恩迈旦龙腊地方，	They arrived at a place called Nmai Dan Lupla.
走过了咱央诗瓦地方；	And then they passed a place called Tsan Yang Shawa.
来到盆都央扎昆戛地方，	They arrived at a place called Hpundu Yang Ja-hkun Ga.
走过了松让暖地方。	And then they passed a place called Sumrang Not.
牵牛的斋瓦们，	The Jaiwa chanters leading the ox
来到阿旦松巴康戛地方，	Arrived at a place called Adam Sumpra Hkang Ga.
来到能让康地方，	They arrived at a place called Ning-rang Hkang.
走过了龙腊康地方；	They walked past a place called Lupla Hkang.
来到勒公旁地方，	And they arrived at a place called Lagum Hpang.
走过了勒公木软地方；	They then passed a place called Lagung Maron.
来到了勒哦木若地方，	They arrived at a crossing called Lagung Maro.
渡过勒刚格坎河渡口；	They crossed the Lakang Gahkan Ferry.
翻过格声格东坡，	And then they crossed over the Gasheng Gadong Hill.
走过了格声寨子；	They passed Gasheng Village
来到赵渊木逃地方，	And then arrived at a place called Jau Yan Mahtau.

跨过了恩先切峡谷。	And then they traveled over the Nsen Hkyet Valley.
牵牛的斋瓦们，	The Jaiwa chanters leading the ox
来到登渊罗昆地方，	Arrived at a place called Ting-yen Lohkon.
走过了罗昆木当地方；	And then they passed a place called Lohkon Madang.
越过能麻央坝，	They traveled over the Ningma Yang Valley.
走过了阿苏枯地方；	They passed the Asut Hku River.
来到崩三省瓦地方，	They arrived at a place called Bungsan Sinwa.
走过了孟暖康戛地方；	They passed a place called Mungnon Hkang Ga.
翻过阿崩渊介空格东山，	They crossed Mount Abrung Yan Kaihkrung Gadong.
走过了依若开屯桥；	They walked past the Numro Hkrai Dun Bridge.
越过农罗乌鲁坝，	They traveled over the Ningro Walu Valley
走过了文蒙仲地方。	And then arrived at a place called Wunmong Jung.
牵牛的斋瓦们，	The Jaiwa chanters leading the ox
来到诗丹木软地方，	Arrived at a place called Shadan Maron.
走过了卡胜克端地方；	And then they passed a place called Hka Shin Hkri-ton.
来到阿刚渊诗邦地方，	And then they arrived at a valley called Agrang Yan Shabang.
走过了荣闪都戛地方；	They passed a place called Rumshat Tu Ga.
来到勒龙腾官戛地方，	They arrived at a place called Lalong Htingkon Ga.
来到依如枯地方，	An then they arrived at the Numru Hku River.
走过了隐浪腾官都地方；	They passed a place called Yunlang Htingkon Tu.
来到乌干省瓦地方，	And then they arrived at a place called Ugam Sinwa.
走过了盆崩诗瓦地方；	They walked through a place called Hpunpom Shawa.

走过乌章开屯桥，	They walked past the Wuchyang Hkrai Dun Bridge.
走过了恩注登散地方。	They traveled through a place called Nju Dingsa.
牵牛的斋瓦们，	The Jaiwa chanters leading the ox
跨过吴苏切峡谷，	Traveled over the Wusu Hkyet Valley.
走过了塔然莱南地方；	They passed a place called Htara Lainam.
越过塔芽扬坝，	They traveled over the Htaya Yang Valley.
走过了迈东登萨地方；	They passed a place called Maitong Dingsa.
来到乌龙登牙地方，	They arrived at a place called Wulum Ting-ya.
走过了恩龙真卡地方；	They passed a place called Nlung Chyinghka.
来到彭干省瓦地方，	They arrived at a place called Hpunggan Sinwa.
翻过了彭干贡山；	They crossed over Mount Hpunggan Gong;
翻过坎道贡山，	They crossed over Mount Hkandau Gong.
走过了鬼旺诗东地方。	Then they passed a place called Guiwang Shitung.
牵牛的斋瓦们，	The Jaiwa chanters leading the ox
来到达荣肯荣地方，	Arrived at a place called Darong Hkinrong.
翻过了恩尊格东山；	They crossed over Mount Ntsun Gadong.
来到载如格列地方，	And then they arrived at a place called Zairu Kale.
翻过了载如格东城；	They traveled over Mount Zairu Gadong.
来到帕然真康地方，	They arrived at a place called Hpa-ra Jinghkang.
走过了格东乌当地方；	They passed a place called Kadung Wudang.
越过了孟东勒央坝，	They traveled through the Mungdung Layang Valley.
走过了木里拜盆洋地方；	They walked through a place called Mali Bai Hpun-yang.

来到鬼占能达地方，	They arrived at a place called Gui Chyat Numda.
走过了能仙达如地方。	And they walked past a place called Ningsen Daru.

牵牛的斋瓦们，	The Jaiwa chanters leading the ox
渡过东邦格坎渡口，	Crossed the Dumbang Gahkan Ferry.
渡过了文里卡河；	They crossed the Wunli Hka River.
翻过了文里山，	They crossed over Mount Wunli.
翻过了昔戛贡山，	They crossed Mount Saga Kong.
来到木章昔玛地方，	Then they arrived at a place called Machyang Sama.
翻过了直卡都依达山，	They crossed over Mount Saga Kong.
来到勒齐贡山，	Then they arrived at a place called Mount Lahkyek Kong.
越过恩东枯地方，	They traveled through the Ndong Hku River.
走过了恩东公地方，	They passed a place called Ndong Krung.
越过了肯直洋坝子，	They traveled through the Hkringji Yang Valley.
走过了能缅开屯桥。	And then they walked over the Ningmyen Hkrai Dun Bridge.

牵牛的斋瓦们，	The Jaiwa chanters leading the ox
来到彭干南布地方，	Arrived at a place called Hpunggan Numbu.
走过了彭干戛地方；	They walked through a place called Hpunggan Ga.
来到恩龙格铺地方，	And they arrived at a place called Nlung Kahpru.
走过了勒杂枯地方；	Then they passed the Laza Hku River.
来到达戛空仁地方，	And they arrived at a place called Daga Hkung-ring.
走过了达戛洛昆地方；	They passed a place called Daga Lohkum.

渡过达戛河，	They crossed over the Daga River.
走过了戛杂戛麻地方，	They walked past a place called Ga-za Ga-ma,
来到高丽切地方，	They arrived at a place called Gauri Hkyet Valley.
走过了刀弄泡夺地方。	And then they passed a place called Daulung Hpaudo.

牵牛的斋瓦们，	The Jaiwa chanters leading the ox
渡过昔马河，	Crossed the Sama River.
走过了背赞峨姜地方；	They walked past a place called Buizan Ngagyang.
渡过闻多格坎渡口，	They crossed the Wonto Gahakn Ferry.
走过荣万切地方，	They passed a valley called Rumwan Hkyet.
来到荣万侬达地方，	And then they arrived at a place called Rumwan Numda.
走过诺浪戛地方；	They passed a place called Nolang Ga.
走过了盆都戛地方，	They passed a place called Hpundu Ga.
来到杂博戛地方，	Then they arrived at a place called Tsap Bo Ga.
翻过了诏蒙崩山；	They crossed over Mount Chyaumong Bum.
翻过诏蒙崩格东山，	They crossed over Mount Chyaumong Bum Gadong.
走过了营盘格定地方。	And then they passed a place called Yinhpan Gadit.

牵牛的斋瓦们，	The Jaiwa chanters leading the ox
渡过商顶卡河，	Crossed the Shangding Hka River
走过了峨敢央地方；	And passed a place called Ngakat Yang.
来到星里开屯桥，	And then they arrived at Sinli Hkrai Dun Bridge.
走过了德弄央地方；	They walked past a place called Delung Yang.
翻过卖包山，	They crossed over Mount Maibau.

渡过了恩布卡河；	They crossed the Npu Hka River.
翻过邦通木达山，	And they climbed over Mount Pranghtum Mada.
渡过了诗雨卡河，	Then they crossed the Shait Hka River.
来到伸然央地方，	And they arrived at a valley called Shing-ra Yang.
走过了巍马央地方；	And then they walked past a place called Woima Yang.
渡过恩泼河，	And then they crossed the Nhpro River.
终于回到了盆代央地方。	And finally they returned to the place Hpuntai Yang.

附记：

景颇族的斋瓦们牵牛的路线，大致与景颇族向南迁徙的路线相符合。据老人们讲，大致是从今天盈江县的卡场开始，到今天缅甸联邦境内的克钦邦，再往恩迈开江逆流而上，一直到今大的四川、青藏高原一带的牧区。

Excursus:

The routes that the Jingpo Jaiwa chanters followed are largely in accordance with the routes that Jingpo ancestors took when they migrated southwards. Based on the stories passed on from old people, the starting place is Kachang in Yingjiang County, and they passed the Kachin area in today's Myanmar, and then walked along the N-mai Hka River until they finally came to the nomadic areas in today's Sichuan Province and Tibetan Plateau.

第六章　大地上的生活

Canto 6　Life on the Earth

一、取　火　　I. Getting Fire

远古，　　In remote antiquity,
大地上的人们，　　People on the Earth
因为没有火，　　Lacking of fire,
吃的是生米，　　Ate raw rice,
嚼的是生肉；　　Chewed raw meat.
生米吃烦了，　　They were tired of eating raw rice;
生肉吃腻了，　　They were fed up with chewing raw meat.
要想煮熟饭，　　In order to cook rice,
要想烤熟肉，　　In order to roast meat,
就得去找火。　　They needed to get fire.

为了找到火，　　To get fire,
每天天一黑，　　Every day when it got dark at night,
东边去找找，　　They went out to search in the east;
西边去看看；　　They went out to search in the west;
南边去找找，　　They went out to search in the south;
北边去看看，　　They went out to search in the north.
终于在一个晚上，　　Finally one night
看到遥远的地方，　　They saw somewhere afar

有一团火的亮光。	There was the light of fire.
可是天一亮，	But when it dawned,
火光消失了，	The light disappeared,
也不知在什么方向。	Giving people no hint of its direction.
等到了晚上，	When night fell,
人们又看到了火光，	People saw the fire light again.
并记住了	They remembered
火光的方向，	The direction of the fire light, which pointed
羌河那边的文浪石洞。	To Wunlang Lungpu near the Qiang River.
火光找到了，	The fire light was found;
火光的方向认准了，	The direction of the fire light was marked.
但不知道派谁能取回火。	But they did not know whom to appoint to get the fire.
有两个叫戛昂拉若拜的年轻人，	There were two young men both named Gaang La Ro Boi,
他们出来说：	Who went forward and said,
“羌河那边的火光，	“As for the fire light over the Qiang River,
我们去找；	We'll go and find it.
文浪石洞的火种，	As for the kindling over the Wunlang Lungpu,
我们去取回来。”	We'll get it back.”
两个年轻人，	The two young men
从戛昂地方出发，	Set out from Gaang

找火光去了，	To look for the fire light
取火种去了。	And to get the kindling material.
翻过一座山，	They crossed over a mountain;
越过两个坝，	They traveled through two valleys.
火光还在远处，	The fire light was far from their reach.
还没有走到羌河边。	They were not near the Qiang River.
翻过三座山，	They crossed over three mountains;
越过四个坝，	They traveled through four valleys.
火光还在远处，	The fire light was far from their reach.
还没有走到羌河边。	They were not near the Qiang River.
翻过五座山，	They crossed over five mountains;
越过六个坝，	They traveled through six valleys.
火光还在远处，	The fire light was far from their reach.
还没有走到羌河边。	They were not near the Qiang River.
翻过七座山，	They crossed over seven mountains;
越过八个坝，	They traveled through eight valleys.
火光还在远处，	The fire light was far from their reach.
还没有走到羌河边。	They were not near the Qiang River.
翻过九座山，	They crossed over nine mountains;

越过十个坝，	They traveled through ten valleys.
来到了羌河边，	They came near the Qiang River.
可是羌河没有桥。	But there was no bridge over the river.
两个年轻人，	The two young men
砍来了木头。	Chopped down a log.
用木头和藤条	And out of the log and rattan
扎成了木筏，	They made a log-raft.
他们坐到木筏上，	They got on the raft
开始渡羌河。	And started to cross the Qiang River.
左边划一下，	They paddled once on the left
冲过两重浪；	And they rowed two waves.
右边划两下，	They paddled twice on the right
冲过三重浪。	And they rowed over three waves.
左边划三下，	They paddled three times on the left
冲过四重浪；	And they rowed over four waves.
右边划四下，	They paddled four times on the right
冲过五重浪。	And they rowed over five waves.
左边划五下，	They paddled five times on the left
冲过六重浪；	And they rowed over six waves.
右边划六下，	They paddled six times on the right

冲过七重浪。	And they rowed over seven waves.
左边划七下，	They paddled seven times on the left
冲过八重浪；	And they rowed over eight waves.
右边划八下，	They paddled eight times on the right
冲过九重浪。	And they rowed nine waves.
左边划九下	They paddled nine times on the left
冲过十重浪；	And they rowed over ten waves.
右边划十下，	They paddled ten times on the right
冲到了河岸边。	And they rowed to the shore.
两个年轻人，	The two young men
把木筏拴在江岸边，	Tied the raft on the shore.
又向着文浪石洞，	Then toward Wunlang Lungpu
不停地赶去。	They hurried their journey without a stop.
翻过一座坡，	They crossed over a slope;
跨过两道坎，	They strode over two ridges.
火光是看见了，	They saw the fire light.
但还不到文浪石洞。	But they had not arrived at Wunlang Lungpu yet.
翻过三座坡，	They crossed over three slopes;
跨过四道坎，	They strode over four ridges.

火光是看见了，	They saw the fire light.
但还不到文浪石洞。	But they had not arrived at Wunlang Lungpu yet.
翻过五座坡，	They crossed over five slopes;
跨过六道坎，	They strode over six ridges.
火光是看见了，	They saw the fire light.
但还不到文浪石洞。	But they had not arrived at Wunlang Lungpu yet.
翻过七座坡，	They crossed over seven slopes;
跨过八道坎，	They strode over eight ridges.
火光是看见了，	They saw the fire light.
但还不到文浪石洞。	But they had not arrived at Wunlang Lungpu yet.
翻过九座岭，	They crossed over nine slopes;
跨过十道坎，	They strode over ten ridges.
终于到了文浪石洞，	They finally arrived at Wunlang Lungpu.
见到了文浪瓦统安木干老人。	And met old Wunlang Wa Htingngan Magam.
统安木干老人问：	Htimgngan Magam asked,
“你们是谁呀，	“Who are you?
你们从哪里来，	Where are you from?
你们来做什么？”	Why are you here?”
年轻人回答说：	The two young men answered,

“我们叫戛昂拉若拜，	“Our names are Gaang La Ro Boi.
我们从戛昂地方来。	We come from Gaang.
大地上的人们没有火，	People on the Earth do not have fire.
吃的是生米，	They eat raw rice;
嚼的是生肉，	They eat raw meat.
生米吃烦了，	They are tired of eating raw rice;
生肉嚼腻了。	They are fed up with eating raw meat.
爷爷呀，	Respected grandpa,
我们向你来讨火。”	We have come here to ask you for fire.”

统安木干老人说：	The old Htingngan Magam said,
“孩子俩呀，	“Well, young men,
你俩的名字，	Your names
与我的不相称，	Do not match mine.
与我的不相配，	They do not go well with mine.
我给你们重新取一个名字吧，	Let me give you a new name.
我的名字叫文浪瓦统安木干，	My name is Wunlang Wa Htingngan Magam,
你俩的名字就叫贡退瓦贡摊吧。”	So yours will be Kumhtoi Wa Kumhtan.”

“孩子俩呀，	“Well, young men,
我这里的火，	The fire here
大地上的人们不能烧，	Cannot be used by people on the Earth
大地上的人们不能用。	And is not available for people on the Earth.

人们用的火，	The fire to be used by people on the Earth
早已埋在竹篷下，	Has already been buried under the bamboo tree
早已藏在石头里，	And has been hidden within the stone.
我虽然不能给你们火种，	Although I cannot give you the fire,
但我能教你们取火的方法。”	I can tell you how to get the fire.”
“孩子俩呀，	“But two young men,
你们先告诉我，	You tell me first
大地上有没有火艾绒，	Whether there is moxa on the Earth;
大地上有没有勒简竹，	Whether there is Lagyen bamboo on the Earth;
大地上有没有起火石。”	Whether there is flint on the Earth.”
年轻人回答说：	The two young men replied,
“爷爷呀，	“Oh, dear grandpa,
我们生活的大地，	On the Earth where we live
有火艾绒，	There is moxa;
也有勒简竹，	There is Lagyen bamboo
也有起火石。”	And there is flint.”
统安木干老人又问：	The old Htingnga Magam then asked,
“孩子俩呀，	“Well, young men,
大地上的人们中，	Among the people on the Earth,
有没有叫戛昂图弄的，	Is there a man named Gaang Htu Lung?
有没有叫申然图贡的？”	Is there a man named Shing-ra Htu Gung?”

年轻人回答说：	The two young men replied,
“爷爷呀，	“Dear grandpa,
我们生活的大地，	On the Earth where we live
有叫戛昂图弄的	There is a man named Gaang Htu Lung;
也有叫申然图贡的。”	There is a man named Shing-ra Htu Gung.”
统安木干老人又说：	The old Htingnga Magam then asked,
“孩子俩呀，	“Well, young men,
既然大地上	Now that on the Earth where you live
有名字相称的，	There are men with well-matched names;
有名字相配的，	There are men with right names.
等你们回到大地，	When you return to the Earth,
就叫戛昂图弄	You tell Gaang Htu Lung
和申然图贡，	And Shing-ra Htu Gung
把艾火绒	To rub the moxa
夹到勒简竹片上擦，	Onto the Lagyen bamboo piece
放到起火石上敲，	And strike it on the flint.
就会得到	Then people on the Earth
大地上的人们用的火。”	Will get the fire for their use.”
两个年轻人，	The two young men
学到取火的方法，	Learned the skill of how to get fire.
又从文浪石洞	Then they left Wunlang Lungpu

往回返大地。	And came back to the Earth.
翻过第十座坡，	They crossed over the tenth slope;
跨过第九道坎，	They strode over the ninth ridge.
还没有见到羌河，	They could not see the Qiang River;
还没有来到渡口。	They hadn't yet reached the ferry.
翻过第八座坡，	They crossed over the eighth slope;
跨过第七道坎，	They strode over the seventh ridge.
还没有见到羌河，	They could not see the Qiang River;
还没有来到渡口。	They hadn't yet reached the ferry.
翻过第六座坡，	They crossed over the sixth slope;
跨过第五道坎，	They strode over the fifth ridge.
还没有见到羌河，	They could not see the Qiang River;
还没有来到渡口。	They hadn't yet reached the ferry.
翻过第四座坡，	They crossed over the fourth slope;
跨过第三道砍，	They strode over the third ridge.
还没有见到羌河，	They could not see the Qiang River;
还没有来到渡口。	They hadn't yet reached the ferry.
翻过第二座山，	They crossed over the second slope;
跨过第一道坎，	They strode over the first ridge.

见到羌河了，　They saw the Qiang River;
来到渡口了。　They reached the ferry.

两个年轻人，　The two young men
解开木筏子，　Untied the raft,
坐到上面，　Got on it
又开始渡羌河。　And began to cross over the Qiang River.

冲过一重浪，　They rowed over one wave,
引来一群鱼；　But there came forward a school of fish.
闯过二重浪，　They rowed over two waves,
招来二群鱼。　But there came forward two schools of fish.

冲过三重浪，　They rowed over three waves,
引来三群鱼；　But there came forward three schools of fish.
闯过四重浪，　They rowed over four waves,
招来四群鱼。　But there came forward four schools of fish.

冲过五重浪，　They rowed over five waves,
引来五群鱼；　But there came forward five schools of fish.
闯过六重浪，　They rowed over six waves,
引来六群鱼。　But there came forward six schools of fish.

冲过七重浪，　They rowed over seven waves,

引来七群鱼；	But there came forward seven schools of fish.
闯过八重浪，	They rowed over eight waves,
招来八群鱼。	But there came forward eight schools of fish.
冲过九重浪，	They rowed over nine waves,
引来九群鱼；	But there came forward nine schools of fish.
闯过十重浪，	They rowed over ten waves
来到了河岸边。	And they arrived at the river bank.
两个年轻人，	The two young men
走到河岸上，	Walked onto the shore.
拴住木筏，	Tying the raft on the shore,
又继续往回赶。	They went on with their journey.
翻过第十座山，	They crossed over the tenth mountain;
越过第九个坝，	They traveled through the ninth valley.
带着取火的方法，	Knowing how to make fire,
越来越快了。	They walked faster and faster.
翻过第八座山，	They crossed over the eighth mountain;
越过第七个坝，	They traveled through the seventh valley.
带着取火的方法，	Knowing how to make fire,
越来越快了。	They walked faster and faster.

翻过第六座山，	They crossed over the sixth mountain;
越过第五个坝，	They traveled through the fifth valley.
带着取火的方法，	Knowing how to make fire,
越来越快了。	They walked faster and faster.
翻过第四座山，	They crossed over the fourth mountain;
越过第三个坝，	They traveled through the third valley.
带着取火的方法，	Knowing how to make fire,
越来越快了。	They walked faster and faster.
翻过第二座山，	They crossed over the second mountain;
越过第一个坝，	They traveled through the first valley.
带着取火的方法，	Knowing how to make fire,
回到了戛昂地方。	They at last returned to their place Gaang.
戛昂地方的人们问：	People in Gaang asked,
“你们去了那么长，	“You were away for such a long time;
你们走了那么远，	You traveled for such a long distance.
可找到了火光，	Do you find the fire light?
可取回了火种？”	Do you get the flint?”
年轻人回答说：	The two young men replied,
“我们没有取回火种，	“We don’t bring back the flint,
但学到取火的方法。	But we have learned how to make fire.

我们渡过了羌河，	We have crossed the Qiang River.
到了文浪石洞，	We have arrived at Wunlang Lungpu.
见到了统安木干老人。	We have met the old Htingngan Magam,
他对我们说，	Who said to us
他那里的火，	That the fire he had
大地上的人们不能用。	Could not be used by people on the Earth,
大地上的人们用的火，	That the fire for people on the Earth
早已埋在竹篷下，	Has been long buried under the bamboo tree
早已藏在石头里。	And hidden within the stone.
只要叫名字相称、	As long as the two guys
名字相配的	Gaang Htu Lung and Shing-ra Htu Gung,
戛昂图弄和申然图贡，	Whose names are compatible,
把火艾绒	And well-matched,
夹到勒简竹片上擦，	Rub moxa
放到起火石上擦敲，	Onto the Lagyen bamboo piece
就会得到	And strike it on the flint,
大地上的人们用的火。”	They will get the fire
	For people on the Earth to use.”

照两个年轻人	Following the two young men's directions
学回来的方法，	For getting fire,
戛昂图弄和申然图贡	Gaang Htu Lung and Shing-ra Htu Gung
找来火艾绒，	Found some moxas
夹到勒简竹片上擦，	And rubbed them onto the Lagyen bamboo piece,

放到起火石上擦敲， And struck it on the flint.
青烟冒起了， Smoke rose up;
火苗升起了。 Flames ascended.

从此，大地上的人们 Ever since then, people on the Earth
不再吃生米， Never eat raw rice;
不再吃生肉， Never eat raw meat.
男人的活更多了， Men have more work to do;
女人的事更杂了。 Women have more chores to finish.

附记：

过去，景颇族认为人间的火和野火神火是不一样的，因此如发生了火灾，就认为是误用了别的火，于是便用竹片、火石、火艾绒，重新摩擦敲打点火。

Excursus:

In the past, the Jingpo people thought the fire used by people on the Earth was different from the wild fire and the holy fire. Therefore, when there was any fire breaking out, people tended to think that they had used the wrong fire, and then they made a new fire by rubbing moxas and the bamboo piece and striking it on the flint.

二、找　水

Ⅱ. Searching for Water

远古， In remote antiquity,

大地上没有水。　　There was no water on the Earth.
因为没有水，　　Without water,
人口不兴旺，　　The population did not thrive.
庄稼难生长。　　The crops did not grow.

为了人口能兴旺，　　For the sake of the population boom,
为了庄稼能生长，　　For the sake of the crops' growth,
大地上的人们，　　People on the Earth
开始到处找水了。　　Started to search for water.

从冬找到春，　　They searched from winter to spring,
没有找到水，　　But they found no water.
从春找到夏，　　They searched from spring to summer,
还是不见水，　　But still they found no water.
直到找到秋，　　They searched for water until autumn.
人们看到蟋蟀，　　They heard crickets
不停地唱　　Singing without stop,
不止地叫，　　Crying with no end,
就去问蟋蟀：　　So they asked the crickets,
"蟋蟀呀，　　"Crickets,
你们不停地唱，　　You sing without stop;
你们不止地叫，　　You cry with no end.
难道口不会渴，　　Don't you feel thirsty?
难道嗓子不会哑？"　　Do you never lose your voice?"

蟋蟀回答说：	The crickets replied,
“到了后半夜，	“After midnight,
天上降下雾，	Heaven delivers fog;
草尖掉下露，	It forms dews on leaves.
我们喝了雾露水，	We drink the fog dew;
口就不会渴，	We do not feel thirsty.
嗓子就不会哑。	We never lose our voice.
这些雾露，	The fog and dew,
在六层天上，	While they are in the sixth sphere of the Sky,
凝结成水珠，	Condense into water droplets
像白色的银泡，	Just like silver bubbles.
你们去拿，	You go and get them.
你们去取吧。”	You go and bring them back.”
大地上的人们，	People on the Earth,
为了取到天上的水，	In order to get water from the Sky,
准备做一只神鹰，	Got ready to create a holy eagle
让它到天上去。	So that it could fly to Heaven.
大地上的人们，	People on the Earth invited
请来了热旺瓦松康木干。	Rawang Wa Sumhkang Magam.
他看着芭蕉叶，	He examined the banana leaf
开始做神鹰了。	And began to create an eagle.

眼嘴做好了，	The eyes and the mouth were done;
耳鼻齐全了；	The ears and the nose were done;
头脚做好了，	The head and the feet were done;
翅膀爪子齐全了；	The wings and the paws were done;
心肝五脏做好了，	The heart and the liver and the entrails were all done.
羽毛长得丰满了，	It became a full-fledged eagle.
开努神鹰做成了。	The Kai-nu Wonder Eagle was created.
大地上的人们，	People on the Earth then invited
又请来生命神松沛瓦勒蒙，	The Deity of Life named Sumjpui Wa Lamum.
给神鹰吹了一口气。	He gave the Eagle one blow.
神鹰有生命了，	The Eagle came to life;
神鹰会说话了。	The Eagle started to speak.
神鹰问人们说：	The Eagle asked the people,
“大地上的人们呀，	“Hello! People on the Earth!
你们让我做什么？”	What do you want me to do?”
人们回答说：	People on the Earth answered,
“开努神鹰呀，	“Hi, Kai-nu Wonder Eagle!
请你飞到天上，	We’d like you to fly to the Sky
为大地上的生灵，	And bring from the Sky the water
取回天上的水。”	For the creatures on the Earth.”
神鹰又问道：	The Wonder Eagle then asked,

“大地上的人们呀，	“Gee! People on the Earth!
等我取回天上的水，	When I return with water from the Sky,
你们用什么报答我，	What will you give me in return?
你们用什么酬谢我？”	What will you give me as a reward?”
人们回答说：	The people on the Earth replied,
“开努神鹰呀，	“Well, Kai-nu Wonder Eagle!
等你取回了天上的水，	When you return with water from the Sky,
大地上的鸟类，	Any bird on the Earth
随便你吃，	Will be your food;
随便你挑。”	Any bird on the Earth will be for you to choose.”
大地上的鸟类，	Ever since then,
从此成了老鹰的吃食。	Birds on the Earth become the eagles’ food.
神鹰离开大地，	The Wonder Eagle left the Earth.
凭着强硬的翅膀，	Due to his strong wings,
飞上了六层天，	He flew above the sixth sphere of the Sky.
找到了天上的水，	He found the water in Heaven.
用嘴含着水，	He kept the water in his mouth;
用爪捧着水，	He held the water with the paws.
向大地回返，	Just before he got to the Earth,
快回到地上时，	All the water was carelessly spilled
水泼到了树梢上。	On the tree top.

大地上的人们问神鹰；	People on the Earth asked the Wonder Eagle,
“开努神鹰呀，	“Hello, Kai-nu Wonder Eagle!
你取回天上的水没有？”	Have you got the water from the Sky?”
开努神鹰回答：	The Kai-nu Wonder Eagle replied,
“取是取回来了，	“Indeed I have got it,
只是还没回到大地时，	But before I landed,
水泼到了树梢了。”	The water had been spilled on the tree top.”
远古，	In remote antiquity,
大地上的人们，	People on the Earth,
为了取到树梢上的水，	In order to get the water from the tree top,
准备做一只破脸狗，	Planned to create a Paguma Larvata
让他到树梢上去。	So that it could climb up the tree top.
大地上的人们，	People on the Earth
请来了热旺瓦松康木干，	Invited Rawang Wa Sumhkang Magam.
他看着自己的肘子，	He had a look at his own elbow
开始做破脸狗了。	And started to create a Paguma Larvata.
眼嘴做好了，	The eyes and the mouth were done;
耳鼻齐全了；	The ears and the nose were done;
头脚做好了，	The head and the feet were done;
指甲齐全了；	The nails were done;
心肝五脏做好了，	The heart and the liver and the entrails were all done.
肢体齐全了，	It had all its legs.

破脸狗做成了。	The Paguma Larvata was created.
大地上的人们，	People on the Earth then invited
又请来生命神松沛瓦勒蒙，	The Deity of Life named Sumhpui Wa Lamum.
给破脸狗吹了一口气。	He gave the Paguma Larvata one blow.
破脸狗有生命了，	The Paguma Larvata came to life;
破脸狗会说话了。	The Paguma Larvata started to speak.
破脸狗问人们说：	The Paguma Larvata asked the people,
“大地上的人们呀，	“Hello! People on the Earth!
你们让我做什么？”	What do you want me to do?”
人们回答说：	People on the Earth answered,
“破脸狗呀，	“Hi, Paguma Larvata!
请你爬上树梢，	We'd like you to climb up the tree top
取回树梢上的水。”	And bring down the water from the tree top.
破脸狗又问道：	The Paguma Larvata then asked,
“大地上的人们呀，	“Gee! People on the Earth!
我取回树梢上的水，	When I return with water from the tree top,
你们用什么报答我，	What will you give me in return?
你们拿什么酬谢我？”	What will you give me as a reward?”
人们回答说：	People on the Earth replied,
“破脸狗呀，	“Well, Paguma Larvata!

等你取回树梢上的水，	When you return with water from the tree top,
树上的果任你吃，	Any fruit on trees will be your food;
树下的果任你挑。”	All fruits on the Earth will be for you to choose.”
大地上的果子，	Since then,
从此成了破脸狗的美味。	Fruits on the Earth become his food.
破脸狗爬上树梢，	The Paguma Larvata climbed up the tree top.
找到了神鹰弄泼的水，	He found the water that was spilled by the eagle.
用嘴含着水，	He kept the water in his mouth;
用爪捧着水，	He held the water with the paws.
返回大地上，	Just before he got to the Earth,
快到地上时，	All the water was spilled
水泼到了树根下，	Into the ground
水钻进了石缝里。	And the stone cracks.
大地上的人们问破脸狗：	People on the Earth asked the Paguma Larvata,
“破脸狗呀，	“Hello, Paguma Larvata!
你取到树梢上的水没有？”	Have you got the water from the tree top?”
破脸狗回答：	The Paguma Larvata replied,
“大地上的人们呀，	“Indeed I have got it,
树梢上的水是取到了，	But before I landed,
快到大地上时，	The water had been spilled
水泼到树根下，	Into the ground
水钻进了石缝里了。”	And the stone cracks.”

大地上的人们，	People on the Earth,
为了找到水，	In order to find the water,
用农丁农若树杆，	With the help of Numding Numro tree branches,
到处去戳，	They poked everywhere;
到处去捣，	They pounded everywhere.
没有找到水，	They did not find the water,
农丁农若树杆却活了。	But Numding Numro tree branches grew into trees.
后来有农丁农若的地方，	Since then, wherever there is a Numding Numro tree,
就会有泉水。	There is spring water.
大地上的人们，	People on the Earth,
为了找到水，	In order to find the water,
用芭蕉树杆	With the help of banana tree branches,
到处去戳，	They poked everywhere;
到处去捣。	They pounded everywhere.
没有找到水，	They did not find the water,
芭蕉树杆却活了，	But the banana tree branches grew into trees.
后来有芭蕉树的地方，	Since then, wherever there is a banana tree,
就会有泉水。	There is spring water.
大地上的人们，	People on the Earth,
为了找到水，	In order to find the water,
用藤篾杆到处戳，	With the help of rattan branches,

用藤篾杆到处捣，	They pounded everywhere.
没有找到水，	They did not find the water,
藤篾杆却活了。	But the rattan branches grew into trees.
后来，有藤篾杆的地方，	Since then, wherever there are rattan,
就会有泉水。	There is spring water.
大地上的人们，	People on the Earth,
为了找到水，	In order to find the water,
用更饶莪戛树枝到处戳，	With the help of Geng-rao Wo-ga tree branches,
用更饶莪戛树枝到处捣，	They pounded everywhere.
没有找到水，	They did not find the water,
更饶莪戛树枝却活了。	But the Geng-rao Wo-ga tree branches grew into trees.
后来，有更饶莪戛树枝的地方，	Since then, wherever there is a Geng-rao Wo-ga tree,
就会有泉水。	There is spring water.
大地上的人们，	People on the Earth,
为了找到水，	In order to find the water,
用更时莪戛树枝到处戳，	With the help of Geng-shi Wo-ga tree branches,
用更时莪戛树枝到处捣。	They pounded everywhere.
没有找到水，	They did not find the water,
更时莪戛树却活了。	But the Geng-shi Wo-ga tree branches grew into trees.
从此，有更时莪戛树的地方，	Since then, wherever there is a Geng-shi Wo-ga tree,
就会有泉水。	There is spring water.

大地上的人们，	People on the Earth,
为了找到水，	In order to find water,
准备做一条乌藏鱼，	Planned to create a cuttlefish
让它钻进石缝去。	And asked it to get into the stone cracks.
大地上的人们，	People on the Earth
请来了热旺瓦松康木干，	Invited Rawang Wa Sumhkang Magam.
他看着自己的手指，	He examined his own finger
开始做乌藏鱼。	And began to create a cuttlefish.
眼嘴做好了，	The eyes and the mouth were done;
鱼头鱼尾齐全了；	The head and the tail were done;
鱼鳃做好了，	The gills were done;
五脏齐全了，	All the entrails were done
乌藏鱼做成了。	And the cuttlefish was created.
大地上的人们，	People on the Earth then invited
又请来生命神松沛瓦勒蒙，	Sumhpui Wa Lamum, the Deity of Life.
给鱼吹了一口气。	He gave the cuttlefish one blow.
鱼有生命了，	The cuttlefish came to life;
鱼会说话了。	The cuttlefish started to speak.
乌藏鱼问人们说：	The cuttlefish asked the people,
“大地上的人们呀，	“Hello! People on the Earth!
你们让我做什么？”	What do you want me to do?”

大地上的人们说：	People on the Earth said,
“乌藏鱼呀，	“Hi, Cuttlefish!
请你钻进石缝，	We’d like you to get into the stone cracks
为我们引出水。”	And get the water out.”
乌藏鱼钻进石头缝，	The cuttlefish got into the stone cracks
找到了破脸狗打泼的水，	And found the water spilled by the Paguma Larvata,
可是它游在水里，	But it enjoyed swimming in the water
再也不愿出来了。	And did not want to get out.
远古，	In remote antiquity,
大地上的人们，	People on the Earth,
为了找到水，	In order to get the water,
准备做一只螃蟹，	Planned to create a crab
让它钻进石缝。	So that it could get into the stone cracks.
大地上的人们，	People on the Earth
请来了热旺瓦松康木干，	Invited Rawang Wa Sumhkang Magam.
他看着自己的巴掌，	He examined his own palms
开始做螃蟹。	And began to create a crab.
眼嘴做好了，	The eyes and the mouth were done;
螃蟹壳做齐全了，	The shell was done;
蟹足做好了，	The feet were done;
五脏齐全了，	All the entrails were done;

螃蟹做成了。	The crab was created.
大地上的人们，	People on the Earth then invited
又请来生命神松沛瓦勒蒙，	Sumhpui Wa Lamum, the Deity of Life.
他给螃蟹吹了一口气，	He gave the crab one blow.
螃蟹有生命了，	The crab came to life;
螃蟹会说话了，	The crab started to speak.
螃蟹问人们说：	The crab asked the people,
“大地上的人们呀，	“Hello! People on the Earth!
你们让我做什么？”	What do you want me to do?”
大地上的人们说：	People on the Earth said,
“螃蟹呀，	“Hi, Crab!
请你钻到石头缝，	Would you please get into the stone cracks
给我们引出水来。”	And get the water out for us?”
螃蟹又说：	The crab responded,
“大地上的人们呀，	“Well, people on the Earth!
要让我钻进石缝，	If you want me to get into the stone cracks
给你们引出水，	And get the water out for you,
先得有一只申拜果艳[①]，	You must find a Shen-bai cicada
做我的照应伙伴。”	As a partner to coordinate with me.”

① 申拜果艳：农历七、八月份鸣叫的一种知了。

大地上的人们，	People on the Earth
请来热旺瓦松康木干，	Invited Rawang Wa Sumhkang Magam.
他照着自己的鼻子，	Modeling on his own nose
开始做申拜果艳知了。	He began to create a Shen-bai cicada.
眼嘴做好了，	The eyes and the mouth were done;
头脚齐全了，	The head and the feet were done;
翅膀做好了，	The wings were done;
肢体齐全了，	The body was done;
申拜果艳做成了。	The cicada was created.

大地上的人们，	People on the Earth then invited
又请来生命神松沛瓦勒蒙，	Sumhpui Wa Lamum, the Deity of Life.
给申拜果艳吹了一口气。	He gave the cicada one blow.
申拜果艳有生命了，	The cicada came to life;
申拜果艳会说话了。	The cicada started to speak.
申拜果艳问人们说：	The cicada asked the people,
“你们让我做什么？”	“What do you want me to do?”

人们回答说：	People on the Earth said,
“申拜果艳呀，	“Hi, Cicada!
螃蟹要为我们引水，	Would you please be the crab’s partner
请你当它的照应伙伴。”	When the crab gets the water out for us?”

申拜果艳对螃蟹说：	The Shen-bai cicada said to the crab,
“螃蟹呀，	“Well, Crab!
等到了直通月、思安月①，	If you cannot bring the water out
你还引不出水来，	Before Lunar May and June,
我就告诉人们，	I'll tell the people that
你被水獭吃掉了。”	You have been eaten by the beaver.”

螃蟹对申拜果艳说：	The crab said to the Shen-bai cicada,
“申拜果艳，	“Shen-bai cicada!
等到石木日月、贡诗月②，	Before lunar July and August,
在出水的地方，	Your voice must be heard.
还听不到你的声音，	If not,
我就告诉人们说，	I will tell people that
你被老鹰吃掉了。”	You have been eaten by the Eagle.”

申拜果艳爬上树干，	The Shen-bai cicada climbed up the tree trunk
等在树枝上，	And waited at the tree branch.
螃蟹钻进石洞，	The crab crawled into the stone cracks
准备引水去了。	To channel water out.

① 直通月、思安月：景颇族历法，即农历的五月和六月。
② 石木日月、贡诗月：景颇族历法，即农历的七月和八月。

到了直通月和思安月，	By lunar May and June
螃蟹引出了清水，	The crab channeled the water out;
到石木日月和贡诗月，	By lunar July and August
申拜果艳在出水的地方唱起来了。	The cicada sang songs at the water source.
树上的猴子	The monkey in the tree
看见清清的水，	Saw the clear water;
没有祭水神	Without offering sacrifices to the God of Water,
就喝下了水，	It drank some water.
所以猴子的声音不好听。	Therefore monkeys today do not have nice voices.
林子里的野猪	The wild boar in the forest
看见清清的水，	Saw the clear water.
没有祭水神	Without offering sacrifices to the God of Water,
就喝下了水，	It drank some water.
所以野猪的声音不好听。	Therefore wild boars today do not have nice voices.
树上的知了	The cicada in the tree
看见清清的水，	Saw the clear water.
没有祭水神	Without offering sacrifices to the God of Water,
就喝下了水，	It drank some water.
所以知了的声音不好听。	Therefore cicadas today do not have nice voices.

洼子里的马鹿	The deer in the valley
看见清清的水，	Saw the clear water.
没有祭水神	Without offering sacrifices to the God of Water,
就喝下了水，	It drank some water.
所以马鹿的声音不好听。	Therefore deer today do not have nice voices.
陡坡上的山驴	The wild donkey on the cliff
看见清清的水，	Saw the clear water.
没有祭水神	Without offering sacrifices to the God of Water,
就喝下了水，	It drank some water.
所以山驴的声音不好听。	Therefore wild donkeys today do not have nice voices.
岩石上的岩羊	The goat standing on the stone
看见清清的水，	Saw the clear water.
没有祭水神	Without offering sacrifices to the God of Water,
就喝下了水，	It drank some water.
所以声音不好听。	Therefore goats today do not have nice voices.
草地上的麂子	The muntjac standing on the stone
看见清清的水，	Saw the clear water.
没有祭水神	Without offering sacrifices to the God of Water,
就喝下了水，	It drank some water.
所以麂子的声音不好听。	Therefore muntjacs today do not have nice voices.

大地上的人们	People on the Earth
看见清清的水，	Saw the clear water.
人们便设起祭坛，	They set up an altar.
摆上甜酒和鸡蛋，	They sacrificed sweet drink and eggs;
摆上糯米和牛肉，	They sacrificed sticky rice and beef
祭献万能的水神①。	To the God of Water.①
人们有了水，	Because people had water to drink,
长得漂亮了，	They became beautiful.
声音好听了，	Their voice became wonderful.
人口兴旺了，	Their population multiplied.
庄稼生长了。	Their crops grew in abundance.

三、打　刀 / Ⅲ. Forging the Machete

远古，	In remote antiquity,
大地上有了水，	There was water on the Earth.
大地上的人们，	People on the Earth,
为了把水引到远处，	In order to draw water to a further area,
准备做引水槽，	Planned to open a diversion channel.

① 祭献水神：在景颇族民众过去的观念中，水中有水神，只有祭献过了喝才不会生病遭瘟疫。

① The Jingpo people used to think that there is a god in charge of water, to whom sacrifices must be offered, so that people can drink water without catching diseases and pestilence.

但是没有刀，
人们准备先打刀。

But they did not have a machete.
They planned to forge a machete first.

木托贡央和登萨勒刚，
开始打木眼刀，
开始造木眼矛。
木眼刀打好了，
木眼矛造好了，
但木眼刀砍不深，
木眼矛戳不成。

Mahto Kum-yang and Tingsa Lakang
Started to forge a wooden machete.
They started to forge a wooden spear.
The wooden machete was done;
The wooden spear was done.
But the wooden machete did not cut deep;
The wooden spear did not stab well.

把木眼刀称原始刀，
丢进深谷，
深谷里长出了给先叶[1]，
直到今天，
人们跳目瑙舞时，
还做一种标志。
把木眼矛称原始长矛，
丢在山坡上，
那里长出了茅草，
直到今天，
人们把它用来盖房子。

The wooden machete was called the primitive machete
And was thrown down into the deep valley,
Where it grew into a plant whose leaves are shaped like a machete.
Till today,
When people celebrate the Manau event.
It is still used as a sign.
The wooden spear was called the primitive spear
And was thrown away on the hill slopes,
Where it grew into thatches.
Till today,
They are still used for building thatched houses.

① 给先叶：一种长在洼子里的像长刀一样的植物叶。

热旺瓦松康木干，	Rawang Wa Sumhkang Magam,
在热旺岔路口，	At the crossroads of Rawang,
守着热旺铁矿坑，	Kept watch on the Rawang iron mine.
支起了铁砧，	He set up an iron anvil;
架好了风箱，	He put up a bellows.
开始打造热旺刀。	He started to forge a Rawang machete.
热旺刀打好了，	The Rawang machete was forged;
热旺刀真锋利。	The Rawang machete was so sharp.
依弄瓦省举，	Nung Nong Wa Singgyi,
在依弄岔路口，	At the Nung Nong crossroad,
守着依弄铁矿坑，	Kept watch on the Nung Nong iron mine.
支起了铁砧，	He set up an iron anvil;
架好了风箱，	He put up a bellows;
开始打造依弄刀。	He started to forge a Maru machete.
依弄刀打好了，	The Nung Nong machete was forged;
依弄刀真锋利。	The Nung Nong machete was so sharp.
木如瓦腊批，	Maru Wa La-hpri,
在木如岔路口，	At the Maru crossroad,
守着木如铁矿坑，	Kept watch on the Maru iron mine.
支起了铁砧，	He set up an iron anvil;
架好了风箱，	He put up a bellows;

开始打造木如刀。	He started to forge a Maru machete.
木如刀打好了，	The Maru machete was forged;
木如刀真锋利。	The Maru machete was so sharp.
贡氏瓦都曼，	Gumdi Wa Tu Man,
在贡氏岔路口，	At the Gumdi crossroads,
守着贡氏铁矿坑，	Kept watch on the Gumdi iron mine.
支起了铁砧，	He set up an iron anvil;
架好了风箱，	He put up a bellows;
开始打造贡氏刀。	He started to forge a Gumdi machete.
贡氏刀打好了，	The Gumdi machete was forged;
贡氏刀真锋利。	The Gumdi machete was so sharp.
掸当贡央，	Sam Tang Kum-yang,
在掸当岔路口，	At the Sam Tang crossroads,
守着掸当铁矿坑，	Kept watch on the Sam Tang iron mine.
支起了铁砧，	He set up an iron anvil;
架好了风箱，	He put up a bellows;
开始打造掸当刀。	He started to forge a Sam Tang machete.
掸当刀打好了，	The Sam Tang machete was forged;
掸当刀真锋利。	The Sam Tang machete was so sharp.
蚌景颇，	Pong Jinghpo,
在蚌景颇岔路口，	At the Pong Jinghpo crossroads,

守着蚌景颇铁矿坑，	Kept watch on the Pong Jinghpo iron mine.
支起了铁砧，	He set up an iron anvil;
架好了风箱，	He put up a bellows;
开始打造蚌景颇刀。	He started to forge a Pong Jinghpo machete.
蚌景颇刀打好了，	The Pong Jinghpo machete was forged;
蚌景颇刀真锋利。	The Pong Jinghpo machete was so sharp.

直黎瓦康康	Jili Wa Hkang Hkang,
在直黎岔路口，	At the Jili crossroads,
守着直黎铁矿坑，	Kept watch on the Jili iron mine.
支起了铁砧，	He set up an iron anvil;
架好了风箱，	He put up a bellows;
开始打造直黎刀。	He started to forge a Jili machete.
直黎刀打好了，	The Jili machete was forged;
直黎刀真锋利。	The Jili machete was so sharp.

蒙嫩瓦锐藏	Mungnun Wa Roiza,
在蒙嫩岔路口，	At the Mungnun crossroads,
守着蒙嫩铁矿坑，	Kept watch on the Mungnun iron mine.
支起了铁砧，	He set up an iron anvil;
架好了风箱，	He put up a bellows;
开始打造蒙嫩刀。	He started to forge a Mungnun machete.
蒙嫩刀打好了，	The Mungnun machete was forged;
蒙嫩刀真锋利。	The Mungnun machete was so sharp.

缅瓦木干	Myen Wa Magam,
在缅岔路口，	At the Myen crossroads,
守着缅铁矿坑，	Kept watch on the Myen iron mine.
支起了铁砧，	He set up an iron anvil;
架好了风箱，	He put up a bellows;
开始打造缅刀。	He started to forge a Myen machete.
缅刀打好了，	The Myen machete was forged;
缅刀真锋利。	The Myen machete was so sharp.
密瓦瓦汤瓦，	Mi-wa Wa Htang-wa,
在密瓦岔路口，	At the Mi-wa crossroads,
守着密瓦铁矿坑，	Kept watch on the Mi-wa iron mine.
支起了铁砧	He set up an iron anvil;
架好了风箱，	He put up a bellows;
开始打造密瓦刀。	He started to forge a Mi-wa machete.
密瓦刀打好了，	The Mi-wa machete was forged;
密瓦刀真锋利。	The Mi-wa machete was so sharp.
蒙岭蒙旁，	Mungling Munghpang,
在蒙岭岔路口，	At the Mungling crossroads,
守着蒙岭铁矿坑，	Kept watch on the Mungling iron mine.
支起了铁砧，	He set up an iron anvil;
架好了风箱，	He put up a bellows;

开始打造蒙岭刀。	He started to forge a Mungling machete.
蒙岭刀打好了，	The Mungling machete was forged;
蒙岭刀真锋利。	The Mungling machete was so sharp.
人们有了刀，	People had the machetes,
但不知道怎样砍水槽。	But they did not know how to make a water channel.
阿真能力拉，	Achying Ning La La
这边去看看，	Went out to observe
那边去瞧瞧，	Here and there.
看见竹鼠咬断给先树，	He saw the bamboo rat biting off a piece of Gasen bamboo
学会了砍竹子。	And then he learned how to cut bamboos.
人们学会了砍竹子，	People learned to cut bamboos,
但不知道怎样破竹槽。	But they did not know how to set up a water channel.
阿真能力拉，	Achying Ning La La
这边去看看，	Went out to observe
那边去瞧瞧，	Here and there.
看见了打卦叶[1]，	He saw the water channel-shaped leaf
学会了破竹槽。	And he knew how to cut bamboos into a water channel.
人们学会了破竹槽，	People learned to cut bamboos into a water channel,
但不知道怎样支水槽。	But they did not know how to set up a water channel.

① 打卦叶：巫师卜卦时用的一种叶子，呈槽状。

阿真能力拉，	Achying Ning La La
这边去看看，	Went out to observe
那边去瞧瞧，	Here and there.
看见竹叶上，	He saw on the bamboo leaf
有水清清流，	There was some clean water flowing.
学会了支水槽。	Then he learned to set up a water channel.
人们学会了支水槽，	People learned to set up the water channel,
但不知道怎样砍水筒。	But they did not know how to cut a bamboo tube.
阿真能力拉，	Achying Ning La La
这边去看看，	Went out to observe
那边去瞧瞧，	Here and there.
看见竹鼠咬断树枝，	He saw the bamboo rat bite off a tree
学会了砍水筒。	And then learned how to cut a bamboo tube.
人们学会了砍水筒，	People learned to cut a bamboo tube,
但不知道怎样通竹节。	But they did not know how to remove the bamboo joints.
阿真能力拉，	Achying Ning La La
这边去看看，	Went out to observe
那边去瞧瞧，	Here and there.
看见竹鼠通竹节，	He saw the bamboo rat biting through the bamboo joints
学会了通竹节。	And knew how to remove the bamboo joints.
人们有了竹水筒，	People had the bamboo tubes,

但不知道怎样接水。	But they did not know how to use them to get water.
阿真能力拉，	Achying Ning La La
这边去看看，	Went out to observe
那边去瞧瞧，	Here and there.
看见土蜂用嘴接水，	He saw the scoliid getting water with its mouth,
学会了用手捧水。	And then learned how to hold water with hands.
人们学着土蜂，	People imitated the scoliid,
用双手捧水，	Held water with their hands,
走不远就会漏掉；	But the water leaked before they could walk a long way.
人们用叶子接水，	People tried to hold water with leaves,
走不到家就泼光；	But the water leaked on the way.
人们用竹筒接水，	People learned to hold water with bamboo tubes,
水不会漏了，	And the water did not leak any more.
可以背到家了，	They could take the water home.
从此人们学会接水了。	Ever since then, people know how to get water.
人们有了刀，	People had the machete;
做出了水槽，	People learned to make the water channel.
可以把水引了，	They could draw water to wherever they liked.
人们有了水桶，	People had the bamboo tube
可以把水背了。	And they could carry home the water.

四、制造用具　　Ⅳ. Making Utensils

远古，
大地上的人们，
没有煮饭锅，
没有烧水罐。
人们想做土锅，
人们想捏土罐，
但不知道哪里有黏土。

In remote antiquity,
People on the Earth
Did not have any pots to cook rice with.
They did not have any jars to boil water with.
People wanted to make cooking pots.
People wished to make boiling jars.
But they did not know where they could get clay.

能先努能年鸟，
飞来对人们说：
"大地上的人们呵，
你们想做土锅，
你们想捏土罐，
你们需要的黏土，
就在根诗河边。"

The Ningse Nu Ningnyen bird
Flew over to say to the people,
"People on the Earth!
You want to make cooking pots;
You want to make boiling jars.
The clay that you want
Is on the Kinshi River banks."

大地上的人们，
跟着能先努能年鸟，
来到了根诗河边，

People on the Earth
Followed the Ningse Nu Ningnyen bird
Until they came to the Kinshi River banks,

找到了细细的黏土。	And they found the clay.
大地上的人们，	People on the Earth
找到了黏土，	Found the clay,
但不知怎样做土锅，	But they did not know how to make cooking pots.
不知怎样捏土罐。	They did not know how to make boiling jars.
阿真能力拉，	Achying Ning La La
这边去看看，	Went out to observe
那边去瞧瞧，	Here and there.
见到资么果[1]，	Seeing fruit shaped like a cooking pot,
学会了做土锅，	He learned to shape cooking pots;
学会了捏土罐。	He learned to shape boiling jars.
土锅会做了，	People learned to shape cooking pots;
土罐会捏了，	People learned to shape boiling jars.
但不知道怎样陶土锅，	But they did not know how to burn on cooking pots;
不知道怎样陶土罐。	They did not know how to burn on boiling jars.
阿真能力拉，	Achying Ning La La
这边去看看，	Went out to observe
那边去瞧瞧，	Here and there.

① 资么果：一种像土锅土罐的野果。

看到路上的拐棍印，　Seeing the prints of a walking stick,
学会了陶土锅，　He learned to print on a cooking pot;
学会了陶土罐。　He learned to print on a boiling jar.

土锅做好了，　A cooking pot was made;
土罐捏好了，　A boiling jar was produced.
但土锅不结实，　But the clay cooking pot was not solid;
土罐不牢固，　The clay boiling jar was not durable.
把它称为原始土锅，　The clay cooking pot was regarded as primitive pot,
扔到坝子上，　And it was thrown away in the flatland.
缅族见了很喜欢，　Myen people saw it and felt so glad;
掸族见了真高兴，　Sam people saw it and felt so happy.
直到今天，　Even today,
土锅和土罐，　Clay cooking pots and clay boiling jars
还留在缅族和掸族家里。　Are still seen in the Myen and Sam families.

土锅不结实，　The clay cooking pot was not solid;
土罐不牢固，　The clay boiling jar was not durable.
人们又用石头，　People found some stones
做出了石锅，　And made stone pots
打出了石罐，　And made stone jars.
但石锅石罐太重了，　But stone pots and stone jars were too heavy.
人们又用铁和铜，　People finally found some iron and copper
做出了铁锅，　And made iron pots

打出了铜罐。 And made copper jars.

五、接谷子回大地 V. Getting Rice Back to the Earth

远古，	In remote antiquity,
大地上的谷子，	The Rice on the Earth
外面没有壳，	Did not have the shell outside
里面没有衣。	And did not have the coating inside.
大地上的人们，	People on the Earth picked up
随心抓来吃，	And ate the Rice arbitrarily,
顺手扯来丢。	And they picked up and threw the Rice carelessly.
谷子生气了，	The Rice got angry;
谷子伤心了，	The Rice felt heartache.
谷子离开了大地，	The Rice left the Earth
到了太阳母亲那里。	And returned to Heaven to its mother, the Sun.

谷子离开大地后，	After the Rice left the Earth,
因为没有吃的，	There was nothing to eat.
大地上的猫狗，	The dogs and cats on the Earth
饿得直哭喊，	Starved and cried.
天上的太阳，	The Sun in the Sky
听到狗和猫的哭喊，	Heard the dogs and cats crying.

就劝谷子说：	He tried to persuade the Rice,
“孩子呵，	“My child,
你还是回去吧。	You'd better return to the Earth.
如果不回去，	If you do not return,
大地上的人们，	People on the Earth
全都会饿死掉。”	Will starve to death.”
谷子回答说：	The Rice Replied,
“不是我不想回去，	“It's not that I do not want to return.
因为没有壳，	Because I do not have a shell,
大地上的人们，	People on the Earth
随便糟蹋我；	Ruin me willfully.
因为没有衣，	Because I do not have a coating,
大地上的冷风，	The cold wind on the Earth
天天来吹我。”	Blows on me every day.”
太阳给谷子，	The Sun dressed the Rice
穿上红衣，	In a red coat;
穿上白衣，	The Sun dressed the Rice
再套上谷壳，	In a white coat;
又让其他谷类，	And he then dressed it in a shell.
做了谷子的朋友，	He also made other grains the friends of the Rice.
这谷子回到了大地。	Then the Rice went back to the Earth.

大地上的人们，	People on the Earth
砍开森林，	Cut down trees
烧出谷地，	And opened up the field by burning the trees.
这边种穿白衣的白谷，	On one side of the field they grew the Rice in the red coat;
那边撒穿红衣的红谷。	On the other side of the field they grew the Rice in the white coat.
谷子发芽了，	The Rice sprouted;
谷苗长齐了，	The Rice seedlings grew up;
谷子丰收了。	The Rice was harvested.
为了报答狗和猫，	In order to thank the dogs and the cats,
每年的新米饭，	Every year when the rice is harvest and cooked,
狗和猫先尝。	Dogs and cats taste it first.

六、盖房子　　Ⅵ. Building the House

远古，	In remote antiquity,
登空铺别拉	Dinghkong Hpap Rep La
和登空铺别木占，	And Dinghkong Hpap Rep Majan
他们最先盖房子。	Were the first to build a house.
登空铺别拉说：	Dinghkong Hpap Rep La said,

“我要用野公猪的肉，	“I will make delicious dishes every day
每天做好菜，	Out of wild boar meat
招待帮忙的客人。”	To treat whomever comes to help.”
登空铺别木占说：	Dinghkong Hpap Rep Majan said,
“我要用筒裙，	“I will use the skirt
铺我的屋头，	To cover my room and
盖我的房顶。”	To cover my roof.”
登空铺别拉	Dinghkong Hpap Rep La
用野公猪肉做菜，	Made dishes out of wild boar meat.
菜少客人多，	The dishes were far fewer than visitors
不够待客人。	And were not enough for the guests.
登空铺别木占	Dinghkong Hpap Rep Majan
用筒裙盖房顶，	Used a skirt to cover the roof.
房宽筒裙窄，	But the skirt was narrow
只够盖半边。	And was enough only for half of the roof.
登空铺别拉	Dinghkong Hpap Rep La
和登空铺别木占	And Dinghkong Hpap Rep Majan
又重新想办法，	Had another idea.
用芭蕉杆做柱子，	They used banana tree trunks as pillars;
用空心树做房梁，	They used hollow trees as beams;

用直八叶做篾子。	They used Zhi-ba leaves as strips.
芭蕉杆做柱子，	The pillars made of banana tree trunks
还没有竖就歪了；	Fell before they were erected.
空心树做房梁，	The beams made of hollow trees
还没有架起就断了；	Broke before they were put up.
直八叶做篾子，	The strips made of Zhi-ba leaves
还没有扭紧就开了。	Came loose before they were twisted together.
他们的房子，	Their house fell apart
还没有盖好就塌了，	Before it was built.
野猪看见塌屋，	The wild boar saw the fallen house
把它做了自己的窝。	And made it its den.
远古，	In remote antiquity,
梯木梯拉	Htip Mahti La
和梯木梯木占	And Htip Mahti Majan
又接着盖房子。	Followed them in building a house.
梯木梯拉说：	Htip Mahti La said,
“我要用遍山的野菜，	“I will use all the wild vegetables
做出最好的饭菜，	To make the most delicious dishes
招待帮忙的客人。”	To treat whomever comes to help.”
梯木梯木占说：	Htip Mahti Majan said,

“我要割回满坡的茅草，	“I will cut all the thatches on the slope.
晒干背回家，	Dry them in the Sun and carry them home
盖上房子顶。”	To cover the house.”
梯木梯拉	Htip Mahti La
和梯木梯木占	And Htip Mahti Majan
开始盖房子。	Started to build the house.
不会做斧子，	They did not know how to make an ax.
思布乌拉枇鸟[①]，	The Si-bu Wu-la-pi bird[①]
在半夜里飞来，	Flew to them at midnight
教给他们做斧子的方法。	And taught them how to make an ax.
梯木梯拉	Htip Mahti La
和梯木梯木占	And Htip Mahti Majan
开始盖房子。	Started to build the house.
不会挖地基，	They did not know how to lay the foundation.
来到草丛里，	They came to the bush.
看见野猪在拱土，	Seeing the wild boar digging the Earth,
学会了挖地基。	They learned how to lay the foundation.
梯木梯拉	Htip Mahti La
和梯木梯木占	And Htip Mahti Majan

① 思布乌拉枇鸟：一种夜间叫的鸟。

① The Si-bu Wu-la-pi bird: a bird that sings at night.

开始盖房子。	Started to build the house.
不会砍木料，	They did not know how to cut trees.
来到树林里，	They came to the forest.
看见竹鼠断树根，	Seeing bamboo rats biting off a tree,
学会了砍木料。	They learned to cut trees to make building materials.
梯木梯拉	Htip Mahti La
和梯木梯木占	And Htip Mahti Majan
开始盖房子。	Started to build the house.
不会立楼柱，	They did not know how to set up the pillars.
来到牛圈边，	They came near the ox den.
看见牛的四只脚，	Seeing the four legs of the ox,
学会了立楼柱。	They learned to set up the pillars.
梯木梯拉	Htip Mahti La
和梯木梯木占	And Htip Mahti Majan
开始盖房子。	Started to build the house.
不会做榔头，	They did not know how to make a hammer.
来到山林里，	They came to the forest.
看见东西迷果[①]，	Seeing the Tong Shiq Mi fruit shaped like a hammer,
学会了做榔头。	They knew how to make a hammer.

① 东西迷果：一种家用木榔头一样的野果。

梯木梯拉 Htip Mahti La
和梯木梯木占 And Htip Mahti Majan
开始盖房子。 Started to build the house.
不会做楔子， They did not know how to make a wedge.
来到水塘边， They came to the pond.
看见乌然乌藏鱼， Seeing the Wu Ran Wu Tsang Fish,
学会了做楔子。 They knew how to make a wedge.

梯木梯拉 Htip Mahti La
和梯木梯木占 And Htip Mahti Majan
开始盖房子。 Started to build the house.
不会甩榔头， They did not know how to use the hammer.
来到牛圈边， They came to the ox den.
看见牛甩尾巴， Seeing the ox wagging its tail,
学会了甩榔头。 They knew how to use the hammer.

梯木梯拉 Htip Mahti La
和梯木梯木占 And Htip Mahti Majan
开始盖房子。 Started to build the house.
不会削柱子， They did not know
他们互相看着对方， How to cut trees into pillars.
光滑的身子， Seeing each other's smooth bodies,
学会了削柱子。 They knew how to cut trees into pillars.

梯木梯拉	Htip Mahti La
和梯木梯木占	And Htip Mahti Majan
开始盖房子。	Started to build the house.
不会砍叉口，	They did not know how to chop trees into fork joints.
他们互相看，	They observed each other.
看到对方的肩膀，	Seeing each other's shoulders,
学会了砍叉口。	They knew how to chop trees into fork joints.

梯木梯拉	Htip Mahti La
和梯木梯木占	And Htip Mahti Majan
开始盖房子。	Started to build the house.
不会架屋梁，	They did not know how to put up beams.
来到山林里，	They came to the forest.
看到搭在树上的蛇，	Seeing the snake resting on the tree,
学会了架屋梁。	They knew how to put up beams.

梯木梯拉	Htip Mahti La
和梯木梯木占	And Htip Mahti Majan
开始盖房子。	Started to build the house.
不会铺茅草，	They did not know how to spread thatches over the roof.
来到牛圈边，	They came near the ox den.
看到牛的毛，	Seeing the ox's hair,
学会了铺茅草。	They knew how to spread thatches.

梯木梯拉	Htip Mahti La
和梯木梯木占	And Htip Mahti Majan
开始盖房子。	Started to build the house.
不会收屋顶，	They did not know how to edge the roof.
对着天上看，	They looked up at the Sky.
看见燕子尾，	Seeing the tail of the swallow,
学会了收屋顶。	They knew how to edge the roof.
从此，	Ever since then,
大地上的人们，	People on the Earth
学会了盖房子，	Learned how to build a house
有了房子住。	And have houses to live in.

七、穿衣穿裤　Ⅶ. Wearing Shirts and Trousers

远古，	In remote antiquity,
大地上的人们，	People on the Earth
上面不沾衣，	Did not have shirts to cover the upper body,
下面不着裤，	Did not have trousers to cover the bottom part.
赤裸的身子，	The naked bodies looked grey and yellow,
又灰又黄真难看。	How ugly they were!

潘格来遮能代	There came Hpan Galai Chye Ningtai,
给人们棉花籽，	Who gave people some cotton seeds,
人们把棉花籽撒到地上，	Which they sewed in the ground.
棉花籽发芽了，	There came out sprouts;
棉花苗长高了，	There grew up sprouts;
棉花可以收获了。	Then the cotton was ready for harvest.
远古，	In remote antiquity,
大地上的人们，	People on the Earth
棉花是有了，	Had grown cotton.
但不会收棉花。	But they did not know how to harvest it.
潘格来遮能代说：	Hpan Galai Chye Ningtai said to them,
“大地上的人们呀，	“Listen, you guys on the Earth.
不会收棉花，	Since you do not know how to harvest the cotton,
就去看山丫口	Go to the mountain saddleback for a look
一团一团的白云。”	At the groups of white clouds.”
照潘格来遮能代的话，	Following Hpan Galai Chye Ningtai’s instruction,
人们来到丫口，	People came to the mountain saddleback,
看着一团一团的白云，	Where they saw the white clouds
学会了收棉花。	And learned how to harvest cotton.
远古，	In remote antiquity,
大地上的人们，	People on the Earth
棉花是会收了，	Had learned to harvest cotton.

但不会做弹花弓。	But they did not know how to create a bow to fluff cotton.
潘格来遮能代说：	Hpan Galai Chye Ningtai said to them,
“大地上的人们呀，	“Listen, you guys on the Earth.
不会做弹花弓，	Since you do not know how to make a bow to fluff cotton,
就到竹篷下，	Go to the clumps of bamboo
看那些弯下的竹梢。”	And observe the curving top of the bamboo.”
照潘格来遮能代的话，	Following Hpan Galai Chye Ningtai’s instruction,
人们来到竹篷下，	People went to the bamboo clump,
看着弯下的竹梢，	Where they observed the curving top of the bamboo
学会了做弹花弓。	And learned how to make the bow used to fluff cotton.

远古，	In remote antiquity,
大地上的人们，	People on the Earth
弹花弓是会做了，	Had learned to make a bow used to fluff cotton.
但不会弹棉花。	But they did not know how to fluff cotton with the bow.
潘格来遮能代说：	Hpan Galai Chye Ningtai said to them,
“不会弹棉花，	“Since you do not know how to fluff cotton,
就到瀑布下，	Go to the waterfalls
看翻起的水花。”	And observe the water spray.”
照潘格来遮能代的话，	Following Hpan Galai Chye Ningtai’s instruction,
人们来到瀑布下，	People went to the waterfalls,
看着翻起的水花，	Where they observed the spraying of water
学会了弹棉花。	And finally learned to fluff cotton.

远古，	In remote antiquity,
大地上的人们，	People on the Earth
棉花是会弹了，	Had finally learned to fluff cotton with a bow.
但不会穿捻线陀。	But they did not know how to use a spinning top.
潘格来遮能代说：	Hpan Galai Chye Ningtai said to them,
“不会穿捻线陀，	“Since you do not know how to use a spinning top,
就去看落下的树枝	Go and observe the way
怎样穿过树叶。”	The fallen twigs penetrate the leaves.”
照潘格来遮能代的话，	Following Hpan Galai Chye Ningtai’s instruction,
人们看着落下的树枝	People went and observed
穿过树叶，	How twigs penetrated leaves.
学会了穿捻线陀。	And finally they learned to use a spinning top.

远古，	In remote antiquity,
大地上的人们，	People on the Earth
捻线陀是会穿了，	Had finally learned to use the spinning top.
但不知道怎样捻线。	But they did not know how to twist threads.
潘格来遮能代说：	Hpan Galai Chye Ningtai said to them,
“不会捻线，	“Since you do not know how to twist threads,
就到有蜘蛛的地方，	Go and observe the way
看蜘蛛抽丝。”	The spider develops silk.”
照潘格来遮能代的话，	Following Hpan Galai Chye Ningtai’s instruction,
人们来到有蜘蛛的地方，	People came and observed
看见蜘蛛抽丝，	How the spider developed silk.

学会了捻线。	And finally they learned to twist threads.
远古，	In remote antiquity,
大地上的人们，	People on the Earth
线是会捻了，	Had finally learned to twist threads.
但不会织布。	But they did not know how to weave cloth.
潘格来遮能代说：	Hpan Galai Chye Ningtai said to them,
“不会织布，	“Since you do not know how to weave cloth,
就到有蜘蛛的地方，	Go and observe the way
看蜘蛛结网。”	The spider spins a web.”
照潘格来遮能代的话，	Following Hpan Galai Chye Ningtai’s instruction,
人们来到有蜘蛛的地方，	People went and observed
看见蜘蛛结网，	How the spider spun a web.
学会了织布。	And finally they learned to weave cloth.
远古，	In remote antiquity,
大地上的人们，	People on the Earth
布是会织了，	Had finally learned to weave cloth.
但不会穿衣裤。	But they did not know how to make and wear clothes.
潘格来遮能代说：	Hpan Galai Chye Ningtai said to them,
“不会穿衣裤，	“Since you do not know how to make and wear clothes,
就到竹篷下，	Go and observe the way
看看裹着竹子的笋叶壳。”	The bamboo covers itself with shell.”
照潘格来遮能代的话，	Following Hpan Galai Chye Ningtai’s instruction,

人们来到竹篷下，	People went and observed
看见裹着竹子的笋叶壳，	How the bamboo covered itself with shell.
学会了穿衣裤。	And finally they learned to make and wear clothes.
远古，	In remote antiquity,
大地上的人们，	People on the Earth
衣裤是会穿了，	Had finally learned to make and wear clothes,
但不会剪头发。	But they did not know how to cut hair.
潘格来遮能代说：	Hpan Galai Chye Ningtai said to them,
“不会剪头发，	“Since you do not know how to cut hair,
就到草地上，	Go and observe
去看杰旺菌。”	What the mushroom looks like.”
照潘格来遮能代的话，	Following Hpan Galai Chye Ningtai’s instruction,
人们来到草地上，	People went and observed
看见杰旺菌，	What the mushroom looked like.
学会了剪头发。	And finally they learned to cut hair.
远古，	In remote antiquity,
大地上的人们，	People on the Earth
头发是会剪了，	Had finally learned to cut hair.
但不会穿耳洞。	But they did not know how to pierce their ears.
潘格来遮能代说：	Hpan Galai Chye Ningtai said to them,
“不会穿耳洞，	“Since you do not know how to pierce your ears,
就去看掉下的树枝，	Go and observe

怎样穿过树叶。”	How the fallen tree branch pierces the leaf.”
照潘格来遮能代的话，	Following Hpan Galai Chye Ningtai's instruction,
人们看着掉下的树枝	People went and observed
穿过树叶，	How the fallen tree branch pierced the leaf.
学会了穿耳洞。	And finally they learned to pierce their ears.
远古，	In remote antiquity,
大地上的人们，	People on the Earth
耳洞是会穿了，	Had finally learned to pierce their ears.
但不会挽发髻。	But they did not know how to coil their hair.
潘格来遮能代说：	Hpan Galai Chye Ningtai said to them,
“不会挽发髻，	“Since you do not know how to coil your hair,
就到林子里，	Go and observe
去看克夺乌蒙鸟的羽冠。”	The crest of the Hke To Wumung bird.”
照潘格来遮能代的话，	Following Hpan Galai Chye Ningtai's instruction,
人们来到林子里，	People came to the woods and observed
看着克夺乌蒙鸟的羽冠，	The crest of the Hke To Wumung bird.
学会了挽发髻。	And finally they learned to coil their hair.
从此，	Ever since then,
大地上的人们，	People on the Earth
有了衣裤穿，	Have clothes to wear and
学会了打扮。	Know how to beautify themselves.

八、男人的手艺　　Ⅷ. Men's Craftsmanship

远古，	In remote antiquity,
大地上的男人，	Men on the Earth did not know
不会做刀壳。	How to make a sheath.
潘格来遮能代说：	Hpan Galai Chye Ningtai said,
“不会做刀壳，	"When you do not know how to make a sheath,
看裹着竹子的笋叶壳。”	Look at the cover of a bamboo."
照潘格来遮能代的话，	Hearing Hpan Galai Chye Ningtai's instruction,
男人来到竹篷下，	Men went to the bamboo clumps.
看着笋叶壳，	Seeing the cover of the bamboo
学会了做刀壳。	They learned to make sheaths.
远古，	In remote antiquity,
大地上的人们，	People on the Earth had learned to make sheaths,
刀壳是会做了，	But they did not know
但不会做刀箍。	How to make a hoop.
潘格来遮能代说：	Hpan Galai Chye Ningtai said,
“不会做刀箍，	"If you do not know how to make a hoop,
就到林子里，	Go to the forest and
去看莱樟树上的白印。”	Find a Lai Jang tree for its white marks."

照潘格来遮能代的话，	Following Hpan Galai Chye Ningtai's suggestion,
男人来到林子里，	Men went to the forest.
看着莱樟树上的白印，	Seeing the white marks on the Lai Jang tree,
学会了做刀箍。	They learned how to make hoops.
远古，	In remote antiquity,
大地上的人们，	People on the Earth had learned to make hoops,
刀箍是会做了，	But they did not know
但不会编刀背带。	How to knit braces for sheaths.
潘格来遮能代说，	Hpan Galai Chye Ningtai said,
"不会编刀背带，	"If you do not know how to knit brace for sheaths,
就到林子里，	Go to the forest and
去看扭在一起的莱樟树根。"	Observe the twisted Lai Jang tree roots."
照潘格来遮能代的话，	Following Hpan Galai Chye Ningtai's suggestion,
男人来到林子里，	Men went to the forest.
看着扭在一起的莱樟树根，	By observing the twisted Lai Jang tree roots,
学会了编刀背带。	They learned to knit braces for sheaths.
远古，	In remote antiquity,
大地上的男人，	Men on the Earth had learned to knit braces for sheaths,
刀背带是会编了，	But they did not know
但不会绕刀背带。	How to tighten the braces to the sheaths.
潘格来遮能代说：	Hpan Galai Chye Ningtai said,
"不会绕刀背带，	"If you do not know how to tighten the braces to the

就到洼子里，
去看藤篾根。”
照潘格来遮能代的话，
男人来到洼子里，
看着藤篾根，
学会了绕刀背带。

sheaths,
Go to the valley and
Observe the rattan roots.”
Following Hpan Galai Chye Ningtai’s suggestion,
Men went to the valley.
By observing the rattan roots,
They learned to tighten the braces to the sheaths.

远古，
大地上的男人，
刀背带是会绕了，
但不会挎长刀。
潘格来遮能代说：
“不会挎长刀，
就到洼子里，
去看藤篾爬树杈。”
照潘格来遮能代的话，
男人来到洼子里，
看着藤篾爬树杈，
学会了挎长刀。

In remote antiquity,
Men on the Earth had learned
To tighten the braces to the sheaths,
But they did not know
How to carry the sheaths on their shoulders.
Hpan Galai Chye Ningtai said,
“If you do not know how to carry the sheaths on your shoulders,
Go to the valley and observe how rattan crawls over tree branches.”
Following Hpan Galai Chye Ningtai’s suggestion,
Men went to the valley.
By observing how rattan crawled over tree branches,
They learned to carry the sheaths on their shoulders.

远古，

In remote antiquity,

大地上的男人，	Men on the Earth did not know
不会编篾篮，	How to weave bamboo baskets,
便学着编篾篮，	So they learned to weave them.
先从篮口编，	They first started weaving the upper part,
没有编出篾篮，	But they failed to make one.
又从篮底编，	Then they started weaving the bottom part,
篾篮编好了。	And they succeeded.
远古，	In remote antiquity,
大地上的男人，	Men on the Earth had learned
学会了编篾篮，	How to weave bamboo baskets and
又学着编篾笆。	Went on to weave bamboo fences.
先从外面编，	They first started weaving the outer parts,
没有编出篾笆，	But they failed to make one.
又从中间编，	Then they started weaving the middle part,
篾笆编好了。	And they succeeded.
远古，	In remote antiquity,
大地上的男人，	Men on the Earth had learned
学会了编篾笆，	How to weave bamboo fences and
又学着编食盘。	Went on to weave bamboo plates.
先从上面编，	They first started weaving the upper part,
没有编出食盘，	But they failed to make one.
又从下面编，	Then they started weaving the bottom part,

食盘编好了。	And they succeeded.
远古，	In remote antiquity,
大地上的人们，	Men on the Earth had learned
学会了编食盘，	How to weave bamboo plates
又学着编篾帕。	And went on to weave bamboo bags.
先从口子编，	They started from the upper part,
没有编出篾帕，	But failed.
又从底子编，	Then they started weaving the bottom part,
篾帕编好了。	And they succeeded.
远古，	In remote antiquity,
大地上的男人，	Men on the Earth had invented a horn-trumpet,
做出骚帕陶光，	But they did not know
但不知怎样吹。	How to blow it.
先从口口吹，	They first blew the bottom part,
骚帕陶光不响，	But the horn-trumpet failed to make a sound;
又从嘴嘴吹，	They then blew the upper part,
骚帕陶光吹响了。	And they succeeded.
有了骚帕陶光，	Having learned how to play the horn-trumpet,
又做出了勒荣桑比，	Men on the Earth invented a flute.
但不知怎样吹。	But they did not know how to play it.
先从大处吹，	They first blew the holes on the two ends,

勒荣桑比吹不响，
又从小处吹，
勒荣桑比吹响了。

But they failed to make a sound.
They then blew the smaller holes on the flute,
And they succeeded.

九、女人出嫁

IX. Women Marrying Off

远古，
大地上的人们，
男人不会串女人，
女人不会找男人。

In remote antiquity,
There were men and women,
Men who did not know how to flirt with women,
And women who did not know how to attract men.

潘格来遮能代说：
“大地上的人们呵，
男人不会串女人，
女人不会找男人，
就去看天上的星星吧。
每一个晚上，
它们从东串到西，
早上又回到东方来。”

Hpan Galai Chye Ningtai said,
“Gee, you men and women on the Earth!
You do not know how to flirt with women;
You do not know how to attract men.
You should look up into the Sky
And observe the stars move
From the east to the west every night
And then back to the east in the morning.”

照潘格来遮能代的话，
大地上的人们，

Following Hpan Galai Chye Ningtai's instruction,
People on the Earth observed the stars.

看着天上的星星，	Men learned to flirt with women;
男人会串女人了，	Women learned to attract men.
女人会找男人了，	Yet still they did not know
但不知道该男人娶亲，	Whether men should bother to marry into women's home
还是该女人出嫁。	Or women should marry into men's house.

有一对兄妹，	There were a brother and a sister.
哥哥对妹妹说：	The brother said to the sister,
“妹妹呀，	“My dear sister,
你留在家，	You stay home,
让我出嫁吧。”	I will marry myself off.”
哥哥出嫁时，	When the brother was marrying himself off,
挎上了长刀，	He put his sword on his shoulder,
还要带弓箭，	But still he wanted
带上了斧头，	To take his bow and arrows along.
还要拿凿子，	He carried his ax,
带上了犁，	But still he wanted to take his chisel.
还要牵拉犁的牛。	He took his plow,
	But still he wanted to take the bull with him.

哥哥出嫁，	When the brother was marrying himself off,
要的东西太多了，	He wanted to take too many possessions with him.
等的时间太长了，	And it took such a long time for him to get prepared.
妹妹便对哥哥说，	The sister said to his brother,

“哥哥呀，	“My dear elder brother,
你出嫁太慢了，	It took you too long to marry off.
还是让我出嫁吧。”	It’s better to marry me off.”
妹妹说完，	Having said that, the sister married herself off,
带上捻线就出嫁了。	Taking only a spinning tool with her.
从此，	From then on,
大地上的人们，	There begins a custom,
女人开始嫁男人。	That women leave home and are married off.

About the Translators

Yang Huifang is an associate professor of English in the School of Foreign Languages and Literature at Yunnan Normal University. Her recent translation publication is *Jingpo Historical & Cultural Photo Album* (Yunnan Nationality Publishing House, 2007). Her research interests focus on literary translation and cross-cultural communication. She worked in 2004–2012 as a coordinator, translator and interpreter on the ADB-funded UNESCO project *HIV/AIDS Prevention Education among Highland Peoples in Sub-Mekong Regions*, which consisted of five programs: *Jingpo Ethnic Program in Dehong, Dai Ethnic Program in Dehong, Dai Ethnic Program in Xishuangbanna, Wa Ethnic Program in Lincang* and *Yi Ethnic Program in Liangshan.*

Chen Ping is an associate professor of English in the School of Foreign Languages and Literature at Yunnan Normal University. Her recent publications include three translations: *Outstanding Brands* (Yunnan University Press, 2002), *Board Secretary* (Huaxia Publishing House, 2004), *Unique Cultural Knowledge of Yunnan Ethnic Minorities* (Yunnan University Press, 2007), and more than twenty articles on translation strategies and translation teaching. Her research interests focus on stylistic translation, literary translation, news translation, conference interpretation, and cross-cultural communication and translation.

Tao Yue is a lecturer of English in the School of Foreign Languages and Literature at Yunnan Normal University. She is also an experienced conference interpreter who has worked with China Council for the Promotion of International Trade, Foreign Affairs Office of Yunnan Province, Transport Canada, Asian Development Bank and many others. Her most recent interpreting assignments include the 13th World Dragon Boat Racing Championships, the 1st China Southeast Asia Business Forum, 2017 International Blueberry Organization Summit, and the 1st South and Southeast Asian Universities Rectors Forum. She combines her interpreting experience with MTI teaching and published several articles of relevant fields. Her research interests focus on interpreting teaching and cross-cultural communication.

(Yang Huifang translated Contents, proper nouns and Cantos 4, 5 and 6, Chen Ping translated Prologue and Canto 1, and Tao Yue translated Cantos 2 and 3. –Translators'note)